MARK MY WORDS

E.L. KOSLO

PROOFING: BRITTNI VAN - The Romance Doctor — @the_romance_doc
Cover: Designed by E.L. Koslo
Depositphotos: marzacz, Forewer, qerest, Kwangmoo, Sanychs, antart

Envato Elements licensed fonts: Barcelony and Baskerville BT
Interior Formatting: E.L. Koslo
Artwork by @irdeinfierno
Depositphotos: huhulin, floral_set, losw, racorn
Shutterstock: stockfour, OPOLJA

Table of Contents

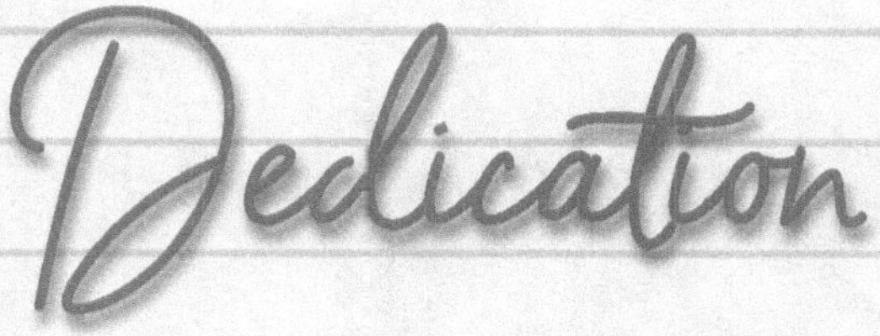

This book is for all the women who have ever been told they are too much.

.

Honey, you're just my kind of too much.

.

Don't ever change.

All content warnings are on my website at ELKoslo.com/words-series

Spice Index 🌶

CHAPTERS THAT TURN UP THE HEAT

Kristine Willard

OCCUPATION: COPY EDITING INTERN

GENRE

Romance

KRISTINE

BOSTON

When I arrived at work this morning, I was looking forward to getting right to work on the manuscript I'd been doing a developmental edit on, but no. Of course not. Today had to be the day that I was voluntold to babysit another copy-editing intern because one of the authors he worked with had gone off the rails. I didn't have time to babysit anyone, I didn't *want* to babysit anyone, and I performed much better alone when I didn't have to deal with other people's bullshit.

The phrase *team player* didn't apply to me because I didn't want to be part of the team. Now Sam, on the other hand. He was the epitome of being a team player and worked for the bane of my existence.

"I can't believe you're making me work with that egotistical waste of perfectly good brain matter. Sam's a first-class douche canoe," I sighed as I looked at my boss, Isobel. I'd worked with her for a while, and she'd asked me to take on some pretty time-intensive projects in the past, but this was too much.

"You'll be fine," she said, rolling her eyes. "If I have to put up with Adrian on this one, you can deal with Sam. He's not as bad as you make him out to be."

"I'm not sure he can dedicate all his remaining brain cells to focus on this project."

"Would you quit pretending he's an idiot? He graduated *Summa Cum Laude* from Duke." Isobel shook her head as she gave me an exasperated look. And he liked to tell everyone about it, or at least his boss did. I graduated from *Harvard*; you didn't see me asking people for a cookie.

"I think he's taken one too many performance enhancements in his time for his brain to work properly. I mean, come on, he played lacrosse." I raised an eyebrow and crossed my arms over my chest. "I bet he does CrossFit. I bet he actually enjoys it. Who *enjoys* CrossFit? I know normal people don't. It's like some millennial form of a torture ritual."

"Lots of intelligent people go to school on athletic scholarships. Not everyone can be born with a silver spoon." She arched an eyebrow back at me, crossing her arms to match my standoffish posture. This was always going to be a point of contention between us. Isobel had worked two jobs and put herself through school, and I...well...

"Hey, I got in all by myself. I graduated with honors, too. You act like I was handed a diploma without working for it." My last name may have ensured my application was reviewed, but I earned my spot at Harvard. I also busted my ass to prove that I wasn't my brother. I didn't need grades handed to me.

"I get it," Isobel told me in that placating tone of voice she used when she was trying to get me to do something she knew I would object to. "I went Ivy League too, but I also ate Ramen noodles my first three years out of school. Anyway—" she sighed. "It's not my choice. When our authors collaborate, we all have to play nice."

"Why is Chase helping that hermit guy anyway?" I knew Evan was a bestselling author, but I thought he might be taking the tortured artist routine a little too far. He rarely came into the office, but when he did, it was all cloak and dagger. Why any of the editors went to all that trouble for one writer was beyond me.

"He's not a hermit. He simply likes privacy and has a touch of social anxiety," she said, shrugging. Yeah, sure. Just a touch. *Right...*

"You told Chase he never left his house. Doesn't that make him a hermit?"

"I prefer the term recluse. It makes him sound more mysterious," Adrian called out from Isobel's open door. Oh, joy. He was my *favorite* person in the whole company. Which was why I rarely called him by his first name, preferring to stick to his official title, *Dickhead*.

"Do you lurk in the hallway waiting to interrupt other people's conversations?" Isobel rolled her eyes, but I saw them lingering on how his shirt clung to his overly large biceps while he leaned against the door frame. I was convinced the big muscles were compensation for something else being *not so big*. His brain surely wasn't his only tiny body part.

"Hey! Your intern was trash-talking my writer and my intern. I was only walking by." He was trying to look innocent, but his stalker tendencies were showing. Over the last few weeks, I'd seen him lurking in the hallway more than average.

"Walking by to where? My office is at the end of the hallway." At least Isobel didn't seem to be falling for his bullshit excuses.

I seriously didn't know how she put up with all these muscle-bound idiots. Adrian clearly had the hots for her and didn't have a big enough pair to do something about it.

Personally, I didn't understand the hype. The expensive piece of hardware inside my nightstand did a better job than any man ever had. And I didn't have to talk to it after. Why waste your energy on morons who only want to get into your pants when you can give yourself a good time? Or at least take the edge off.

"Evan's sent me some new pages," he told her, his voice a little guarded, but I could tell he was secretly excited about something from the gleam in his eyes.

"Already?" Isobel's eyes widened.

"Yeah, your girl has been working her magic," he said, looking mildly impressed.

Isobel's mouth dropped open dramatically, and she made a fake little gasping noise. "Was that an actual compliment about Chase?"

"Well, she is pretty flirty, so I can see how it'd be easy for her to write about sex." And just like that, the sleaze shoved his foot in his mouth three sentences into a conversation. That had to be a new record for him.

"I'm gonna pretend you didn't talk right now, so my knee doesn't have to slip into your nuts—accidentally, of course." His head swiveled comically in my direction, and I narrowed my eyes at him. Chase was a professional, and he was a giant douche who needed to watch himself.

"Are you really going to let your intern talk to me like that?" he asked Isobel, pointing at me.

"Are you still talking?" I scoffed, sitting down and facing away from him.

"I'm sure the two of you can figure out how to get along," Isobel sighed, exasperated.

She may have been able to put up with his childish bullshit, but I didn't have to. There wasn't enough bonus pay in the world to put up with Adrian regularly. "Hard pass."

"She'd better watch her mouth around my intern," Adrian told her, clearly pretending I wasn't in the room. "He's good at his job, and I don't want the fire this dragon spews out to scare him off. Quality talent shouldn't be stifled because you won't control your pet bully of an intern."

"Are you implying that I'm not good at my job?" I turned in my chair and pinned him with a scathing look. I was not about to put up with him degrading my work. He was not my boss, and I *did not* and *would not* ever report to him.

"You can infer whatever you'd like from my comment," he said dismissively, swallowing hard as I glared at him. He may be trying to play the tough guy, but I wasn't intimidated by him.

"If your intern can't handle my fiery personality, then he can take a flying leap off of—" I started in on him.

"Kristine! Stop." Pausing mid-rant, I looked over at Isobel's outburst.

The death glare she was giving Adrian even shriveled *my* balls. "Seriously? Must you fight with everyone, Adrian? We get it. You think your shit smells like roses."

"At least it doesn't smell like—"

"Eh!" She warned, putting her hand up in front of his mouth. "Knock it off. If you tried hard, I'm sure you could be a professional."

"I am professional," he huffed, his voice taking on an annoying, whiny quality. Clearly, he didn't like Isobel calling him out on his behavior.

"Pffft…" The noise came out of my lips all on its own, but Isobel's head still swiveled in my direction.

"You're not helping." Damn, I might have pissed her off. I still wasn't Dickhead though; she was super angry at him.

"Well, sorry if I can't help but laugh when someone says something stupid." My face also apparently did this thing where my top lip curled and my eyes showed my unimpressed thoughts. My brother had given me a shirt for my birthday last year that said, 'If my mouth doesn't say it, my face certainly will.' My mother had been horrified, but it wasn't wrong.

"You could learn something as well about knowing when to stop." She pointed at me just as Adrian made a face at me over her shoulder. He was lucky I couldn't reach the stapler. "Not every sarcastic remark sent in your direction needs to be returned with something ten times worse."

I snapped my mouth shut and crossed my arms over my chest. This was turning out to be a shit day. Chase was supposed to be writing another steamy romance novel, not helping a mystery writer—with a limp noodle—figure out how to pleasure a fictional character.

"Alright, what exactly do you need from me?" Isobel wasn't letting me off the hook with this project, and I knew I was pushing the envelope of her tolerance.

"Adrian will send you the first draft of the manuscript. Check it for plot holes and start marking up copy with edits."

"Sam's already done that," Adrian said smugly. Of course he'd give his intern a head start. Lord knows what Sam had done to that markup.

"Did she ask you for direction?" Isobel gave him a pointed look, and he opened his mouth but shut it again before he responded.

"No, but he's my—"

"If you want to continue to utilize my writer when she's mid-contract, and taking time off from her book, not to mention my copy intern, then we do this my way," she told him, leaving no room for interpretation.

"But—"

"Either Kristine checks the first draft, or we're wasting our time." We would see if I could salvage whatever Sam had done to the original draft.

"Evan has been on the New York—" Adrian sputtered, pulling out his usual line of 'my author is more important than yours…blah blah blah.'

"Times bestseller list, we get it," Isobel finished for him, not sounding the least bit impressed. "You've beaten that horse to death. Enough with the macho posturing. You asked for help. We're providing it, but you don't get to dictate how this goes."

"There's a reason they put me with Isobel. I'm good at combing through the text to ensure the plot is cohesive." I had better attention to detail than some of the more experienced senior editors and certainly the pool of other interns. He may not like me, but I was damn good at my job.

He turned to look at me with an eyebrow raised. "Mystery and suspense novels..."

"Are still novels," I pointed out in a bored tone. "They all have a formula, and it's my job to find the holes."

"There are no holes that need to be filled." He tried to look intimidating, crossing his arms over his broad chest.

I snorted as I tried to hold back the laughter. Adrian didn't realize what he said could be taken in an entirely dirty manner. "Well, obviously, some holes aren't filled right if you need Chase as a consultant."

"How dare—"

Isobel laughed, shooting him an unimpressed look. "She's right."

"Thank you." I smiled over at Isobel. At least she didn't let the jerks in this office walk all over her.

"Fine. I'll send Sam down with a hard copy," he sighed.

"Great." I nodded. Not meaning it at all. Hard copy meant that I had to interact with Sam. And he'd probably want to work with me in person. *Ick.*

"Thank you, Ad. Now, why did you come down here to begin with?" Isobel asked after we all agreed.

"Does she have to sit there in the corner and stare at me?" he asked, glancing at where I was seated.

Widening my eyes, I sat forward, resting my chin on my hands, batting my eyelashes. He gave me a weird look and focused on Isobel.

"Kris..." she warned as she pointed at my computer.

"I don't *have* to. It's enjoyable for me to make you uncomfortable." Making sure to maintain eye contact, I smiled innocently. He blinked and looked away—*chicken shit.*

"Go get some coffee or something. Please?" Is requested, and I narrowed my eyes at her.

"My mug is full." I shrugged and held it up for her to see. I knew hers was also full because I wasn't a total amateur.

"Kristine. Go get me some coffee. Either at the café downstairs or the one down the street, your decision." *Fuck.* She was dismissing me.

"Fine," I sighed. Most of the time, she didn't mind if I sat quietly in the corner while she met with other staff, but apparently, Isobel needed privacy with the king of the dicks.

Gathering my bag and laptop, I stepped out and made a show of closing the door. I could hear lowered voices as I walked away but knew she'd bust me if I eavesdropped. I didn't like being out of the loop. Everyone in the office was aware of my reputation. I was always listening. I knew the dirt on everyone. The weird fetishes of some authors, the dirty secrets people whispered in their office when they thought no one could hear. I knew it all.

"Where are you going?"

God, not again. We had a few unpaid interns who were still undergraduates who worked around the office during the school year. They were usually scouted from some of the top English lit programs locally, or in Carson's case, they were related to an executive.

"Coffee. Nothing that should interest you. Don't you have some copies to make?" I rolled my eyes at the tall, good-looking jackass who enjoyed asking me pointless questions all day.

"Oh, come on, Kristi, you secretly love having me around." My lip curled up at all the white teeth on display as he smiled at me.

"Nope."

"Why are you so grouchy today?" He started following me down the hallway, not even breaking his pace when I glared at him over my shoulder.

Most of the guys in the office were the same. Tall, attractive, mildly intelligent, over-educated, and thought the world adored them.

"Go away." *Shoo...*

"I can come with you," he offered as he tried to keep up with my brisk walk.

"Those copies aren't gonna make themselves. The whole office will shut down without you, Carse," I teased in a faux pleasant voice. He really couldn't take a hint.

"Ha-ha. We both know this office is mostly paperless. You're one of the only copy editors who still insists on marking up a physical copy." He looked so proud that he knew that. It only showed how creepy he was for watching me. We all had a preferred method of how we worked.

"And that's why they keep me around. Because I catch things that the tablet jockeys miss."

"And because you know how to wear the hell out of a pencil skirt."

I stopped in my tracks, turning to face him as my bag hit the floor with a dull thunk. "Listen here, you little—"

"Kris! There you are. Adrian sent me to find you." Sam gripped my elbow and tugged me back from where I'd stepped toward Carson. He bent down and grabbed my bag, thrusting it into my arms.

"Let's get going on that special errand," he said—a little louder than his normal voice—before he looked over his shoulder and gave Carson a warning smile.

"Since when is coffee a special errand?" Carson asked as he tried to follow us.

"Take a hint, Carson." Sam placed his arm around my waist and pushed me toward the elevators. "You're out of line. Again."

"Fine. I'll come find you later, Kristi." Carson winked before he turned, walking in the opposite direction.

Sam quietly urged me into the elevator, and then I rounded on him as soon as the doors were closed. "What the hell was that?"

"You're welcome," he told me, leaning against the wall and staring at his phone.

"I didn't ask for your help. That twerp is one sexual harassment claim from getting my foot up his ass."

"We both know that wouldn't end well." He raised an eyebrow, not looking up. Jerk couldn't even be bothered to look at me. This dismissive nature was why I didn't want to work with him. I grew up with arrogant assholes whose egos made him look mild in comparison, but I wasn't about to put up with his shit either. Sam and I had the same job. He was my equal and wouldn't get away with treating me like I wasn't.

"Yeah. I might lose a shoe if it gets lodged up there," I growled.

"Why must you always be so hostile?" His voice wasn't accusing. It was simply curious—like he was trying to figure me out.

"I don't recall asking for your opinion," I replied defensively. I didn't need to justify my actions or attitude to anyone, much less him or his dickhead of a boss.

"Well, I'm giving it," he shrugged, glancing up in my direction.

"Seems like you MAST idiots are all for forcing your opinions on people today."

He nodded, giving me a small smile before he pocketed his phone and finally looked into my eyes. His division of Vivid Words Publishing covered the Mystery/Action/Suspense/Thriller books. It was common to shorten his division to MAST. And it was likely also a comment on how tiny their employees' masts must be. Adrian was the perfect poster child. Sam...well, the jury was still out on him. "So, I take it you've talked to Adrian this morning."

"Unfortunately."

He sighed, and I took the opportunity to lean into the elevator's corner and pull my phone out. I had the usual messages from Isobel asking me to go through various manuscripts. At the bottom of the unread messages was the email from Adrian with Evan's manuscript. Clicking on the link, the shared document on the central server opened up, and I scoffed as I noticed that I had read-only permissions.

"What?" Sam asked curiously as he looked over.

"The asshole has locked me out of commenting on or editing the manuscript." I turned my phone for him to see.

"He wants any text edits to go through me first," he replied. He didn't have that usual cocky smirk Adrian loved giving everyone, but I still didn't like that they seemed to think they were running the show on this one. "If you email me notes, I can look over them to see what changes need to be made."

"God, he's a jackass."

"He's only looking out for Evan." Sam shrugged as he continued giving me that same slightly amused look. It irritated me that he wasn't acting like an asshole. If he behaved like Adrian, then my anger was justified. But he didn't seem bothered by my attitude.

"What exactly does he think I will do if I can mark up the digital copy? He does realize I'm a professional. This is my job," I insisted.

"I don't think he meant it as a slight. He thought it'd be easier to have controlled access. Less chance for error."

"Whatever. I don't make errors," I growled, looking away from him. His eyebrows shot up, but he still wouldn't look up to make eye contact with me.

The elevator stopped in the lobby, and I walked out without looking back. I continued to be frustrated by some of the men in this building. Boys club could be an understatement sometimes. They continued to think that *romance* authors needed a feminine touch, despite an increase in male writers.

Isobel was hard as nails and took shit from no one, which was the only reason she'd survived as long as she had in this world.

As I reached for the main door, a hand closed on the bar before I could push it.

"After you." Sam smiled as he waved me through. Another thing I didn't like about him. I was perfectly capable of opening a door, but he insisted on being overly polite. No one had manners that good, or maybe that was my cynical inner New Yorker talking.

"Why are you following me?" I narrowed my eyes at him as he fell into step a few paces behind me, heading in the same direction down the sidewalk.

"You think awfully highly of yourself, don't you?" He chuckled at my drawn-out sigh, following me to the crosswalk at the nearest corner. When the signal changed, he was still only a few paces behind me, an annoying smile on his equally annoying handsome face.

I spun around as I reached the door to the café, and he was right behind me, as I expected. "What was that about following me?"

Sam simply smiled and walked right past me. He stopped to pick up a drink carrier from the quick pick-up shelf and winked as he paused in the doorway on his way back out. "Have fun waiting in line."

Ugh. Jackass. Annoying, frustrating, infuriating, egotistical, *handsome*, jack ass...

Samuel Langley

OCCUPATION: COPY EDITING INTERN

GENRE

Mystery, Action, Suspense, Thriller

Chapter

TWO

SAM

BOSTON

"Dammit," I muttered, pressing the button on the console of my treadmill to slow it down to a three. I reached forward to where my phone was propped in the water bottle holder. Pressing the green button on my phone to accept the call, I tried to sound cheerful as I heard it connect in my AirPods. "Hey, Mom."

"Don't *Hey, Mom* me," she scolded, and I knew I was in for an earful. My sisters must have relayed that I wasn't coming home for the twins' birthday in a few weeks. I don't know why it still bothered me that she got upset when I missed family functions, but I didn't have the flexibility in my schedule to fly back home for every little thing.

"I know, you're mad..."

"I'm not mad, Sam. I'm disappointed." Even worse. Lay on the mom guilt. She didn't understand why it was so vital for me to 'sacrifice' family time for my career. She'd met my dad in college—which was within a half-hour of both their hometowns. She settled into the role of homemaker and mother quickly, having my sisters in rapid succession within the first six years they were married. "I know Claire told you it was alright to see them when you come home next, but the boys are disappointed."

So that was the angle she was taking, using my nephews as ammunition. I'd already mailed their gift, knowing it would drive my mother insane all summer for two six-year-olds to have super soaker water guns. They lived down the street from Nana and Pops, so I was sure they'd be the unwitting victims of my nephews' inevitable water fights.

I didn't intentionally plan it like that, but it worked out in my favor that my brother-in-law, Brad, had mentioned that they wanted Nerf or water guns and not the lame shit my sister put on their Amazon wish list for their birthday. No six-year-old wanted a handwriting practice book or a series of educational apps for their iPads. Especially not Felix and Alex.

"The boys have a Facetime scheduled with me for the day after their party, and their cards and gifts were in the mail days ago."

"Sam," she sighed. Here we go.

Rolling my eyes as I reached for my water bottle, I remembered why I'd dodged her calls. Another one of my friends from high school had sent out a wedding invitation, and my youngest sister—who was five years older than me—had recently told her that she was done having kids.

"Brett's invitation came today. You *are* coming back for the wedding, right? If you two stayed in touch, he would have chosen you for his best man."

After high school, I'd gone off to college on an athletic scholarship. It happened to be across the country in North Carolina while several friends had gone to the local community college in Michigan instead of a major university. They still all kept in contact with each other. Some of them even started popping out kids a few years ago. I hadn't talked to some of them in years. As a scholarship athlete, I'd had to stay focused on training and my grades to stay eligible, and sometimes trips home had to be delayed or cut short.

That was when my mother had perfected the 'when are you ever coming home?' guilt trips. It only worsened when I graduated from Duke and landed a job in Boston. It'd killed her that I wasn't moving back home, or at least closer to home.

"Mom, yes, I'll try to come back for the wedding. But Brett and I haven't really hung out since high school." We'd been best friends in middle school, and she wouldn't let some things go. It was a long time since our twelve-year-old selves had ruled the neighborhood.

"It'd just be nice to see my son once in a while," she sighed like she hadn't seen me recently for Easter. "I know your job is important, but I feel like maybe you're sacrificing your chance at a future for this career you have planned out."

Rumor had it that one of the major genre editors was retiring. One of the mid-level editors would probably fill his position, but I wasn't shooting that high yet. I was hoping for an interview for one of the full-time copy editor positions. I'd been a copy-editing intern for Adrian for two years—since I finished undergrad—but I was ready to move up. I was also not going to argue with having another supervisor. Two years with Adrian was a long time.

"I'm twenty-four, Mom." Just because most of my sisters were engaged or married by twenty-four didn't mean I needed to be.

"Well, I know that men don't have the inconvenience of biological clocks ticking, but what if it's too late once you finally settle down with someone? A woman's eggs—"

"Mom, stop!" I half whined as I cut her off. I understood she only had girls before I came along, but I did not need the biological clock argument. She already had ten grandkids; I was sure she could wait for a few more. "I have a decade before that is even relevant. Stop worrying about me settling down to have kids. I'd need to have a girlfriend first."

"So, you won't be bringing a plus one to the wedding?"

"Oh my God, just stop." I didn't know how my sisters put up with her meddling. They all lived within an hour of home, which made Mom happy, but I couldn't even escape her being halfway across the country. "Was there anything else you needed?" Checking the time on my watch, I knew I needed to get showered and back upstairs. I needed to find Kristine to go through more pages, and I was not looking forward to being put in her crosshairs again.

"No," she sighed dramatically. "I guess I can let you get back to work. Not that it's going to keep you warm at night."

"Love you, Mom," I rushed out, not waiting for her to respond before disconnecting quickly. She didn't need any more opportunities to pick at my life choices.

Deciding that my run would have to wait until later, I pressed the stop button, hopping off quickly to grab some cleaning wipes. I knew they had a cleaning crew that came through here regularly, but I wasn't leaving my residual sweat behind for the next person.

As I headed toward the locker room of the corporate gym, I smiled at the girl at the desk who'd started working there a few weeks ago. She was young, probably still in school since she spent her afternoons with a notebook open in front of her, but not young enough to be illegal. My mom was right that my job wasn't keeping my bed warm at night—not that I would tell her that—but I wasn't a fan of the *intraoffice* dating scene. I'd dated a fellow intern at one of my summer internships during college, and it had gotten awkward when she'd taken our relationship as being more than what it was at face value. Now I tried to be upfront about my intentions with potential dates.

The lacrosse intramural club I participated in often had social outings, but I'd been trying not to end up in strangers' beds at the end of the night. Maybe I was maturing with age, but one-night stands weren't my thing anymore. I'd had plenty of those with the lacrosse-stitutes on campus at Duke.

"Have a good afternoon, Sam." She smiled as I wiped my towel up the back of my hair while opening the door.

I was sure I smelled nasty and knew I had sweat dripping down my neck, but I winked at her and gave her a slight head nod anyway. No point in burning bridges I never intended to cross. "You too, Sara."

Thankfully, I'd taken my lunch a little late today, so I didn't have to worry about any weird, half-naked locker room talk. I only wanted to get in, wash my junk and get out. It still amazed me how much some guys gossiped in the locker room. I knew high school and university athletes did, but some hard-nosed professionals who worked for other companies in our building weren't much better than fifteen-year-old girls.

As the hot water beat down on my scalp, I pressed my hand against the wall and tried to relax. Adrian had been a total dick lately when Evan's first draft came back and was a disaster. This was the first novel of his that I'd edited where I was left shaking my head. His plot was well developed—having the usually detailed finesse of his other books—but there wasn't any spark between the main characters.

Being on Adrian's team, I hadn't worked with Chase—Chastity—whatever her name was, but she had a big following. If she could get through to Evan, she'd save all of us the hassle of scrapping a novel past its due date. Unfortunately, it meant subjecting myself to being in Kristine's crosshairs until we were done.

With her tall, lithe body—that packed a surprising number of voluptuous curves—dark auburn hair, and those captivating hazel green eyes, I could admit that I was physically attracted to her the first time that I saw her, but that viper tongue of hers worried me. She was an expert at cutting people down to size with a few well-placed barbs, and I was not looking forward to dealing with her temperamental nature. That was one bear you did not want to poke.

But imagining riling her up to the point that she used her tongue for another kind of lashing made me pause my soapy hands to will away my response. Kristine was likely to be a minx in bed, or at least the fantasy version of her that'd been appearing in my head lately. No, that was a dangerous line of thought. Any attachment to her, especially a sexual one, would be not only suicide for my career–my cock as well.

I'd worked with plenty of attractive women in my career and kept things strictly professional; this was no different.

ADRIAN HAD SENT THROUGH the first round of edits to Evan's manuscript, and I was scrolling through to fix any minor grammatical errors. Evan's writing was typically pretty clean, but there were still things that you missed in your own writing that editors caught with a fresh eye. Adrian couldn't be fucked with going through the first draft of anything, typically refusing to look at a manuscript past a three-chapter preview until it'd been sent back as a second draft.

He'd earned it, though, working his way up from the bottom of the company as he played baseball on scholarship to pay for school. That was part of why I understood him. I knew how hard it was to earn a degree and deal with the rigorous schedule of a college athlete. I respected his work ethic, even if the chip on his shoulder had turned him into a prick.

"It's good, right?" He was seated behind his desk, hands clasped behind his head, shiny dress shoes propped up on the corner of his worktop. I'd expected his office to be a disaster along with his personality, but he was meticulous about filing, and his desk was always tidy. It freaked me out when I needed to pull something from his filing cabinets when I started working for him, and everything had neatly labeled tabs in his handwriting. He was either the world's neatest jackass or a secret serial killer.

Or both...

"Yeah, the text is clean. You can tell the writing style is a little different, but I wouldn't have been able to tell that someone else helped him write this." Authors changed their style slightly as they honed their craft; trying a new writing technique on a new project wasn't unheard of. Given that the subject matter was a departure from his usual, passing the changes off to his readers would be easier.

"I have to admit, I thought he'd get all anxious and refuse to work with her, but they've already gotten through quite a few scenes we told him needed to be reworked."

It irritated me a little how he spoke about some of the writers, but I knew he ultimately respected them. Creating characters out of your imagination took talent. The environments they developed with only a few sentences could transport readers to another world, sometimes literally. Editors were the backbone, polishing those stories so they shined, all while keeping the writers happy so they had something *to* edit.

"I'm marking up a few things I've noticed, but this shouldn't have too many changes going back to him."

Adrian nodded and swung his legs down, propping his elbows on the edge of his desk and leaning forward. "Oh, I'm supposed to have you send all your edits through *her*."

My heart rate kicked up slightly, remembering my response to thinking about her earlier. Tamping it down quickly, I saved my notes and closed my laptop, looking up at Adrian. "Like *every* edit, or only the major ones?"

He sighed, pushing himself back in his chair and rolling his eyes. "Everything. Isobel told me you both needed full access."

With her little tantrum in the elevator, Kristine had indicated she wanted more permissions to edit the files, but I was still controlling access to the document, which meant...I had to go to her.

"Am I supposed to email them to her, send them on the shared server, or—"

He started shaking his head, and I could tell by the self-satisfied smirk that he already knew what I'd deduced. I'd have to seek her out.

"Sucks to be you, man."

THREE

KRISTINE

BOSTON

MANY PEOPLE IN THIS building couldn't handle multitasking, especially those lacking an X chromosome. I found focusing on one task at a time tedious, always working through issues with multiple projects. Isobel preferred to complete things one storyline at a time, but I could often edit or proof three, four, and even five manuscripts simultaneously and keep the storylines separate. I prided myself on knowing all the tiny details the authors threw into their plots to keep things interesting. Very few plot points slipped past me, and I often found some of the novels predictable, but I think some readers enjoyed that.

It wasn't my job to judge if the story would sell to the general public; that was up to Isobel and the marketing department. I simply ensured that when they hit the shelves, there weren't any glaring formatting issues that would make the publishing house look bad. Many authors had moved to self-publishing, and I found myself virtually pulling my hair out that some didn't understand the value of having a good editing team behind you. Plenty of indie authors were kicking ass with the help of their editors. It didn't make you weak to get help. It made you look like a professional.

"You ready to go through these new pages?"

My fingers tapped the table's surface to the song's beat in my ears as I scanned the page to ensure the punctuation issues had been resolved. It blew my mind how many people forgot spaces, missed commas, and omitted periods. It made me wonder how they made it through an introductory English class in high school.

"Kristine..."

I knew that quite a few authors hated working with me. I wasn't naive to the point that they resented all the little notes and red marks I left all over their precious pages. I also didn't give two shits. They excelled at their job of developing the plots and characters and all the tiny details, and I excelled at making sure they were written so people could understand them.

"Kris!"

My head swiveled toward the open door of Isobel's office as Sam's loud shout drew my attention. So rude. I untucked my legs from my chair and pulled out one of my wireless earbuds. "Hey."

"Really?" Sam did not look impressed with me, yet again. He kept showing up in random places around the office and pinning me down with that look that I couldn't quite classify. Was it resentment? Boredom? Disdain? I wasn't sure, but I was a little jealous of the warm smiles he bestowed upon the other people working in our office.

"What?"

Sam sighed loudly, his full lips pursed as his eyes narrowed slightly. "I've been standing here trying to get your attention for several minutes."

"Maybe you should've tried harder," I replied, shrugging. He could have at least walked further into the room so he was in my line of sight. He had to have seen the white earbuds sticking out of my ears. Did he think they were only for decoration? These babies had the best noise-canceling properties my meager paycheck could buy.

"I also sent you an email this morning to schedule a time to sit down and review these. You read it. You just never responded."

I rolled my eyes and pulled out the other earbud, tucking them into the case inside my messenger bag. Obviously, some people couldn't take the hint when I was ignoring them.

"Don't roll your eyes at me," he warned in a deep voice, my stomach clenching at his tone. Very few people in the office would ever think of speaking to me like that. Of course, he saw the eye roll; he watched everything. "I know you don't like me. I'm not the president of your fan club either, but we need to work on this together."

This was getting incredibly annoying. My schedule was my own. The only person I rearranged things for was my boss, and the six-foot-tall, dark-haired, blue-eyed man currently standing in the doorway was not Isobel. Although at times, her balls may be bigger.

"I prefer to work alone. You make your notes; I make mine. We can let them go over both sets," I told him dismissively, returning to where I had been working.

"No." The way he said it wasn't with the petulant defiance I would have expected but a firm expression of his disagreement with my methods.

"Excuse me?"

"I was given precise instructions from your boss and mine that we were to go over these together," he responded with an exaggerated lift of one eyebrow.

Why did Isobel insist on torturing me like this? Was I not a model employee?

"Did you look them over?" I sighed. I was sure he probably had, and I had as well, but I wasn't expecting to have to go through them line by line to compare notes.

"Yes."

"Did you make notes?" I knew that I sounded condescending, but the way he looked at me was irritating. His deep blue eyes probing mine with that semi-bored expression were unnerving.

He sighed as he took my bag off the chair beside me, placing it on the floor.

"Excuse me," I scoffed as I grabbed my bag from him, yanking it a little too hard. "You could've asked if you could sit."

"Your bag doesn't need its own chair," he said dismissively, rolling his eyes.

"And gentlemen ask if they can join someone," I pointed out. He had barged in here, interrupted my work, and expected me to jump because he command-ed it. That was not how this was going to work. I didn't buy into it when Adrian did it. Why would I with his mini-me?

He growled under his breath and gripped the back of the chair with both hands, staring me down. "Kristine. Am I allowed to sit in this chair that is your boss' property, not yours, and go over these pages we were both assigned to edit?"

I had to admire the snark in his voice. I intimidated most people in this office with my *oh-so-pleasant*—note the sarcasm—outer demeanor, but he didn't seem to be one of them.

"By all means..." I gestured to the now empty chair as I pulled my bag around behind my seat and closed the document where I'd been working.

"My tablet work alright, or do you want to use your laptop?"

His tablet was sufficient. It's not like I had permission to make actual edits to the manuscript anyway. "Your copy will work. Since you're the lead on this."

Sam sighed and rolled his eyes again, taking a deep breath as he looked at me. "Would you get the chip off your shoulder already? It wasn't a slight on your work quality. It's simply the protocol to keep the document secure."

I knew he was right—that didn't mean I had to like it. Admitting Sam was on my level didn't come easily to me. He was my professional equivalent in Adrian's office, but I didn't consider Adrian to be anywhere near the same caliber of an editor as Isobel.

"Let's pull up the new section and read through it," I rolled my finger in a circle in the air to indicate that he needed to get on with it. I had other things that needed my attention.

"It's a little..." His cheeks turned a rosy shade of pink, and he bit his lip before he glanced in my direction. Interesting...

"Oh, my God, give it here. I'm sure I can handle reading a sex scene without turning into a bumbling, blushing mess."

Sam sputtered as I pulled the tablet from his hands. "I'm not...uh..." He cleared his throat before he shifted in his seat.

"Grow a pair, Sam. Just because Evans kept it PG all these years doesn't mean Chase has done the same. I can handle a little bit of racy dialogue."

He pushed the tablet toward me, and I started reading the highlighted passage. The scene involved a detective and a prostitute getting into an argument that ended up with them angrily fucking against her couch. It was in the original manuscript pages that Chase was sent when Adrian asked for her help. I'd read it before, but the dialogue flowed better this time. It was more provocative, and you could tell that the characters had real explosive chemistry.

The vague descriptions of awkwardly moving body parts and semi-clothed interactions had been morphed into a choreographed dance of passion. I had to admit that I was pleased with how well Chase's style had meshed with Evan's.

"Well..." I sighed as I licked my lips and ran my finger along the edge of my collar. I usually was desensitized to this kind of thing, but it had painted a vivid picture of the torrid act with the edits.

"There were a few comma splice errors that I marked, but otherwise..." he trailed off.

"Yeah, I saw those." I nodded, swallowing as my mouth dried out a little. I cleared my throat, my voice huskier than it usually sounded. "Nice catches."

"Was there anything else that needed to be addressed, or should I leave it?" He still wasn't looking at me; his cheeks tinted a soft shade of pink.

"Well, maybe suggest eliminating the repetitive words a little. He says..." I pointed to a paragraph toward the middle where the word cock was used at least three consecutive times.

"Please don't tell me you're going to suggest 'pulsating member' or something cliché," he laughed as he scooted closer and tried to glance at the paragraph I had highlighted.

"No." I rolled my eyes again; if I spent much more time with Sam, they might get stuck there permanently. He looked relieved, and I laughed as I typed up a few alternative sentences that could be swapped out. "Let's restructure the paragraph to avoid mentioning it so much."

"Cock," Sam smirked.

I frowned at his random use of the word, wondering if he secretly had Tourette's. "What?"

"You want him to take out the word cock."

"Well, yes." Another eye roll. Had he not been involved in this conversation?

"And replace it with what?" he asked, his bright white teeth chewing at his lower lip a little as he stared at me.

"Not replace, just reword. Allude to it." If the whole page were full of cocks, readers would tune out at the repetitive phrasing.

"This isn't some flowery love scene," Sam said in a low voice, his fingers nervously tapping on the table's edge.

I cleared my throat and sat back in my chair, turning to face him. He didn't seem to be messing with me, but I didn't understand why he'd want to repeat the word so much. It lessened the impact if every fifth word was cock. "Yeah, thanks, Mr. Obvious. I'm aware."

"You realize that many of his readers are male, right?" He asked curiously. I knew that a large part of the market segment was male, but it wasn't an exclusive hold on the subject.

"Women read mystery novels," I pointed out in a bored tone. I was tired of the MAST writers and editors pigeonholing their female readers. They needed to embrace that thousands of women loved a good suspenseful plot.

"I wasn't saying that; I was only pointing out that this is a scene being written for a sixty percent male audience."

"And?" I wished he'd get to the point and say what he wanted instead of dancing around it.

"Women may like the flowery allusion of a penis, but men want to read things written a certain way," he said with a shrug.

"So, the word cock needs to be on the page..." I looked over and counted the times it appeared on the page. "Eight times."

"I know he used it often, but I fail to see an alternative."

He wanted some other options that men would respond to, fine. "Dick."

"Hey, you don't need to call me names." He smirked as he bumped my shoulder.

The eye roll and head shake caused him to laugh at me and tap his stylus on the screen. "Whatever, Sam, so substitute 'dick' a few times."

"But it doesn't have the same impact," he mused, pulling his lip to the side and looking up at the ceiling. He looked simultaneously foolish and adorable when he was thinking. At least, I assumed that was his thinking face. Either that, or he was plain ridiculous.

"It's fine. I'd rather have the scene read easier than being a cockfest." I found myself giggling along with him as he burst into laughter.

"Cockfest? Really?"

"Oh, shut up," I scoffed. "You know what I meant."

"No, I'm not sure what you meant. Please elaborate on this cockfest situation," he sputtered, trying to keep a lid on his amusement.

"I hate you." I narrowed my eyes at him and crossed my arms, my nipples deceiving me with their hypersensitivity. The words on the page had gotten to me, not the man across the table. I hated it when people mocked me, mostly when they were mildly attractive, cocky men who thought that they were better than me.

"I'm aware." The annoying smirk stayed on his face as I went in and put a few suggestions for rephrasing on the page that helped the sequence read a little easier. "I still think it was fine the first time."

"Well, fine isn't going to get him on the Times list again," I pointed out, only slightly mocking. Fine wasn't acceptable with something that would have Chase's name attached to it, either. It was ten times harder to break into the big time for women writers than men, and since she was a romance novelist, she was already devalued. We weren't about to give anyone any excuses to think Evan's work with this book was subpar and blame her.

"Let's move to the next section," Sam suggested as he scrolled down the page to the next scene.

"Whatever," I sighed. I was already bored with this. Sam would argue with my suggestions no matter what they were simply because he didn't like how I did things.

"Do you want me to read it aloud, or do you want..." he trailed off, his cheeks turning a tiny bit red. Hmm. Now there was something that would make things interesting. Reading side by side had obviously affected us somewhat with the first scene, but it was, by far, one of the tamer selections we were editing.

"That's a great idea," I agreed, trying to keep the excitement out of my voice. I had a feeling Sam would be flustered within a few sentences.

He cleared his throat, put his arm across the back of my chair as he leaned in, and started scanning the page for the start of the next scene. "Is it okay if I start right here?" He pointed his stylus at the beginning of the scene, where the prostitute goes into the man's office they suspect of murder and fellates him to get information.

"Looks perfect. Go right ahead," I choked out, biting my lip to keep from laughing. This was going to be good.

"Kallie had always known that using her body as a weapon was the best way to protect herself..." Sam read clearly in his deep timbre. I squeezed my eyes shut for a moment to keep a shudder from trailing down my spine as his warm breath flowed over the side of my neck. *"If you wanted to survive in a male-dominated world, you had to learn what made them tick. What their motivations were. And where their weaknesses lie..."*

Sam cleared his throat softly, the hair on the back of my neck standing up at the sound. *"Donald Harrell's weakness had always been in his pants, and every one of the girls who worked in his club knew it. Having a big dick was something that could either get you a lot of attention or become your greatest asset..."*

"Pfft..." A soft sound of disgust slipped through my lips before I could help it, and I could feel Sam's chest bump against my shoulder lightly as he tried to smother a laugh.

"Something funny?"

"No..." I shook my head as I released a sigh. "It's just. Really? The bad guy has to have a giant dick?"

Sam couldn't contain his laughter this time, and I gripped the stylus in my palm more firmly as his body brushed against mine again. "What does it matter?"

"I don't know," I sighed, "it seems a little gimmicky."

Sam pointed at the following sentence. I knew what Evan was trying to set up, but I was not too fond of it when men let the appendage in their pants determine how gigantic their other head became. "She manipulates his inflated ego to get him to admit things."

"And you can't appeal to the ego of a guy with a normal-sized penis?" There were far more of those than the ones with anacondas in their pants.

"You can, but being well endowed made him...*cocky*," Sam laughed softly.

"Oh, my God." I couldn't help the laughter that slipped out. I honestly didn't understand men sometimes. They all had ego issues. Why did they have to be tied to what was—or wasn't—in their pants?

"Okay, poor choice of words, but she's using what she knows to manipulate him. I don't think the size necessarily matters; it's that he's got that whole big dick energy thing going on."

"Excuse me? What?" I laughed, hating that Sam was funny when he wanted to be. Donald's weakness may have been his penis, but mine was a man with a good sense of humor.

"Don't play dumb, Kristine. I know you've heard of Big Dick Energy. It's not an uncommon term." Knowing that if I looked back, he'd see my expression.I imagined the eye roll that I knew Sam was performing.

"It's a stupid term," I muttered, trying to rein in my wayward thoughts.

"Why?"

"'Cause men are always looking for stupid excuses for inflating their already over-inflated egos." And appointing oneself as important based on what lay between your legs was getting old. The cliché could die already; I was tired of beating down other men's egos. Sam's boss being one of them.

"Sociologists have said it's an actual phenomenon," Sam explained, and then I was eye-rolling. Yet again. Of course, it was.

"Yeah, I know, but it doesn't make the way men's brains function any less ridiculous." It always seemed to come back to an ongoing, perpetual dick-measuring contest. "Do you let the size of what's in your pants make you act like a douchebag?" I asked with a pointed glance at his slacks.

"You think *I* have it?"

Well, that backfired.

"I never said that..." The smug grin I could see out of the corner of my eye made me clench my teeth.

"But implying that I should be acting like a douchebag means that you think I've got something to warrant it."

I rolled my eyes and raised my voice, trying to downplay the reaction he was trying to get out of me... and that he was succeeding. "Okay, Sherlock. Let's pretend this conversation didn't happen. Can we get back to why this whole sentence is unnecessary?"

"He's using it as justification for why his character acts as he does," Sam explained thoughtfully. Usually, when I questioned an author's reasoning, I got that condescending glare from other editors, but Sam wasn't like that. I wasn't sure if I liked how that affected my image of him. I wanted to believe he was cut from the same cloth as his sexist supervisor, but he appeared to take our discussion seriously, not simply humoring me because I was challenging him.

"So, he's a 'cocky' jerk with a huge...*ego*...because he's got impressive equipment. What if he didn't? He wouldn't still be capable of being a sociopathic jerk?"

He tilted his head and pursed his lips before he responded. "Well, it can go both ways. Sometimes men act like jerks because they're overcompensating."

I laughed and didn't even need to think to identify a man like that. "So, Adrian."

"No comment," Sam chuckled, winking at me. "Other times, having a large member can instill someone with an innate confidence that they might not have if they..."

"Had a micro-penis."

Sam's lip quirked at the corner with my blunt appraisal of some members of the male species. We may have disagreements, but Sam seemed to enjoy my commentary, even if it wasn't always the most diplomatic assessment of a situation. "Or simply below average. Doesn't have to require a magnifying glass to find it."

"Also, like Adrian," I giggled, and his mouth pulled into a more genuine smile, his eyes connecting with mine. The dark blue almost seemed to sparkle with humor, and I liked that while I couldn't always read his facial responses, I could read his eyes.

"Stop," he laughed as he made a few notes about the impact of penis size affecting character development. "All we can do is put in the suggestions. It's up to Evan what he wants to use as a plot device."

"Fair enough," I agreed with a nod. Evan didn't seem the sexist type of macho man, so if he was using the word, and Chase wasn't browbeating him into changing it, using it in his story was intentional.

"I need to return a few emails, you look through the last section, and I'll be back in a few minutes." Sam took his phone out of his pocket and stood up, avoiding eye contact as he approached the door. He seemed a little nervous as he left, and I wondered why he was acting so uncomfortable.

Then I started reading.

Kallie was taunting the detective about what methods she'd used to get the information he needed for his investigation. He was forceful with her, and I found my nipples reacting against my will as I kept reading. Evan's dialogue was all the same as before, but you could feel the frustration and pent-up energy in their coupling with the changes he'd made.

"Damn..."

There was a part where he pulled her hair, and she hit her head against the wall while he pinned her on her knees. The description of the act caused a noticeable reaction in me as I kept reading. My skin prickled, my breathing picked up, and I could tell my eyes were dilating. Chase had truly worked her magic on him to get this kind of reaction. Her grasp of seduction was what made her so successful. With a few well-placed words, she could turn on the heat. No wonder Sam left the room. If this was managing to turn me on, I could only imagine what it'd done to him.

"You finished?" He peeked in the doorway and scanned my face, probably noticing the changes. I had the horrible tendency of having a very noticeable flush to the skin of my neck when I felt aroused. The tenor in his voice was lower than it had been before he retreated to the hallway, but maybe that was only my imagination.

"Close enough," I squeaked.

"And?" He sat next to me and turned the tablet, glancing at the few notes I'd left—nothing substantial, simple wording and sentence structure suggestions.

"It was...good... I guess." I cleared my throat, trying to banish the breathy quality it'd taken on. I wasn't one of those girls who poured on the charm with breathy voices and fluttering eyelashes. I needed to get my head back in the game. I was a professional.

"You guess?"

I wasn't about to admit to him that it was a good thing I was wearing a padded bra. I also wouldn't be telling him about my slightly damp panties. "It'll work."

"So, he didn't use cock too many times?"

"Um, nope." I narrowed my eyes at the smug look on his face and softly cleared my throat again. "I think it was just enough cock."

He laughed as he saved the document and flipped the cover closed on his tablet, turning those disarming blue eyes on me. "I'll let you know when I hear back from him."

"Uh..." I cleared my throat yet again. Why was it so dry suddenly? He was studying me, and I didn't particularly appreciate how it made me feel.

"Evan," he led, and I gave a single, curt nod. "I'll send him the edits and let you know when we've got something else to review."

"Sure, yeah—sounds good."

Was my voice still breathy?

"Sorry to interrupt your work earlier... I guess you can get back to that now." He nodded to the laptop I had abandoned when he ambushed me earlier.

"Yup. Thanks for the permission." Except I wasn't going to be able to focus now because I imagined Sam in place of Detective Raines—pinning *me* to the wall with his cock in my mouth...

And that was all kinds of fucked up because I didn't *like* him...right?

FOUR

SAM

BOSTON

"Dude, are yah gonna spot me or what?"

Shaking my head, I looked back down at my boss, who I somehow got dragged into spotting on the weight bench in the gym downstairs. Typically, a few personal trainers floating the weight room floor took care of this, but Adrian caught me as I came in the door and roped me into being his bitch. Like I didn't spend all day doing things that weren't part of my job for him.

"Yeah." My hands moved into position, past the edge of the bar, and I counted out the reps as he tried to max out the heavy bar. People liked to trash talk that he was soft, but one thing Adrian excelled at was looking good. He didn't always want to focus on doing his job to the best of his ability, but his physique never suffered.

Being naturally athletic, I lifted sometimes, but I preferred running and using the press and cable machines rather than racks or weight benches. Lacrosse players had to focus on overall strength and speed; over-inflated muscles would only slow you down on the field, and as an attacker, I needed to hone my speed at an early age.

"Yah gonna stand there with a blank look on yah face or tell me about how much of a pain in the ass Isobel's attack dog is?"

"Your grasp of the English language befuddles me," I muttered. Adrian was constantly using slang and ending his sentences in prepositions. It drove me insane. I wasn't expecting him to speak in proper English 24/7, but he could at least sound like he deserved his master's degree.

"Whateva, we're not on tha clock. I can speak how I want to," he bit back, the faint sound of his born and raised Boston accent slipping through his typical veneer. You could pull the boy outta Southie, but he had that culture in his DNA. I knew he hated being reminded of his humble beginnings, having worked his ass off to get scholarships to Boston College. Without an Ivy League education, gaining respect from others in our world was hard enough. My family had never struggled, and I earned good grades in high school and college, but certain boys' clubs never had openings if you didn't have that elite pedigree.

"Yah never answered my question."

Holding in the cringe, I refocused on his sweaty face and tried to come up with something to appease him. "Kristine is fine. We work well together." *Lies, so many lies.* "It's refreshing to work with someone so professional."

Adrian scoffed, and as I watched his eyes roll back in his head, I knew I'd laid it on a little thick. Kristine wasn't terrible to work with, but the snark was strong with that one, and I often wondered if I should wear a cup under my trousers just in case I angered her unintentionally...or intentionally. Take your pick. Her feistiness appealed to me, having grown up surrounded by strong women.

Her voice also did something to me, especially when it got that little growly quality to it, like when I'd saved her from getting fired for assaulting the nephew of one of the higher-ups. She didn't seem to realize that nepotism, while complete bullshit, also ensured some idiots were untouchable. I knew she could defend herself, but he was a jackass and sexually harassed everyone who came near his desk.

"Just watch yah self around that one; she's got an ego problem." Like he didn't. "Yah'd think having a loaded daddy would get her whatever she wanted, but she's a real man-eater."

Daddy? "Do you mean like she has a sugar daddy?" She didn't seem like the type to cater to some older guy's whims.

Adrian laughed as he pushed his way through his rep, groaning slightly at the end. Another reason that I hated working out with him. He was a grunter. "No, her pops is some bigwig at a hedge fund in New York, old money, loaded yacht party shit. Fairly sure Kristine summers in the Hamptons. But she's no *daddy's little princess.*"

She'd never given me that elitist kind of vibe. Sure, she was difficult to talk to and often abrasive in social situations, but it wasn't because she was a snob. I knew he meant to give me the information as a warning, but it was like peeling back another layer on the onion; I was curious about what was inside.

She'd enjoyed teasing me when we read through the pages the other day, and I could tell from the subtle physical cues she gave away that she was aroused yet angry about it for some reason. It was like she didn't want to show anyone she could be attracted to them. I'd kept my cards close to the vest, but she was locked up tight.

"She'll have yah balls in a vice before yah can blink if yah try something."

"Why would I try something?" While I was friendly with my colleagues, I didn't make it a point to openly flirt with any of them, especially those who weren't interested. Adrian was the one who had a reputation for skirting the line of professionalism. He wasn't as blatant as Carson, but he was one inappropriate comment to the wrong person away from getting reported to Human Resources.

"Yah two are both about tha same age," he said with a shrug like that was the only reason to be interested in someone. "Yah don't have a girlfriend, right?"

"Not right now." I shook my head. I don't even know why I was confiding in him. It wasn't like my personal life was any of his business.

"Or a boyfriend?"

I frowned as I looked down at the smirk on his face. "No, not one of those either."

"No judgment here, man. It's cool if yah like dick."

You *are* a dick. "And you wonder why people around the office think you're a jerk."

"Hey, I only call 'em as I see 'em. You're kinda a pretty boy."

As he racked the bar and sat up on the bench, I hoped I could step back and make my escape. My run the previous day had been crap since my mother got into my head with her 'abandoning the family' rhetoric. I knew she was wrong, but it still bothered me to think that I was letting people down.

"Are we done?" I asked him as he moved to a weight rack and picked up a seventy-pound free weight. I stuck to the forties or fifties and tried to fatigue the muscle by maxing out my reps. Whatever floated his boat—and his obnoxious biceps—and got me out of here faster.

"Yeah, I guess yah can go do yah aerobics class or whateva," he joked.

"I'm headed to the treadmill, but I'm sure I'll catch you in Zumba later this week."

I knew that Isobel could be found in the dance studio sometimes. Adrian was almost creepy enough to stalk her if he knew that information.

Trying to focus for once, I headed to the treadmill, set it to a seven, and started running. The last week had wreaked havoc on my mental and physical health. Sometimes I watched the people behind me in the mirrors, not in a creepy way, but simply general observations on human interaction. But today, I was trying to stay in my lane.

In my peripheral vision, I saw a toned, pair of pale slender legs start to move on the treadmill next to me. There were plenty of available machines in the room, but apparently, this person couldn't respect personal space. It was unwritten gym etiquette to leave space on either side of a runner unless the machines were all occupied.

After I'd clocked my first mile, I slowed to a jog, wiping my face with my towel and glancing up as I placed it back into the cupholder. The pair of slender legs belonged to Kristine. Her face was intensely focused as I watched her out of the corner of my eye, those white earbuds shoved into her ears again, the swing of her long ponytail hypnotic to watch as she kept a steady cadence.

Female athletes were typically bulkier than Kristine's slim but curvy build, but it was clear that she had an innate athletic ability. I wondered if she'd been in sports when she was younger. She'd have made an impressive distance runner with how her arms naturally carried while she ran. The momentum of your body could be a powerful thing. Part of our conditioning had been learning proper running form and then fine-tuning it with a stick in our hands.

Watching Kristine's hands pass by her lower cheeks as she increased her speed drew me to the fact that she had on a pair of tiny shorts—extraordinarily little shorts—with venting slits up the side that revealed a good amount of thigh. In the office, she was always buttoned up, wearing long-sleeved blouses and fitted slacks, rarely skirts, but she wasn't exactly the epitome of girly.

Trying not to be utterly creepy in my observation of her, I quickly resumed my jogging pace. I returned my focus to my reflection in the mirror or the numbers on the panel of my treadmill. My brain wasn't even registering the music in my ears because I wondered what kind of music she listened to while she ran. I usually pulled up an app with playlists suited to keeping an even cadence, but I knew she created her own running soundtrack.

I didn't even know what was wrong with me. My fixation with her was growing the more time we spent together. She was a piece of work sometimes.

I let out a harsh breath—my steps faltering—as I recalled how her soft pink lips had parted when I read to her. I'd had to leave the office after that before my voice started squeaking like a pubescent boy's. The scene had been steamy before I found myself reading it aloud to a woman whose eyes had dilated to the point they appeared a deep hunter green. Add to that the flush that appeared on the creamy skin of her neck, and I was fucking adjusting myself like a high school boy caught in gym class with a hard-on.

A cough from my right startled me out of my dangerous thoughts, and I pressed the button to slow my treadmill as I looked over at Kristine, who had finally noticed I was running next to her. She glanced at me before screwing the cap back on her water bottle, eyes guarded.

"Who is stalking who, now?" I challenged as she settled it back into her cup holder. She must have turned her music down when she slowed, her fingers tightening on the water bottle and causing a plastic crinkling noise.

The glare she gave me should have corrected the situation in my shorts, but it only caused a flare of heat to surge through me as I raised an eyebrow at her reflection in the mirror.

She huffed, readjusting her earbud, then took off at a steady jog, averting her eyes to the open tread on her other side.

Fine, I could ignore her too. Glancing down at her screen, I noted the speed and set mine a bit faster, my legs burning as I broke into a run. She narrowed her eyes as she glanced back at me, and I watched her hand reach forward to adjust her speed again. So competitive.

She didn't know who she was challenging. I ran six miles daily—as long as I could fit it into my schedule—and my stamina would surely outlast hers.

Waiting until she wasn't looking, I snuck my hand forward and sped up again, welcoming the burn in my lungs as I watched the mileage start to track faster on my screen.

Of course, she couldn't help herself, so moments later, I smirked, trying to keep myself from laughing as she sped up again. I knew she was competitive, but this wasn't only in reaction to some office rivalry.

Half expecting her to fly off the back of the treadmill, I watched as she pushed herself off the belt and settled into a steady run. A novice could never maintain that cadence without fatiguing quickly, so I was impressed at how well she held her form.

Tiny beads of sweat had started to build at her temples, and I watched one track down her flushed cheek and onto her neck. The same pink mottling she had in the office the other day was visible on her skin right above the low-cut neckline of her tank top. Fumbling, I reached forward and slowed down my tread, picking up my water bottle and taking several large gulps as I tried not to focus on how her modest chest appeared as it bounced under that athletic tank.

I was glad I wore compression shorts regularly because otherwise I'd now likely be showing off my hard bouncing cock to anyone who was watching.

A glance at my screen showed I had clocked three and a half miles. Deciding that I'd hit my six and get out of here, I placed my water bottle back in the holder and pushed a few buttons, settling into a steady run so I could finish.

Kristine had also slowed to a fast-paced walk to take a drink, but I could see the challenge in her eyes as my belt started to pick up speed. She tightened her ponytail, her arms pushing her tits together in that damn tank top, and I held in a groan as I looked forward at my reflection again. I was trying—and failing—to keep myself from imagining pushing them together in the same manner with my hands.

One more mile. Only one more mile and I could go home. *Fuck.*

She settled into a fast run next to me, matching my pace, and I found my competitive streak kick in as I pushed my button two times in quick succession. Her tongue peeked out of the corner of her mouth as she followed suit, and I watched her expressive eyes narrow in the mirror as she matched my pace.

Almost there, a quarter of a mile left to go. It was on.

Pushing myself into a sprint, I pressed the speed button several times and watched the numbers climb as I pushed my legs to their limit. My muscles were burning as I saw her in my peripheral vision sprinting just as quickly. Deciding I could go over my mileage goal, I kept up the speed, smirking as I watched her hand move to the button to lower her speed. But before I could reach forward to slow myself down, her fingers pushed the button to max out my treadmill speed.

My legs flexed to compensate for the quick change of pace, and I heard her loud laugh as my eyes widened. Bracing my hands on the handrails, I jumped, my feet lifting off the belt and bracing on the side rails as I coughed loudly.

Before I could turn to respond to her little joke, I watched as her body drifted down her treadmill belt and jumped off the back in one smooth motion. She gave me a jaunty little salute in the mirror as she burst into laughter and strutted toward the locker room doors.

"Oh, I don't think so," I growled as I reached forward to press the stop button on my treadmill and hers, quickly grabbing my things and jogging after her.

She looked over her shoulder, eyes wide as she saw me coming after her, and quickly changed direction, weaving through a set of burly men joking around next to a leg press machine. I quickly side-stepped them, coming around to the transition in the flooring that led straight into a path to intercept her.

"Right where I want you." A dark chuckle escaped my lips as I sped up, and I would have caught her if...

"Hey, where's tha fire?" Adrian laughed as he grasped my shoulder, causing me to jerk back and turn in his direction.

"What?" His eyes widened at my tone, and he frowned over my shoulder as he looked over to the locker room doors and then back to my face.

Mine followed, and I watched as Kristine glanced back over her shoulder, her slender middle finger raising into view as she winked and disappeared behind the door. Fuck.

"What did she do now?" he laughed, taking in my clenched jaw and pinched expression.

Closing my eyes and taking a deep breath, I schooled my features and turned back toward him, shaking my hands at my sides. "Nothing, don't worry about it."

"Didn't look like nothin." His eyebrow rose, and I shook my head slightly.

"It's fine," I bit out, turning out of his grasp and attempting to walk at an average pace away from him. "I'll see you tomorrow."

"See yah." His laughter followed me, and I tried to calm myself down as I headed toward the door to the men's room.

I don't even know what my plan would have been if I caught her. But her little aggressive attempt to rile me up had worked in more ways than one.

"Fuck," I grunted as I threw open a changing stall door and quickly latched it behind me. The space was too small to pace like I wanted to, but my adrenaline was sky-high as I slapped my hand against the wall. That smirk she aimed at me as she escaped made me want to do dangerous things to her. Punish that smart mouth of hers. Have her begging for it. I wasn't sure what *it* was yet; mercy, my mouth, my dick—take your pick.

I hated that I couldn't control my body's reaction to her, but goddamn, did she work me up like I seemed to do to her sometimes. Recalling those luscious lips and how her toned legs flowed out of those tiny shorts was doing nothing to control the situation on my own. Not wanting to be that *cliché* guy, beating off in the locker room, I tried to will it away, but the tenting of the mesh material wasn't going away. It was only getting harder the angrier I got with myself for responding this way.

It seemed like there was only one way out of this situation. Angrily tearing at my waistband, I pulled open the curtain to the private shower and shoved my shorts the rest of the way down, throwing them onto the bench in the corner before I yanked off the rest of my sweaty clothes and chucked them in the same direction.

The blast of hot water had me hissing at the burn, but I didn't give a fuck as I grasped my solid cock and started angrily pulling it through my fist as I clenched my teeth. Unbidden images of that troublesome mouth started flashing behind my eyelids as I clenched them shut tightly. The way her tongue wrapped around my name when she was irritated. The tone of ire in her voice made the hair on the back of my neck stand up. How her mouth looked when the word dick escaped her lips made mine throb as I set a punishing pace, working my hand rapidly under the hot spray of the shower head.

"Ahh," I gasped angrily as I thought back to the way her eyes flashed with anger when I teased her, those green orbs shooting death glares at me. My heart pounded, and my bicep burned as I pushed myself closer to climax, grunting with the motions of my hand.

I was so close and hated myself a little as I imagined what it'd look like if she were on her knees in front of me, teasing me with that wicked tongue of hers in a much more sensual way. Sucking and licking me until I couldn't control myself anymore and grasped that ponytail on the back of her head to...

"Fuck," I groaned as I felt my balls contract and paint the shower tiles with my release. I tried to maintain my balance with a hand braced against the cool surface, flashes of color dancing across my field of vision.

What the hell was wrong with me? Fuck... I knew *exactly* what was wrong with me.

Her.

FIVE

KRISTINE

BOSTON

For the first time in my professional career...I was feeling regret. I'd broken Sam. Gone were the teasing sighs and the tiny barbs he normally tossed in my direction to wind me up. He was the perfect mask of indifference. Approaching each of our interactions with a calm, polite, professional demeanor, often opting for brief emails instead of showing up in doorways and scolding me for being rude.

I should have been in heaven, not having to deal with another male ego, but I found myself formulating ways to get the veneer he'd fastened in place to crack.

I knew I should have given him space when I'd gone down to run that day. He looked like he was concentrating while those long legs of his beat down on that treadmill belt. He was trying to outrun something, and I felt empathy as I often did that myself. I found myself trying to push my body to the point where my brain stopped overthinking.

We didn't *know* each other—not well enough to confide in one another—but I found myself wanting to ask what was bothering him. Which only served to piss me off because I never wanted to have small talk with anyone, never mind Sam. We weren't friends... We were barely coworkers, temporarily thrown together for this project.

Isobel was right. He wasn't as bad as I'd made him out to be, but now he was broken, and I wanted to shake him out of it. This stoic behavior, in turn, made me angry all over again because I didn't want to socialize with him; I only wanted to hear his teasing voice instead of the detached one he'd adopted.

"Kristine?" Isobel was working on formatting an e-book at her desk for another author, her eyes intensely focused on the computer monitor in front of her. Usually, we had a department of desktop publishers that worked on that kind of layout and design work, but occasionally, Isobel refused to pass a project off to them.

"Yes?" I'd been trying to get into this new manuscript I was doing a structural edit on, but I couldn't concentrate. Maybe I'd broken myself as well. I'd already read forty pages, the right side of my tablet screen full of notes, but I couldn't tell you what the main character's name was off the top of my head.

"Chase messaged me that she's going to be out of the office, out of town, whatever you want to call it, for a few days. She's been dodging my emails. I think something is going on there, but I can't force her to tell me. Can you check the chapters she sent in a few weeks ago so I have something to give back to her once she's done with this little break?"

The chapters were already sitting on the shared server, full of my notes, but I was waiting to tell Isobel until I'd seen more of the manuscript. "They're on the shared drive. I worked on them last week."

She nodded as her fingers paused on the keyboard, looking up to make eye contact for a few silent, loaded moments. "Would you ever change your professional goals for a relationship?" *Whoa*. That was some deep material to think about on a Monday morning. She must have sensed my hesitation, waving her hand in the air. "Never mind. Ignore that."

But I couldn't. Isobel had been a little scattered the last few days, so I wondered what was going on in her personal life, which was weird because we typically had a distinct barrier between our personal and professional lives. We were friendly, but we weren't friends, just like everyone else in my life. They only saw what I wanted them to, which wasn't much.

"Is this for a manuscript?"

She sighed before she leaned back in her chair. "No. Like I said, forget it."

It seemed everyone in this office was broken this week, and I didn't like it. I didn't like it one fucking bit. Isobel was the one I counted on as the solid foundation in this office, so we were all screwed if she faltered.

"You can't drop a question like that and recall it—that's just fricked up, Is. Seriously? Has everyone lost it this week?"

"Excuse me?" Her eyebrow arched higher than I'd probably ever seen it rise, her intimidating *business-lady bitch face* appearing. It made me cringe inside, but she needed to answer for herself. What in the actual fuck was that question?

"You heard me. Don't ask me shit if you don't want me to answer it. No, I wouldn't sacrifice my goals for a man. We work hard to get where we are, much harder than the dicks between their legs will ever get. I would not let some man derail my career to suit his ego."

She sat back in her seat, swiveling and chewing her bottom lip. This entire day kept getting weirder and weirder. First, Chase missed a deadline—she never missed a deadline. Then Adrian was friendly to me this morning, Isobel was having an existential crisis, and the pod people had captured Sam.

"Seriously, you all have lost your ever-loving minds. I just can't. I can't deal with any of you today," I huffed as I started packing away my laptop and shoving my tablet into my bag. I would find somewhere else to work. This crap was toxic to my mental health. I didn't have the energy or patience to deal with other people's problems today. "When you can tell me why you'd ever change your career goals, for Adrian—I'm assuming—of all people, then I will come back into this office. Until then, email me if you need me to work on something."

"Kristine," she admonished, and I shook my head. I was not getting dragged into this office romance bullshit. No. *No.* Hell to the nope.

"I'll see you in a few hours. Text me if you want me to pick something up for your lunch."

Swinging my bag onto my shoulder, I started toward the door, halting when I noticed the prominent figure striding down the hallway.

"Oh yay, it's Dickhead," I muttered under my breath.

"Morning, Kristine, I wanted to see if I could borrow you for a favor..."

Shit.

"What do you need?" I sighed as I tried to step around him.

"I put in an order at that sandwich shop over on High Street. Would you mind picking it up for me? Sam has something going on and is returning after lunch today."

Great. Now I was expected to be Adrian's snack bitch. Why couldn't he use DoorDash like the average person? "I've got things I need to get through."

"Actually. Would you mind, Kristine?" Isobel asked, and I turned to give her a death glare. "You can take my corporate card, and I'll call in an order too. Would you like anything?"

Yeah. I want my boss not to treat me like a delivery driver for someone when he should have his intern do his errands. "Fine. But you're paying for mine too." I knew if I argued, she'd only get pissy.

"That's fine. Take an Uber, and I'll reimburse you."

Fuck. This was annoying.

"Sure thing, *boss.*" I smiled tightly, taking a few steps to snatch the card from her hand before dodging Adrian in the doorway.

As I walked down the hallway, Carson looked up from his desk, and I gave him a death glare as he started to push himself out of his chair. "Not today, Car-satan. Sit back down."

"Rawr," he teased as I walked past him, my eyes widening as I looked toward the reception desk where Sam was leaning against the counter—smiling and laughing with Andrea, the receptionist. Was he fucking kidding with this?

"I thought you were supposed to be working a half day?" I asked as he looked over his shoulder toward me. "Thanks for leaving me to be Dickhead's errand girl."

"Hey, Kristine, it's nice to see you too this morning. Can I help you with something?"

My jaw clenched as I tried not to flare my nostrils. Maybe Sam wasn't so broken—that teasing glint was held in check, but it was back.

"Frick off, Spam," I growled as I turned and stalked off toward the elevators.

Heavy footsteps followed me down the hallway, and I quickly jabbed the button and hopped into the first open elevator.

"Hey," Sam called out as his hand shot into the open door, quickly followed by his body before it slipped closed. "What's going on? You're unusually surly this morning."

"Thanks." I let out a sarcastic laugh. "*Surly*, that's just what every woman wants to be called."

"Seriously, are you okay?"

Rolling my eyes, I sighed and leaned into the back corner of the elevator, pulling up my email on my phone.

"You're ignoring me now?" That obnoxious smile was back, and I regretted feeling bad for thinking that I had broken him with my little treadmill prank.

"No."

"It kinda seems like you're mad at me."

Sighing as I rolled my eyes, I leaned into the corner of the elevator and pinned him down with a stern glare. "Not everything is about you, Sam."

"But I think this is." He took three steps forward, right outside of the bubble of invading my personal space.

"Or maybe it's not." My eyes dropped to my phone's lock screen, and I pretended to be reading something as he took another step forward. I didn't particularly appreciate how my breathing picked up as he approached, but I couldn't help it. The bastard smelled good, and I *liked* how he was invading my personal space, but from enough of a distance that I didn't feel caged in by him. If I asked him to back up, I knew he would, which said a lot about his character.

"Do you need me to accompany you on whatever errand Adrian has sent you?"

"I thought you had things going on. Since I'm the one being forced to give up my morning to go pick up food for your narcissistic boss, you know. Must be nice to ditch work whenever you want to."

He pursed his lips as he looked down at me, seemingly fighting with himself about how to respond.

"You can punch me if I'm out of line with this because I know that I probably am, but I'm going to ask it anyway," he said in a deep voice, leaning in toward me, his breath warm against the side of my neck. "Is reading about all that sexual tension driving you a little crazy too?"

What? I was not expecting that to be his question.

"Are you seriously asking me this?" I bit my lip as I tried to hold in the laugh that wanted to escape. It seemed poor Sam was having trouble with a little bit of spice. "That isn't exactly a professional thing to ask me, Sam."

"I know, but I can't help myself. After we read that section together..." He paused before he continued. "It's kind of messing with my head. I keep picturing us as..."

Heat flashed through me at his quiet admission, but I chose to ignore that he'd said it was making him think about *us*. There was no us.

"Is that what's been wrong with you this week?" Here I thought it was because I'd riled him up. "You can't handle reading about a little dick?"

"Well, I thought we talked about that part before." He leaned in even closer, his hand coming forward to rest on the elevator wall next to my head. "You told me I had big dick energy."

I most certainly did *not* tell him that, but now I was wondering...

The hairs on my neck stood up as I gazed at his intense stare. His lips parted slightly, and I couldn't stop looking at them. Would they feel as soft as they looked? Was he one of those soft sensual kissers, or did he push you up against the wall and take over until you felt like your lungs would explode? I wasn't sure which one sounded more appealing.

"I don't think I've ever seen you at a loss for words," he whispered as his other hand reached toward my face. My lips parted, and I held my breath as his finger touched my cheek—tucking a wayward strand of hair behind my ear—his hand lingering and then pulling away. I'd always thought that was only a cliché in the romance novels I edited, but it still made my pulse skyrocket.

"Who..." I breathed out, suddenly having an Amy Farrah Fowler moment. I could understand her involuntary noises around attractive men on a soul-deep level. It took a lot to get me flustered, but Sam whispering the word dick in my ear was making something other than my jaw clench.

"Use your words, Kristine. I know that you are familiar with quite a few of them."

I can't right now, Sam. But keep up the teasing, and I might be able to use my kneecap.

"I...uh..." Couldn't form a complete sentence to save my life as his masculine scent clouded my brain cells and, apparently, my judgment as I kept staring at his mouth. What in the fuck was wrong with me?

The elevator stopped, and Sam stepped back, shooting me a teasing grin over his shoulder before holding out his hand and gesturing for me to walk out ahead of him. "After you..."

Dodging the people waiting just past the door, I wove through the building lobby, unlocking my phone and trying to see if there was an Uber nearby. I could tell by the beating of my heart that the thought of Sam coming after me again excited me. I already knew that because I'd slumped against the locker room door the other day in the gym, panting as if I'd run a marathon instead of three miles.

Maybe I was the one who'd been broken. My physical reaction to Sam was precisely why I liked to stay in my own lane. Adrian and Sam had forced their way into my life, and now those little shits were screwing everything up.

"Hey, wait up," Sam's voice carried across the lobby as I pulled open the door. His hand grabbed the frame and held it while he followed me out onto the sidewalk.

"What do you want?" I asked and watched as his gaze swept down my body before he looked back into my eyes.

"I'm going to the dentist. I wasn't trying to skip out on work. Andrea asked me about something for one of her classes, and I was helping her out before I left." He seemed a little flustered, and I wasn't sure I was happy I'd gotten what I'd asked. It made me want to return to the days when we just passed each other in the hallways with a nod and sat across the table in department meetings. Being thrown into proximity to him was messing with my head. "Next time, just tell Adrian to send Carson to get his food."

"I would have, but he cornered me in Isobel's office, and she told me to go. I'm sure she was trying to get rid of me. Have you been getting some weird vibes off them lately?"

"Yeah, I have, but..." A loud honk from the street drew our attention. It appeared my ride was waiting.

"I should go," I said awkwardly and watched as he shoved his hands in the front pockets of his pants.

"Yeah, I guess I'll see you around." He nodded, and then I awkwardly nodded back, not knowing how to navigate this new dynamic in our relationship. His body language indicated that he was nervous around me, but I'd also noted minor signs of attraction. I knew I'd felt the same way, but it was probably because of what we'd read together. I was projecting the chemistry that Chase and Evan had produced onto Sam.

It couldn't possibly be that he was attractive, vaguely funny, had gorgeous eyes and broad shoulders. It most definitely was not because I wanted to run my fingers through his hair to see if it was as soft as it looked.

"You better go." He gestured toward the waiting car as the driver rolled down his window and gave me the stink eye.

"Yeah." Before this got any more awkward. "See ya later, I guess. Are you coming back this afternoon?"

"I should be, but..."

"Yeah?"

"Are you planning to hit up that bar where the graphic design team is throwing Carrie's birthday party on Friday?" I looked up at him in surprise. While he may have been social with others we worked with, I tended to stick to myself. Even friendships got messy when you worked together; it was easier not to form attachments.

"I wasn't, but..."

"You should," he encouraged. "It'll be fun. They've got karaoke and darts."

Another honk from the curb, and I knew this guy would ding my rating if I didn't hurry up.

"Just text me the details, and I'll think about it." I held my phone up like a giant dork and shook it before I hustled across the sidewalk and into the waiting car.

"Sorry," I apologized as I buckled myself in. I'm sure the driver probably already started the clock, so my awkward little exchange with Sam cost me more than just my sanity. At least Isobel's expense account was the one paying for it.

"No worries, address still the same?"

"Yeah," I nodded as I unlocked my phone and returned to my emails. Chase cc'd me on the email she had sent Isobel when she decided she needed to drop off the grid for a little while. It wasn't like it was the first time she'd done it, but typically only during the rough editing process, not when she was starting a project.

Trying to focus on being productive was becoming increasingly difficult as I found my mind wandering on the ride across town.

"You need a ride back, right?" he confirmed as he turned the corner on High Street and found somewhere to park near the restaurant.

"Yeah, not sure how long the food will take, so I'll try to be quick."

"Hey, it's your wallet, not mine," he laughed as he pulled out his phone and started to scroll through some social media app.

"Gotcha."

When I walked inside the small restaurant, I scanned the room. Thankfully, there was only a short line, but most tables were filled with people out for breakfast. Seeing if I knew anyone when I walked into a room was a habit. My mother had taught me that you needed to be aware of your surroundings at an early age so people who may not have your best interests in mind didn't catch you unawares. It was part of the reason I hated visiting home. Living in Boston, I didn't have to live up to my last name. I wasn't 'Mason Willard's daughter,' and I could be a badass at work all on my own without people using me to get to him.

As I walked toward the end of the line, a distinct feminine laugh caught my attention, and I scanned the tables in the back corner of the room.

"Are you kidding me?"

Chase Rodgers, known by the pen name Chastity Rose, was sitting in the back corner at a table with a guy who looked vaguely familiar. So much for her being out of town. More like she was dodging her editor. I could walk away and pretend I hadn't seen her, but as she glanced at me guiltily and held her hand next to her face, my feet automatically changed course and headed in their direction.

"Chase," I sighed as I stopped next to their table, narrowing my eyes at the guilt that crossed her face. She was up to something. "So, you are alive. I was beginning to wonder."

"Yup," she nodded. "Still here. What are you doing here?"

"Picking up an order for dickhead. He claimed he had a craving, and his intern..." His annoyingly charming intern. "...was 'busy.'" I tried to keep the disdain out of my voice as I mimed air quotes at *busy*.

Chase seemed a little shocked. "Is actually let him send you on an errand?"

Sighing, I rolled my eyes. "Those two are being weird. She's super distracted lately, and to be completely frank, she's pissed off at you."

Her face pinched as she cringed. "Crap."

Raising my eyebrow, I looked at the guy across from her, who'd been silent until then. "So, are you the reason that Chase isn't meeting her deadlines?"

"Kristine, be nice," Chase admonished.

"It's just a question, Chase. He's a big boy. He can answer questions." His eyes widened as he looked over, and his mouth twitched as he stared at me.

"Uh..."

"Okay, so maybe he can't." I returned his stare, squinting as I studied his face. His eyes seemed familiar, but I couldn't quite place it. "I know you."

He started shaking his head, looking mildly panicked. I almost felt bad for the guy as he stuttered. "I...uh. I've never met you."

"No..." I tilted my head to the side, studying him. "Your face is familiar. Where do I know you from?"

"Kristine," Chase scolded. "Leave the guy alone."

Turning back toward her, I relented. "Fine. Maybe I'm mistaken, but I doubt it."

"Anyways," I took a breath and sighed again. "You better come up with something, or she's gonna take it out on me."

My phone started buzzing in my pocket. Fuck. Pulling it out, I sighed as I looked at the screen seeing a text from Isobel. "Damn. I'm being summoned. Good to see you, Chase. I'm sure I'll see you around."

Quickly unlocking my phone and pulling up the messages, I saw that Dickhead was getting impatient.

Isobel: Adrian is getting hangry. Any idea of when you'll be back?

Kristine: Just getting food now. Be back ASAP.

Thankfully, the Uber driver hadn't taken off by the time I picked up the to-go order. He quickly maneuvered through traffic and managed to get me back to the office in less than ten minutes. After quickly rating him, I hustled to the elevator and recalled the exchange that'd happened earlier.

Sam was getting under my skin, and I didn't like it. I knew I'd tried to rationalize it as proximity and exposure to the racy scenes we'd been editing together, but deep down, I knew I was full of shit.

SIX

SAM

BOSTON

Loud music filtered over the speakers as I sat at the bar, aimlessly picking at the label of my beer, occasionally glancing toward the door like a desperate stalker. This whole week had been one giant ball of awkwardness. Mostly from me, which was unsettling. All because a particular snarky coworker had laid off the snark for once.

We'd finally gotten through the last round of edits on Evan's manuscript and handed it off to the formatters. Typically, that was the time we celebrated. Another job well done, and then we'd have the build-up to a book release. Sometimes it was a little anticlimactic with Evan because he refused to do book tours, but the marketing team usually orchestrated a big social media push.

Most authors would manage their social media accounts and add graphics Vivid had provided them, but Adrian managed all that. Evan didn't want anything to do with social media. He let Adrian have free reign of his fan group, Facebook, and Instagram pages, and I was confident all the media graphics were also getting posted on TikTok. Someone from marketing had set up his Goodreads account. Part of me admired that he could hand those parts off to professionals to manage, but that always seemed like the fun part to me.

Adrian often had me working the local events for his authors, occasionally traveling to the New York branch of the office to help with promotional tours. I found it entertaining to interact with the readers, learn about which parts of the books they enjoyed, and travel to new cities. I always felt like a proud parent watching the readers fall in love with a book I helped make shine.

"Hey, Sam," Andrea greeted me as she sat on the stool next to me at the bar. "Why are you over here all by yourself? There's plenty of space over at the tables if you want to come to join us."

Glancing to the back corner, I could see a large group of my coworkers joking and laughing, some already well on their way to being drunk. It appeared they were all having fun, especially the birthday girl, who was in a corner booth kissing her boyfriend with more tongue than was appropriate for public consumption.

"Nah," I sighed, looking toward the door again and hating myself for doing it. "I'm good here for a while. I'll come join you in a bit."

This whole inner turmoil was really starting to be obnoxious, and it was killing what was supposed to be a fun evening, all because I had to open my huge mouth and invite Kristine to come tonight. I knew she probably wouldn't show up, but I wanted to see her in an environment outside the office. I needed to see if the appeal was still there or if it was just the idea of getting her to shed that hard professional outer shell.

"Thought you'd be out trying to pick up chicks."

Kristine sat down on the stool Andrea had just vacated, crossing her legs and showing off a generous amount of bare skin that her short, pleated, red skirt revealed. Now that was something I had never seen on her. And it was not helping my conflicted feelings at all. Fuck, she looked hot.

Her makeup was darker than I was used to seeing. Her hair flowed down around her shoulders with chaotic waves, a stark contrast from her usual sleek bun. And she was showing more skin than I'd seen outside the gym in a form-fitting tank top highlighting her athletic build. It was too bad the skirt wasn't plaid because she would be fulfilling a naughty school-girl fantasy for me if it was. I'd love to bend her over my knee and grab hold of that...*no, Sam, stop imagining her ass.*

"Who says I'm not?" I shot back as I leaned toward her, hesitating before I said. "I wasn't sure if you would come."

"Well," she replied with a grin, leaning toward my ear. "If you can't get a girl to come, you may need to reevaluate your technique."

My mouth dropped open slightly, my dick certainly noticing how good she smelled, as she started laughing at my expense.

"I don't think I've ever seen you at a loss for words, Sam."

"Ha-ha, Kristine, aren't you cute?" She was, and I was starting to think I was in some serious trouble. This crush, fixation, obsession—whatever it was—had really started to fuck with me.

Don't think about fucking, Sam. And don't think about how you can see down Kristine's tank top when she leans in toward you. That would be an epically bad idea.

"Why, yes, Sam. I am pretty damn cute."

Shaking my head at the sudden playfulness I wasn't expecting, I couldn't help teasing her. I only hoped it wouldn't come back to bite me in the ass later. I leaned in, brushing her hair behind her shoulder as I whispered in her ear. "I was thinking more along the lines of pretty damn fucking sexy."

"Wha..." she made the little squeaking noise she'd made in the elevator, and I couldn't hold in the smirk that she had a physical tell when she was flustered.

Leaning back, I picked up my beer bottle and took a healthy swig of the cold liquid before I looked back toward her. Kristine was clenching her jaw and staring at me with trepidation like I was a predator, her gaze flickering between my eyes and my mouth.

Now that we were out of the office, picking up on her signals was easier. The way she initiated eye contact, the teasing tone of her voice, and the nervous habit of bouncing her foot all indicated what I knew she'd never say. She was just as attracted to me as I found myself to her.

"Now, who can't find her words?" I teased, watching as her eyes flashed with annoyance.

"Oh, I know plenty of words, Sam. Let's see if I can list them off, shall we?" She tilted her head to the side in the manner I'd learned meant that she was about to lay into you.

I couldn't wait.

"Cocky."

I wasn't going to comment on that one, but she'd gotten the attention of the piece of anatomy in question.

"Arrogant."

It was probably wrong of me to get a little turned on at how her eyebrow arched and how when she'd started counting off on her hands, it caused her arms to push her tits together in that tight tank top.

"Egotistical."

"Wait," I interrupted, "Aren't those all synonyms of each other? Do they even count as different things?"

"Maybe that's the point, Sam." She turned on the stool to face me head-on, shifting forward so her leg nestled between mine. "You're a brat."

"Oh, Kris," I laughed as I whispered in her ear again. "We both know I'm not the brat in this situation." I paused momentarily and then pressed my lips against her ear, roughly whispering. "And brats are designed for one thing—getting put over my knee."

At her quick inhale of breath, I was almost afraid she'd throw her knee forward into my crotch, but she grasped my leg with her hand, turning her mouth toward my ear. "You say that like it's a terrible thing. Sounds fun. Wonder if you'd have the nerve to follow through."

"Fuck." I exhaled softly, grasping her wrist to halt the forward motion of her hand.

"Don't play a game you can't win, Sam," she taunted as she leaned back, turning toward the bar and signaling to the bartender.

There were two ways that I could handle this situation. I could pull back and stop flirting, even though imagining what it'd feel like if Kristine rode me in that skirt was now running on a loop in my head. Or...I could go for it and fuck the consequences. Well, hopefully, fuck something.

After the bartender slid a tall glass of what looked like a mojito across the bar to her, I leaned close to her ear as she wrapped her lips around the straw. "I'm not playing a game, Kristine. I think you'd look hot with my handprint right about here." I grazed my palm along the back of her skirt, just enough that she could tell where I was talking about but not enough that I was that creepy guy grabbing a woman's ass in a bar.

She choked on the sip that she'd taken of her drink, coughing a few times before she turned and glared at me. "You can't just whisper things like that in a girl's ear, Sam. Holy fricking shit."

Leaning in toward her again, I made sure my lips grazed her earlobe, secretly enjoying the shudder I saw go through her at the contact. I don't know if it was the beer or that I hadn't gotten laid in a few months, but... "So, I shouldn't whisper that I'm imagining what it'd be like to flip up the back of that skirt and bend you over the end of my bed?"

I could tell by how she tensed up that she'd heard me clearly, but the question was... Would she play along or twist off my nuts?

"Do you want me to keep going?"

Her hand grasped my thigh again as she gave me a subtle nod.

I leaned back toward her, running the tip of my nose along the side of her neck. "I bet you taste as sweet as you smell..." Her breath caught as I softly kissed beneath her ear, loving how her fingers clenched my leg, her nails biting into the denim of my jeans.

"Would you leave marks on my back when I make you come?" I whispered, "I wonder what you'd sound like if you moaned my name."

"Sam," she breathed out in a quiet moan, "What..." Her hand shook on my thigh as she turned her head to the side to look into my eyes. "What's going on?"

"I'm telling you what I've been thinking about this week and hoping it's not one-sided because then I'd feel like a giant jackass."

"It's," she sighed, as her eyes shut slightly. "This is a terrible idea, but..."

"Mmhmm," I hummed as I pushed a stray curl over her shoulder, tracing the soft skin with the tip of my finger.

Kristine leaned in, grasping my earlobe with her teeth and tugging, eliciting a low groan out of me. "We should ditch these losers and get out of here."

"Are..." Now I was the one at a loss for words. "You..."

"Aw," she smiled as her hand pressed further into my lap, and she grazed my cock, which was trying to break out of my zipper now. "Did I make you nervous, Sammy? I thought you wanted to bend me over something. We don't have all night."

"Fuck," I groaned as I looked at the teasing grin on her face. She was enjoying turning the tables on me, yet again.

"Yes," she whispered, licking her lips. "That's the idea. Come on."

She grabbed my hand and tugged as she slid off her stool, dropping my hand as I stood behind her. My fingers grazed the exposed skin on the side of her waist, and she shook her head as she stepped out of my reach, nodding to the corner table where our coworkers still celebrated.

"We don't need to be a topic of gossip on Monday," she told me, leaning in toward me but not touching. "You go request a ride, and I'll be out in a few minutes. I need to powder my nose." Then she was off toward the bathroom with a wink, swinging her hips as she disappeared down the back hallway.

Holy shit, this was happening. I told myself I'd stop doing this. I was old enough to be over the whole one-night stand at a bar thing. That's what this was, right? One night to get her out of my system, and then Monday, I'd return to my little bubble in the office. I wouldn't have to think about what she looked like naked anymore. Except I'd *know* what she looked like naked. How it felt to be inside her. What it sounded like when I made her come. Because I was going to make her come.

Kristine: Quit overthinking. Go outside.

Glancing over my shoulder, Kristine stood in the hallway leading to the bathroom with a hand on her hip. She held her phone with the other, an amused smirk plastered across those full lips.

Sam: Someone is impatient.

She laughed as she looked down at her phone, pulling it into both hands to text me back.

Kristine: Someone promised me a spanking, and I'm waiting to see if he can deliver.

Sam: Oh, I can deliver and then some.

Kristine: Promises. Promises. Let's hope you're not all talk.

Laughing at the playful snark in her texts, I glanced back up, and my heart pounded at the sincere smile I saw aimed in my direction. It was rare for her to give a smile that was anything but condescending or caustic. She was beautiful—dangerous—but beautiful, nonetheless.

Sam: I guess you'll have to come with me and find out.

Kristine: I hope you can make me come. But you're wasting time.

Nodding at her, I threw a couple of bills on the bar and headed toward the doors. As I stepped away, I briefly caught Andrea giving me a curious look from the other side of the room. Right...don't turn this into office gossip.

The wait time said ten minutes for the Uber to show up. Hopefully, I could keep my hands off her that long. I wanted to kiss that teasing smirk right off her. Steal her breath until all she could do was moan my name. God, I hoped she was loud. There was something about a woman unashamed to embrace their pleasure that turned me on.

> Kristine: Let me know when you want me.

> Sam: Right now...

> Kristine: I meant when the car gets here, you goober.

> Sam: My place okay?

> Kristine: You think I'm letting you know where I live?

> Sam: Such a brat.

I attached a gif of a hand miming a spanking to see her reaction.

> Kristine: I'm still waiting to see if you have the nerve. Sometimes men are all talk.

> Sam: You want me to come back in there? I can talk, alright, while I count the number of times I spank that mouthy ass of yours.

> Kristine: God no, Andrea is trying to figure out where you went. I think someone has a crush. And I wasn't aware my ass had a mouth.

Checking the arrival time on my phone, I laughed as I leaned back against the building wall—five more minutes.

> Sam: Are you jealous?

> Kristine: You wish...

> Sam: Maybe I do.

> Kristine: You know what this is, right?

> Sam: ?

Part of me was starting to develop fond feelings toward her, but I needed to shut that down now. She wouldn't be my girlfriend, but I didn't want her to be a notch on my bedpost either. Shit. I think I liked her.

Yes.

I checked the map and saw that the Uber was only a few blocks away. My pulse kicked up when I felt her slender hands slide along the side of my waist and her head rest between my shoulder blades.

"Thought you didn't want to be a topic of gossip."

My hand closed over one of hers, enjoying this rare moment of affection coming from her. She'd barely taken two sips of her drink, so I knew it wasn't fueled by alcohol. I wasn't sure how to handle this suddenly affectionate behavior. Just when I thought I had her figured out, she'd surprised me.

"Shut up, Sam."

There she is…

Smiling at the annoyance in her voice, I grasped Kristine's hand and pulled her in front of me, using my fingertips to push the hair out of her face. Her eyes were open and unguarded, a hint of vulnerability I had never seen when she looked at me. "I think you like it when I tease you."

"You run that mouth of yours too much. You should use it for other things—like kissing me."

Like she was one to talk about running her mouth.

"My bad. I'll shut up now." Slowly leaning toward her, giving her a chance to pull away, my eyes flickered between her eyes and her lips.

"You should," she whispered, her eyes fluttering closed.

Maybe I should have expected the shock that ran through me as our lips touched—retreating briefly before pressing together again as if drawn like magnets—but it hit me all at once and heat blossomed in my chest as I slid my fingers through her hair, grasping the back of her head as I tilted mine to get closer. Her tongue pressed against my bottom lip, and I groaned as I let her inside, seeking the heat of her mouth.

The sound of a car approaching broke us apart, and I smiled, watching her hold the tips of her fingers to her kiss-swollen lips. She'd felt it too.

Holding my hand out toward her, I smiled as she grasped it without hesitation. I don't think we knew what to do with ourselves in the quiet car. I kept obsessing over what that brief kiss had felt like, but she was staring out the window, a vice-like grip on my fingers.

"Just drop you at the curb?" The driver broke the tense silence in the car as he maneuvered through traffic and approached my building. It was a split unit in a brownstone right at the edge of Back Bay. Hopefully, my roommates would be asleep or out. I didn't want them to give me shit for bringing home a girl or make Kristine feel self-conscious.

"Yeah, that's fine. Thanks, man."

As the car stopped, Kristine pulled her hand from mine and was out on the sidewalk before I could get to the door handle.

"Hey," I coaxed as I walked up behind where she was pacing. "What's wrong?"

She shook her head and continued to pace, refusing to look at me. Shit. She was second-guessing this.

Reaching forward to grasp her hand, I pulled her back into my chest, smoothing her hair away from her shoulder and softly kissing the exposed skin on the side of her neck. "Calm down. Nothing needs to happen. I can take you home, or we can go upstairs and talk."

"Goddammit, Sam," she groaned, and I chuckled at the petulance in her voice. It appeared she was fighting with herself just as much as I had over the last few weeks.

"What?" I laughed. "What's bothering you?"

"Quit being so fucking nice all the time," she growled as she spun in my arms, her hand firmly grasping the back of my neck. "Take me upstairs and fuck me until I can't remember my name."

Fuck...

SEVEN

KRISTINE

BOSTON

SAM BLINKED A FEW times as he looked down at me, seeming to process my words before something clicked inside him. It was only a fraction of a moment before his lips crashed into mine, this kiss much more demanding than the last one. I let myself go and reveled in the feel of his mouth on me.

"Oh God, upstairs, take me upstairs," I panted as our lips broke apart, his mouth nipping at the sensitive skin beneath my ear.

He groaned as he leaned away from me, digging in his pocket to pull out a set of keys before he tugged me up the front steps of his building. Two apartments were inside the entryway off to the right, and a long wooden staircase led to a small landing at the top. He grasped my hand as he took the steps two at a time, failing to account for me wearing heels.

"Slow down," I laughed as I yanked my hand free, pausing to reach down and pull them off before I hurried up after him. It seemed someone was in a hurry. I hoped that wasn't telling for what would happen when he got me into his bed. Sam may have been frustrating at times, but I never took him as someone who would be a selfish lover. At least, that's what I was hoping. Not that I thought of Sam as a potential lover all the time...because I didn't.

He was unlocking the door at the top of the stairs when I joined him, bouncing a little on my bare toes. I hated to admit it, but I was nervous. I never did this. I didn't go home with men on the first date. But this wasn't a date. There hadn't been any romantic lead-up to what was about to happen. I'd hardly call him paying for a mojito I'd taken two sips of as showing me a fun time. But, God, I hoped that was precisely what he was about to do. It'd be disappointing to have to break into my toy arsenal once I got home.

It wouldn't be the first time I'd had to take care of myself when yet another guy proved disappointing in bed. Another reason I hated dating.

As the door swung open, Sam reached behind him and grasped my wrist, tugging me inside and pressing his palm hard on the door until it slammed closed, quickly backing me against the wood surface.

"Last chance," he whispered as he boxed me in, one hand on my hip, the other on the side of my neck. "If you stay, I'm going to fuck you, Kristine. I can't deny I want you anymore."

I appreciated that he was giving me a chance to back out, but I was seeing this through, no matter how much the saner part of my brain was telling me to cut and run. Run from the way he looked at me. Run from the way I felt when he touched me. Run from the blistering intensity of his kisses. Sam was nothing like I expected, and I wasn't sure what to do with that information.

"Fuck me," I whispered, grasping the waistband of his jeans, tugging him toward me, and leaning up to nip at his bottom lip. "I want this. I want you."

He groaned before flattening himself against me, his fingers tugging lightly at my hair as he slipped his tongue past my lips and stole my breath. Fuck, he was making me lose my mind. That was the only explanation for the feelings that coursed through me at Sam's touch, at the insistent pressure of his lips and tongue. My heels dropped to the floor with a thud, but the sound didn't faze him.

My fingers made quick work of the buttons on his shirt, parting it with my hands and yanking his undershirt from his jeans. I needed to see him. I needed to feel skin and for him to take me to his room and do everything he'd promised me in that bar.

"Bed," I panted, leaning my head back as he scraped his teeth against the sensitive skin of my neck, leaving chills in his wake. "Now." As much as I would be a fan of him taking me against the front door, we could save that for later. If there ever was a later. I wasn't thinking that far ahead right now. Now I just needed to get his clothes off...and mine.

"It doesn't always have to be on a bed," he breathed into my ear, apparently having the same thoughts I was having. "But whatever the lady wants."

"We both know I'm not a lady."

"Could have fooled me." His fingers crept under my skirt and pressed into my panties, rubbing lightly as I gasped.

"You're stalling."

"I'm doing no such thing," he chuckled, as I pressed my hands against his chest. "I'm just enjoying getting you worked up. The tease is half the fun."

Expecting him to back off, I squealed as he reached down and grasped my thighs, hoisting me against his chest before he turned and headed further into the apartment. Thankfully, it was empty, with a few beer bottles and books abandoned on the coffee table surrounded by three oversized leather recliners. It appeared Sam had roommates. I hoped they weren't home because I had a feeling Sam would make good on his promise to make me moan his name.

He set me down just inside the doorway to his room, the interior dimly lit by the moonlight casting in through the open curtains. I don't know if I expected a nerd den with gaming consoles everywhere, but it was surprisingly neat. He had a queen-sized bed that took up most of the space along the wall by the window, with a small desk in the corner with dual computer monitors and a plush leather desk chair.

As I quickly scanned the space, I heard him close the door and flick the lock, lifting the handle until it clicked. He shrugged as I turned in his direction, "It doesn't always stay locked. I figured you wouldn't want any accidental interruptions."

"Roommates?"

"Yeah," he nodded. "Two. They're out at a party." He held up his phone awkwardly, a text message screen visible. He tossed it toward his small dresser before tentatively taking a few steps toward me. "So..."

I smiled, shaking my head at how he could go from seductive flirt to shy in moments.

"So..." I took two steps forward, grasping the hem of my tank top as I peeled it over my head and dropped it to the floor.

Sam shrugged his button-up shirt from his shoulders, lifting the hem of his white undershirt, winking at me as he pulled it over his head and dropped it next to my tank top on the floor. "Where were we?"

"I'm not sure," I whispered as I flattened my palms on his abdomen, slowly running them up his chest, reveling in how his defined muscles flexed as I grasped the sides of his neck and pulled lightly.

He took the hint and leaned forward, pausing before our lips touched. "Oh, I remember...I was about to bend you over that bed."

Before I could react, Sam had spun me around and walked me forward, pinning me to the end of his bed with his hips, his hands coming up to massage my lace-covered breasts. My chest heaved as he toyed with me through the material, pinching and caressing as I ground myself into the distinct hardness I felt pressed into my ass.

"You looked so fucking hot in this skirt when you walked in tonight," he whispered as he reached between us, unclasping my bra with deft fingers and discarding it on the floor. His skin seared mine as he flattened himself against my back, his fingers more insistent as he teased my nipples. "I couldn't see anyone but you."

"Like you can talk, Mr. Sleeves Rolled up to his Elbows."

He chuckled as he placed open-mouthed kisses along the side of my neck. "I heard you girls have a thing for forearms," he teased, grinding his hips against mine.

One comment a few weeks ago about how I'd rather watch a guy roll his sleeves to his elbows than pose shirtless, and he was using it as ammunition against me. The cocky bastard remembered everything.

"Tell me to stop," he whispered, cupping my breast with one large hand, flattening the other against my stomach, and teasing the waistline of my skirt with his fingertips. "God, why do I want you so fucking much? You drive me crazy, but I can't stay away from you. You make me so fucking hard, and I can't stop thinking about you."

"Don't stop," I panted as they delved under the material, sliding into my panties and right to where I wanted them. He drove me crazy too, but sanity was overrated, it seemed. "Oh, God, Sam. Don't stop."

"Told you I'd have you moaning my name." He parted my folds, slowly teasing my lips as he played with the moisture he'd inspired there with his dirty mouth. "Fuck, you're so wet. I bet you're tight. I'm going to make you come so hard. This skirt is just evil. I bet you knew it'd make me want to rip it off you. You're a fucking tease without even realizing it. Or maybe you realize it and are just trying to drive me insane."

"Fuck," I exhaled in a whisper as he leaned me forward, hooking his fingers inside of me and starting a slow grind against my ass as he fucked me with his long fingers.

"Not yet," he whispered against the back of my neck as he picked up the pace, the muscles in his arms flexing as he drove me to oblivion. I never came this fast. Never. Even when I did it to myself, I had a tough time relaxing, but within moments, I was panting, leaning forward to grasp his comforter tightly as he pushed me toward the edge. "I want you just as wild as you make me. Fucking beg for it."

"Oh...*oh*...more, please," I panted as I fell over the edge, pulsing against his insistent fingers, colors flashing behind my closed eyelids as my chest heaved. He'd barely done anything, and I'd gone off like a rocket.

"Fuck," he groaned, steadying me before he pulled his hand out. I slumped against the bed, turning my head to look at him as he licked his fingers. Shit. Why did I find that so hot? And why was I now picturing him with his head buried between my legs?

"Come here," he whispered, helping me stand, wrapping his arms around my waist, and burying his face into my neck. "Fuck. That was so hot. You sound exactly like I imagined you would when you came. So desperate. Trying to remain in control but finally letting me push you over the edge. God, I need to be inside you. Are you ready for me?"

"What do you think?" I laughed, wiggling my hips against him.

"Goddamn," he exhaled sharply, turning me around and sitting me on the edge of his bed.

His fingers quickly popped open the button on his jeans, pushing them to the floor before he stepped out of them and placed his hands on my knees.

"Something needs to go," he whispered, toying with the hem of my skirt. I reached for the zipper on the side, but he shook his head. "Not that. The skirt stays on. I've been fantasizing about flipping that thing up for too long. Don't deny me my fantasy." His fingers skimmed my thighs, grasping the sides of my panties as he slowly drew them down my legs, kneeling on the floor at my feet as he helped pull them off. "You're fucking soaked." I thought he'd stand back up quickly, but that was not what happened as he slowly pushed the front hem of the skirt up and out of the way.

"What are you...? *Oh*," I moaned as he used his hands to tilt my hips backward, causing me to hold myself up with outstretched arms. His long fingers parted me as he took a slow lick up my center, those haunting blue eyes watching my reaction as he tasted me.

"What was that?" he asked his voice smug as he leaned back and licked his lips.

"Never mind, keep going," I commanded in a harsh whisper that tapered into a moan as he slipped his tongue inside me. I don't think I'd ever associate the word selfish with Sam Langley again, as he worked me up. My voice was harsh as I failed to hold in the moans he created when he latched onto my clit and sucked. Hard.

My head fell backward, and my eyes closed, hair brushing the mattress as his fingers joined in, finding that spot inside that made me pant and squirm. Sam was already putting my toys to shame. His name was on the tip of my tongue as he sucked, bit, and licked me into a frenzy, my face numb and my brain fuzzy as I called out his name. "Fuck, Sam. Oh my God."

He kept going, not letting up, until I grasped the hair at the back of his head in my fist and pulled him away.

"Take those off," I moaned, nodding to the substantial tent in his boxer briefs. "Right fucking now."

"Yes, ma'am," he chuckled as he stood and pushed them to the floor, his length springing forward. He wasn't huge, but from what I'd seen, I bet he knew how to use what he had. His whole body was long and lean, cut with tightly packed muscles, and I wanted to explore it with my tongue, but right now, I wanted that cock inside me.

"Protection?" I asked as I watched him slowly grip his cock in his large hand, working the rigid flesh in a way that made me want to suck it into my mouth and feel it throb on my tongue. The pill was a part of my nightly regime, but I had no idea who else he'd had in this bedroom.

"On it," he nodded as he took a few steps around the bed to his nightstand, ripping open a box of condoms and pulling out a string of them. He tore one off with his teeth and threw the others toward the pillows as he sheathed himself. Stepping between my parted legs, his hands grasped the sides of my neck. "Can I kiss you?"

Generally, if a guy asked me that after going down on me, my automatic answer would be no, but I wanted Sam's lips on mine. I'd barely started nodding, and his mouth was slanted across mine, tongue in my mouth as he ground his hard cock between my legs. One of my hands grasped the side of his face as the other guided him to where we both wanted him to be.

"Fuck," I whined against his lips as he pressed inside, hot and hard. His tongue thrusting in my mouth as he rocked his hips back and then pushed forward again.

"God, Kristine," he panted as his head fell to my shoulder, his hands grasping my hips as he kept his slow but insistent pace. "You feel so good. God, why does this feel so good?"

"It could feel better," I whispered, hooking my feet around the backs of his legs and pulling him into me harder. "Don't hold back. Fuck me like you mean it. Fuck me like you despise me."

"But I could never despise you," he whispered, eyes wide as he leaned back slightly, pulling me to the very edge of the mattress and tilting my hips up. He scanned my face, waiting for something, but I wanted him to use me. "Never."

"Fuck me harder," I whispered, and he nodded, his fingers digging into my waist. I could tell something was still holding him back, so I ensured he knew I was serious. "Now, Sam. Hard."

His control snapped as he pulled me toward him, setting a punishing rhythm of thrusts that had me gripping his sheets for dear life, my knuckles turning white, and my arms burning with the exertion of holding myself up. Sam was a giver, and I took every fucking inch of it as he wound me up again, using my hips as leverage.

"Oh..." I moaned as I felt myself start to get close again, the angle he was holding me at hitting just the right place. "Right there..." I panted and almost laughed aloud at the satisfied smirk that pulled at his lips as he continued to work me over. Sam knew he was good at this, and I hated him a little for making me react so intensely to his touch.

"I don't know. Maybe I should slow down," he teased, pulling out and sliding back in slowly, grinding his hips against me in a way that sent tingles down my spine.

God, he was good at this. Cocky bastard.

"Don't you dare," I growled as I tightened my legs around him and began bucking my hips into his movements. I was so close. He wasn't stopping now.

"I thought I was supposed to be bending you over the bed?" he laughed as he slowed down again, teasing me with the head of his cock. He was trouble, but I loved it. Goddammit, was one night going to be enough with him?

"Make me come first, and you can do whatever you want..." I moaned, my eyes closing as he picked up the pace again.

"I'll hold you to that," he panted, thrusting into me repeatedly, the pleasure worth the fingertip-shaped bruises I knew I'd have on my hips tomorrow.

"Shut up and fuck me," I moaned as I arched my back, feeling the sheets pop from the corner of the bed as I gripped them for dear life and held on as I felt myself start to fall over the edge again. A loud groan tore out of Sam as I pulsed around him, adding to the intense satisfaction.

It took me a few moments to return to earth, opening my eyes to see Sam clasping my hips, eyes wide as he throbbed inside me, still hard. Holy shit, he had stamina. "That was fucking hot. The way you..." He was panting, holding back as he watched me. It almost seemed he got as much enjoyment from watching me come as I had doing it.

I was reasonably sure I blushed as I bit my lip, returning his intense stare. Now was when I usually ran, hopped into an Uber, and fled back to the safety of my apartment, but he hadn't come yet, and I wanted him to use me as he'd promised in that bar.

Pressing my hand on his chest, I urged him to step back as my legs fell limp to the edge of the bed. Summoning all the strength I had left, I rolled over and shook my ass as he stood there staring at it.

"Come on, don't get shy on me now, Sam. You have a promise to fulfill."

That seemed to snap him out of it as he stepped forward, using his foot to spread my legs a little wider and stepping in toward me, teasing me with the head of his dick before he pushed back inside, groaning loudly. "Fuck, you're still so tight."

I grasped the loose fabric above my head, pushing onto my toes as he thrust inside me hard, using one hand on my hip for leverage as he held my ass firmly in his other hand.

"Do it," I taunted as I looked over my shoulder at him, using my hands as leverage to push my shoulders up from the mattress.

He squinted as his pace slowed, his eyes flashing to mine as realization crossed his features. "Shit," he groaned as he drew his hand back and swung it forward, a loud smack joining the sounds of him fucking me. I moaned as I watched his chest heaving, his eyes riveted to where I knew his hand had left a mark.

"Fuck, that looks..." he groaned, closing his eyes and tilting his head back. Both hands held my waist as he picked up his rhythm again, forcing my hips into the mattress with every thrust. "I'm...uh...*fuck*..."

"Come," I moaned, my forehead falling to the fabric in front of me, my thighs burning with the effort to hold myself up as he used me for his pleasure.

"Fuck. Kristine," he groaned as he held me flush with him. "Gonna come so hard inside you. And you're going to take it." I felt him pulse inside me seconds later. He kept me there for a moment before he leaned over my back, his lips kissing my shoulder blade as he pulled out.

It was hard to catch my breath as I lay there and realized that maybe I didn't know who Sam was at all. He seemed like he'd been almost embarrassed when we were reading through all those scenes, but tonight he'd shown me a completely different side of himself. Not knowing how to manage this, I closed my eyes, enjoying his weight on my back and the soft kisses he lazily placed across my shoulders.

"I, uh..." I cleared my throat as I felt the bed shift, and Sam sat along the edge of the mattress next to me. He placed his warm palm in the center of my back and softly rubbed circles as I tried to form a coherent sentence. "Um. I can go home now if..."

Sam shook his head as he leaned toward me, grasping my shoulders as he pulled me up to sit next to him, his arms closing around me as he kissed my forehead. "It's late. You don't need to run away. Stay."

I started to shake my head, but he stopped me, cupping my cheek softly and leaning in to kiss me lightly. "Stay, Kristine. I promise not to make this into something it's not."

"I..."

"Stop thinking so much. I'm offering a warm bed and maybe breakfast if you play your cards right in the morning, but I'm not looking for a relationship either."

I don't know what about that statement made me feel a little disappointed, but he was right, it *was* late, and it would be nice to curl up with him in this big bed and pretend that tonight meant something more than it did. Before we'd worked together, this was the last thing that I wanted, to depend on someone. But now he was in my head, and I was beyond confused after that performance.

"But..."

"And I wouldn't be opposed to you waking me up in the middle of the night for a repeat performance," he teased, tilting my chin with his finger and kissing me. "But you're in charge next time."

"Who says I wasn't in charge this time?"

"Try me."

Oh, Sam. You don't know what you're asking for...

Chapter

EIGHT

SAM

BOSTON

Today was starting off so well until Kristine opened her eyes. She was, surprisingly, a cuddler. It wasn't something I'd ever expected, but when I stirred awake in the middle of the night, her slight form was curled against my arm, her hair fanned across my chest, and her legs intertwined with mine. She'd passed out cold after fulfilling my fantasy of riding me in that skirt, looking spectacular in the moonlight streaming through my window with her wild curls falling around us. We didn't talk, just watched each other as she moved over me, using my body to please herself. I was afraid to pop the bubble of silence, quietly reveling in the feel of her, in awe of how sensual she was as my hands cradled her hips.

She'd given me a long, sweet kiss after we'd finished, rolling off to the side and quietly asking to use my bathroom. I wasn't sure what had changed between the 'get this out of our system' fuck that'd happened after we left the bar, but this new vulnerable side of her was starting to work its way under my skin. I half expected her to be gone when I'd passed her in the bathroom doorway, coming out a few moments later to her curled up in my sheets, fast asleep.

"What are you doing?" she yawned, lifting her hand off my chest like it was on fire and shifting across the bed.

"Lying in my own bed, getting groped in my sleep," I teased and watched the shutters slam down on her defenses. Apparently, we were back there, the place where she was going to keep me at arm's length. It didn't matter that I'd been inside her, that I knew what she tasted like, and had heard her moan my name as she pulsed around me. She was putting that distance between us again.

I should have been okay with it, happy that she wasn't getting clingy or acting like we were now in some relationship, but I wasn't. I didn't want to date her, and I wasn't sure I could survive dating her without my ego taking a severe beating, but I thought we'd at least be able to talk to each other.

"I was *not* groping you," she hissed quietly, pulling the sheets to her chest, her fingers clutching the fabric tightly.

"Calm down, Kris," I smiled, hoping to get her to let down those walls a little. This didn't have to change the way we acted around each other. I liked the teasing banter and her response to winding her up. She wasn't as uptight as I'd initially thought her to be, with a wicked sense of humor and a strong sense of self. But those damn protective instincts were showing again, her barbed armor fully back in place, despite the fact I'd already seen her in action. "It was just a joke. And I've seen you naked...well, mostly."

"It's not funny, Sam."

"It was a little funny. You don't need to be shy." I gestured to the white-knuckled grip she had on my sheets.

"Stop staring at me. You're being creepy."

She hadn't seemed to mind my staring last night, but pointing that out would only get her more riled up. I shook my head, sliding backward off the bed and reaching down to grab my boxer briefs from the floor. I would look for my athletic cup, a little scared that the aggressive look she was giving me would mean she was about to injure my nuts, but it was in my lacrosse bag in the entryway.

"Oh, my God, Sam. Cover that up," she whined as I faced her, bending over slightly to pull them up my legs.

"I am covering it up, but it's not like you didn't see it last night."

"Put a damn shirt on." She waved her hand wildly, pulling the sheets over her face and burying her head into the pillow.

"I never took you to be a prude, especially with how you teased me about how I felt reading about *a little dick*."

"Shut. Up."

Chuckling at the high-pitched voice from under my sheets, I walked toward the dresser and grabbed a T-shirt, throwing it on before I grabbed an extra clean towel from the bottom of my closet.

"Here. Feel free to take a shower if you need to. I think there might be some girly shit under the sink that you can use."

Her face peeked out the top of the covers, and she glared at me. "I am not using one of your hook-up's crap. Gross."

"It's not from an ex. Calm down. I have four sisters. They visit sometimes. And when my sister and her husband visited me last summer, my sister left her tropical body wash behind." I didn't think Kristine would be into Coconut Mango Oasis, although it was better than the masculine-smelling stuff I used. But...I wouldn't mind her smelling like me.

No. Shutting that down. This was just one night and one slightly awkward morning. That was all.

"I'll leave something for you to wear on the dresser if you want it."

She frowned as I pulled a pair of shorts from my drawer that skewed toward the short side and a compression tank I wore to the gym underneath shirts in the Winter. It was probably the only clothing I had that would possibly fit her.

"Go away," she moaned, waving her hand in the air again, face still buried in the sheets.

Biting my lip to hold in the laughter, I quietly closed the door. My cringe was immediate when I noticed my roommates sitting in front of the TV, headsets on, and beers already on the table. I got that we were still in our twenties, but beer for breakfast should have ended in college.

"Sup," Taylor nodded as I headed to the fridge, hoping they hadn't cleared out the groceries again.

"Hey, how late were you guys out last night?" I asked as I started pulling out ingredients for omelets.

"Not late enough to avoid the 'Oh, yes! Harder, Sam!' coming from your bedroom," Caleb laughed, lifting his beer bottle and tipping it in my direction with a wink.

Shit.

"Who you got in there?" Taylor teased as he wiggled his eyebrows and nodded toward my bedroom door.

"I don't know what you're talking about," I deflected as I reached under the sink to pull out the cutting board.

Of course, Kristine decided to take advantage of my offer, and the shower turned on at that moment, sending my roommates into fits of hysterical laughter.

"Yeah, right. Who is she? Some random hottie from the bar last night?"

You could say that. She had looked hot last night. But Kristine was far from random.

"Don't be dicks."

"We'll leave the dicking to you," Caleb tittered as he killed his bottle and reached into the cooler between their seats to twist open a new one. My roommates were so immature sometimes. Both were super smart, working in computer programming and information technology systems, but they were having trouble letting go of their teens and realizing that we were adults.

"Do not say anything if she comes out here," I warned, pointing the knife I'd been using to chop an onion in their direction. "I will end you two."

"Geez, dude. You must like this one," Taylor laughed as he mimed cracking a whip in the air.

"I..." wasn't even sure how to answer that. I did like Kristine much more than I should, but this wouldn't turn into a relationship or anything. She'd been adamant that last night was it, and with her reaction this morning, I wasn't expecting any repeat performances. It didn't matter that I now had a highlight reel from last night to fuel my imagination. So many things we didn't do kept scrolling through my mind.

"Shit." Caleb looked at me with wide eyes, taking in my expression. "You DO like this one. Who is she?"

"No, no." My head shook as my eyes darted to my room, where the shower had turned off. "It's not like that. I work with her. Please don't be jerks about this. She'll castrate me if you embarrass her."

"Damn, who knew Mr. Aloof Professional had it in him to hit the office dating pool."

They both knew that I refused to date within my office. We'd run into coworkers at bars before, and they knew I was not likely to hook up with someone and make it awkward, which was what my dumb ass had decided to do last night. But Kristine wasn't just some random assistant or intern. I'd thought we were becoming more friendly toward each other, but then I hadn't been able to keep my hands or mouth off her last night, the sexual tension that'd been building as we edited Evan's book finally reaching a boiling point. We'd both been helpless to resist it anymore.

"She's a friend, I guess." I wasn't sure what we were anymore. "I'm begging you, don't say anything to her. She's..."

"I'm...?"

My eyes flashed with panic, sending my roommates into giggles as I twisted to look back at my door. Kristine's hair—loose, damp curls—fell around her freshly washed face. The shorts I'd given her were rolled up at the waist, showing off her long, toned legs, the compression tank tied in a knot, hanging slightly over her shoulders, and revealing a sliver of her abdomen. Last night she'd looked fucking hot, but now...

I was in so much trouble.

"Well, hey there." Taylor grinned as he sat upright in his chair, threw his controller toward the coffee table, and combed his hair back from his forehead.

"Hey." Kristine looked toward me nervously, that rare vulnerability showing through her eyes, and then slightly waved in their direction.

"I'm making breakfast," I jerked my head back toward the ingredients I'd prepped on the cutting board, trying not to scare her off.

"I see that," she said with a smile as she looked down and tucked her damp hair behind her ear. When she looked back up, my breath caught at the soft smile aimed in my direction. The shower had reset her from her earlier panic mode. Part of me was glad she wasn't putting the walls back up, but the other part was entirely out of its depth.

"You can sit at the table until it's ready," I offered as I glanced toward my roommates. They'd both turned their chairs to watch, Taylor's chin propped on his hands. I caught him admiring Kristine's legs and glared at him. He glanced up and cringed as he shifted in his chair, turning back around and smacking Caleb in the arm as he put his headset back on.

"I can...uh. Can I help?" She shifted awkwardly, biting her lip as she glanced up from beneath her eyelashes.

"Sure."

This interaction should be interesting.

She tentatively walked toward me, her teeth still worrying her lip as her eyes darted to where Tay and Caleb had resumed their video game.

"So..."

"We don't need to have awkward small talk, Sam."

"Would you just relax for once?" I teased as I bumped my hip against hers. "Maybe I like talking to you."

"Pfft. Yeah, okay." Kristine rolled her eyes, and I wanted to kiss her to shut her up. She wasn't used to letting people in past all that armor. "Because we have so many deep conversations."

I refrained from commenting on things that had been deep between us but didn't want to risk our temporary accord for a quick laugh.

"There's bread on top of the fridge if you want to make toast. I'll get this going."

She nodded, stepping away and pushing up onto her tiptoes to reach the loaf of bread, exposing a sliver of her back beneath the hem of my shirt. I should have given her one of my jerseys. That'd be a sight to have Langley splashed across her shoulders. She'd never wear it, and it was a total cliché, but I found myself picturing it. nonetheless.

Whisking the eggs, I kept glancing in her direction, watching her move around our tiny kitchen, finally relaxing a fraction. She was stunning when she let her guard down and let herself be comfortable. I knew it'd probably be short-lived, but I still wanted to peel more layers off that onion. She didn't realize that she checked all the boxes. She was naturally attractive without trying, took care of herself, seemed to be athletic, competitive, was funny—even when using her vocabulary to eviscerate you—and her work ethic and attention to detail were admirable. When she let down those walls, she was easily the sexiest woman I'd ever been with intimately.

"Stop staring at me. You're going to burn that." I blinked, and Kristine smiled, pointing a butter knife toward the skillet I should have been paying attention to instead of watching her.

Quickly flipping the eggs in the pan, I grabbed a few plates from the cabinet above the sink and tried to focus on not burning our breakfast. I was still shocked she'd stayed this long. I'd never expected her to be here when I woke up this morning. She continued to surprise me.

"How'd the dentist go?" she asked quietly, leaning her hip against the counter next to me, waiting for the toast to pop.

"Seriously?" I laughed as I smiled over at her. "What happened to no awkward small talk?"

She returned my smile, shrugging her shoulder a little, looking more approachable than I'd seen her in a long time. "We can stand here in silence if you prefer."

"It was fine, just a cleaning, but my mom was harassing me to make sure I was taking care of myself."

"Aww," she cooed. "Is Sammy a momma's boy?"

I normally would have cringed at that name coming from someone other than my older sisters, but at least she'd temporarily refrained from the maybe-meat based nickname.

"No," I laughed. "But if I don't humor her, she'll just harass me until I do what she wants."

"You do strike me as a people-pleaser," she commented, grabbing the toast as it shot up and quickly buttering the surface as she glanced back.

"I do like to please," I confessed in a low voice as I leaned in.

Reveling in the shudder I saw her try to suppress, I quickly slid the second omelet out of the pan and grabbed both plates, nodding toward my room. Taylor and Caleb were still absorbed in their game, but I wasn't in the mood for an audience. Plus, we needed to talk about what happened the night before.

"We can eat in my room. Forks are in the top drawer."

She grabbed a couple of forks and followed.

I don't know why I was surprised to see my bed made as I nudged the door open with my shoulder, but it was, the pillows upright against the headboard and her sexy skirt folded neatly on my desk chair.

I sat on the edge of my bed, waiting until she'd climbed over the covers before handing over her plate.

"Thank you for breakfast." She flashed me a shy smile as she sat cross-legged, leaning against the headboard.

"I told you I'd make you breakfast if you played your cards right."

"Hmm," she hummed as she took a bite of her toast, shaking her head at me. "Is that what I did last night?"

"Mmhmm." I smiled, swallowing the bite I had in my mouth. "You played all your cards last night."

"Not all of them," she winked, and I found myself treading into dangerous waters. I knew she didn't want a relationship, but I didn't want last night to be it. I wasn't looking for a girlfriend either, much to my mother's dismay, but I was attracted to Kristine. Much more than I should have been.

"You'll have to show me your hand later," I laughed as I settled back against the headboard next to her.

"Sam..." She frowned as she leaned her head against the dark wood and looked over. "You don't need to flirt with me. I know what the score is. Last night was fun, but..."

"But?"

"We work together, sort of."

"And?"

"We don't do this."

"Do what?"

"My God, Sam. Stop that," she growled, reaching over to settle her plate on my nightstand.

"Stop what?"

"Quit trying to be cute."

I laughed at the scowl on Kristine's face, the fierce little glare she aimed in my direction making my heart speed up. "I don't know what you're talking about."

"Of course you don't," she scoffed, crossing her arms over her chest, my tank riding up and showing a sliver of her navel.

"You don't have to hide from me."

Kristine turned toward me, picking at the comforter and refusing to meet my eyes. "I'm not good at this, Sam."

"You're good at everything, and you know it."

"That's the problem."

"Hey," I whispered, turning to place the plates on the floor before I pulled her toward my chest. She hesitated for a moment before she tucked her head under my chin. "There's no pressure here."

"There's pressure everywhere."

"Not from me."

Her head started shaking against my chest, and I held her tighter, kissing the crown of her head. Part of her behavior was making sense to me, cogs clicking into place as I realized that maybe she didn't have everything in her life put together. She didn't seem to have anyone in her corner to support her without strings attached.

"You don't mean that. There's always expectations, always someone working an angle."

"Hey," I leaned back, framing her face with my hands and tilting her head to look at me. "There's no hidden agenda here."

Her eyes rolled, and I shook my head.

"I mean it. Obviously, if you want to sleep with me again, I'd be on board with that," I laughed. "But I don't want anything from you. I don't have any nefarious plans or ulterior motives. I just happen to think you're not as big of a bitch as you want everyone to think you are. And I happen to like the person you've let me see in the last few weeks."

"Don't get all mushy on me now, Spammy."

"God, would you quit with the passive-aggressive nicknames?" I sighed, smiling to let her know I could see right through her trying to goad me. "I'm just making it clear that—" I leaned in and placed my mouth next to her ear, barely grazing her skin. "If you want to use me for my body, I'm on board. If you want to talk, I'm down with that too. Just let me know what you need, and we'll figure it out."

"That sounds an awful lot like something someone would say if they were expecting a relationship from me."

She was right, and I did want a relationship of a sort with her. I liked having her around, and if we just returned to friendship, we'd make that work too. But the baser part of me wanted her naked against my sheets as often as fucking possible.

"No strings, I mean it."

"We'll see..." she sighed, pushing me back as she looked up at me with the most open expression I'd seen from her yet. "So, what was that about me using your body?"

Laughing at the naughty glint in her eye, I slid down the mattress a little and flopped onto my back, the rest of my breakfast forgotten.

"Do with me what you will."

NINE

KRISTINE

BOSTON

"Hey." Isobel nodded as I walked into her office on Monday morning. "Don't run off. We need to chat. Let's go over something before the staff meeting this morning."

Shit. I'd read the memo that there was a multi-genre-wide meeting before lunch today, but I'd been so distracted that I'd failed to figure out what it was regarding. It wasn't in my nature to go into meetings unprepared, so I was sweating a little as I waited for Isobel to look up from her computer.

Pulling my phone out of my pocket, I glanced at the text message that'd come through while Isobel had requested a word with me.

> Sam: You forgot something at my place.

Frowning, I tried to figure out what I'd possibly left there.

I'd left Sam's apartment well after lunchtime the day before, after eating several slices of greasy pizza and learning that Sam was his apartment's mature, responsible resident—not that I'd been surprised. I'd also taken him up on his offer to use him—a few times.

The outer jock exterior did not match the person he showed me, which was a hard pill to swallow. I hated Dickhead for his refusal to see my work past the flowery genre label of contemporary romance novels, yet I'd judged Sam on his. He knocked down all my defenses and could flip the switch from sexy to tender in a heartbeat.

> Kristine: Is that your sneaky way of trying to get me to come over after work?

> Sam: No. But that would be a good angle to try in the future.

Kristine: There is no future. One night, Sam.

Sam: And one morning.

Sam: And one afternoon.

Kristine: Details, details.

Sam: You know as well as I do that details make the story.

Kristine: You going to the meeting?

Sam: Yup. Do you know the deets?

Kristine: Deets? Really?

Sam: So, no?

Kristine: No clue. Waiting for Isobel to clue me in.

Sam: Adrian is clueless.

Kristine: Uh...duh.

Sam: More so than usual.

"Don't let me interrupt," Isobel sighed loudly as she tapped her fingers on the top of her desk.

"Sorry," I muttered, locking my phone screen and tucking it back into my messenger bag.

"You don't know this—" she started as she leaned back in her chair.

Batting my eyelashes at her, I tilted my head to the side, playing along. "Know what?"

"Exactly." She grinned as she stood and walked to the front of her desk, sitting on the edge and crossing her ankles. "Word on the street is they are scouting for at least one of the head copy editor positions."

"Genre?"

"Not sure yet, but it's looking like fantasy."

She chuckled as my lip curled up, knowing it wasn't my favorite. I liked it well enough and often read fantasy novels, but they were hard to do developmental edits on sometimes because you were working outside of the constraints of the known universe. Worldbuilding was a tricky subject to do well, and fantasy authors hated when you picked apart their work.

"When?"

"Three to six months."

"Internal interviews only, or are they opening up this one?" Sometimes management cast the net wider if they were looking to pull in new talent, but occasionally, they'd pit us against each other and let us fight it out. I swear they had a popcorn machine in the executive lounge they broke out to watch when they did shit like this.

"As far as I know, they're only interviewing candidates internally and requiring a recommendation from their direct supervisor."

I bit my lip, hoping my little outburst at her last week wouldn't cause her to hold a grudge.

"Don't worry. I already submitted your name."

Not one to get excited and start flapping around, I nodded, flashing her a bright smile. "Thank you, Is. I mean it."

"Adrian put in Sam's name as well."

Fuck.

I mean, I knew that he was much more competent than I'd initially believed, but this meant I might have legitimate competition, and our thing—whatever it was—might make it a touchy subject. Or a no-touchy subject. I wasn't going to pursue Sam, but it'd been a rare treat to find a guy who knew how to use the equipment in his pants and didn't mind taking a little direction in the bedroom. His dirty mouth had been an added bonus.

"Good to know." She narrowed her eyes but said nothing about him or his boss.

"Chase is still out of contact. I'm starting to get a little worried."

"Is it the new boyfriend?" I asked, wondering what was going on there. She'd been a little shifty when I saw her last.

"Boyfriend?"

Oh, shit. Apparently, Isobel was not aware of Chase's new friend. My bad. I was usually the one finding out the gossip, not spreading it. I needed to get my head together.

"When you sent me to get..." *Don't call him Dickhead.* "Adrian's food last week, she was there with a guy. He looked familiar."

"Hmm." She pursed her lips as her jaw clenched. This was not a good sign. "Let's see what she has to say for herself."

"Don't shoot the messenger," I replied with a cringe.

"I'll see you at the meeting." She pulled out her phone and quickly typed out something on the screen. It seemed I was dismissed.

"See you there. Want me to save you a seat, or...?"

"Don't bother, Adrian said he'd save me one."

I wasn't even going to comment on that one. I wasn't sure what those two had going on, but it wasn't like I could judge anymore. Sleeping with Sam had been a wild departure from my normal behavior, but after this past weekend, I didn't regret it—not even for a moment.

MY LEG BOUNCED NERVOUSLY against the conference table's underside as the room filled. I wasn't nervous, per se, but this could be a step up for quite a few of us in this room. A chance to build a team, spread our wings and start overseeing the projects that were dropped into our laps. We could also begin to scout manuscripts and see if we could find the next big bestseller. Okay, so maybe it was a huge deal.

"Let's settle down, people." Sloane Graves, the head of digital publishing, stood at the front of the large conference room on the floor above the editing offices. She was tall and curvy, a no-nonsense bronze-skinned woman who didn't take shit from anyone. If I admired Isobel for her backbone, I practically fangirled over how Sloane could work a room. She was ruthless when working on a project, not settling for mediocre work and insisting the entire publishing outfit came together to give the new launches for her A-team talent authors the best send-off into the world possible. "I'm sure the gossip has already started filtering through for this one, but I'm here to give you all the pertinent details."

A tall, stoic, dark-haired man stood from the front of the table and stepped forward to her left. *Shit.* This was not what I was expecting. He hadn't said anything. I didn't even know he was in town—that little shit.

"This is Gregory Willard." She motioned to my elder brother, who smiled warmly at the room, ready to turn on the Willard charm. And stomp all over my decision to do this on my own. A few heads turned in my direction as the connection clicked in their heads, but I just fastened on my trademark glare and dared them to say something. You could easily tell we were related, but I'd let them draw their own conclusions. It wasn't any of their damn business. "He works for a firm the marketing department in New York has been trying to acquire to start doing in-house promotions for all our book tours. You might recognize his work from the last Whitmore Carlisle release, which has remained at the top of all the major book sales lists for the last six weeks straight."

"Hello all," Greg said with a smile as his gaze swept the room, briefly pausing on me with a wink. Great. *Thanks, Jackass. Make it obvious, why don't you?* "I'll keep my time here brief. Thank you, Ms. Graves, for letting me address your team."

"The floor is yours for a few Mr. Willard." Judging the smile she aimed in his direction, she'd bought his nice guy routine. *Ugh.* Charming prick.

"We will work closely with your Public Relations department over the next several months, ensuring we have enough people on the ground to keep the momentum going with Vivid Press. That means that some of you may be taking on extra roles with your authors, as you know their projects as well as they do." He wasn't wrong. The editing teams often read through the material dozens of times and knew it, as well as the creators. All the little intricacies and plot points, what parts might draw the reader in to look for more.

"We need our teams to start flagging parts of manuscripts that would be good for readings, social media promotion, and previews on digital media. That's where all of you come in. The marketing experts need material easily accessible to start making ad copy to release to our network of street teams and ARC readers to promote before the book ever hits the printing press."

"Mr. Willard is saying that we are rolling out a new software system that will make it easier for our copy editors and their interns to mark parts of the book for the marketing team without combing an entire manuscript to find the juicy parts."

"Hey." My chair shifted as a body settled into the seat next to mine, a warm hand grazing the outside of my kneecap. Judging by the spark that shot up my leg at the contact, even through the material of my pants, I knew it was Sam without glancing back.

"You're late," I hissed out of the corner of my mouth.

"Sorry," he laughed, his warm breath fanning across my neck. *Don't look at him, Kristine.* "What did I miss?"

"Just my brother invading my space," I muttered. And he did it with absolutely no warning whatsoever, because the Willard men did what they wanted, when they wanted, even if it meant bombarding someone by surprise. Not to mention invading others' professional bubbles without remorse. Stupid prick being good at his job. It wasn't a surprise his firm had been hired, but he still could have told me he'd be coming here instead of ambushing me at a staff meeting where he knew I couldn't—and wouldn't—make a scene.

"What?"

"Nothing, just new computer software that we have to learn."

"Hmm."

Clapping drew my attention back to the front of the room, Greg smiling widely, eating up the attention. I still couldn't believe he'd come into my office without giving me a heads-up. I knew he'd been working with the New York office, but this was a little much, even for him. He'd told me about how he landed my publisher as a client a few months back, and I asked him how Vivid was even on his radar, but I knew how. Our father. Mason just couldn't help himself.

"Alright, settle down," Sloane called the room back to order, and my brother sat down at the far end of the table, flashing me a raised eyebrow and a smug smile with a head nod in Sam's direction. Shit.

"Showtime," Sam whispered, nudging his leg against mine.

"Quit touching me, Spam."

I knew I was being bitchy, but my brother was an expert at reading my emotions. Sam could not be obvious around him because that meant my mother would know about him within minutes of my brother leaving the room. He had a big mouth and couldn't help feeding my mother the juicy gossip. He'd been doing it all our lives, part of why I left New York. Everyone worshiped at the altar of Gregory Abernathy Willard. Even his middle name was pretentious.

Fucking douche had been making my life complicated from day one.

Why can't you be well-behaved like your brother?

Why won't you go to Yale like your brother?

Your brother wants to stay in New York because he loves his family...

Yeah, and he also liked the big fat check my parents gave him to pay for his living expenses. And the way our father had dropped his resume on the desk of the head of marketing of the company of his choice. The job he now held, the position I'm sure our father paid for before he even had his first interview.

Gregory was brilliant, with enough charisma to fuel his enormous ego, and he was classically handsome and good at sports; everyone loved him. And then I was born. The child who didn't do what she was told. The one who talked back and told teachers they didn't know what they were doing. The little girl who was kicked out of dance class for not listening to the instructor. The daughter who refused to wear dresses or play nice with the little trust fund babies they threw in her path when they decided it didn't matter if she was smart because they were determined to marry her off to a rich idiot before her twenty-first birthday.

"You alright?" Sam whispered, and I looked down at my lap, my hands clenched in fists as whatever Sloane was talking about at the front of the room went in one ear and right out the other. *No, Sam. I'm not okay.*

"Fine."

The backs of his fingers brushed against my pant leg again, and I batted him away, trying to keep my expression neutral as my brother continued to smirk at me across the room, studying my face.

"Now that we've taken care of the standard business," Sloane continued from her place, standing at the head of the long table. "We need the candidates for the copy editor positions to stay behind for a few minutes. Sam, Kristine, Cole, Sofia, Nate, you all need to hang out here with your supervisors for a few moments."

As everyone filtered out of the room, leaving the ten of us at the table, I watched my brother cross the room and stop behind my chair. Sam's hand was perched on his knee, a respectable distance away from me but still close enough to put me on high alert.

"We've got reservations for 7:00," Greg told me quietly as he leaned over my shoulder. I glanced back at him, hating that he didn't even check to see if I had plans. The fact that I didn't wasn't relevant. He expected me to drop everything to accommodate him. "Just the two of us, or...?"

I frowned, and then he glanced over at Sam, who was looking down at his phone. He briefly looked up and locked eyes with me before he nodded at my brother, holding his hand out toward him. Shit. *Quit being polite, Sam.*

"Sam Langley," he smiled as my brother gave me a loaded look, slowly shaking Sam's outstretched hand. "Kristine and I just finished working on a project together."

"I'm sure you did," Greg laughed. "This one is a handful, isn't she? How often did she try to tell you that you were doing your job wrong?"

"Oh, only a few," Sam laughed as he kicked his foot out under the table, grazing my heel with the tip of his shoe. "She knows what she's doing, though, so I tend to listen when she's bossing me around."

"Alright, that's enough," I interrupted, pinning Sam down with a loaded stare before turning on my brother. "Just text me where you want to meet, and I'll show up. I'm assuming Daddy is paying."

"Oh, come on, Krissy," he smiled, knowing I hated that name. "I'm a big boy now. If you haven't noticed, I have my own job and everything."

Don't worry, I noticed. I also see your five-thousand-dollar suit that screams, 'My mommy picked this out.'

"You should bring your friend." Greg lifted his chin toward Sam, and my eyes widened.

"I...uh...what...he's not." Fuck. Now he was going to know something was going on. I was stuttering like a pubescent boy discovering porn for the first time. "Sam's busy."

"And you know this how?"

Glancing around the room, I noticed Sloane off to the side with Adrian and Isobel, curiously watching Greg talk to me. She had to know he was my brother. The last name was a dead giveaway, as well as our matching hair color and hazel-hued eyes. We may have had wildly different personalities, but we looked like siblings. Another Willard trait that I couldn't shake, the gene pool was as dominant as the personality traits.

"I just do. I'm sure you're busy, and Sloane needs to..."

"Krissy, relax. I've got the afternoon free. And Sloane looks occupied." He glanced over his shoulder, making eye contact with her and smiling. She grinned back, obviously another powerful woman to add to his fan club. Ugh. "What do you say, Sam? Want to join my sister and me for dinner? You can fill me in on what it's like to work with this little troublemaker."

I felt my face flame as I twisted in my chair to face Sam, mouthing 'NO' with a slight shake of my head. He looked a little nervous, his eyes shifting to Gregory and back to me.

"I was going to go to the gym to run a few miles after work," he started.

"See, Greggy? Told you he was occupied."

"I told you to stop calling me that," Greg narrowed his eyes at me, and I gave him a wide smile in return.

"And I told you to stop calling me Krissy when I was five. It's annoying when people don't do what you want, isn't it?"

"Anyway," he smiled, looking back toward Sam. "I'm sure you can go hit the treadmill another time. I'd love to get to know my sister's friends here. You should join us."

"Let it go, Greg."

"You seem adamant about keeping me away from your friend Sam here, Krissy. I'd hate to have to ask Mom why that could be."

Fuck. That was low. She'd have our wedding planned before Greg could even hang up the phone. She'd assume he was rich because why else would you ever date someone? Boy, would she be disappointed to see me cavorting with a man without influence. In her eyes, I was already a failure, refusing to take a job in New York so she could continue to try to marry me off to her friends' pretentious offspring. Add in that I earned my career on my merit, and I was the feminist outcast.

"Fine," I growled, looking over to Sam. "Would you like to join my obnoxious brother and me for dinner, Sam?"

"Well, when you put it like that, how can I refuse?" he laughed as he kicked his toe against my shoe again, his eyes twinkling with amusement. He had no idea how much of a shit show my family was.

"Great." Greg clapped, reaching forward to squeeze my shoulder. "I'll text you the address. Make sure to wear a dress, Krissy. I need to make some calls. I'll see you tonight." He glanced at Sam, smiling widely. "I look forward to picking your brain about this one."

Fucking nosy-ass bastard. He was almost worse than our mother with digging for dirt.

Sloane called the small meeting to order, telling us about the three new positions coming available in the next several months. First, two copy editor positions within the Boston branch, in non-fiction—*ick*—and fantasy. Then another in the New York office in the contemporary romance division. That would have been a perfect position, but I was never moving back to New York. It just wasn't going to happen.

"Hey, you okay?" Sam cornered me in the hallway outside Isobel's office, pulling me in the door and leaning his arm on the wall next to my head as I sagged into the corner.

"I'm fine," I muttered, trying not to look into his concerned eyes. I didn't want to need him for comfort. I didn't want to need him, period, but he'd been on my mind nonstop for days, and not even the parts I expected. I could have compartmentalized better if it was just a physical attraction, but this was different. I wanted his arms around me and to have him tell me he'd protect me from my brother's prying. That he'd listen as I vented about how my family wouldn't let me have my own life, far away from theirs. I could explain to Sam that my father was probably behind my brother's visit to our office.

He'd let me yell that I suspected my father was behind the position at the New York office since I knew that Isobel's counterpart had just been hired two years ago. Sam thought his mother was annoying when she tried to control him from across the country. He had no idea what it felt like to not know for sure if your professional future was something you earned or was just an orchestrated move on my father's chessboard to try to draw me back.

"Look, if you don't want me there tonight, I can devise an excuse, but maybe it wouldn't be the worst idea to go with a little backup."

"That's not..." I sighed, unsure how to phrase it without sounding like a self-centered bitch. "I appreciate your being willing to take one for the team, Sam, but I'm not sure if you going will just complicate things more."

"As a friend, Kristine. I told you there wasn't an agenda here." Those words may have come out of his mouth, but the sincere look of compassion in his eyes, the way he was leaning into my personal space, and the fingers on his other hand gently grazing mine indicated that we'd gone beyond being able to pretend we were just friends or coworkers. The lines were too blurry now, and being under the Willard microscope would only magnify our chemistry.

"You say that now, but—"

"I think I can manage to keep my hands off you for one evening."

"Can you?" I nodded to his fingers as I pressed my hand against the center of his chest.

"The question is—"

He leaned in close, his lips grazing my ear. "Can you?"

"*One* night, Sam."

He nodded as he straightened up, clearing his throat and stepping backward. "Got it."

Chapter
TEN

SAM

BOSTON

KRISTINE WAS RIGHT TO tease me. I *was* struggling with the compulsion to touch her—even if it was to calm her down. She'd been so tightly wound in that conference room that it shook me a little. She was known around the office for being an ice queen, an emotionless robot who didn't smile, much less socialize with the rest of us in a way that made her appear human.

I'd known, of course, that she was capable of much deeper emotions than scathing sarcasm or surly indifference, but as her brother was ruffling her feathers, she'd been positively panicked. When Sloane had announced the position in the New York office, I thought she'd jump all over the contemporary romance position, clearly the front runner with her experience, but she'd frowned as if someone had just killed her puppy. Wouldn't she jump on the chance to go home?

I knew if a position in the Chicago office became available, I would be all for it, regardless of genre, at the chance to be closer to my family. If she could, my mother would beg, borrow, and steal to get me an opportunity like that.

After I returned home from work, I texted Kristine to check on her. She'd seemed upset and distracted the rest of the meeting, and I couldn't get the haunted look in her eyes out of my head when I'd cornered her in Isobel's office.

Sam: Are you sure you're alright?

Kristine: Fine.

Sam: It's okay if you're not. You can talk to me.

> *Kristine: Would you just lay off it, Spamela?*

And we were back to the aggressive name-calling. That was never a good sign.

> *Sam: Fill me in. What topics do we avoid this evening?*

> *Kristine: The first one would be that you've seen me naked.*

> *Sam: While one of my favorite topics, noted.*

> *Kristine: Quit being cute and only stick to our professional relationship. If I steer the conversation correctly, Greg will spend most of the night talking about himself.*

> *Sam: Got it. You're in charge. ;)*

> *Kristine: Don't be a smartass.*

> *Sam: I'm not. I liked it when you were in charge.*

A lot. So much so that I couldn't stop myself from reminiscing about what it'd felt like when she rocked her hips over mine in that sinuous rhythm. Back and forth, round and round, and okay...I could see her point. No imagining her naked, no matter how tempting it got...

> *Kristine: He cannot know that we are more than colleagues.*

> *Sam: Are we more than that? He must suspect something. He was somewhat suggestive.*

> *Kristine: He's a nosy asshole who will tell my mother everything. Do not give him ammunition against me.*

> *Sam: Are you ashamed of me?*

I asked just to see if I could get a reaction, but I knew that her family was loaded, and sometimes with that came expectations of a certain caliber of suitor. Not that I was her suitor or anything. That was laughable. She'd have to let me in first.

> *Kristine: Don't be such a girl.*

That didn't answer my question.

Sam: And here I was, ready to wear my sexy high heels.

Kristine: While you paint an enticing picture, let's go with dress shoes. Please. Ones made for men.

Sam: You spoil all my fun.

Kristine: Just call me a killjoy.

Sam: I'll be there in dress shoes, pressed slacks, and a tie.

Kristine: And I'm hoping for a shirt that buttons.

Sam: You are a joy killer.

Kristine: I need to wash my hair. Leave me alone.

Sam: Already blowing me off with clichés.

Kristine: Maybe if you play your cards right, it'll be another variety of blowing.

Sam: Do tell. Someone told me to keep my hands to myself.

Kristine: A lady never divulges such information.

I couldn't help it, I burst out laughing, earning a raised eyebrow from Taylor, but he didn't ask me who I was texting. Of course, he probably didn't need to. Both my roommates had given me shit about how I'd acted around her over the weekend.

Sam: Sorry, sweetheart. You already told me you're not a lady.

She didn't respond, but she didn't need to either. Tonight would test our acting skills because I wasn't sure if I could pull off platonic, especially since she'd planted the seed of blowing things afterward.

"Wow, you do know how to listen to instructions." Kristine had texted me her address after she'd washed her hair, surprising the shit out of me because just the other night she hadn't wanted me to know where she lived. She still didn't invite me inside the sleek-looking apartment building in Boston Landing.

Caleb, Tay, and I looked at the area last year, debating whether we should stay in our current building, but the $8000 rent on the three-bedroom units had been a little bit of a deterrent. The three of us made decent salaries, but they wouldn't even cover living expenses in a place like that.

"Quit staring at my building, Sam. It's creepy."

"Sorry." I shook my head, trying not to picture where she lived. I had a feeling she wouldn't invite me up any time soon. Then, glancing back toward where she stood on the curb, my eyes widened when I took in the sleek bun she'd pinned her long hair into and her face carefully painted with sophisticated makeup.

My sister Fiona always called her makeup for going out 'war paint,' and I wondered what kind of battle Kristine was preparing herself for. It wasn't that she didn't look gorgeous, because she did, but it was much more polished than I was used to her looking.

"Wow..."

"Oh, stop it," she hissed, smacking me in the shoulder with the back of her hand. "It's just makeup."

"You look..."

"I said knock it off, Langley. Don't say another word." Her voice rose as I scanned her from head to toe, pausing on the way the silhouette of her dress hugged her hips, tapering down to her long slim legs. "Quit staring at me like that. You've seen me in a dress before."

Laughing as she swatted at my shoulder again, I caught her hand, tugging her forward until I could lean down to whisper in her ear. "The dresses you wear to the office, while rare, don't look like this, Kris. You're a knockout, and you know it."

Her breath caught as I ghosted my lips down the side of her jaw, her fingers clasping the open placket of my sport coat. "You're playing dirty, Sam. And I don't like it."

"But I think you do," I laughed as I stepped back, gently prying her fingers from me and shoving my own in the pockets of my pants so I didn't touch her again the way I wanted. "I think you like me dirty, and I love giving you what you want."

She was quiet again in the Uber, scooting across the back seat and keeping her fingers twisted together in her lap. I kept stealing glances at her profile, the lovely curve of her mouth, her exposed neck, and how her skirt had ridden up to show off a generous amount of those shapely thighs. Kristine didn't even know how sexy she was, which was a good thing, given her arrogance about her caliber of professional talent. I knew tonight I needed to turn off my attraction and keep things distant and platonic. Still, when I noticed her nibbling on her lower lip, I desperately wanted to pull her into my lap and kiss away every speck of lipstick she had painted across those same full lips.

"You need to get a hold of yourself," she hissed as the car pulled up to the valet stand in front of her brother's hotel. "Quit staring at my mouth, and for the love of God, don't touch me."

I chuckled, mainly at how she was so indignant and partially because she had my number. I did want to kiss her. I wanted to do more than brush her shoulder with my fingers and clasp her hand as we sat side by side. I fantasized about pinning her to the door of the restaurant bathroom, pushing aside whatever scrap of lace I knew she had on under that dress, and fucking her with my fingers until she screamed my name into my shoulder. Then she'd be begging me to fuck her...

But I needed to get those thoughts out of my head and put on the best damn show I'd ever put on in my life because I had a feeling it was important to her that her brother did not know that I'd seen her naked. That'd I'd been closer to her than coworkers should be. As close to her as a man could be to a woman.

It was just going to be so damn hard, pun fully intended.

"You look lovely," Greg complimented Kristine as he walked toward us while we approached the heavy wooden doors to the steakhouse inside his hotel. She stiffened up as he leaned in and kissed her cheek before stepping back and nodding at me over her shoulder. "Good of you to join us, Sam. I'm looking forward to getting to know Krissy's friends here. You are friends, right?"

Nodding awkwardly, I kept my hands in my pockets, afraid that I'd do something stupid like graze my hand against the small of her back as he led us toward the host station. Of course, the young hostess fawned all over him. "Mr. Willard, your table is ready. Right this way. Would your wife like a cocktail?" she asked, glancing down at Kristine's fingers before conspicuously looking back at Gregory's hands.

"She's my baby sister," he chuckled as he leaned toward the pretty blonde's ear. "No Mrs. Willard, yet."

"Barf," Kristine muttered under her breath, but I heard her, biting my bottom lip to hold in a laugh at the blatant disgust in her tone.

"What was that?" Gregory asked as he stared toward the retreating hostess as he pulled out his sister's chair at the table.

"Nothing, Greggy. Just said I'm in the mood for beef."

"Still eating like a lumberjack, I see."

Kristine's hand balled into a fist in her lap as her smug brother took the seat to her left, leaving the one to her right open for me. I could tell she was trying to hold in a retort and failing as I took my seat, keeping a respectable distance between us.

"Just because your anorexic girlfriends eat like two carrot sticks a day doesn't mean I have to keep myself from enjoying the costly cut of meat that my brother is going to buy me for ambushing me and making me go to dinner with him."

"Well, if you returned our mother's phone calls, you'd know I was going to be in town, and then maybe you could've made an effort to welcome me like a normal sibling."

"Oh, I'm sorry. Are you too busy to tell me yourself, or is it just that hard to detach yourself from our mother's teat?"

Wow. I watched the two of them hiss back and forth across the table, suddenly thankful for the playful banter I shared with my sisters. The Willard clan played for keeps in the game of sibling resentment.

"So, Sam." Gregory cleared his throat, making eye contact with me from across the table. Great. Now he was pulling me into this little battle of barbs.

"Leave him alone." Kristine glared at him before he could say anything else.

"Afraid he's going to tell me your dirty little secrets?" Greg taunted before he motioned toward a server walking by the table. "Bring us a bottle of Chivas Regal, the 25. I don't want any of that watered-down crap you serve the people at the bar. Three glasses."

She nodded and turned toward the bar, hurrying around the tables and flagging down a bartender.

"You didn't even say please, or thank you, you dick," Kristine sighed as she reached for her water glass.

"She works here, and I'm tired of waiting for a drink."

"We just sat down."

"Exactly, we're seated. Do servers in Boston not expect their patrons to need drinks?"

"God, you're almost worse than him."

I expected another retort, but Greg just laughed, glancing over his shoulder and motioning for the returning server to give Kristine the first glass.

"Is there anything else you'd like, sir? I can send over your server if you're ready to order."

"No, this is great. We can wait a few more minutes to order. I'll let you know when we're ready."

Neither of them had cracked open their menus, and I wished I could hide behind mine. The thinly veiled hostility that Kristine was trying to suppress put her behavior into clarity for me. She had vipers within her own family to contend with; no wonder she refused to put up with anyone's shit. I didn't know whether I wanted to hug her or grab her hand and make a run for it. Or... *No, Sam, don't even think about doing other things with her right now.*

"Are you a scotch drinker, Sam?" Greg asked as he lifted his glass to his lips, holding the amber liquid in his mouth for a moment before he swallowed.

"I've been known to imbibe from time to time." That seemed like a safe enough answer.

"Kristine here doesn't have the palate for it."

"No." She shook her head and tipped her drink back, taking two healthy pulls from the glass, never flinching as she swallowed. "I like scotch just fine. I hate that you have adopted our father's pretentious taste. It's as if you can't keep your lips off his ass long enough to have an original thought."

"Which one is it, Krissy? Mother's teat or father's ass? Don't pretend you hate that fancy apartment of yours. I know family money paid for that," Greg chuckled with a pointed look in my direction. I was aware that her family had money—probably much more than I could imagine—but that wasn't why I was so drawn to her. I'd be compelled by her scathing wit and eyerolls much more than her bank account.

"Nana paid for my apartment, not Mason. I don't need to sell out for our parents' approval."

"Still from the Willard coffers, sweetheart. They've got their hooks in you too, and once you get offered that promotion, I won't even say a word when you move back in with Mommy Dearest."

"That—" she growled, narrowing her eyes. "Will never fucking happen. I'm not coming back to New York, and I am not marrying fucking Trevor like it's some arranged marriage. No matter what our father wants."

My fingers clenched the glass before me, the amber liquid swaying as I tried not to read into their conversation. *Who the fuck was Trevor?*

"Sam." My head snapped up as Gregory gave me an appraising look across the table. "You're up for one of the copy editor positions, right?"

I glanced over at where Kristine was scowling in my direction now. "Yes. I am."

"Are you a fantasy man or a non-fiction man?"

Kristine scoffed as she rolled her eyes, throwing back the rest of the contents of her glass.

"Why can't I be a romance man?"

"Oh." Greg's eyebrows raised. "Is that why Kristine kept insisting you two aren't together? I didn't realize you weren't into women."

The sound of choking turned our heads toward Kristine, whose face had turned red as she tried to hold in her laughter at her brother's comment. He seemed to be the poster child for toxic masculinity.

"Of course, Greg, you caught us. A straight man couldn't possibly edit a romance novel. Sam is my super, super gay office friend. He pulls in all kinds of tail. Gay, gay tail."

"That's nice," he replied, not picking up on her obvious sarcasm. "My assistant is gay."

I wasn't sure what to say to that, but if Kristine was using falsifying my sexuality as a ploy to keep her brother from prying into her love life, I could live with a bit of a harmless lie. It'd also seemed to diffuse the sibling-pissing match they had going on. That was more awkward than failing to correct him with the news that I'd been inside of his sister. And that I was imagining spanking that tight little ass of hers right this moment.

"Then maybe you would be a better fit for the job in New York. I could always introduce you to Preston if you need to make a new *friend*."

My eyes widened as Kristine's hand grasped my knee, her chest shaking with silent laughter as she tried not to look over at her brother.

"Kristine working with romance books never made sense to me anyway. Wouldn't you need to believe in love to be able to edit it?"

The smirk that had been on her lips moments before fell into a flat line, her eyes taking on that dead quality that I hated, which meant that she was pushing her armor into place.

"Kristine is a professional. Her editing skills aren't reliant on her personal life. A good editor can handle any genre, regardless of their own experiences."

"Don't they always tell writers to stick to what they know? Shouldn't that apply to their editors as well?" His narrowed eyes scanned her face, looking for a reaction she refused to give him.

"There are plenty of writers whose imaginations are vivid enough to fill in the blanks." I'd never met a serial killer or an FBI agent, yet I could edit manuscripts that painted detailed portraits of both those types of characters. If the emotion was conveyed clearly enough, the reader could imagine it. You could fake anything with enough research. I highly doubted that Evan had sexual encounters like the ones described in his last book, but with Chase's help, he'd knocked it out of the park.

"Well, now that I know you're not screwing my baby sister—" Greg started, smiling at Kristine's exaggerated eye roll. "You need to fill me in on the office dirt. Who is she spending her time with?"

"Why is my sex life so important to you, Greggy? Still having issues getting it up? You know they have prescriptions for that sort of thing."

He narrowed his eyes at her before he refilled both of their glasses, mine still largely untouched as I tried to keep a clear head in this tête-à-tête they had going on. I was simply an observer watching it all unfold, occasionally getting dragged into the conversation by way of a device they used to poke digs at one another.

The server eventually wandered over to take our orders, Kristine ordering an outrageously expensive porterhouse cut of aged beef and Greg following suit. Not yet knowing if I needed to dip into my savings for this meal, I stuck with a more sedate eight-ounce New York strip with a side of julienne potatoes and mixed grilled vegetables.

"Exactly how long are you going to be here?" Kristine asked as she placed her silverware down across her plate. The only remnant of her meal was the small bone in the middle of the delicate porcelain.

"Love you too, Krissy," he retorted with a smirk as he leaned back in his chair, smiling fondly at her.

"Oh, quit with that bullshit," she smiled, clearly more relaxed than when we arrived at the restaurant an hour earlier. "We both know why you're here in person. Sloane could have introduced that software to the office without your little spiel. But you're too much of a narcissist to resist getting the credit for something."

"Just a few days. I'll fly back on Friday morning."

"Please stay out of Sloane's ear on the promotion," she requested, her voice ringing with quiet sincerity. "You can tell Mason I'm just fine without him meddling in my professional life. You know Nana would lose her shit if she knew what you two were trying to pull."

"You know Ms. Graves will put you wherever you want if you ask. Sloane thinks very highly of you. Almost makes me proud."

Kristine scoffed, sipping from her glass of water after they'd exhausted half the bottle of scotch. "If I have to cheat to get it, I don't want it. I don't need things handed to me because your father has a superiority complex. Not with the strings Mason would attach to it."

"He's *our* father."

"I said what I said." Clearly, Adrian was right about Kristine having some *Daddy issues*.

It must be nice to have that kind of sway. Having the flexibility to call in favors just because of who you were. I would have been a little bitter about it, but Kristine was perfectly capable of earning the promotion without her family interfering. The only thing that worried me was that she was determined to stay away from New York, and I knew she'd never be interested in being a non-fiction editor. Most likely, I didn't want that position for the same reason. It wouldn't present the same challenges in developing a fiction manuscript.

Which left us with a bit of a dilemma, we both wanted the same job, and neither one of us would submit to the other.

I casually listened to the siblings bicker about much more mundane topics while we waited for the check. Gregory insisted on paying, and I thanked him while Kris continued to stare daggers while he signed for our meal. He wasn't a terrible guy, but I could tell he enjoyed his privilege and the things he could get away with because of it. She never leveraged her family's wealth like it seemed he did.

After everyone had finished their drinks, he bid us goodbye and disappeared into the hotel bar staring down at his phone as Kristine and I headed out the doors to wait for a ride.

"Do you want to ride back to my place?" She asked, leaning into my shoulder slightly as we stood side by side outside the restaurant, both pleasantly numb from the rich food and the alcohol.

"It'd make sense to have them drop you off first. It's closer."

"Not what I meant, Sam."

"I know." I smiled as my fingers reached for hers, barely ghosting against the soft skin before I pulled away, trying to respect her boundaries.

"Thank you for behaving yourself in there," she said, smiling softly as she glanced up at me, her eyes soft as she momentarily glanced toward my lips.

"Wish I could say the same for you." She laughed as I shook my head at the memory of her and her brother lobbing verbal grenades at each other. "You might have just as well stabbed him with your fork."

"Don't think I wasn't imagining it. He irritates me sometimes."

"I couldn't tell." She rolled her eyes as she leaned against my shoulder, tucking her hand in the crook of my elbow. "I wasn't sure if I needed some protection against your barbed tongue in there. You're scary when you're worked up."

"I'd be happy to demonstrate how not barbed it is if you join me for a drink at my place."

"Well—" I grinned as I leaned in closer, grazing my lips against her cheek. "Maybe I'll let you. However, I do recall someone not wanting me to see her apartment. And I also seem to recall something about only one night, and that's it."

"If you don't want to see me naked, Sam, that's fine." Her voice was calm, but she tried to let go of my arm and gasped when I held her fingers in place. "I'll just pull out one of my battery-operated boyfriends that don't talk back."

My eyes widened as I realized she was telling me that she'd get herself off with a vibrator if I didn't come home with her.

"Close your mouth."

Giving up on keeping a polite distance from her, I snaked my arm around her waist, pulling her into my chest. "Ever have a threesome with one of those boyfriends?"

It was her turn for wide eyes as she scanned my face, her eyes lingering on my lips. "There's a first time for everything, Sam."

Chapter

ELEVEN

KRISTINE

BOSTON

Sam's hand clasped mine tightly as I pulled him toward the entrance to my building, ignoring the stares from the other residents gathered in the small lobby area. The front desk clerk was long gone, and only a few people were seated on the plush couches just inside the building.

This place tended to attract young professionals as tenants, mostly arrogant fuckboi types that hit on me in the elevators at least once a week, whereas I only wanted one particular young professional to execute some very wanted advances on me in the confined space.

"No doorman?" Sam teased, tucking me into his side while we waited for the elevator to return to the lobby.

"No, Sam." I rolled my eyes, toying with one of the buttons on the front of his dress shirt. "I'm not that pretentious."

"Hmm," he hummed as he leaned toward me, kissing the side of my head.

"What does that mean?" While I'll admit that I did like nice things, I tried to live on my income, apart from letting my grandmother subsidize my apartment. She'd seen it as a way to keep me away from my father, understanding that I was suffocating under his thumb in New York. She'd been forced into marriage to a man she barely knew at nineteen to ensure the family fortune remained in the family, so she could empathize with my parents trying to push me into the same thing. They'd been allowed to marry for love—when they still loved each other—and they weren't pressuring Gregory into getting married yet, but as soon as I had my degree in hand, my parents started matchmaking.

After a dozen horrendous dates with their wealthy friends' sons, I knew I needed to get as far away from them as possible. I'd been set on finding a copy-editing position in California, but I'd met Isobel at a trade conference and knew I wanted to work with her. I'd still had to go through the complete hiring process and started in a lower position than desired, but I loved my job.

Which was why I was so pissed off that the only role for me to move forward in my chosen genre would be to move closer to the family compound. I couldn't call that place home anymore. It brought back too many memories of fighting with my intoxicated, narcissistic mother and hyper-controlling father. But I was refusing to dwell on them right now.

"Sorry, I didn't mean anything. I'm just not used to people throwing money around, and I guess I never associated you with someone like..."

"Someone like my arrogant douche of a brother?"

"Yeah, like him..."

He hesitated like he wanted to say something else, and I hated to be that person, but I asked him anyway because I hated people who wouldn't communicate. "Go ahead and finish the sentence, Sam."

He glanced down at me, hesitating just long enough for the elevator to arrive, causing him to close his mouth again and urge me into the small metal box.

Once the doors closed, I turned toward him, leaning my hip against the wood railing. "You're not getting off that easy, Langley."

"Well, I didn't think it was going to be easy, but we should at least get into your apartment first," he joked.

Shaking my head, I arched an eyebrow. He was telling me what I wanted to know before he got off—that was for damn sure.

"Fine. Who the fuck is Trevor?"

Surprised laughter bubbled up my throat as he narrowed his eyes at me, not expecting that reaction. "Oh, come on, Sam. I never took you for the jealous type."

"I'm..."

"Yeah, you hear me make one off-hand comment about an arranged marriage, and you get all alpha male on me. I'm not anyone's property, Sam. We aren't even dating."

Anger—or maybe annoyance—flashed in his eyes, and I looked off to the side, watching the numbers go up, my floor rapidly approaching. I hadn't wanted to start a fight. I just wanted to see if the second—well, I guess technically the fourth, or was it the fifth?—time would be as explosive as the first.

"That's...ugh. Why do you do this?" Sam sighed, deflating from his momentary frustration.

"Do what, Sam? Not let myself be treated like someone's property?" I knew I was pushing him away again, but I wouldn't be some submissive girlfriend. That wasn't what this was, and even though Trevor was just some rich asshole I *never* thought about, Sam would not be allowed to play the jealous boyfriend card with me.

"That's not what this is, and you know it, Kristine. You're pushing me away because I asked you a question you don't want to answer. I'm not asking for your life story, but this guy must have been important to you if marriage was in the picture."

My eyes widened as I looked at the frown pulled across his lips. It didn't look like it belonged there. Sam wasn't some taciturn guy. He was always smiling or smirking in that irritating way of his. "Fine," he sighed, and I hated that he kept using that word. It was a filler word that conveyed nothing other than vague annoyance.

The doors to the elevator parted, and I stepped forward, watching as his hand clenched the railing and he remained rooted in his spot.

"Oh, come on, Sam. That isn't what this is. Get out of the damn elevator," I laughed as I stood in the hallway with my hand on the elevator door so it wouldn't close.

"Maybe I should go home."

Fuck. *Come on. Play with me, Sam.* I didn't want him to go, but he was trying to blur the lines.

"*Fine...*" I teased, turning toward the side of the hallway my apartment was on and taking a step forward. "Guess it's just me and the silicone stud tonight. See you at work."

The doors closed, and I heard a muffled 'Fuck.' Well, that wasn't very reassuring, but if he wasn't respecting my boundaries, I wasn't going just to let him push them aside. I allowed enough people in my life to push my limits, and I didn't need the guy I was...*shit*. So, what were Sam and I doing?

Before I could push myself too far down that path of thought, the elevator chimed, and I turned from where I was standing in front of my apartment door.

"Don't think this means you're getting out of answering the question," Sam called out as he approached me, his face serious. "But I'm not interested in talking right now."

"And what are you interested in, Mr. Langley?"

"Just open the fucking door, Kristine."

"Geez," I laughed nervously, hoping he'd smile at me, laugh, and show me some indication that he was willing to be my Sam. Wait...no, not *my* Sam. Just the fun, friendly Sam. The one who'd asked me if I wanted to have a threesome with a faux phallus. "Maybe I need to use a toy on you, Sam. It might lighten you up."

A low grumbling growl built in his throat, and his palm pressed hard against the door as soon as I turned the door handle. "You have any roommates?"

"No." I shook my head as he placed his palm on my back, urging me across the threshold.

"Good." He stepped into the apartment behind me and pushed the door closed behind him, the soft snick of the lock engaging in contrast to the loud sound of my heartbeat in my ears. "Then no one will hear you scream."

"If I didn't know any better, I'd think you were threatening me," I laughed, but my voice was strained as he stepped in behind me, carefully pulling down the zipper at the back of my dress. His fingers parted the material, and it fell to the floor in a puddle around my heels.

"Oh, I am, Ms. Willard. I am threatening you," he chuckled, placing one palm on my stomach and the other loosely around my throat. He applied a modest amount of pressure there—not enough to constrict—just enough to let me know he was in control right now.

"With what weapon?" I whispered. "It seems like you're just threatening me with a fun time."

His hips pushed forward, a distinct hardness pressing into my lower back. "I think you can figure that part out."

"I don't know. I need to compare your weapon with my arsenal."

"Arsenal?" He chuckled, his hand loosening and stroking down the skin on my throat and settling between my heaving breasts.

"Do you think you can handle the comparison, Sam?"

His stern veneer cracked entirely as he flexed his hips forward, slowly grinding against me. "Is that supposed to make me feel threatened?" he laughed against my ear, slowly sucking on the skin beneath. "It may be able to make you come, but does its weight press you into the mattress as it slowly grinds between your legs? Does it make you wet by whispering how good you taste against your lips before it slowly slips inside you?"

"Fuck..." I panted as the hand on my stomach trailed between my legs, pressing the lace of my panties into where I was already wet for him.

"Does it wrap your legs around its head and make you scream until you're hoarse and begging it to stop?"

"Uh..." *My words aren't coming right now, Sam. But if you keep pressing your fingers into me, I might.*

"Why don't you get out your favorite, and let's see if I can make you come harder than it does?"

Was he serious with this? Most guys cringed at being compared to a sex toy. Something about women using toys, even large toys, made them insecure about their bodies.

"Who..." Goddamn that noise.

Sam chuckled against my hair, slowly rubbing another slow, torturous circle with his fingers against my soaked panties. "Go, let's see what you've got."

"But..."

"If you think a piece of silicone will intimidate or emasculate me, you clearly don't know me. Didn't you know that toys are friends?"

He dropped his arms from around me, placing his hands on my waist and turning me toward the hallway where my bedroom was. "We don't have all night," he laughed. "Well, I guess we do, but the longer this takes you, the fewer orgasms you'll get."

Holy shit. And I'd thought the last time was intense. Irritated Sam was bringing his A-game tonight. Once I'd disentangled my feet from my discarded dress, I glanced back at Sam's challenging smirk before taking off toward my room with as much grace as my uncomfortable footwear allowed.

"You've got two minutes," he taunted as I pushed my partially opened bedroom door, flinging it into the wall with a thud.

"Shit," I whispered as I got down on my hands and knees at the side of my bed and pulled out the black trunk I'd purchased to house my growing collection, courtesy of Chase's submissive friend, Talia. I'd insisted on fact checking parts of Chase's steamy BDSM novel with her directly, and she'd welcomed me into her fold. She was a sex toy blogger who loved giving her friends new things to play with. There was no way for her to test out everything some of the companies sent her for free, and I was not about to turn down her kind of gifts.

"What is that?" Sam asked wide-eyed when he walked through the door a moment later, watching me turn the dials on the lock after I'd hauled the small black trunk onto my mattress. "I didn't think you'd have an actual arsenal. But, damn, Kristine, I've got to say, I never took you to be the kinky type."

"There's a lot you don't know about me, Sam," I teased as I pulled the lock from the metal loops and carefully placed it on my nightstand. There was no way I'd be leaving anything in the contents of the box just lying around. The house cleaner that Nana insisted on providing me with cleaned everything. She did not need to know what was stored under my bed. "A girl can't always rely on competent men to meet their needs. They're harder to find than you think."

"When was the last time you were in this little Pandora's box?"

He'd already taken off his jacket and unbuttoned his shirt before he joined me, smooth, bare skin showing between the open buttons. Sam's attire at work wasn't casual, but tonight, he wore fitted dress pants that made his ass look positively sinful. And I wanted to sin with him so badly.

"A few weeks ago." The day he'd trapped me in the corner of the elevator and whispered vaguely suggestive things in my ear, to be exact. I had to relieve the tension somehow.

"Did you make your selection yet?"

I pulled open the lid and surveyed the contents; over a dozen small black silk bags were lined up in the case, a little tag on each one. Talia was terrific at ensuring you had proper storage for her generous contributions. "Hold on, give me a moment."

I picked up a bag I knew held my first battery-operated boyfriend, a simple, anatomically correct model in matte black. It wasn't the largest toy I owned but it had a strong motor. It'd never failed to get things in motion.

Deciding that it wasn't what I wanted Sam to use on me, I put it back inside and picked up a smaller bag, peering inside as I glanced at him just standing there a few feet away, watching me. This toy was smaller but could make me come in under two minutes. It had a suction feature that pulsed on your clit and could induce some of the strongest orgasms I'd ever had. It would be fun to let him play with, but not tonight.

I pushed aside the largest toy in the arsenal, a dark purple waterproof model I didn't use very often, to pull out the mid-sized blue rabbit that I knew usually provided an enjoyable time.

"This isn't Goldilocks and the three dildoes, Kristine. Just pick something and get naked," he laughed as he slowly unbuckled his belt and stepped out of his dress shoes. "But you can leave those heels on if you'd like."

"You're so impatient," I laughed as I laid the bag with the rabbit down on the nightstand and pushed down the latch on the lock of my trunk, spinning the dials and lowering it to the floor before I pushed it under the bed with my shoe.

"Really?" he laughed as he nodded to where I'd pushed the trunk out of sight. "You had to lock it again? Afraid I'll see what else you've got stashed in there?"

"No," I shook my head as I reached behind myself to unclasp my bra, but I think he could tell I was lying. I didn't want Sam to explore the contents of the trunk. There were also some toys I only played with if I was feeling extra frustrated. He didn't seem put off by the fact that I owned toys, but I'd never had a guy interested in using them *with* me.

"Mmhmm," he hummed as he pulled his shirt out of his pants and pushed them to the floor, stepping out of them and shrugging off his dress shirt. He approached me in only his dark, tight-fitted boxer briefs, his excitement visible through the thin material.

"Maybe it's none of your business what's in there," I said quietly, suddenly feeling shy about the things I typically only got out when I was alone. The last guy I'd tried to date had made it clear that he wasn't comfortable with anything outside of the 'norm' in the bedroom, so I hadn't done much experimentation with a partner.

Talking a big game and having experience were two separate things. It wasn't that I was inexperienced, but my limited partners were clueless or selfish. I knew Sam was neither of those things, and it scared me. He wanted me to open up to him and seemed determined to ensure I was satisfied. Still, with every encounter, I found myself unable to resist revealing things to him emotionally as well. I *wanted* to talk to him.

This promotion was going to kill things between us. I felt the tension already at dinner, and now I knew he'd eventually want to talk about it. Unfortunately, despite the bullshit he'd fed my brother, he wasn't a romance man, and I wasn't returning to New York. That spelled disaster if we were actively competing for the same job. However, it wasn't enough to keep me from having sex with him. Not tonight, and most likely not any other time he was interested. My brain told me to bail and keep him at a distance, but other parts of me were already desperate for his attention.

"You don't need to be embarrassed around me, Kristine," he whispered as he stepped in behind me, fingering the lace along my hips before he knelt behind me and pulled my flimsy panties down my legs, helping me step free. He kissed a trail from my lower back up to my shoulder blades, his hands reaching around to cup my breasts as he stood to his full height behind me. "I think it's hot when a woman knows how to get herself off." He paused, gently rubbing the pads of his thumbs across my nipples. "Now, get on the bed."

With one last gentle pinch, he pushed me forward, turning me before he urged me back to the pillows, climbing on the bed and settling his weight against me. The soft friction of his briefs pressing between my legs had me panting as he kissed along my shoulders and licked a path up my neck and behind my ear. How he knew exactly how to excite me remained a mystery, but I rubbed against him like a cat as he grasped my hands and pinned them to the pillow above my head.

"Keep these here," he whispered as he reached toward the nightstand, picking up the little silk pouch and pulling open the drawstring. "Hmm. Interesting choice."

My teeth worried my lower lip as he pulled the toy out of the pouch, turning it over in his hand before experimentally pressing the buttons, testing the different functions. I was practically panting as he knelt between my legs, his muscular body on display. I was halfway tempted to tell him to ditch the toy and just fuck me, but I could see the gears turning in his brain as his eyes glanced to mine and then back to the rabbit.

"I..."

"Ah, ah, ah. Nope. You lie there with your arms up, and I've got it from here." The devilish glint in his eye was indication enough that I was in for quite a ride. "Close your eyes. No peeking."

Scanning his face, I nodded, letting my eyelids slip closed as I waited to see what he intended to do to me. He was almost silent, but after a moment, I heard the telltale buzz of him setting the lowest vibration. I think he enjoyed teasing me, prolonging the anxious wait as I tried to keep myself from squirming.

Lifting my hips, I rubbed my thighs together. Sam slowly trailed it down the inside of my arm at an achingly slow pace. By the time it was at my side, another had joined on the opposite arm, and the two fingers slowly teased inward, softly grazing my nipples. I could still hear the buzzing, but it was muffled like he'd laid it on the bed somewhere.

"You're so soft," he whispered as the fingers changed course and trailed across my stomach, teasing my mound briefly before tracing along the crease between my thighs. Finally, he pressed his hands against my thighs and gently spread them apart, exposing me. The bed shifted as he moved briefly, and then I felt a warm stream of air against my thigh before he started raining small kisses everywhere but where I wanted him.

"Please," I whispered, desperate for him to touch me there. Usually, I'd need a few drops of synthetic moisture when I played, but I could tell he wouldn't meet any resistance with how aroused I already was from the dirty words he'd practically growled in my ear and his teasing touches.

"Relax," he whispered, but he must have been just as anxious as I was because it wasn't long before I felt the first touch of the low humming vibrations at my entrance. I half expected him to just thrust it in there, but he teased me with the tip, slowly drawing it through my arousal and spreading the wetness he found there.

My back arched as I felt the tips of the rabbit ears graze my clit, the subtle hum ratcheting up my blood pressure as he continued to taunt me with no intention of pressing the teasing toy inside me. My hands grasped the pillowcase as I tried to fight the urge to mindlessly reach forward and grab his hands, telling him to get on with it. He had to know I was waiting for it at this point, the sighs and slightly desperate moans I could not hold in filling the silence in the room.

"So beautiful," he murmured as he finally poised the tip at my entrance, thrusting it inside teasingly a few times before pressing forward, seating it deep inside me. The vibrations increased, the toy pulsing and buzzing as he skillfully manipulated the controls, driving me closer and closer to release until...

"Oh, God..." I moaned as he turned up the intensity of the small rabbit, the ears insistently pressing against my clit as he twisted the toy, pulling out momentarily before thrusting it back inside. Sam even knew how to manipulate my toy with more skill than I did, using it to draw out my pleasure, getting me to the edge before pulling it back and lowering the settings, causing me to thrash against the bed as I got closer and closer to release.

I could hardly breathe as he worked me up, pushing me toward the brink and changing direction, teasing me until I was moaning loudly, trying to close my thighs to keep it in place. But he had other ideas, one hand pressing my thigh to the mattress as he began to fuck me with the toy earnestly, pushing the intensity to the highest setting and then holding it inside me, twisting it side to side as my pulse pounded. Finally, I detonated against the pressure, calling out his name as my hips shot up, writhing against him as I came apart.

The vibrations stopped abruptly, a dull thud sounding against the floor. I couldn't open my eyes, still buzzing with pleasure as I felt Sam's strong hands grasp the backs of my thighs, pulling me down the bed slightly. The sound of a crinkling condom wrapper and Sam's soft groan only intensified my excitement as I waited for what came next.

My eyelids fluttered open as I felt him stretch above me, his warm bare skin doing nothing to calm the fire I felt racing through my veins.

Sam's eyes were dark in the dimly lit room, glittering with quiet intensity as he leaned in and kissed me. His hips aligned with mine, and his rigid cock pressed inside me as he plunged his tongue into my mouth, his lips moving feverishly as he drove his hips forward into me.

"Fuck," he groaned as he turned his face, leaving me gasping against his cheek as his fingers weaved with mine, holding them to the pillow as Sam flexed his hips insistently, pressing me down into the mattress as he chased his release. "You are so fucking sexy when you come."

"Oh, God," I moaned as my hips pressed up toward his, something explosive building as I felt him drive us both toward an intense peak. It'd always seemed like some cheesy romance novel cliché when authors described couples orgasming simultaneously.

I was wrong. So, so wrong.

As Sam captured my lips again, thrusting his tongue into my mouth, he drove my body right over the cliff again, my head pressing back into the pillow as my hips pulsed frantically against his. He groaned in my mouth as my body clenched around him, setting him off, his cock throbbing deep inside me.

I didn't like to admit it, but I was wrong about sex not being worth the trouble. With Sam, it was worth it. It was worth everything to feel the weight of him as I pulsed around his hard flesh.

And that scared the shit out of me.

But not enough to stop.

SAM

BOSTON

SOMETHING SHIFTED WHEN SHE opened her eyes. The walls were gone, even for just a moment, and she was with me, utterly present as I pressed inside her. Afraid of what else I'd confess to her in the throes of passion, I kissed her with abandon, surrendering myself to the feel of her body. She was slick and tight, hugging me exactly right as I thrust inside, close to exploding but wanting to prolong her pleasure.

There was something about being able to watch her fully as I used the toy on her, not distracted by the sensations in my own body, but as she started coming, it was hard to keep myself from following her simply from watching. I'd succumbed fantastically only moments after getting inside her, emptying myself into the condom while she pulsed around me.

Tonight's events had steered us in a dangerous direction. Even though Kristine's brother was a smarmy douche, I'd seen inside the walls. She was vulnerable despite the intensity of her words. I could see the broken woman desperate to find her way in the world, pushing back against the pressures of her uncaring family. It was such a stark contrast to the loving home I'd grown up in, and it made my heart ache for her.

"Why are you so quiet?" she whispered, tracing a small circle around my nipple. It almost tickled, but I liked her hands on me. Maybe the sleep snuggling hadn't been an anomaly. Kristine was curled against my side, tucked under my arm as I lay in the middle of her ridiculously comfortable bed.

"Hmm," I hummed as I turned my face into the top of her head, inhaling the scent of whatever products she'd used to style her hair. "Just enjoying this."

It was the truth. I was enjoying this new closeness. She kept me at arm's length so often that being able to hold her felt good. All the reasons to stay away from her disappeared whenever I spent time with her alone. The potential problems the possibility of promotion would surely cause between us didn't seem to register. I wanted her, and she wanted me, and it seemed easy.

"He's no one," she whispered into my skin, kissing my side as her legs wound around my thigh.

"Who?"

"Trevor."

"Kristine..."

Her head shook, the loose strands of her hair rubbing against my arm. "I'm serious. He's the eldest son of my mother's best friend. She tried to get me to date him, but there's a reason he's still single and over thirty."

"Is he gay? Like you told your brother *I* was?" What sane man would let Kristine slip through his fingers?

"No, definitely not," she laughed, squeezing my side as she tilted her head to look up at me. "He's a jackass who screws all his secretaries and is looking for a submissive woman to be his baby factory while he fucks anything under twenty-five in a skirt. He's a disgusting pig with a small dick."

"You slept with him?"

Her giggling surprised me. "Oh, fuck no, but good ol' Trev pressed his hips into me while we were waiting outside a club, and I was underwhelmed."

"Maybe he wasn't, you know..."

"Fuck, Sam, I think we've spent enough time together to be comfortable saying the word cock without blushing," she laughed. "He told me he was hard and asked if I'd have a quickie with him in the bathroom."

"Wow," I responded—a little shocked—loving the amused twinkle in her eye. "Sounds like a real winner."

"Yeah, that's it. Even if I could find his dick with the assistance of a microscope, I still wouldn't touch it for fear of all the venereal diseases he's most likely contracted."

"So, I read too much into that comment about an arranged marriage?"

"Way too much. It was never serious, just a handful of dates with tiny-dicked Trevor and a few others. My mother pushed for it, and my father saw it as a business opportunity. My happiness didn't matter to them."

"I'm sure that's not true," I whispered, hugging her closer because I *wasn't* sure if it were true. If her parents acted like older versions of Gregory, maybe they didn't have her best interests at heart.

She was quiet for a few moments, holding me just as tightly, her body slightly tense. My mother wanted me to settle down and start giving her more grandbabies, but she'd never try to get me to marry as some business arrangement. It'd never crossed her radar for me to marry for anything but love. She'd probably try to run off any woman who wasn't madly in love with me. I *know* my sisters would.

"Are we going to talk about it?" Her fingers had resumed tracing my chest, but she kept her face down, her chin tucked so I couldn't see her eyes.

"About the promotion?" I clarified a few moments later.

"Yeah, you're planning to go for the fantasy slot, right?"

Lying to her wouldn't help anything, and I was planning to throw my hat in the ring for that position, no matter the competition. I knew there was still a chance neither of us would get it, but there was also a strong possibility one of us would, and the other might resent that.

"I am," I confessed, hating that she tensed up momentarily. It wasn't personal, and I did want her to succeed, but I didn't want to push my career goals aside because we wanted the same promotion. It wouldn't be fair to either of us to step aside, nor would I want her to. If I got the position, I wanted it to be because I earned it, not because I didn't have competition. "Where does that leave us?"

"They won't be announcing anything for three to six months. We might hate each other by then." I could tell by her tone that she was forcing sarcasm into her voice, but she was right; neither of us could predict the future.

"Doubt it."

"Sam, I'm not pulling any punches on this one, and you shouldn't either." She pushed herself up, leaning against the headboard as she looked down at me. It felt like she was already putting up a wall between the two of us.

"Can I ask one question?"

"I'm sure I can guess what it is." She chewed on her bottom lip nervously, looking adorably mussed with her loose bun and wisps of hair framing her face. "But go right ahead."

"Why won't you go for the romance spot? Despite what your dipshit brother said, you excel in that genre."

She sighed as she looked up toward the ceiling, tucking her legs against her chest and wrapping her arms around them. I wanted to force her to lay back down and stop hiding, but if she needed to hold herself together to talk to me, so be it.

"If I get the job in New York, he wins."

"Your dad?"

She nodded, looking back down and resting her chin on her knee. "Yeah. He will use it to manipulate me if I have to move back to New York. He already managed to get Greg's company a foothold with Vivid, and I won't take a job he is responsible for creating. I've met Meg from the New York office, and she loved that job. If she's moving on already, it's because someone made that happen."

"Surely Sloane wouldn't compromise her integrity or the publishing house's with something like that." Sloane didn't seem the type to let people get away with nepotism. She'd started in our position as a copy-editing intern and worked her way up, which is why she liked to cultivate talent internally when it was possible.

"Not her, Sam. It'd be higher than that. Mason doesn't lower himself to calling in favors with middle management. He would have approached the executive team, if not higher."

That almost sounded paranoid, but her world was different than mine. She'd grown up with a rich father who came from what sounded like old money and endless connections. The only nepotism my parents executed was being able to choose my elementary school teachers because my mom was the president of the PTA.

"So, we both want the same job."

"I guess we do," she confirmed.

"Am I supposed to say something like 'May the odds be ever in your favor?' Tell me what to do here, Kris."

"This isn't *The Hunger Games*, Sam. But I'll understand if you want to stop doing..."

"Each other?" I filled in when she paused for too long.

Kristine nodded, chewing on her bottom lip again.

"*I* don't want to stop, but I'm not the only one making the decisions here."

"Maybe we need a little distance?" she suggested, looking slightly upset, but that wasn't what I wanted.

"Maybe we both need to say fuck it and see where this goes instead?" Pushing myself up to a seated position next to her, I tucked Kristine under my shoulder, pulling her as close as her posture would allow.

"I don't want you to resent me if I get this job, Sam."

"Let *me* worry about that, Kristine. But I understand if you don't want to label this."

"You might get chosen for the New York position," she teased, tucking her head beneath my chin and curling against my chest. "And then Gregory will set you up with Preston."

"Preston doesn't have these," I laughed as I reached over and cupped one of her breasts, lightly pinching the nipple.

"But I bet my balls are still bigger than his," she chuckled as she crawled into my lap and framed my face with her hands.

"Oh, I'm sure they are." Smiling as she leaned forward and kissed me, I looped my arms around her back. "They might even be bigger than mine."

"Can we keep this between us a little longer?"

"Your giant balls?"

She smacked me in the chest. "I'm trying to be serious here."

"If that's what you need," I offered, gently urging her back against the mattress and settling between her legs.

"It is..." she whispered, moaning when I ground my hips into her.

Keeping things platonic at work was more manageable since we didn't have to work directly with each other in the following weeks, but Kristine spent at least three nights a week in bed with me.

Adrian and Isobel had filtered us more information about the interview process, but it became an unspoken rule not to discuss it. There were eight candidates for three positions within the two branches, and I had a feeling that Kristine and I were among the top three. Adrian seemed sure the fantasy position was mine for the taking, but he didn't know Kristine wasn't interested in the romance position. Isobel was mad at her for letting family drama get in the way of her career, but Kristine's feelings were valid.

There were still times when we were together that I felt her putting up barriers, but she always seemed to drop them after sex. Something about the endorphin release freed up her typically stubborn tongue.

My mother had been calling more, still trying to guilt me into coming home, but I'd been able to redirect her so far. My middle sister's accidental pregnancy was an easy way to deflect her attention from me. A few times, she'd been sent to voicemail when Kristine was over, and I had a feeling she suspected there was a woman. My sisters had all tried to sneak my dating life into texts in the last week or so, which meant she was trying to use them to get information from me.

"Hey," Kristine whispered as she stood at the coffee pot in the empty break room, filling her travel mug.

"Morning," I smiled. It *had* been a great morning. Kristine had woken me up an hour before either of us needed to get ready for work with her head between my legs, which led to us having to shower together to conserve water because I'd insisted on returning the favor, twice. As a result, we were both a few minutes late to work, and her hair had been wet when she shoved it up into a bun this morning before we shared a ride into the office.

"Did they schedule your interview yet?"

I nodded, anxious now that Human Resources was starting the ball rolling. "Wednesday morning."

"Me too."

"Nice."

Shit. It was getting awkward. *Change the subject, Sam.*

"Have you seen any more pages from Chase's manuscript?" I knew it was random, but Adrian was freaking out that Evan was super secretive about his current project. He usually pitched a new project within weeks of his last release date, but he wasn't showing Adrian any pages this time.

"No." Kristine rolled her eyes. "She's been completely flakey lately. She told Isobel she was working on something different but won't give any details. She's pushing for an extension on her new series. It's bizarre. She hasn't missed a deadline since I've worked here."

"Do you think…?" I trailed off, my brain trying to make strange connections where there probably shouldn't be one.

"Think what?"

"That something is going on there?" I paused, trying to collect my thoughts. "So, Chase and Evan work on his book—which even you have to admit messed with our heads a little—and suddenly, both of them are acting out of character and blowing off their editors."

"God, Sam," she chuckled. "Not everyone is screwing each other. You need to check your libido."

"Doesn't seem to bother you," I smirked suggestively, but she smacked me in the chest, glancing around me to ensure no one was within earshot. "But what if they are?"

"Then good for them, but they both better start submitting pages because I'm tired of Isobel acting like she has a permanent case of PMS every time Chase dodges her calls."

"Evan dodged Adrian's calls before all this happened." Not that I blamed him. Half his calls were Adrian trying to convince Evan to come into the city more, which rarely happened.

"Wonder why?" Her scathing sarcasm wasn't lost on me.

"Evan has an automated out-of-office response set up on his phone. It pisses Adrian off so much," I laughed. There had been a few times he'd had me text Evan, but I never got the out-of-office response. So, it had to be something Evan set up expressly for Adrian's number and email.

"You'd think by now your smarmy boss would figure out half the people who work with him think he's a gigantic dick," she sighed.

"Oh, he does know everyone thinks he's a dick. He wears it like a dickish badge of honor, making him look like even more of a dick. It's a continuously perpetuating cycle of dick."

"Sam, stop saying that," she giggled. Kristine actually giggled—not a sardonic laugh, not a sarcastic laugh, an honest-to-God giggle came out of her mouth.

"Say it, Kristine. I want to hear you say it. What is Adrian?"

"A sparkly vampire?" she laughed as she placed her hand in the middle of my chest, but then she froze, stepping away from me and shooting a nervous look toward the door to the hallway.

Carson was standing in the doorway, frowning as he watched us. I could not wait until the universities let out for the semester, and that little shit was sent home for the summer. He'd been a jackass since they announced which university interns were getting paid positions this summer break. Despite his uncle's connections, he wasn't chosen for placement and was taking it out on everyone in the office. He'd also gotten a little more careless with his suggestive comments.

"Speaking of dicks," Kristine muttered as she stepped past me, refusing to make eye contact as she headed toward the door.

"She's never going to sleep with you, Sam," Carson taunted with a smirk as he approached me. "That one is locked up tight."

Well, she did have some things locked up tight...under her bed...

"Carson, a word of advice." I motioned for him to step closer. He hesitantly obeyed, and I leaned forward, lowering my voice. "Quit being fucking creepy to all the women in the office, and you might get them to stop hating you."

"Hey, Carson," Kristine called out from the doorway.

"Yeah?" he turned in her direction and smiled, winking at her.

Her lip curled in disgust, but she responded anyway. "I know a guy with a tiny dick that sounds like an owl..."

"Who?" he responded, and I unsuccessfully tried to choke down a laugh.

Kristine was spectacular as she winked and waved, walking out of the room.

He turned back toward me, a frown on his face. "What was that? Who is this guy? That was random."

"Not important, Carse. I'm sure you'll figure it out eventually," I chuckled, patting his shoulder as I headed out of the break room, checking to make sure he wasn't following me before I jogged down the hallway toward Adrian's office.

Pulling out my phone, I fired off a quick text to Kristine. I was almost disappointed she didn't stay to see his reaction. If he still wondered why he didn't get a paid summer position, he really was *that* dumb.

Sam: That wasn't nice.

Kristine: He didn't get it, did he?

Sam: Not even a little.

Kristine: Well... I would say it was fitting, but we both know it's so tiny it wouldn't fit inside anything without falling out.

Sam: Ouch.

Sam: Speaking of fitting things inside... Do you want to crash at my place tonight?

Kristine: I can't. I need to work on this manuscript Isobel just sent over.

Trying to tamp down my disappointment, I shoved my phone back into my pocket and finished the trek toward Adrian's office, cringing when I heard him laughing loudly along with the muted tones of a feminine voice.

"Hey, Sam." Isobel laughed nervously as she stood from where she'd been perched on the corner of Adrian's desk, straightening her skirt and running a hand down the back of her hair. "We may have a new project for you next week."

"Oh, come on, Is," Adrian chuckled as he also stood, grabbing something from his printer and handing it to her before he sat back down. "You know as well as I do this is getting signed."

"What's getting signed?"

"Chase and Evan wrote a book together." Isobel beamed as she looked over at Adrian. He gave her a wolfish grin, and I couldn't believe they were so blatant about their flirtatious behavior. Typically, Isobel was just as buttoned up as Kristine, at least until you got to know her better.

"And it's fucking insane, man," Adrian chuckled, shaking his head. "It's gonna be a bestseller for sure. So, you ready to brave the dragon again to work on this one?"

"Ad, seriously, we talked about this," Isobel scolded as she rolled her eyes and sighed. "Stop talking like that. Sam isn't the only talented copy-editing intern."

"It was a joke." He was trying to defend himself, but I knew he was referring to Kristine.

"I'm sure we can manage to work together again," I confirmed, and Isobel smiled at me before reaching forward to squeeze my hand.

"Thank you, Sam. At least someone in this office acts like a professional. I'll update you with details after I run this one through Sloane."

"She's not gonna turn it down, Is."

"We'll see," she shrugged, stepping around me and heading toward the door.

"What kind of book?" I asked curiously. Evan had never worked outside of the mystery and thriller genres. I wondered how the romance could be introduced, since I knew that was Chase's forte.

"It's kinky as fuck." Adrian tapped on his phone screen and then tossed it in my direction. "We didn't get to read through more than a few chapters, but it's hot, man. Check out the fifth chapter."

I pulled open the chapter navigation on the PDF and selected the fifth chapter, quickly scanning the dialogue, my eyes widening when I got to the character's narration.

Frances slowly circled Dominic as he knelt on the cold concrete floor, his hands bound lightly behind his back. Red rope trailed up his forearms and muscular biceps, creating an enticing pattern of exposed flesh and intricate knots. Shibari was always one of Fanny's favorite forms of expression in their bondage sessions.

The way the stark contrast of his pale skin looked against the rope was uniquely bewitching, with slight indentations from the twist of the ply crisscrossing the ivory canvas of his arms.

He marked so beautifully, and his fair skin was flawless, just waiting to be turned pink with one of her implements.

While she could appreciate disobedience, Dominic was the ideal sub for Frances. He was always eager to please, even after almost a decade in their current dynamic. She'd never felt compelled to find another primary submissive because they worked so well together, and he was always open and honest in communicating with her.

It also didn't hurt that he was endowed with the perfect equipment for her slender build. It was like the gods smiled on her the day Dominic had entered her dungeon for the first time. He was built just for her pleasure. She'd thought her life was fulfilled, granting other people's fantasies, but he'd been a welcome reprieve—a safe harbor in the storm of her thoughts.

He'd made her a better Domme. She'd never told him the depth of her feelings, but the love they shared within their dynamic had kept her alive more than once when the darkness threatened to suck her back into her previous life of addiction.

"Are you ready for me?" she whispered as she trailed the soft leather of the crop across the bottoms of his feet.

"Yes, Mistress..." His voice was soft but powerful enough to bring her to her metaphorical knees.

"Stand, my angel," she commanded and watched as he slowly rose to his feet without the assistance of his bound arms. The muscles in his back and bare cheeks flexed as he stood in front of her, stark naked, the red rope his only adornment.

Frances circled Dominic, thinking of all the places she wanted to leave her marks on his body; his lean muscles and soft skin were her favorite canvas.

"Count for me," she murmured as she made her first strike against the firm muscles on the back of his left thigh, just below his clenched fists. "One strike for every time you teased me this week."

"One," he breathed out, his cock hardening, the pink flesh taunting her as she slowly walked around to his front after rubbing the sting out of

> *his thigh. His jaw clenched as she tipped his chin up, looking into his expressive green eyes.*
>
> *"It's not nice to tease your Mistress and fail to deliver..."*
>
> *He nodded, releasing a shaky breath as she stepped back and surveyed him for the next strike. His body was tense as she striped the backs of his thighs, her arousal building with every gasp and visible pulse of his engorged member.*

Blowing out a breath, I shifted from side to side, not wanting to adjust myself in front of my boss outright. I hated to admit that Adrian was right about something, but damn, this was some spicy material. Kristine owed me an apology. There was no way Chase and Evan drafted this book without fucking. There was just no way. And I wondered how I would get through the next several weeks of copy-editing the same material with Kristine and keep my hands off her.

"Fucking gold, right?" Adrian laughed as he reached his hand back out for his phone. As I handed it back, a text message scrolled across the screen. It seemed that maybe Kristine and I were right about something else.

> Is: Don't bother going home tonight after work. We're going through this one at mine.

It disappeared quickly but was followed by another one.

> Is: Bring the cuffs. They go on you this time.

Well, that was interesting. Gross, but interesting.

"It's got some potential," I agreed.

I just hoped it wasn't the potential to be disastrous. Kristine's earlier texts indicated she wanted some space, but I didn't want this to be what finally caused her to distance herself from me for good. I knew there would be an expiration going in, but I didn't want it to be so soon.

Chapter
THIRTEEN

KRISTINE

BOSTON

I KNEW IT WASN'T fair to Sam, putting on the brakes and trying to distance myself slightly. We'd settled into this non-relationship that felt a lot like a real relationship. It wasn't just sex with him, although that continued to surprise me. Sam was tender in some moments and demanding the next, consistently amazing me with his attentive nature.

A few nights this past week, we'd even fallen asleep talking, fully clothed, and I didn't panic the following morning when I was curled up against his chest, his nose buried in my hair. If I wanted to be his girlfriend, I had a good idea of what it would entail. Even his goofy man-child roommates hadn't managed to scare me away. It terrified me that I'd let him in, but something about how he treated me fulfilled this need for companionship and validation I didn't even know I had.

Sam's life had been a stark contrast to my life of privilege, and he'd experienced what it was like to grow up in a loving family. He sometimes grumbled about how his mother meddled in his life, but she was simply concerned for her youngest child. The meddling I dealt with involved manipulating my career, using the lure of financial security to get me to bend to their will, and borderline emotional abuse when I didn't comply with what my parents wanted for my life.

I'd joked about my mother planning a wedding if she found out about Sam, but the sad truth was that when she found out he was just an average hard-working guy from a middle-class family, she'd tell me I was wasting my time. The more attached I got to Sam, the more I wondered if it was *me* wasting *his* time. He was bound to find out I had the potential to be just as toxic as my fucked-up family.

An early morning text pulled me out of the cycle of overthinking. I found myself frequently trapped inside similar paths of thought on the nights I spent away from Sam.

> Isobel: Did Sam tell you about Chase and Evan's new manuscript?

> Kristine: A new manuscript? No, why would Sam tell me?

> Isobel: He was in the office right after we got their email. I thought he would have told you because you'd be working together again. I knew you two were friendly and wanted to make sure you didn't think he was getting an unfair advantage.

Fuck me.

> Kristine: Isn't telling me assignments your job?

> Isobel: Yes, but I was waiting until the contracts were signed.

> Kristine: What genre is it?

> Isobel: Thriller, serial killer trope, romantic subplot with BDSM.

Wow. That was quite the departure from both of their previous works. Evan had never explored kink in his novels, and his more thriller-like mysteries hadn't involved serial killers. I was excited to see the first draft, and it sounded like Isobel was hyped up about the project.

Part of me was anxious that I would be working up close and personal with Sam for the next several weeks. I knew it wasn't fair of me to think of us collaborating again as a hardship, but it wouldn't help my tumultuous thoughts. If I kept my heart guarded, I stood a chance against this situation blowing up in my face.

Still, if this book was even half as sexy as Evan's last project, I knew we wouldn't be able to keep our hands off each other. The last time had been hard enough—pun intended—when we hadn't seen each other naked yet. Now that I knew his tells when he was turned on and had permission to touch him, it spelled disaster for my willpower to remain distant.

"Did you get a chance to look at the manuscript yet?"

Sam picked up my messenger bag and settled it on the floor as he dropped into the chair next to me at the small table in Isobel's office. It was oddly reminiscent of one of our first interactions when we started working on Evan's book together but with much less hostility on my part.

Despite her early morning texts, Isobel had barely greeted me before telling me she'd most likely be out of the office all day. I didn't need her to hold my hand, but I thought she'd at least debrief me on the document before she dropped it in my files and ran.

"Not yet. I just finished my coffee," I confessed. Part of me was scared to open the file, knowing it would be another intense edit. Chase's typical romantic comedies were spicy reads, but when she dove into BDSM, there was another level of intensity to the writing that worked its way under my skin, and I couldn't hold back my physical reactions.

"Want to camp out in one of the private conference rooms and dive in?"

"Is that wise?"

"Oh, come on, Kris," he chuckled, his hand closing on my bare knee and squeezing lightly before he trailed it along my thigh. My breath caught in my throat at how it felt for him to touch me casually. My brain took it to a suggestive place, but his smile was easygoing, lacking the intent it usually did when he was trying to get me naked. "I think we can keep our hands off each other long enough to do our job."

"Shh," I hissed, glancing toward the open office door. There wasn't anyone standing in sight in the hallway, but I knew how easy it was to eavesdrop outside offices without anyone suspecting. My own voyeuristic nature regarding office dirt made it easy for me to watch for potential drama undetected. The last thing either of us needed was a comment to be repeated. It'd spread like wildfire. I knew neither of us was far enough up the chain of command for it to be scandalous, but I didn't want to compromise my professional integrity. At the same time, we were both being considered for a job with much more responsibility.

While we were editing interns, we were often nameless and faceless past our pay grade, but if one of us secured this full-time copy editor position, we'd have a team to manage, and we couldn't do that if people thought we screwed around in the office. Sloane didn't have any specific policies prohibiting intra-office dating. Regardless, it was an actual written rule you couldn't fraternize with other employees considered subordinates. Another reason I felt the expiration date quickly approaching with Sam. If one of us snagged this position, we wouldn't be equals, which could complicate things.

"Calm down. Carson was at his desk, and Andrea was talking to him about something. He was too busy staring down her blouse to see me sneak in here. That dude isn't subtle about taking great interest in her chest."

"Still. Isobel might come back in here and hear…"

"She has no room to talk," he interrupted. "When Adrian showed me the manuscript, those two were texting some interesting things to each other."

"What?" I laughed, trying to process how Sam managed to look at Adrian's text messages undetected. "How do you even know that?"

"He had me read part of a chapter on his phone, and a text scrolled across the top. If they're trying to be covert, he needs to change her contact in his phone to something besides her first name." Sam smiled and shook his head, rolling his eyes as he looked at me.

"That's all you're going to tell me?"

The teasing smile that stretched across his face was both adorable and obnoxious. "You look nice today."

"Oh my God, you ding dong," I laughed. "What did the fricking text message say?"

"Something about going to her place to look over the manuscript and it being his turn to wear the cuffs," he said with a shrug—like he didn't just reveal our bosses were handcuffing each other outside the office. At least, I hoped it was outside the office. And not anywhere near where I worked. Maybe using one of the conference rooms wasn't such a bad idea.

My eyes widened as I tried to stifle a laugh. Maybe Sam was right about it all. Everyone around here *was* fucking, including us. The thought would have been laughable a few months ago, but now. Now I didn't know what to think about any of it, my own out-of-character behavior included.

"So...you...me...closed conference room...this manuscript and some more coffee?" Sam smirked as he placed his hand on the back of my chair, leaning in close. "There aren't any windows in there, and we can wedge a chair under the handle to keep the door closed. You know I love it when you wear a skirt."

"Sam, what the frick is wrong with you?" I hissed, trying to keep myself from blushing. I couldn't tell if he was joking or not, but the idea of doing things in the office was getting me a little hot under the collar.

"I was kidding," he winked, but how his eyes trailed down the length of my bare legs made me question if it was just a joke or him trying to manifest something happening. "I'll grab some coffee from the break room if you claim a room."

Pulling my now empty travel mug from my bag on the floor, I handed it to him, hesitating momentarily. "Put this in your bag after you fill it. We don't need the gossips seeing you bringing me coffee."

"Fine," he sighed, only looking a little annoyed. "But I don't think anyone will think that we have some torrid affair going on because I filled your coffee mug. Now, if they knew what else I filled..."

He was right, I knew he was, but I still felt anxious about people at work potentially finding out we weren't just two interns working together on a project. "It's hardly that torrid," I deflected, but the image of him aggressively pinning my wrists to my mattress after he'd made me see stars with that rabbit flashed through my mind regardless. Okay, *maybe* it was a bit torrid.

"You go first. I need to pack up the rest of my things and ensure I have the right files."

He leaned in as he stood, brushed my hair over my shoulder, and lightly kissed beneath my ear. I held my breath as he pulled away, glancing down so he wouldn't see how much a simple kiss could affect me. Even the tamest of Sam's touches ignited something primal inside of me that I had difficulty concealing. I was sure he could see their impact if he tried, but it helped me maintain the illusion of having any resistance against him.

"See you in there," he said with a nod as he tucked my mug into the bottle holder on the side of his bag.

As soon as Sam had stepped through the door and out of sight, I sank back into my chair with my hands over my face. This 'work friends with benefits' situation was getting out of hand. I didn't think about sex all day. I never had, but every time he was in the same room, it was like a fucking pornographic slide show on repeat in my brain. I blamed Evan. It was all that fucker's fault. If he didn't need Chase, I never would have been sucked into this whole intra-office literary orgy.

Carson was still trying to use his X-ray vision on Andrea's blouse to get a glimpse of her generous cleavage as I crossed into the shared office cubicles that filled the central part of our floor. The poor girl didn't seem to realize how much of a pig he was. He was nice to look at, but I could see him abusing that with her if she got too close.

I quickly passed by the other genre editors' offices, keeping my head down as I approached the back wall that held half a dozen small conference rooms. I rarely used them, only sneaking off occasionally if Isobel was meeting with someone in her office, and I couldn't be bothered to walk to the coffee shop down the street.

They were small, housing a round table with four chairs and a small bookcase filled with office supplies. Checking over my shoulder to ensure I wasn't drawing any unwanted attention; I chose the room in the corner closest to the storage room. The door was cracked open and appearing unoccupied, so I quickly flipped the magnet on the door that indicated a meeting was in progress.

The office manager only required people to schedule the larger conference rooms ahead of time, so these were first come, first serve, but they all appeared unoccupied. It always struck me as odd that the main conference rooms had glass walls, and these were like glorified closets without any exterior windows, but I was thankful for their privacy.

My phone chimed with a text as I sat down in one of the chairs and started pulling out my laptop.

Isobel: Adrian told me Sam was starting edits today. Maybe you two should schedule some time to get through some chapters together.

Kristine: On it. We're comparing notes right now.

Isobel: Thank you for being so agreeable toward working with him again. I know it's not easy to accommodate working with other teams.

Yup, Isobel, spending alone time with Sam was a real *hard*ship. I wasn't sure how I'd survive it.

> Kristine: No problem. At least he's not as stupid as Dickhead.

I probably shouldn't be winding her up, now knowing that she was most likely fucking said dickhead, but I didn't want her to think I enjoyed working with Sam as much as I did.

> Isobel: Be nice to him.

> Kristine: I can be a professional.

> Isobel: No nicknames.

> Kristine: Too late. Spamela stays.

> Isobel: Adrian will be pissed off if you're mean to him, and I'm not dealing with that tantrum.

Just cuff him to your bed, and I'm sure he'll get over it—was what I wanted to type, but I wasn't supposed to know that they were doing kinky shit in their spare time.

The door opened inward as I sent her an angel emoji and quickly shoved my phone back into my bag.

"Your caffeinated beverage, ma'am." Sam grinned, pushing the door closed with his foot and passing my stainless-steel insulated mug across the table. "Ready to get down and dirty?"

"Sam," I scolded with a roll of my eyes, but I found myself glancing at the height of the chair across from me and gauging if we *could* shove it under the door handle to keep it closed.

"I'm just teasing you. Lighten up, Kris. We've managed to keep it PG at the office this long. I think I can hold out until later."

"Later, huh? Already got plans for me, Mr. Langley?"

"Always, Ms. Willard. Maybe we can break into your little black box again and try some things you don't want to show me."

"Uh." *Fuck.* The blush couldn't be stopped as I pursed my lips together and held my mug to my face. Damn him for throwing my brain right back into the gutter.

"Ah, I can see you're thinking about it," he teased. He hadn't pushed further on what was inside the box before now, but I knew it was only a matter of time.

"I thought we were working." My voice was a little strained as I tried to redirect him, but now I was running an inventory through my head of what I could show him inside my black toy box. I already knew he'd be a quick study.

"We are," he shrugged, putting his bag on the table and pulling out his laptop. He grabbed a small notebook and pencil, setting them in the middle of the table before he closed his bag and tossed it into the corner. "You want to use mine?" He gestured to the sleek silver piece of equipment. "It's got a larger screen than yours."

Rub it in that my department didn't get new tech when they rolled it out, Sam. "Must be nice to roll with the big boys over in MAST," I teased.

"Like you couldn't get IT to give you one of these if you wanted to," he laughed. "I'm sure if you went down there and intimidated them in that skirt, they'd find a way to sneak you one."

"You act like I just terrorize everyone in the office daily."

"Not everyone," he shrugged, but I could tell by the grin he was trying to rile me up.

"Fine. We'll use your stupid laptop. We've already covered that sometimes bigger isn't better."

"Sometimes it is, though," he said with a wink, pulling open the lid and starting to type, probably logging into the system to access the shared document server.

"It's not *that* big, Sam." Arching an eyebrow, I made a suggestive glance at his crotch, and he narrowed his eyes.

He scooted his chair closer to mine, placing his arm around the back and grazing his lips against my ear. "You didn't seem to mind when you were moaning for me to take you so deep it hurt last week."

"Fuck me," I blew out under my breath, willing my pulse to slow down. I was never going to survive this edit. Sam would keep distracting me until I couldn't take it anymore, and my brain exploded from pent-up sexual frustration.

"I will," he whispered, his hand settling on my thigh, his thumb dragging across the skin on the inside until it met the hem of my skirt. My legs widened fractionally, and my head turned to the side, his lips grazing my jaw as I reached forward to turn the laptop in my direction. "You have no idea how badly I want to fuck you on this table right now."

"Stop," I whined, my mouth going dry as he slipped his hand underneath the hem, grazing the scrap of silk covering me.

"I just want to see how wet you are," he whispered in a muffled voice. "You haven't looked at the book yet. I bet you'll be drenched by the time we get through a few chapters."

Despite my better judgment, I parted my legs as far as the chair legs would allow, gripping the arms and closing my eyes as he slipped a finger beneath the edge of my panties. He was right, I was wet, and we hadn't even gotten into the spicy stuff yet.

"Fuck," he groaned before he withdrew his hand and helped pull my skirt back into place.

"God, you're such a fricking tease," I growled as he used a hand to adjust himself, his hips shifting side to side in his chair. He licked his lips and unbuttoned the cuffs on his dress shirt, quickly rolling them up and pushing them up past his elbows. "That's just playing dirty."

"I would say I was sorry, but I'd be a fucking liar," he laughed, pulling the laptop to the edge of the table and starting to read aloud.

> *"The lights flickered momentarily, the deep red fading and plunging the room into darkness before returning as Frances stepped closer to her bound captive. She was watching with keen eyes as his chest expanded in a shaky breath before he let it out in a stuttering pant. He was blindfolded, arms stretched enticingly across the bed, wrists enclosed by black leather as he lay prone and vulnerable to her whims.*
>
> *Glancing at the table to her left, she quickly pulled a small metal harness with leather straps from the wooden surface and turned it over in her hands as she tried to gauge if she could maneuver the equipment into place without injuring her submissive.*
>
> *He was a good boy, his cock laying flaccid against his thigh, but she knew the longer she left him bound, the more his mind would be prone to wander, awakening the beast between his legs. But he had a job to complete first, and sacrifices needed to be made.*
>
> *"Hold still, pet," she soothed as she approached the bed, carefully pulling the metal cage around his member, fastening the buckles, and securing it behind his balls, rendering his equipment useless to her now. But that wasn't the part of his body she intended to use; his tongue would suffice for her current needs.*
>
> *His breath was still even as she climbed onto the large bed, throwing one leather boot encased thigh over his shoulder as she straddled the area around his neck.*
>
> *She longed to look into his pretty brown eyes, to see the excitement in them as she untied the strings on the sides of her panties and pulled the wet silk from between her thighs, but that would have to wait for his next session. They were enacting his fantasy of being bound and rendered partially senseless.*
>
> *Being a Domme was what she did and who she was. Frances made strong alpha men beg her to take away their freedom and use their bodies for her entertainment. When she'd gotten into the community at an early age, she'd tried to submit, but it became clear she wasn't good at following orders, craving the adrenaline rush from being in a position of power.*
>
> *It helped her harness confidence when powerful men trusted her enough to control their fantasies, and she was good at it. Her clients often clamored for her attention well past when their dynamics ended, but this was just a fantasy realm for her; her heart had turned to stone long ago.*

"Open," she commanded as she tugged on his lip, smiling as he complied, his mouth falling open softly.

"Good boy, you're such a good listener," she cooed, watching as his arms shifted fractionally against the restraints with her praise. The ones with the praise kinks were her favorite, so eager to follow instructions. This particular client thrived on positive feedback and often tried to anticipate her commands. Sometimes, it got him into trouble, but he also enjoyed impact play, so a spanking wasn't a deterrent to him.

"Are you ready, my pet?" She was practically straddling his face already, he had to know what was coming despite the blindfold, and she grinned as she watched his tongue peek out between his full lips. "That's right, my boy, Mistress wants you to make her come with that wicked mouth of yours before she lets you out of these restraints. Think you can manage that with only your tongue?"

She waited a fraction of a second, watching his lips move, but he caught himself, nodding with his head back against the pillow.

"You may speak freely," she told him softly. "But it might be difficult with your tongue in my pussy."

"Get up here, Fanny," he growled as he bit down on his lower lip, her thighs shifting as his broad shoulders lifted from the bed.

"Ah, ah, ah," she scolded. "So impatient. I think you forget who is in charge here, young man."

"Fuck my face," he whispered as he licked his lips, the soft moan Frances could not conceal ringing loudly in the dimly lit room.

"Oh, I plan to," she told him huskily, shifting forward to hold onto the metal headboard and lowering her bare skin to his greedy mouth."

"Are they fricking kidding me with this?"

Sam's voice cut off suddenly as I stood up from my chair, the legs teetering precariously before he reached out to keep it from falling.

"What? What's wrong with it? I thought it was an interesting hook," he laughed, watching me pace in front of the door.

"Seriously?" I tried to keep my voice low, but I was a little too wound up to be worried about potential eavesdroppers at the door. "The protagonist has a guy tied up to a bed naked and sits on his face in the first thousand words."

"I'm failing to see the problem here," he laughed as I tried to understand what he'd just read. Isobel had told me it was a thriller, not the script for porn.

"It's just..." I couldn't even form a coherent sentence, and it didn't help that I wanted to climb into Sam's chair and ride him until I could push the sound of his voice reading that opening scene out of my head.

"Weren't you the one teasing me about not being able to handle a little spice a few months ago? Why are you getting so worked up about this right now?

Both Adrian and Isobel are on board with this. I've read up to chapter six, and despite the racy beginning, the plot is solid."

"Because I don't know how I'm fricking supposed to concentrate on work with this, Sam. I already want to rip your clothes off every time you roll up your damn sleeves..."

"You do?" He looked surprised, standing up from his chair, his hands framing my hips as he halted my pacing. Even with my heels on, he was still a few inches taller, and my pulse slowed as he looked down into my eyes.

"Yes," I whispered, watching as his lips curved into a smile. Sam leaned forward, and I arched backward, keeping his lips from contacting mine. "Hold up there, Casanova. We need to go through at least four more chapters today if we're going to keep a decent schedule to get edits back to Chase and Evan."

"How about we come up with an incentive system?" Sam suggested in a whisper. His palm pressed into the center of my back, drawing me into his chest and tucking his face close to my neck. "Every chapter we finish editing today is an orgasm I get to give you later."

"Sounds like a one-sided arrangement," I whispered back as my hand trailed down his side and cupped him through his dress slacks. He was already hard, pressing insistently against my palm as I tried to remember why we were in this room. Suddenly our jobs didn't seem quite as important as the need to touch him.

"Your pleasure is my pleasure," he murmured, trailing his lips up my neck, biting the tip of my earlobe. "Or I can fuck you against the door of this conference room right now while you try to keep quiet so the rest of the office doesn't hear you scream my name when you come."

"Holy shit," I panted, squeezing the bulge in his pants. Before I could form a coherent sentence, Sam was backing me into the door, biting at my neck as he pulled up the hem of my skirt.

"Fuck it, we can work later," he growled into my skin before unbuckling his belt.

"What are you...?" I trailed off, watching him shove his pants to the floor and lower his boxer briefs. "Are you seriously suggesting that..."

Was this some alternate universe where our office had somehow turned into a set of low-budget porn? Fooling around at work was such a bad idea. But as he reached around me to make sure the door was securely closed, I realized this was happening, and I needed to snap out of it and follow along because it wasn't every day you got to enact one of your dirtiest fantasies at work.

"How do you want it?" he asked as he pulled my skirt to my waist and fingered the lace along the side of my panties.

"Hard," I breathed out, grabbing hold of his tie and pulling his lips to mine, surrendering to whatever magic Chase and Evan had unlocked with their words using Sam's rich voice.

My other hand reached down blindly to push down the waistband of his briefs just enough to free him, taking his hard flesh into my palm and pumping my hand as I bit his lip, holding his face to mine with his tie. Thank fuck he'd worn one today. It made it that much easier to keep him where I wanted him.

"You have to keep quiet," he warned, prying my hand loose and pulling on the knot of his tie—loosening it fractionally. Seeing him standing there with his pants around his ankles, briefs haphazardly pushed down his thighs, and his tie hanging askew against his fully buttoned dress shirt was almost comical. His eyes widened, and he held up a finger, reaching down for his pants and pulling a condom out of the back pocket. Biting my lip to keep from laughing, I reached for his tie again, but he stopped me before our lips met. "I'm serious, Kris. Mouth shut, or I'll find something to keep it shut."

Fuck. Why was that so hot?

Nodding as I watched him roll the condom into place. I pulled him in, kissing him with abandon as he reached forward and grabbed the back of my thigh. He wrapped it around his waist while his other hand pushed my panties to the side.

"Shit, you're so wet," he whispered against my lips, his breath coming out in harsh pants between us. "Did my voice do that to you, or the thought of Fanny sitting on his face?"

"Oh God," I moaned as he stepped forward and replaced his fingers with his cock. "You. It's always you."

"Shhh," he scolded, using his hand to rub against my clit, my head falling back against the door with a soft thud. "If you can't handle this, we can stop."

"Don't you fucking dare," I growled under my breath, grasping his shoulders and using them for leverage to push up onto my toes. Thank God I'd kept running when we weren't together because otherwise, I'd never have the stamina to hold myself up like this. "You can't tease me like this and back out, Sam."

"Oh, I won't be backing anything out," he smirked as he slipped inside, drawing his hips back fractionally before he pressed forward, his pelvis pinning me to the door. "So fucking tight. Every goddamn time."

"Faster," I urged, pulling him forward, my hand grasping the hair at the back of his head. Maybe if our mouths were busy, we could keep quiet.

"Mmm," he hummed against my lips as he reached down and coaxed my other leg forward, using his chest to pin me to the door as he wrapped my legs around his waist. "Too much noise."

My other hand reached for the tie again, wrapping it around my palm as I held his mouth to mine, frantically kissing him as he pressed his pelvis into me before drawing back slowly and forcing his way back inside. The pace was torturously slow, but the way he was grinding his hips into me with each slow thrust was working.

"Why can't I get enough of you?" he whispered against my lips, looking into my eyes, keeping eye contact as he continued his slow thrusts. "You're fucking embedded in my brain."

Nodding, I gasped as he gripped my hips in his large hands, tilting my pelvis fractionally and hitting a new spot inside me. I agreed wholeheartedly. Sex with Sam was an addiction, and I had no idea how to quit. Every rational thought that told me this would never last was pushed out every time he was inside of me. We should have kept our hands off each other for many reasons, but nothing else seemed to matter when we were together.

"Fuck me," I panted, my back arching against the door as he pulled me into him more forcefully. With each thrust, the door shifted slightly in the frame, and I hoped it wasn't enough to draw attention from the rest of the office. I was sure we most likely weren't the first people to fool around in these rooms, but doing it on company time and getting caught was not on my list of workplace rules to break.

"Are you close?" he panted, leaning back and grinding into me in a way that made my eyes roll back into my head.

"Yes," I moaned softly, concentrating on the feel of him so deep inside of me and the pressure his movements focused directly on my clit. "Just keep doing that."

"God, I wish I could see your tits," he groaned quietly as his head fell into my clothed chest, his pace increasing as he pushed me closer and closer to release.

"Later." My voice was a breathy moan as I shifted my hips into his movements, chasing that high I knew he could give me. "Make me come."

My eyes were clenched shut, my back arched, and my fist clenched tightly around the material of his tie as he drove me over the edge. A moan slipped out before I bit my lip, trying to hold it in as I clenched around him, pulsing as he braced his hand against my back, the other slapping against the door as he thrust into me repeatedly.

He groaned into my chest as his hips faltered, pinning me to the door as he came.

My heart pounded frantically as he peeked at me from beneath his lashes, his face still half-buried in my chest. "There's something wrong with us."

"We're a pair of sex addicts," I agreed, laughing at the wolfish grin that formed on his lips.

"I think we found our new workspace."

"Sam." I frowned. "I'm not fucking you in the conference room every day."

"Well, not every day..." he laughed, helping me lower my shaky legs back to the floor. I wobbled on my heels momentarily as he reached behind me and freed my hair from its messy bun. He leaned in and kissed my lips, briefly cupping my cheek. "I'm sure it won't turn you on this much once we get to the serial killer content."

"Clearly, you underestimate me."

SAM

BOSTON

AFTERNOON EDITING TIME IN the private conference room had become the highlight of my days. It also didn't hurt that Kristine had been wearing skirts to work for weeks. Every time we went into that room, we told ourselves we'd stop doing it, *but* we kept doing it. Fun fact: the conference room chairs were tall enough to keep the door handle from opening. I'd also started carrying a pencil case full of condoms in my messenger bag for work.

"Would you stop smirking over there," Kristine scolded as she threw a piece of popcorn at me from across the table. We'd settled into a routine of working together in whatever office Isobel and Adrian weren't using during the morning, heading into the corner conference room while half the building was out for lunch, and spending a few hours editing in there afterward before we headed back to check in with our respective supervisors. "It makes you look creepy when I know you're editing her finding a dead body."

"I'm not smirking. This is my face." I laughed as I did a faux smolder in her direction. "Is this better?"

"Why, yes, Zoolander, that one is *so* much better." It was hard to maintain it while she was rolling her eyes at me, but I managed. "You're making it hard to concentrate."

"Well, it is hard being really, really, ridiculously good-looking," I responded, adopting my best Blue Steel impression.

"Oh my God, Sam, we were barely toddlers when that movie came out."

"You forget I have four older sisters. My oldest sibling is twelve years older than me. I've seen all kinds of movies, and Becca worked at a video store in high school."

She cringed, "Do they still have those?"

"Not many, but I remember her taking me there to pick out *Shrek* and the original *Harry Potter*." She'd gotten her license around the time I turned four, and my parents had made her drive me places when they needed alone time. My mom had called them 'Big Sister Dates,' but I'm sure they kicked us all out of the house on Saturday afternoons to fuck. My dad's vasectomy was the only reason there weren't a dozen of us. Langley men—and women—multiplied like rabbits.

"She's probably the reason I got into reading. She always gave me copies of books she'd read once I'd learned how to read. Harry Potter, Percy Jackson, she was really into fantasy novels. I was her little sidekick until she started dating, then I was just a tiny cockblock who wanted to play sports with her boyfriends."

"Yeah, you are a bit of a cockblock," she laughed, tucking her stylus above her ear, a loose tendril of hair falling in front of her face.

"I know," I smiled, reaching across the table to brush it back into place with the tip of my finger. "I'm the worst."

"At least you're self-aware. It's always good to be in touch with your true self."

"I'd like to touch your true self," I smirked, and she threw more popcorn at me.

It was moments like these when we were alone and just talking to each other casually that I found myself wanting more from her. Sitting in the same room with her wasn't as tension-filled as it had once been. We didn't need to talk to fill the silence, but I was comfortable sharing parts of myself with her.

Occasionally, she'd even reveal trivial things about herself and her child-hood, and it made my heart hurt thinking about this lost little girl, raised by nannies with two parents who ignored her until it suited them and a brother who made it a point to be horrible to her on a regular basis. I tried not to react to the things she'd told me, just being an ear to listen, but it still made me angry. She'd developed a thick armor, hiding away the best parts of herself, and I found myself resenting her family for how emotionally guarded she'd become.

"What?" she asked self-consciously as she caught me continuing to watch her from across the table.

Shaking my head, I leaned back in my chair, forcing myself to concentrate on our work. "Nothing, you just seem relaxed today. It's nice."

"Are you getting soft on me, Spammy?"

"No, don't worry," I teased. "No getting soft over here. I know you'll go back to criticizing how I insert my notes in the margins any moment now."

"You know I don't have any issue with your insertion techniques," she winked.

Her mind was such a curious place for me. One minute she was playful and making borderline dirty jokes. The next minute she was pinning me to the wall, practically tearing off my pants and telling me to shut my mouth. Then there were other times when I could see the shutters slam down, and she'd actively keep me at a distance no matter how much I tried to show her that I enjoyed her company.

Studying the notes already marked in this scene, I shook my head at some of the sentences Adrian had left in the margin.

> Adrian: Do you realize the connotation of the nickname Fanny outside the US? It seems a little sexually suggestive, not that I'm opposed to it.

Looking over at Kristine, I highlighted the note and turned my laptop so she could see my screen. "Did you see this one?"

"Hmm?" she hummed as she pulled the earbud out of her left ear. She typically had one earbud in when we worked together. I had no idea how she could read and listen to music simultaneously and still concentrate, but it worked for her.

Using my stylus to tap on the note, I watched as she read it, holding back a laugh at the loud sigh and eye roll that followed.

"He really does not understand irony, does he?"

"You think they named her that on purpose?" Evan was infamous for looking up the meanings of names to develop his characters. Still, I could see Adrian's point on this one. The slang equivalent for pussy in the UK *was* fanny, so they'd effectively named their female main character after a vagina.

"Have you met Chase? Of course, this was intentional. She probably thought it was hysterical to name the character who uses her sexuality as Frances does after the female genitalia."

"Evan's pretty anal about knowing what his characters' names mean."

"Anal," she giggled.

"Have you looked up what her name means?" I asked. Out of habit, I looked up the main character Frances and her submissive, Dominic. Her name meant 'free one,' and his meant 'of the Master.' Those seemed fitting for a Domme who was very free with her innate sexuality and her long-term submissive who was very devoted to his Mistress.

"Hold on..." I watched as she pulled out her phone. "Hmm. Okay, I can see it. But Adrian is still an idiot. Chase made that her nickname because it probably made her laugh. They could have called her Franny or something similar, but they didn't."

She continued to look down at her phone, typing something else onto the screen. "Pffft."

"What?"

"Do you know what your name means?" she smirked.

"Yes." And I knew why my parents named me that. My dad had been desperate for a son and begged my mother to have one last child before he got a vasectomy. "Name of God or heard by God." My mother felt God answered my dad's ongoing prayers for a boy while girly girls surrounded him.

"That's a little much."

"Well, yours can be interpreted as a follower of God, so..." I laughed as I looked down at my phone.

"You're not a god, Sam." She rolled her eyes but kept typing. "And I'm hardly following you, but your last name is hilarious," she giggled.

"Yeah, yeah, laugh it up." In English class in my senior year of high school, we had a unit on Onomastics, which was the study of naming things. It frequently occurred in literature for authors to try to use intentional naming of characters, items, and places to add depth. My last name had been an endless source of entertainment for my classmates with its suggestive connotations. It was bad enough that we lived near a small town called Climax, MI, and discussed all the different meanings of that word in the same unit. Plus, my middle name was Ethan, which means firm. So there were endless jokes about my firm long wood for months afterward.

"I don't know, Sam. Maybe there is something to this naming thing. It seems like a self-fulfilling prophecy. Wonder if all the Langley men have *long wood*?"

Pulling up a quick Google search, my eyes widened as the meaning of the surname Willard appeared. "Same seems to go for your last name, *strong-willed*. Wonder if your ancestors already knew how much of a pain in the ass you'd be."

"Doesn't seem to keep you away," she teased, reaching her bare foot across the space underneath the table and suggestively rubbing my thigh with her toes. She often sat with one leg tucked underneath her in the chair, so one or both of her heels were usually abandoned underneath whatever surface she used to work.

Placing my phone on the table, I caught her foot, pulling it into my lap and digging my fingers into the arch.

"Oh, that's nice," she groaned, leaning back against the chair and closing her eyes.

Glancing toward the door, I urged her other foot up, gently removing her heel before scooting my chair a little closer. She made soft humming noises as I rubbed her feet, reminding me of the happy sighs she often let out when we were cuddling in bed, with much less clothing involved.

"Shh," I scolded as she groaned when I rubbed a particularly sensitive part of the sole. It was one thing when we were shut up inside the private conference room, but we were in the middle of Isobel's office with the door open. "Unless you want Carson to come running down the hallway to see what's going on in here, you need to be quiet."

"Shut it and just keep rubbing," she laughed, wiggling her toes close to my zipper. Much more stimulation from her and my dick was going to think it was conference room time.

"When is Isobel supposed to be back?" I asked. The last thing we needed was her or Adrian walking in on me giving Kristine a foot massage. They still thought we only tolerated each other as coworkers. Kristine was often irritated they both kept telling her to play nicely with me. She played very nicely with parts of me, but I doubt that was what they had in mind.

To everyone outside our alone time, we were working on a project together, forced into spending time with one another to edit. Kristine still acted indifferent when others were around, throwing sarcastic jokes around at my expense. If I thought she was serious, I would have been offended, but I knew she didn't mean them. At least, I hoped she didn't.

"Why are you talking?" she sighed, avoiding the question.

"Because I don't want to risk her walking in here at an inopportune time and seeing this."

"You're too uptight, Sam," she said, eyes still closed.

"Yeah, *I'm* the uptight one."

"She's meeting with Sloane. She's not supposed to be back until after lunchtime, and I'm sure your limp-dicked boss is following her around like a puppy."

Adrian had been finding reasons to be in Isobel's office more often, but she was in his just as much. Those two weren't fooling anyone, especially since they'd also been spotted in the gym downstairs together more often. Isobel hadn't been an avid gym goer before, so her showing up and leaving with Adrian was conspicuous.

"Do you want to get dinner somewhere after work tonight?"

She frowned, her eyes slipping open as she glanced up at me. "I like that Indian carry-out restaurant that's near my place."

"That's not what I meant. Would you be interested in stopping at that little Italian place a few blocks from here?"

"I don't think they offer carry out."

"I know," I smirked. "I was asking you to sit down to dinner with me in an actual restaurant."

"Like a date?" Her voice was pinched as she looked at me with wide eyes. I knew I was taking a chance by asking her to go out in public with me, but she had to see our relationship was changing.

"If that's what you want to call it. I'm fine with just calling it dinner. No pressure. Just two people who happen to enjoy each other's company enjoying a meal together at a real table in public. Maybe with some wine."

"Sam," she sighed, and I leaned forward, my fingers cradling the side of her jaw, the pad of my thumb softly rubbing against the skin beside her lips.

"If you don't want to call it a date, I'm alright with that. I'm just tired of hiding."

"It's not that..."

Waiting a few seconds, I watched the nervous twitch of her eyes, knowing I was pushing her out of her comfort zone, but I knew if I didn't nudge her, we'd continue as we were. As much as I enjoyed our bubble, I wanted to spend time with her outside the office, not holed up in our apartments.

"Please, just this once. If we have a terrible time." Which I doubted. "Then I'll never ask again."

"I'm holding you to that," she smiled, nodding.

I shifted her feet off my lap, and they fell softly to the floor. Glancing toward the door, I slipped my fingers into the loose hair at the back of her head, leaning in and stealing a kiss before I sat back into my chair. "I need to check in with Adrian and work on a few other things this afternoon, but I'll pick you up here at 5:00 pm."

"Okay."

"Don't even think of leaving early because I'll just come to your apartment and drag you back out."

"Sounds kinky," she laughed.

"Seriously," I warned, pulling my laptop off the table and shoving it into my bag. "I'll find you."

Chapter
FIFTEEN

SAM

BOSTON

"And I like the suggestions you two have made about the ending scene. It does read a little shallow. If they spice up the dialogue and try to keep the tension high, it will draw the reader in."

My eyes shifted to the clock, watching as it ticked closer to 4:58, wishing Adrian would shut up already. I wanted to be at Isobel's office at 5:00, so Kristine didn't try to pull a runner.

"I'm sorry, am I keeping you from doing something?" he asked, sitting up straighter in his chair and interlocking his hands on the desktop. He looked vaguely like a buff version of Mr. Burns from The Simpsons, but I dismissed that thought as I tried to focus on him instead of the clock on the corner of his desk.

"No. It's fine," I assured him. Making your boss mad by tearing out of the office mid-conversation never went over well, even if I was sweating that Kristine would bolt.

"Alright, if you say so," he replied with a shrug. "But I need to get out of here. Business dinner."

Thank God. However, I wasn't convinced that 'business dinner' wasn't a secret code for his plans with Isobel for the evening. Those two had been having lots of 'business lunches' and 'business dinners' lately and judging by the state of their hair as they returned—often late—the only eating being done was of each other.

"See you tomorrow," I bid him good-bye, grabbing my bag from beside the chair and walking as quickly as possible without running out the door and down the hallway. There was a cluster of interns by the elevators as I turned toward the hallway leading to Isobel's office, avoiding eye contact with Andrea, who was packing her belongings as I passed the main desk. She was a nice girl, but she'd try to rope me into a conversation if I gave her a chance, and I didn't have time.

As I approached, Isobel was stepping out her door, too preoccupied with pulling on her blazer to see me until I was right in front of her.

"Oh, Sam. Hi. Was there something I could help you with? I'm heading out, but I'm sure Kristine can help if you need her. She's still working."

Thank God she hadn't left yet. Crap. Now I needed to devise an excuse for why I was down here.

"I misplaced my water bottle and thought I'd check in here to see if I left it earlier while I was reviewing the manuscript with Kristine."

A momentary flash of what I assumed was suspicion crossed her features, but she stepped aside anyway, gesturing toward her door. "Help yourself, have a nice night, Sam."

"You too," I smiled as I stepped around her and through the door, biting my lip at the look Kristine was producing as she barely restrained her laughter at my expense.

"You're such a goober," she whispered, shaking her head, closing her laptop, and sliding it into her open messenger bag on the seat next to her.

"What?" I mouthed as I grabbed the bag and placed it on my lap as I sat down on the edge of the seat, my bag behind me.

"She doesn't care if you're in here. You don't need to make up bullshit excuses. Your water bottle was sticking out the flap of your messenger bag."

"Shit. Oh well. Maybe she didn't notice. You ready?"

"We're leaving together?" she frowned.

"I told you that I was meeting you here at 5:00."

"And you're late, by the way."

"By four minutes. I couldn't get Adrian to shut up."

"Sure, blame Dickhead for your perpetual tardiness."

"I'm not the one rolling into staff meetings with only a minute to spare."

"Yeah, you're right," she laughed. "You're usually the one who comes in after the meeting has already started."

"That was once." The day that Gregory had been in the office.

"This month." Maybe she had a point. Sometimes I did have a challenging time getting to a stopping point with my work to make it to scheduled meetings on time.

"You ready?" I tried changing the subject, watching as she bent over the table, the collar of her blouse shifting to expose the top of her cleavage. I knew precisely how soft that skin was, but we weren't in the conference room, so I didn't have permission to touch.

"Stop looking down my shirt, Sam."

I didn't even know how she knew that was what I was doing, but I winked in response, loving the way her eyes softened as she looked over at me. She didn't want to admit it, but she felt something for me. I knew she did.

By the time she'd finished packing up, most of the office had cleared out already, the sea of cubicles and the reception desk empty. It made it easier for me to feel brave enough to place my hand on the small of her back as we approached the open foyer by the elevators. She didn't stop me either, so I chose a spot close to her as we waited for the elevators to return to our floor from the lobby.

I knew I was pushing her past what the current barriers between us were, but I didn't want to be her dirty secret anymore. If she gave it a chance, I could see us having a real relationship down the line.

The sidewalks were crowded with people making their way toward the public transit stops and the T-station not too far from our office. Kristine watched the crowds around us, quietly navigating the traffic as we walked to the restaurant. It was still a little early for the dinner rush, but I'd called ahead to secure a table anyway.

"Come on," I grasped Kristine's hand, pushing through the small crowd by the door and approaching the host station. She surprised me by interlocking our fingers as we waited, her teeth worrying her bottom lip as she looked up from beneath her lashes.

"It'll be about twenty minutes for a table," the hostess told us, not looking up from where she'd been wiping down menus.

"I reserved a table for Langley."

"Ah," she smiled as she looked up. "You're a few minutes early, but I can make sure they've got it ready for yah."

"That sure I'd agree to this?" Kristine asked quietly, leaning into my shoulder.

"I had a hunch," I winked, but I'd only called around three after I left Isobel's office.

After a few minutes, the hostess returned, leading us to a booth in the corner of the restaurant tucked behind a pillar. I knew Kristine was self-conscious about the two of us being seen outside the office, and I thought this would make it a little easier for her to relax and enjoy herself.

Turns out I was sorely mistaken. When the server showed up at our table a few moments later, I could see Kristine slam down the walls she'd been lifting bit by bit for me over the last several weeks.

"Sam? Hey!" Andrea greeted as she approached the table while tying an apron in place, not noticing Kristine on the opposite side of the booth. I'd had no idea that she also worked here. I knew some office staff had other jobs, but I'd never seen her here.

"Andrea." My voice was slightly strained, and I could see Kristine getting visibly agitated as my eyes flitted between the two women. "I didn't realize you worked here."

"Oh, it's only a little side gig. My uncle owns the place. I work a few nights a week to pick up some extra cash to pay for my books. What brings you in here tonight?" Andrea absently glanced at the other occupant of the table, her face sobering as she realized who was dining with me. I didn't think she had anything in particular against Kristine but seeing her sitting here with me was a surprise.

Kristine chimed in before I could formulate a response, her voice pinched. "Sam here lost a bet, so he had to buy me dinner tonight."

"A bet?"

I narrowed my eyes at Kristine, wishing she didn't have to push me away so often. I knew we'd never defined what we were to each other, but she made spending time with me outside the office sound like an obligation.

"Yeah, I bet he couldn't get through the first draft of the manuscript we're working on without crying, and I caught the poor bastard sobbing into his tablet last week. So, I'm making him buy me carbs."

"Oh," Andrea glanced at me, looking uncomfortable at Kristine's made-up bullshit, but I wasn't about to correct her. "It's a thriller, right?"

"Yeah," I nodded, my hand reaching under the booth and squeezing Kristine's knee, making her leg slightly jerk. "There's a side character that gets killed by the serial killer, and it just tore me up a little reading about the lead character finding him."

"Sam's really in touch with his feminine side, a little too much, sometimes," Kristine remarked, digging her fingernails into the back of my hand until I released her knee.

"Alright, well, do you two know what you'd like to order?" Andrea looked like she was about to bolt, as eager to escape this awkward exchange as I was.

Scanning the menu, I quickly rattled off my order of Chicken Parmesan, and Kristine ordered some truffle ravioli dish and two glasses of wine. I'd planned to treat her since I was the one who'd asked her out, but this was feeling less and less like a date and more like a disaster.

"What is wrong with you?" I hissed as Andrea headed toward the back to put our orders in at the kitchen pass thru.

"You didn't tell me that people we knew worked here. I panicked."

"Is it that horrible to be seen with me in public?"

"Sam," she sighed, leaning back into the wall of the wooden booth, crossing her arms over her chest. "This isn't part of our arrangement. We don't *date*. This wasn't a good idea."

"I know, but I thought maybe things were starting to change between us. It's not just..." I wasn't even sure how to phrase how my feelings had been evolving toward her. It wasn't just physical anymore, and she couldn't deny it with how many nights she ended up in my bed without sex being involved.

"Maybe we need to slow things down. We've been spending too much time together. It's just going to make things messy."

"What? That's what you want?"

Her eyes were in her lap when she nodded, pulling her bag from the side of the booth and pulling it over her shoulder. "Yes. We work together, Sam. Why did we think this was a good idea?"

"At least eat your food first. God, why do you have to be so dramatic about everything?"

"It's fine, Sam. I..." she paused as she looked up into my eyes, conflict visible in her expression. "I think we've been confusing our relationship lately. It started as just scratching an itch. For both of us. But..."

"We both know it's not like that anymore," I hissed.

"Well, I'm not sure if I'm ready for what it's turning into."

I wasn't sure how to respond to that. Seeing someone from the office outside of work had unsettled her, but Andrea didn't seem to suspect anything. She thought we were here because of Kristine's BS story about a bet. Like I'd cry over the death of a character—please, I wasn't Adrian.

"Alright, if that's what you need, we can take some time to figure things out."

"It's not like you're my boyfriend, Sam. I'm not breaking up with you. I need to sort some things out, and this is making everything more complicated than it needs to be. People will talk if she says something, and I can't afford to have that kind of gossip hanging over my head."

Once our food arrived, we were both quiet, and I laid off bringing up anything suggestive for fear that I'd push her right over the edge. Clearly, she was in panic mode, and I knew nothing I said would get through to her.

The relationship I thought we'd been building was slipping through my fingers before I could admit how deep my feelings for her had grown. Did I let her push me away and accept this wasn't going anywhere, or did I call her bluff and make her admit she felt something too? Neither option seemed like it'd turn out how I wanted, so my only alternative was to do what she asked and take a step back to let her figure out her feelings.

"Can we talk about this?" I asked as I slipped my card into the payment folder, impatiently waiting for Andrea to return and take care of the check. I knew once she brought it back, she'd stay away until we left, and every time she stopped at the table, it just made Kristine that much more anxious.

"What exactly is there to talk about, Sam? You don't seem to understand how this stuff works," she sighed, crossing her arms tightly over her chest. She'd closed herself off again, and all I desperately wanted to do was pull one of her hands across the table and stroke her fingers until she calmed down.

"How what works?" I mean, I got that it would make the rounds with the gossip mill, but it was hardly scandalous. We liked spending time together, and it wasn't anyone else's business what we were to each other.

"It's so easy for you. You're a guy. No one cares who you screw around with. You could fuck half the office, and no one would care."

"But I'm not fucking half the office. I'm..."

"Don't," she threw her hand up, her eyes flaring with annoyance. "Don't even say it."

"Fine," I sighed, waiting for her to continue. "Go on."

"You sleep around, and you're some kind of stud. I sleep around, and suddenly I'm the recipient of rude and suggestive comments from the Carsons of the office. Don't you think that kind of thing gets back to the executives? The same people who sit on the panel for the full-time editor positions. If they think I'm..."

"Wait," I interrupted her, holding up my hand while she frowned at me. "None of them are going to hit on you. That's a sexual harassment claim waiting to happen."

"I didn't say that. If you would have let me finish," she paused as Andrea awkwardly stopped beside the table and snatched up my card, promising she'd return it quickly.

"If you would have let me finish, I would tell you that it affected my professional integrity. Do you think they will take me seriously if I'm boning my way through the interns? They will question my ability to manage a team if they think I'm the office bicycle."

"It's none of their business who you have a relationship with, sexual or otherwise," I argued but snapped my mouth shut, nodding at Andrea as she handed me back the check. She didn't try to stick around to talk, obviously sensing the tension between Kristine and me. But at least she couldn't misinterpret it as something scandalous if she thought we were fighting.

"No, it's not, but it'll be there in the back of their minds while they're making the decisions anyway. It's not fair and sexist as hell, but it'd be there, Sam. And it's fucking horrible. I refuse to let a few stolen moments in a conference room fuck up my entire career."

I wasn't sure what to say to refute what she was saying. Part of me wanted to dismiss it as paranoia, but I knew what she said had some validity.

"No one needs to know our relationship outside the office is more than just friendly colleagues. I can see why you're worried, but it's a leap for people to assume we're sleeping together if we spend time together. And we both know the conference room didn't define the depth of our time together."

"But we *are* sleeping together, Sam," she sighed. "The lines are all blurry. One slip and a fling turns into something dangerous. We had sex together *in* the office."

"Stop calling it a fling. It wasn't that for me. No one saw anything."

"But what happens when someone does? We can't keep doing this."

"So, where does that leave us?" She seemed to have a retort for everything but pushing her too hard on this wouldn't end up in my favor.

"I don't know. And I'm not sure if I can afford to find out."

KRISTINE

BOSTON

"Did you put those edits on the shared drive, Kristine?"

"Hmmm?" My stylus tapped absently on the corner of my tablet as I scanned through Sam's notes in the margins of the twentieth chapter. He was slowly coaxing me to the dark side with his technology of choice. There was something about this passage that didn't sit right with me, and I couldn't figure out what. We'd both looked through it separately, and Isobel had made some notes as well, but I kept scanning the text for something to jump out at me.

"Hey," Isobel's voice rose as I glanced in her direction briefly. "I think you need to take a break. Now."

I'd been throwing myself into edits for the last few weeks, still avoiding talking to Sam about where our thing was going. He'd tried, refusing to let me avoid him after I'd left the restaurant that night. The problem was that he was distracting me from my work. Add that to the fact that today was the day Human Resources was letting us know which candidates had been chosen to continue the interview process for the fantasy position. I was officially not myself.

It may have been horrible of me, but I was praying one of us wouldn't be asked to continue. My competitive nature was at odds with the new feelings building inside me toward Sam, despite me throwing on the brakes. He continued being patient when I needed space and affectionate when I needed reassurance, but I didn't know how to voice that, and I found myself drawn to him whenever we were in the same room.

It was fucking frustrating to be developing these feelings, but I couldn't stop them. I'd never tell him, but I was almost certain I might be falling in love with him. I knew I was the one who'd initially constructed boundaries, but that bastard had wormed his way into my heart. I was turning into a lovesick fool inside my mind and a cranky bitch to everyone else with my self-imposed hiatus. It needed to stop, so I had no choice but to avoid him until I got my head together.

"I'm fine." I waved at Isobel dismissively, my eyes running over the text again, still not knowing why I couldn't make this passage flow.

"You are not, and if I have to restrict your privileges on the document, I will. You've been acting like a hormonal teenager for weeks, and I'm sick of it. What's your problem?"

My jaw clenched as I put down the stylus, locking the tablet's screen and crossing my arms as I looked toward her. "Fine. Happy now?"

"You've got to snap out of this. I expect better from you." Her tone was curt, but I could tell by her face that Isobel was concerned about me.

"Better than what?"

"Kristine," she sighed, standing from her desk and sitting across from me at the table in the corner of her office. "Sloane wants you in New York."

"No." I shook my head. We'd been over this a dozen times in the last few weeks after my first interview, and I'd told Sloane as much when I'd spoken to her.

"You still won't consider it?"

"Do you want my honest answer?"

"Let me guess," she laughed. "Oh, frick no."

"Bingo." I nodded. My response had been the same when she brought it up the day of my interview. "I do not want to live in New York, ever. I've been there, done that, and have the emotional baggage to carry around for the rest of my life to show for it. If there isn't a position for me to advance here, I'll stay where I am until there is."

"Sloane told HR to keep you on the candidate list for the manuscript trials for both positions."

"What? Why?" I whined. They'd told us the next part of the interview process would be editing a several-chapter manuscript excerpt for the hiring team to evaluate. All the applicants were to be given the same chapters, so it'd be a head-to-head comparison using identical material.

"Because she's seen your work, Kristine. She knows you have an aptitude for romance and wants to see your skills compared to the other applicants. This is a huge opportunity for you. I'd hate to see you sabotage it."

"I'm not sabotaging it." I was so full of shit, but there was no way I'd survive going back to the city. Even if I got my own apartment on the other side of Manhattan—or braved the Bronx or Brooklyn—Mason would still find ways to insert himself into my life. He'd done it while I was at Harvard from a few hours away. If I were that accessible, he'd probably put a tail on me. Nana reading him the riot act was the only reason he'd left me relatively alone when I moved to Boston instead of returning to New York.

"Is there another reason you want to stay here? Don't get me wrong, I love having you on my team, but this isn't what you want to do forever. You have too much drive to stay at the bottom of the totem pole indefinitely."

Pushing Sam's face out of my mind, I shook my head. There wasn't a way to keep him that I could figure out in my head. He'd either resent me for getting the job, or I'd be bitter he got the job. Or worse, if neither of us got the job, and it all fell apart anyway, or one of us left, and it didn't work out long-distance. There was no future for us, but I was too selfish—or too damn stubborn—to stop leading him on.

"There will be other opportunities. I'll wait for the next one if this doesn't work out. Sometimes it's all about timing. While I want to move up, I'll be patient for the right position."

"Bullshit," she shook her head as she sighed.

"It'll be fine. I'll wait if I don't get one of the positions here." I'd fucking hate it, but I'd wait. I didn't need a fancier title and a pay raise, and a team to lead to inflating my ego or my bank account. I would succeed on my own terms and no one else's. Not even Sam's.

"Alright, I'm not going to force you to talk about this, but you've given yourself twice as much work by staying in the running for the fantasy position."

"I don't mind a challenge." That part was true; while it'd be more work, I wasn't worried about editing either manuscript. I could handle both to prove myself. If they still didn't promote me afterward, I could reevaluate then.

"You might if I can convince Chase and Evan to do this book tour."

Frowning, I sat back in my chair, crossing my arms. "Why does that matter to me?"

"Because PR wants more people on the ground for this promotional push, and it's all hands on deck."

"Isn't that typically your job to wrangle the writers?"

"Not this time." She shook her head, and my eyes widened. I loved the ease of working with Chase since she never complained about my edits, but I hated book tours. There was a shit ton of traveling and sometimes back-to-back events for days on end. Isobel often took a few days' leave after returning from a busy tour. I also didn't see how I'd be able to complete what HR expected of me with the manuscript trials if I was on the road. It could be done remotely, but I would have all kinds of other work duties to take care of on tour. That was the only drawback I saw to stepping into a higher position. With all the benefits, there were also job duties I was content with not to be responsible for in my current position.

"What about PR? Can't they send one of their interns?"

"They're all busy working on that new software training with Gregory Willard." My asshole brother. Great. Even once he'd returned home, he was making my life difficult.

"Shit."

"It's not definite, but Adrian will probably send Sam if we can persuade Evan to go. This would allow you to show what other skills you can handle outside the office."

"I thought Evan didn't do events?"

"That's why I need to convince Chase. This is coming from above Sloane. They have to do this tour. Vivid wants the press, which doesn't hit the same with a social-media-only promotional push. We want this on everyone's radar."

Part of me hoped they'd refuse because I couldn't handle trying to edit these manuscripts for the copy editor positions, managing the shit show book tours could turn into, traveling cross country and living out of hotels for weeks, and surviving being on the road with Sam for that long. I was already having a tough time keeping my feelings—and sometimes my hands—to myself when I knew it would end up crushing me when it was over.

This was exactly why I emotionally distanced myself from men. I didn't *need* anyone. I didn't *need* Sam.

But I wanted him despite all my efforts to keep him at a distance. He'd started thawing the frozen thing in my chest where my heart ought to be, and I couldn't risk letting him finish the job.

"Stop giving me that look, Kristine. If they agree to this, it's good for all of us. And you get access to a company credit card with a travel and food stipend for six weeks. That's six weeks of getting to be outside this building. Trust me, all the headaches that can pop up on the road are worth the perks."

"Six weeks?" That was a *long* time. If things between Sam and I fell apart, I'd still be forced to work with him every day for six weeks. At the office I could hide on my side of the floor. Our relationship was already strained enough, with me avoiding him over the last several weeks. I could only push him away for so long before one or both of us got hurt.

"They'll put you up in nice hotels, too," she winked. Like I hadn't spent half my childhood on extravagant vacations in luxury hotels that I hated. Fuck me; this was not going to end well.

"And there isn't any way I can get out of this?"

"Nope, I've got too many projects to be out of the office for that long. Sloane wants you and Sam if they agree. It'll be a valuable experience for you both."

The real question was, for which one of us? Because at the end of those six weeks, one of us would be left without that promotion.

SAM FOUND ME IN the coffee shop down the street later that afternoon, probably when he realized I'd stood him up for our standing conference room date. I couldn't shake this sense of anxiety that had been developing inside me since he had tried to take me out to dinner.

Was he interested, or was I convenient? Since we'd spent so much time together lately, both in and out of our clothes, I wasn't sure what we were anymore. My insistence that we only sleep together once had been pushed aside when he'd been so damn good at it. I'd convinced myself it was purely physical initially, but now I didn't know what was happening anymore.

"Hey, I thought I might find you here." Sam smiled, pulling out the chair beside me and moving my bag into the seat across the table. I knew he'd done the same thing dozens of times over the last several weeks, choosing the chair closest to me whenever we were together, but the proximity made me feel a little crowded.

"Yup." I clenched my teeth, giving him a tight smile, then returned my focus to the laptop on the table before me.

"You alright? I tried to text you about where you wanted to order lunch from today but never got a response."

He wasn't going to leave me alone. Didn't he see how hard this was for me?

"I'm trying to get work done."

Sam was quiet for a few moments, staring at me with a little frown pulling at his mouth as I stared at my laptop screen, entirely unable to focus. I knew it was rude, but I needed space.

"Do you want me to go?"

I didn't know how to answer that. Part of me wanted to say yes, pushing him even farther away. But the other part of me wanted to go home and cuddle up in bed with him, pretending that the advancement of our professional careers wasn't in direct competition with each other.

"Hey." He pressed the lid on my laptop shut. I sat back in my chair and pulled my coffee cup up for a drink. Anything to avoid looking at him or touching him. "What's wrong? Did you hear something from HR already? They were supposed to send information to the people going forward in an hour or so."

"No," I shook my head. "I haven't heard anything."

"Do you want to try to get some work done in the conference room until we find out? Keep our minds busy while we wait?"

"What do you think I was doing here, Sam? I'm trying to work, but you won't leave me alone. If I wanted to work with someone else right now, I would have stayed at the office."

"Seriously?" He was looking at me like I was acting unreasonably, and maybe I was, but I wasn't used to all these feelings that had been developing under the surface. This was why I had only wanted one night with him. Now it was complicated, and there were feelings involved I wasn't sure how to process.

My parents weren't exactly great role models for conducting a relationship, choosing to plaster on fake smiles and avoid spending time alone together.

Once that new love luster had worn off when I was a toddler, my parents barely tolerated each other.

I didn't know how to be in a relationship, and Sam had grown up with June Cleaver for a mother and a slew of older sisters who all were in happy marriages and had kids they weren't actively fucking up. We weren't from the same world, and eventually, he was bound to see how emotionally stunted I was and would walk away.

Maybe it was better if I did it first.

"I'll email Isobel to let her know I will be out of the office for the rest of the day. Congrats if you get to the next round. I'm sure they loved you."

"Are you brushing me off? Again?" Sam reached forward to grab my hand, but I jerked it away at the last second. I wouldn't be strong enough to follow through if he touched me.

Leaning over to grab my bag, I shoved my laptop inside and pushed the trash from my lunch back inside the paper bag from the coffee shop. "Sam, I asked for space, and you're not giving it to me. You're not my boyfriend, so please stop acting like you are."

"Wow, nice, Kristine. Fine. Whatever. Run away. That seems to be what you do best."

My eyes stung as I strode toward the exit without looking backward. I knew I was fucking this all up, but I didn't know how to stop.

SEVENTEEN

KRISTINE

BOSTON

My phone chimed with a text message as I went through the small stack of mail I'd retrieved from the lobby of my apartment building when I got home, and I looked at my bag like a bomb had gone off. Was it going to be him? Did it matter?

> Nana: When are you coming to see me?

My heart dropped as I looked at the message on the screen. It wasn't him, but my grandmother didn't deserve to be ignored because of my disappointment at blowing up my nonexistent love life.

> Kristine: Hey, Nana.

> Nana: Don't Hey, Nana. me.

> Kristine: Are you at the house on the Cape?

My phone started ringing, her name filling the screen. *Oh, come on, Nana. I don't want to talk.* She hated texting. She'd do it to get my attention, but she didn't like to have conversations via text messages.

"Oh, you're going to answer this time, I see," she laughed as the call connected.

"You act like I don't answer your calls most of the time, old lady." We didn't talk frequently, but she'd call me every few months to check in and see how I was doing. My mother never called me to talk. There always had to be something she wanted from me, and she accused me of being a terrible child if I didn't answer her calls while I was at work, so I just stopped responding altogether. She could pull her toxic codependent crap on Gregory. She loved him more anyway, and everyone knew it. I'd always be her disappointment.

"Who are you calling old?" Nana laughed, her voice husky. She'd stopped smoking years ago, when I was a little girl, but her voice still had that deep, gravelly tone of someone who used to chain smoke when they were younger.

"I'm not the one turning eighty this summer." It felt unreal that she was that age already. It didn't feel like we had a fifty-five year age gap between us. But Mason hadn't settled down until he was over thirty-five, and my mother was already pregnant with Gregory then. Sometimes I wondered if their relationship would have died off without my brother. They claimed they loved each other, but as a person who grew up living with them, I wasn't sure how they considered how they treated each other love, more like grudging tolerance that included a side of avoidance.

The only consistent person in my life I could say that I loved was my grandmother. She was affectionate without being clingy, supportive without an agenda, and respected my boundaries. Sort of like someone else... No.

I was not going to think about Sam. Our *relationship* had been about fulfilling an attraction, not love. I often doubted I was even capable of feeling love toward someone romantically. Maybe Gregory was right. I *was* a fraud.

"Do you have plans this weekend, or are you too busy to visit me?"

A few weeks ago, I would have told her I'd have to get back to her, but since I'd flushed my only source of alternative weekend plans down the toilet, my schedule was wide open.

"I've got time. I can take a bus to the ferry and be there sometime on Friday."

"Work keeping you busy these days?" she asked, but I knew she was fishing. Despite her dislike of my mother and her nonexistent parenting skills, she still socialized with them. My mother also had a big mouth. A trait my brother often mimicked.

"It's a little hectic. I'm up for a promotion."

"I'd heard that. Something about you refusing to take a position in the city?"

"Let me guess," I sighed. "My asshole brother told Mommy dearest all about it."

"Something like that," she confirmed. "Your mother tried to convince him to step in, but he told her he was staying out of it."

I knew Nana would never pressure me, but I wanted her opinion on my decision to stay away. "Do you think I'm making a mistake?"

"Do you?" Of course, she'd throw it back on me while telling me the truth. She also liked to force me to face my own decisions like an adult without her opinion swaying the outcome.

"I don't know, Nana." Part of me wanted to start crying again. This shouldn't be a difficult decision. I was distancing myself from a toxic family situation. But I felt like I was being stubborn and choosing the hard path because it meant I didn't have to deal with my feelings. It was also a convenient excuse to push Sam away from me before things got too difficult for me to deal with.

We weren't supposed to be together for more than one night, but then that night turned into a weekend, which turned into it happening again—and again—and now here we were, three months later, and we'd settled into this relationship that seemed so easy, but it wasn't real. None of this was real.

"Is there something else going on? You seem a little down. Does it concern that nice gay boy you work with?"

I couldn't hold in the laugh at the fact Nana even knew about Sam. Greg must have told my mother every detail of his last visit. He couldn't help himself despite his claims of *staying out of it.*

"He's not gay, Nana."

"Hmm..." she hummed, and I knew she would ask. "How do *you* know he's not, *you know?*"

Well, Nana, because I've been sleeping with him multiple times a week, sometimes even multiple times a night, for months now, and Sam Langley is most definitely not batting for the other team. However, his bat-handling skills were quite impressive. His home run percentages were flawless. Although he played lacrosse and not baseball, so a better analogy would be that his stick-handling skills were legendary, and he scored goals all over my five-hole.

"He's just not."

"Your brother thought you might have been involved with him. He said you seemed different around this young man. But then he started talking about how he'd found out he was more interested in men when he took you two to dinner."

"It was a misunderstanding, Nana. Greg was an asshole, and Sam called him out on it. We just didn't correct him."

"We, huh?" Of course, she'd pick up on that.

"He's a friend." Well. That probably wasn't true now, but I'd done that to myself. I also felt like Sam would never have tried to be my friend if we hadn't been attracted to each other.

"Mmhmm. Sure he is, honey."

"He doesn't like me romantically." Not anymore.

"Are you a mind reader now?"

"Do you want me to visit you or not, you nosy old crone?" I sighed, desperately wanting to change the subject.

"I'll send the car service to get you," she insisted.

"Nana, it won't kill me to take the ferry."

"Suit yourself. If I'm not at the house, I'm probably at the club watching the lifeguard training."

"Holy shit," I sputtered. Nana knew when to get me to laugh, but she wasn't joking. Nana would watch the lifeguards at the country club returning from university for the summer tourist season. "Aren't they a little young for you?"

"Eh, I'm just looking. I wouldn't know what to do with one of those young sporty types." *But I did, Nana, and it was hot.* "There's no harm in a little window shopping," she laughed in her husky chuckle.

"I'll let you know when I'm planning on heading down," I told her, changing the subject before she started to stray off-topic. "I have a few vacation days saved up. Maybe I'll come down early." I needed a break. Something had to give if I wanted to get through this mock manuscript trial without losing my mind. It's not like I had any other commitments besides work. I distanced myself from everything so I could focus, not that I'd had many close relationships, to begin with. My entire childhood had been spent determining which of my friends was using me to get to my brother or father.

"Sounds good, sweetheart. I'm looking forward to seeing you. It's been too long since it's been just us." Which made me feel guilty because when I'd stayed away from New York, I'd also unintentionally neglected to visit her.

After we hung up, I texted Isobel, asking if she needed me in the office in person for the rest of the week. I could still work if I didn't go in. There were tons of editors and their interns who worked remotely. If I had internet, I could access everything on the shared drive if IT knew to let me have remote access.

> Kristine: Can I work remotely until Monday?

> Isobel: Something wrong?

> Kristine: My grandmother is at her house on the Cape, and I wanted to visit before the tourist season starts.

> Isobel: I'll email IT. Just make sure you're checking your email regularly. I'll need your eyes on Chase & Evan's final draft before I can send it for formatting.

> Kristine: Email me the details when you have them. I'll head back to the city Sunday.

> Isobel: You haven't taken any vacation this year. Why don't you take a few days of PTO so you're fresh for your sample edits?

> Kristine: I'll work remotely.

> Isobel: Let me repeat that, take the next few days as PTO. I don't need you in the office until next Wednesday. Take a break for once.

> Kristine: I'll think about it.

I guess I wouldn't have to worry about avoiding Sam at the office if I took a few days off. Maybe we both needed some distance from each other, and Nana could help me figure out what to do with the mess I'd created for myself.

SAM

BOSTON

WHENEVER I OPENED MY text messages, I wondered if it was her. It was stupid, really. She'd looked serious when she stormed out of that coffee shop. I thought she'd get a hold of me once she had time to think about whatever was bothering her. Kristine clearly needed more space, so I was trying to be patient and let her have it. Whenever things got too serious for her, she reminded me that I wasn't her boyfriend, so I didn't have the right to act like one. But she'd been pushing me away for weeks, and I didn't like it. I wasn't ready to let go of the hope we could make this work or at least see it through to its natural conclusion. I was still attracted to her—more than just physically—and wasn't ready to give her up so soon.

We'd both been asked to continue in the interview process, Adrian confirming with Isobel that Kristine had made it to the next round when I was too afraid to walk down to her office to ask.

Blake: You down to sub in a game Friday after work?

It'd been a while since a lacrosse game had fit into my schedule, and it would feel good to push myself outside the gym. I could run and lift, but there wasn't a workout that could mimic a good game.

Sam: What time?

Blake: 6:30. Beers after?

The last time I'd gone out with the guys on the intramural team, this petite little blonde hit on me at the bar. It'd been fun to go back to her place and fool around. She'd been more than eager to give me a blow job in her kitchen, but I wasn't interested in returning to that hook-up lifestyle. I liked figuring out what made Kristine pant and squirm, and afterward, when she opened up and let me see inside that locked-up brain of hers, I knew I was in a precarious place.

She'd thrown on the brakes hardcore, but if she felt as drawn to me as I was to her, I hoped it was only a matter of time before she reached out to me. I hated feeling like a desperate teenage girl waiting by the phone for my crush to call. I knew it was fucked up, but I also knew that she'd shut down and stop things entirely if I chased her. I'd settle for her body and part of her mind and heart rather than nothing.

She'd been so adamant that this wouldn't work between us, but it was working, or at least it had been until she tried to push me away. I could understand her reservations, we were actively competing for the same job, but I'd be happy if she earned it. I wanted to keep progressing with my career trajectory, but there would be other opportunities if this fell through. I wasn't going to put all my eggs in one basket. I'd started keeping an eye on other publishers in the Boston area. Working with Adrian was a good experience, but I wasn't married to Vivid. I'd take it if something better came along at the right time.

I wasn't sure what that meant for my future with Kristine, but I wasn't ready to walk away yet. She was interesting and sarcastic, with a quick wit that constantly kept me guessing. I enjoyed her little barbs, even when they were aimed at me. Her independence was sexy, and she didn't make me feel guilty for spending so much time focused on my job. Call me a glutton for punishment, but she'd gotten under my skin and into my heart, and I couldn't imagine not having her in my life.

I texted Blake back, hoping that distraction would keep me from dwelling on this. She needed time, and since we'd likely be thrown together working on the book tour, it was only a matter of time before she was forced to talk to me.

> Sam: I'm in. Text me the location, and I'll be there.

WHEN I GOT INTO the office on Thursday, I was tempted to peek in Isobel's office to see if Kristine was ready to talk to me, but Adrian already had a list of documents he'd shared that needed my attention this morning.

> Adrian: You ready to dive into this one?

A message on the intraoffice chat awaited me when I booted up my computer at my small desk in the corner of Adrian's office. He wasn't anywhere to be found, but he'd been logged into his laptop at 7:00 am. I was a little nervous about the final draft of Evan and Chase's new manuscript, but if Adrian and Isobel were both excited about it, it was bound to be a success. Sloane was looking at promoting candidates with solid, well-rounded portfolios, which could give Kristine and me the edge against some of the others.

After combing through the first few chapters to ensure the new edits they'd made flowed well, I pulled open the chat on my laptop and looked to see if I could get Kristine to talk to me. When I got to her name, it showed her offline, which was weird because it was already after 10:00 am. I tried sending her a message, but it bounced back with an out-of-office reply.

> Samuel Langley: Hey, you up for comparing notes on the final draft? You haven't left any comments yet.

> Kristine Willard: I'm not in the office today. If you need to contact me for something time-sensitive, please send me an email, and I'll get back to you as soon as possible.

The little green light was lit next to Isobel's name, so I shoved my tablet into my bag and set off toward her office. Slowing down as I reached the doorway, I listened to see if anyone was talking. I'd interrupted Isobel and Adrian's little mating dance a few times over the last several weeks, and I didn't want today to be the day I walked in on them doing something I couldn't unsee.

"Isobel?" My hand reached across the doorframe and knocked, ensuring she was alone.

"Hey, Sam," she smiled as I peeked around the frame and saw her seated, thankfully alone, at her desk. "What can I do for you?"

Not wanting to sound desperately needy, I went in with the manuscript angle, not immediately asking why the table in her office was empty, and Kristine was nowhere to be found.

"I saw the final draft of the manuscript had editing permissions for both Kristine and me. I wanted to ensure it was alright to start verifying the original edits and proofreading without her. Does that work for you?" There, that sounded like a legitimate reason to ask her a question. I could have done it by email or chat, but then I couldn't subtly figure out why Kristine wasn't in the office.

"It does, I scanned through the document, and it looked like they revised everything important, but they'll appreciate it if you and Kristine go over it with a fine-toothed comb before we send it to be formatted."

"Do you know if Kristine has looked it over yet?"

Isobel smiled, closing the lid of her laptop and swiveling back and forth in her chair. "She's on a little vacation for the next few days. I told her she needed to take a break and recharge. Hopefully, she'll come back next week a little more relaxed."

"She's gone?" *God, Sam, could you sound any more desperate?*

"Kristine assured me she has her laptop and tablet with her, but I told IT to restrict her permissions to the shared server until Friday. She's been a little stressed about everything lately, and I need her fresh if you two are going to manage the book tour."

"I thought Chase and Evan hadn't agreed to anything yet."

"They haven't, but they'll both be in the office next Thursday, so we have until then to devise a strategy to convince them. It's in everyone's best interests to maximize the publicity on this project," she answered with a smile. "And Sloane is counting on you and Kristine to prove you can handle more responsibility. None of the other candidates are being given this opportunity, so you need to be ready to hit the ground running on this one."

"Alright, sounds good." I'm sure Kristine would be dragged out of the office kicking and screaming, but this was a once-in-a-career opportunity to show we could handle it, or neither of us would get that promotion. "Let Kristine know I should have my notes put in by Friday if she wants to get a hold of me to discuss edits."

"I'm sure she knows how to get in touch with you by now, Sam," she smirked, and I tried not to fidget as I thought about all the ways Kristine had touched me over the last several months. Dwelling on our previous arrangement would not help me figure out how to get her to talk to me.

EVEN THOUGH I WAS productive—Adrian only made a few appearances in his office throughout the day on Thursday and Friday—I still felt like I should have been doing more to contact Kristine. She'd been completely silent, both in a professional sense and a personal one. Isobel would probably fill me in if she heard something of importance, but I found myself opening new texts to her, pouring my heart out, and then deleting them before I got the courage to hit send. I missed her, but I wasn't sure what to say to her to keep her from shutting me out for good.

My sisters would probably have good advice on what I should do, but I couldn't bring myself to reach out to any of them. My mother would just harass me about when I was bringing Kristine home with me and the arrival of the wedding invitation I knew was coming. I was surprised she wasn't already blowing up my phone with constant questions about who I would bring as a plus one.

It was still several months away—well after we were scheduled to return from the book tour—if we could get Chase and Evan on board, that was way too far out for me to even consider asking Kristine. She already had one foot out the door, and since she may not even be talking to me by then once the promotions were announced, I was leaning toward going alone.

"Hey, man." Blake smiled as I approached him on the sidewalk outside the field house we were allowed to use for our league play. It was a little way outside the city, but I could walk to a T-station from the office and take the subway a few blocks from the stadium. Adrian had made fun of me for bringing all my gear to work today, but I wouldn't have time to go home and get outside the city in time to make the game.

"What's up, B?" I slapped his outstretched hand and pulled him in for a hug, regretting not making more effort to be present for more games. When I'd first moved to the city after graduation, I was a regular on the roster, but they'd put me in as an alternate with my busy work schedule. I typically picked up a few games a season, but I missed the team's camaraderie from when I was more active. "Who are we playing?"

"Rockets," he cringed. Most of our team was either old high school or university players who'd moved to the city for work and wanted to try to hold onto the sport they loved. The Rockets had four former U.S. Lacrosse athletes, two of whom had been on previous Olympic teams. They typically scouted from the local universities and pulled in seniors each year to round out their line-up.

With the four semi-pros being older than Blake and me, you'd think they'd have slowed down with age, but they were brutal, taking the tournament championship for the last four consecutive years. For a millisecond, I'd considered their offer to join their team in my second year in the league, but they wanted too much of a time commitment. I'd left early morning daily team sports conditioning behind when I'd graduated from Duke, and I wasn't trying to relive the glory days. I just wanted some guys my age to hang out with and go to the bars with me when I'd still been into drinking away my weekends.

"Long time no see, Langley. How's corporate life treating you?"

"I'm a book editor, B. It's hardly corporate life. I spend most of my day correcting grammatical errors and working on plot development."

"Dude, you still have to report to an office daily and get health benefits. That's about as corporate as you get."

Blake was the manager at a sporting goods store, having played lacrosse competitively in high school, but he'd dropped out of college after a few semesters to help raise his little sisters when his dad died.

"We can't all have Peter Pan syndrome. Some of us have to work one of those stuffy corporate jobs to have somewhere to live."

"You think I like living with three teenage girls? Are you kidding me? They're insane, and I want to commit murder every time one of them brings some punk-ass kid home with them for a date. I can't wait until I have enough saved up to get my own place. I don't care how many roommates I have to find. I'm not living at home forever."

"Yeah, I can't even imagine living with all my sisters again," I commiserated. My eldest sister had almost been in high school when I was born. Now, her kids were in elementary school, which made me feel ancient because I was in their wedding at the same age my nephews were. "Having roommates isn't so bad. You want mine? Tech-heads with the maturity of adolescents."

"Dude, I would kill to live at your place." While my building wasn't anything fancy, it was much cleaner than some of the dumps we toured, and it was easy to get to by public transportation.

"I'll keep an eye out and let you know if anyone is looking."

"Thanks, man. I appreciate it." He slapped me on the shoulder and laughed. "You ready to get our asses handed to us?"

"Yeah, might as well get this over with so we can get to the after-game drowning our sorrows."

WE MANAGED TO KEEP up with the Rockets in the first quarter; one of our other attackers, Foster, got early possession of the ball and scored before their goalie could react. That was the only easy point we scored as both teams lobbed the ball back and forth, the other team tiring out our goalie quickly with shot after shot. They only managed to make a fraction of them, but it still put them up by three going into the second quarter.

I scored a few points at the beginning of the third quarter, but then we had several bad turnovers, and the Rocket's lead expanded to eight. During the fourth quarter, we were all fucking exhausted, but they didn't stop, scoring three more goals, and we finished the game getting spanked 14-6. Despite the crushing loss, I felt good—sore and tired—but it'd been a good distraction from all the stress I'd been carrying around, waiting for the other shoe to drop in my personal life.

The locker room was lively; my teammates were excited to go out and get hammered to make up for losing. They probably would have gotten just as drunk if we'd managed to pull off a victory, but that's just how they were. Most of us were single in our early to mid-twenties, but a few more seasoned players were on the cusp of their thirties and had wives or babies at home.

"You coming out?" Kent, our goalie, asked as he pulled a clean shirt on and started fastening the buttons on the front. He'd gotten married the year before, and his wife was pregnant last I heard. He was a firefighter for the BFD and is still in ridiculous shape despite being five years older than the rest of us.

"Yeah, I need to get out of my head this week," I nodded, rubbing a towel over my damp hair.

"Work?" he asked with a smirk. "Or pussy?"

I held back the laugh that wanted to tumble out, knowing that Kristine would castrate me if she knew I was talking about her using that terminology. "Little bit of both."

"You got a girlfriend, Sam?" No. I guess I didn't, but I also couldn't fathom looking for someone else to warm my bed right now—or give me shit or criticize my work.

"Not really," I admitted, pulling on my jeans and buttoning them up. "I was sort of seeing someone from my office, but it was complicated."

"Ah, the good ol' office fuck. Fun until it's not anymore."

"Something like that." *Fun, until you let your guard down and start feeling things.*

"Just enjoy it, man. Before you know it, you'll be stuck in the burbs with a cranky wife who eats everything in sight and threatens to rip your dick off if you ever get her pregnant again." By the smile on his face, he looked like he was joking, but damn.

"Married life not what you were expecting?"

"Nah, man, it's great. We fucked like bunnies for the first two months. That's probably why I won't get laid until this kid is out. Karma," he laughed. "It probably also doesn't help that I keep getting called out on jobs whenever she wants me to start fixing shit around the house. Nesting is no joke."

"Oh, I know. Four older sisters, remember?"

"You ever gonna settle down?" He arched an eyebrow, sitting on the bench across from me and tying the laces on his shoes. "You're not getting any younger."

"Fuck, Kent. I'm twenty-four. Don't start acting like my mother."

"Just kidding. But is this girl you're torn up over *the one*?"

"Man, married life has made you soft. The one? Really?" I teased. But it was a valid question. Was Kristine someone I could see myself with long-term? What would happen if a position became available at the Chicago office? I didn't see a long-distance relationship working out all that well.

"You're thinking about it. That must mean she has some wifey potential."

Before I could respond, Blake threw himself onto the bench next to me, a waft of potent cologne filling my nostrils. "Fucking get dressed already, Langley. The drunk coeds of Boston College wait for no man."

"Fine, give me five minutes, and we can get out of here."

"Damn, dude. If you only last five minutes, no wonder the office girl is blowing you off," Kent teased.

"Fuck you," I laughed as I flipped them both off.

"Nah, I'm good," Blake laughed as he got up and grabbed his bag from under the bench. "I'll wait outside so you two can finish spilling the tea."

"You coming with us?" I asked Kent as he zipped up his bag.

"Maybe for one beer, can't stay out too late, or she'll threaten to change the locks again."

"You sure I should get married?" Between the shit my brothers-in-law said about my sisters, and now Kent talking shit about his wife, maybe I was alright being a bachelor for a few more years...or a decade. Men could father children at any age, right?

"If you find the one you can't imagine living without, definitely."

UNLIKE THE LAST TIME I was in a bar, I wasn't waiting for someone to show up. Kent and Blake drove back into the city to meet up with us while the rest of the team shared an Uber XL to a sports bar near Boston College that we typically went to if we played on the campus field.

"Who's up for shots?" Blake asked as he signaled for one of the young female servers.

"Don't you have to drive home?" I laughed as I looked at his eager expression. You could tell these guys' nights out were the highlight of his week.

"Nah, my sister is on campus with a friend. They're gonna meet me later and drive back to Mom's."

"So, you're using your teenage sister as a sober driver?" Kent laughed before he tipped back his beer bottle.

"Don't tell me you haven't used your pregnant wife for the same damn thing," Blake shot back.

Kent lifted his bottle in a salute. "Touché. That I have."

For a Friday night, things hadn't picked up yet around 9:00 pm. By 11:00 though, this place would be crawling with desperate young college students out to drink and hook up. It was hard to believe that three years ago, I'd been one of them. So many things had changed since then, and now I had to think about where I wanted my future to lead, not how to get the hot girl in the corner booth's phone number.

"You looking for a hookup tonight?" Blake asked as he slid a shot glass across the table.

"Why are you guys so concerned with my love life today?"

"We're living vicariously through the unattached successful bachelor among us," Kent teased as he continued to nurse his beer.

"Not that successful and not that unattached," I laughed before I threw back the shot, grabbing another one off the tray at the edge of the table.

"Ooh...so office girl is more than just a casual piece?" Blake chuckled as he turned in his seat and scanned the college students crowding the bar.

"Can we not talk about this tonight? I just want to have a drink with you and go home. I'm getting too old for this shit."

"Damn, Sam is a little pissy bitch when he's in love." Frankie, who was a defender, taunted from across the table.

"I'm not in love. It isn't like that," I denied, shaking my head.

"Then prove it. Pick up some chick tonight and take her home. If the office girl is casual, she won't care."

"Nah, man, don't be like that," Kent scolded him, throwing a wadded-up cocktail napkin in his direction. "That's a dick move, and you know it."

"You're just pissed your lady cut you off," Frankie shot back.

"At least I have a lady," Kent smirked. "At last count, wasn't it two failed marriages under your belt before thirty? How's that division of assets thing turning out for you? Didn't the last one take your truck?"

"Fuck you, asshole," Frankie shot back, and I shook my head at the turn this conversation had taken. So much for a relaxing night out with the guys.

"Tinder is where it's at," Todd, another defender, chimed in, changing the subject. "The girls on there know the score, and you can just block 'em if they get too clingy. You got an account, Sam?"

It'd been months since I'd even opened it, but I did have a Tinder account. I'd only gone on two dates with women on there, and both had been mediocre. We were at that awkward age where most chicks wanted too much commitment or none. I'd stopped trying to be a mind reader, and then Kristine had fallen into my lap.

Maybe they were right, though. If things with Kristine fell apart, it would be a good place to try to get back out there. It'd make my mom happy if I finally settled down. I just wasn't sure where to even find dating material anymore. Bar chicks were either too young or too desperate, dating apps had turned into hook-up apps, my work schedule didn't leave too much time for hobbies, and my lacrosse league was for men. Maybe I did need to put myself out there more.

But I hesitated to try when I didn't know where things were headed with my job. I'd never expected the last few months to take the turn they had when Adrian dropped that editing collab in my lap, much less getting to know Kristine the way that I had. Which also meant I didn't know where my romantic life was heading either.

THE REST OF THE night, I was distracted. Half listening to conversations, avoiding eye contact with women on the dance floor, and checking my phone to see if I had any text messages.

By the time I got home, I was ready to say fuck it all.

Taylor and Caleb were missing from their usual perch in their armchairs, the apartment dark and quiet. Grabbing a bottle of water from the fridge, I headed to my room and threw myself face down on the bed, wishing I had more answers.

I didn't want to seem like a whiny bitch, but this *does she, doesn't she* crap was really getting on my nerves. It wasn't Kristine's fault, she had just as much going on as I did, but I hated being stuck in limbo. I was also horny as fuck when I was drunk, and my hand wasn't going to cut it.

I unlocked my phone screen on a whim, tapping the little flame icon and waiting for my phone to re-download the Tinder app. It wouldn't hurt to see if there was anything else out there. As she'd repeatedly reminded me, Kristine wasn't my girlfriend, and I needed to stop acting like that.

After it loaded, I absently pressed the little x icon, comparing every woman who appeared to Kristine.

Too blonde. *Nope.*

Too skinny. *Nope.*

Too much makeup. *Nope.*

Obviously too into themselves. *Nope.*

After nixing about fifty women, I was zoning out as a side profile picture popped up that made me lose my breath.

The screen read:

> *Kris, 24*
> *Don't waste your time if you're just looking for a quick fling. Himbos and idiots need not apply. If you need to ask, you are one.*

It had her interests listed as reading, running, and comedy.

The sarcasm and scathing insults part of the comedy routine she had down pat. There were only two pictures on her account—both profile shots taken from the side—with her hair shielding half of her face in the first, and she had a book held up over half of her face in the second, but I knew it was her. When had she done this?

Hesitating for a fraction of a second, I clicked the blue star icon, watching as the photo was stamped with a Super Like. We'd see if I got a reaction out of that. I wasn't sure if she even used the app, but I felt like it was some sort of signal that maybe I shouldn't give up yet.

NINETEEN

KRISTINE

CAPE COD

As THE FERRY SLOWED and turned into the harbor at Provincetown, I quickly closed the cover on my tablet and stashed it inside my messenger bag. I'd brought a small duffel for my trip, not bothering with a suitcase since I was only here for a short visit.

There was still a month until peak tourist season started, so there were only a handful of other people on the first ferry, most choosing to take in the sights of the trip from the upper deck. I'd opted for a quiet corner of the boat's interior, using the time to catch up on my emails and make sure all the files I needed to work on were still functional. I knew that Nana's internet service could be spotty from past trips, but I still needed to have work access if I needed it.

Isobel had been vague about when they planned to send us the manuscript trials. I didn't want to risk missing it and end up being days behind the other candidates, especially since I had to mark up two manuscript samples.

After half the impatient passengers had filed off the gangplank and onto the long pier that took you into Provincetown, I made my way behind them, heading for the taxi stands. Nana's house was tucked into a cove further down the peninsula, just south of Chatham. It'd been in her family for several generations, undergoing a large restoration when I was in my teens, and she'd begun to spend more time down here, away from the city.

Once my grandfather had passed away, she didn't feel the need to keep up the façade of a dutiful society wife, deciding that spending her days lunching with the ladies and chairing various philanthropies were too politically driven for her tastes.

It only took about ten minutes to be tucked inside a local taxi and headed down Highway 6. I could have easily taken a chartered flight from Boston to the small airport near where she lived, but something was calming about the drive from Provincetown to Chatham. The roads alternated between winding through some quaint little New England villages and stretches of marsh-land. The Cape Cod National Seashore a calming natural beauty within view out the window for most of the trip.

The taxi driver wasn't a talker, which I appreciated—I often used car rides to get work done—but I kept my bag tucked in my lap and just enjoyed the mid-morning sunshine and the fact that this road wasn't crowded with tourists yet.

The drive took over an hour, the taxi finally stopping on the gravel drive that wrapped along the rear part of Nana's property.

Her house was tucked along a quiet stretch of rocky beach just a little north of Tern Island. A few neighbors were within walking distance, but typically only locals used the beach this time of year.

"Nana?" The front door was unlocked, another habit I found bizarre after growing up in the city, but one which seemed commonplace here. She was a little more cautious during the tourist season but didn't bother the rest of the year.

"Is that my wayward traveler?" she shouted from the direction of the kitchen, which was located along the back of the house, facing the water.

The scents of her apple strata wafted in my direction, warm cinnamon and brown sugar making my stomach grumble, reminding me that I hadn't eaten much before I caught the bus to the wharf this morning. I was sure she'd cringe at me using public transportation, but I always felt like a douche riding in the back of a town car. It was sometimes necessary for Manhattan, but I tended to walk now that I lived in Boston or catch a bus.

A gilded picture frame caught my eye as I turned the corner into the kitchen, my eyes widening. Hanging there in the middle of my *almost* eighty-year-old, widowed grandmother's kitchen—for all the world to see—was a painting of a pineapple. An *upside-down* pineapple.

"Just in time. I pulled it out of the oven a few moments ago," she smiled as I looked over to where she was seated at the kitchen island. Her sleek silver bob framed her slight face, her skin just as luminous as ever. She may have hated the trappings of wealth and the headache that came with it, but Nana was a hot grandma. Her complexion was near perfect, subtle laugh lines around her mouth and smile lines at the corners of her eyes the only indication of her age. I knew some of it was cosmetically enhanced, but I only hoped I'd age as gracefully as she had.

"So, you got some new artwork," I commented, glancing back at her painting. I knew I was probably reading too much into it, but really? It was upside-down. What was I supposed to think?

"Oh, yeah. I found that on the gallery walk last week with Georgia. Isn't it lovely?"

"Any particular reason it's hanging like that?"

She stepped over in front of the painting, peering at it while I stood off to the side, watching her reaction. It was clear Nana had no idea.

"Is it crooked? Pietro hung it without a level." She paused at my frown. "I'm not sure what you're getting at."

"Who's Pietro?" The last time I talked to her, the young guy she used to take care of the landscaping and repair person work was named Rodney. "The pineapple is upside-down, Nana."

"And? That's where the mounting bracket was." She ignored my first question, but if he was helping her around the house, I was sure I'd meet him eventually.

"So, you went to the gallery walk and bought an upside-down pineapple painting and didn't ask why the hardware was upside-down?"

Shaking her head, she walked back to the island and carefully scooped two servings of strata into bowls. "Come sit down with me and stop obsessing over my painting. I like it like that, it gives the kitchen a little more character."

Yeah, character and let people think Nana was into some partner swapping.

"But why upside-down? I'm sure Pietro could have easily changed the mounting bracket."

"Georgia and Paul's is hung upside-down too. I think it's a new vacation house trend or something. They also have a new bronze sculpture they commissioned on the table by their front door of an upside-down pineapple."

"Oh my God," I sputtered, unable to keep in my laughter any longer. Nana's other geriatric friends were swingers, and she didn't even realize it. The upside-down pineapple had become the secret symbol of swingers, but I doubted my grandmother knew that, given the placement of her new painting. I knew because there were no limits to some of the plot devices romance authors used.

"Are you feeling alright, dear?" she frowned, looking at me with alarm.

"I'm fine, Nana." I waved my hand in front of my face, trying to calm myself down.

"No, no," she fussed. "Something is going on with you. Why are you so distressed by upside-down pineapples?"

"It's not a big deal, really. Forget I said anything."

"Kristine, you tell me right now, young lady."

"Nana..." I started, not sure how to broach this subject. "How well do you know Georgia and Paul?"

"I've been friends with them for twenty years."

Long before my grandfather passed away five years ago. Interesting. "Did Georgia and Paul ever suggest any couple activities with you and Grandfather?"

"We played in a Bridge league and went to dinner every Friday night."

"And in all that time, they never tried to...get to know you and Grandfather more...*intimately?*"

"What nonsense are you going on about? You're making no sense right now."

"Do Georgia and Paul have a lot of friends who are couples?"

"Well, I guess so, but it's pretty common for the people at the club to intermingle."

"Oh, they're *inter*mingling, alright." With each other's spouses.

"Kristine, I don't appreciate the run-around. Get to the damn point already."

"Fine," I laughed, glancing back at the painting again. "Georgia and Paul are swingers, Nana."

She paused for a moment, frowning, still not connecting the dots. "Well, they do like to dance. I believe they took salsa lessons last spring."

"Not that kind of swinger."

Her frown deepened as she looked down at her bowl for a moment, and then it was like a light bulb went off. "Oh, that's hysterical," she chuckled. "No wonder Georgia is always popular on the senior social nights."

You couldn't make this shit up. But to her credit, Nana did march over to her new painting and pull it down, turning it right side up and leaning it against the wall. "I'll have to look into some new mounting hardware in the morning. You know us Willards don't share well. Maybe you can help me rehang that while you're here. If you're not too busy with work, that is."

"I'd be happy to help, Nan. I've got a few days off to relax." Although I wasn't sure who Nana wouldn't be sharing.

"I'm so thrilled you were able to make it down. I've missed you, Chicklet."

"Oh, God, not that, Nana," I groaned. "That's almost worse than Greg still calling me Krissy."

"Yeah, well, your brother is an ass."

"Something we can agree on," I laughed, standing up and throwing my arms around her slight shoulders. "I've missed you, Nan."

"Alright, no more being mushy," she deflected as she sat up and smoothed down the front of her blouse. "Eat before it gets cold."

As I dug into my warm apple-loaded treat, I closed my eyes and took a deep breath, content that I'd been forced out of the office for a few days. Spending time with Nana was just what I needed to get myself re-centered before facing Sam again.

Turned out Pietro wasn't a repair person. He was the new next-door neighbor. He was tall, nearly six feet, with almost black hair, generously sprinkled with gray, and striking light green eyes. He was over a decade younger than Nana, but he'd moved to the Cape after his wife had died, around the same time as my grandfather. He'd kept to himself for the last several years but had recently become a member of the club to which Nana and all her friends belonged.

"Kristine, would you mind handing me the level?" he asked, his voice carrying a mild Italian accent.

"Sure." I handed him the small spirit level we'd found in the shed, idly swinging the hammer Nana had given me between my fingers. I'd been ready to rehang her painting, but Pietro was already sitting at the kitchen island when I'd come downstairs this morning, prying off the old hardware and carefully transferring it to the opposite end of the frame.

Nana claimed he'd just come over for coffee, but the hair at the back of his head was flattened, and his clothes were slightly wrinkled. The coffee pot was also suspiciously bone dry, and the distinct aroma of coffee was absent in the kitchen. I didn't want to think about my grandmother sneaking men into the house while I was asleep upstairs, but her personal life wasn't my business. She was single, obviously above the age of consent, so if Nana wanted to be a cougar to the handsome gentleman from next door, she could have at it.

"There we go. *Perfetto*." He stepped back, appraising his work, the painting now featuring an upright, abstract pineapple. I absently wondered if Pietro knew the symbology of the previous orientation, but I would not be the one to ask him. Nana already told me she didn't share, so I had a feeling Georgia and Paul hadn't gotten their hands on Pietro. "Is there anything else you need me to do for you this morning, Daphne?"

Nana had been dicing vegetables on a cutting board next to the sink, but she hadn't gotten very far, becoming distracted once Pietro started rolling up his sleeves to get her picture straightened out. My grandmother and I appeared to share the same forearm fetish, which was hilarious and disturbing. But I couldn't blame her because Pietro was a silver fox.

"Maybe you could look at that leaky faucet in my bathroom later today? Kristine said she needed to go into town to get a better Fi-Wi signal this afternoon."

"Wi-Fi, Nana. Not Fi-Wi."

She waved her hand in my direction, rolling her eyes, "Whatever you kids call that nonsense. Our generation didn't have the interwebs and AOL to turn us into zombies."

"It's the Internet, Nana, and AOL hasn't been popular since I was in elementary school."

"Whatever that garbage Mason insisted I get was…"

My father had always kept up with the latest technology because his firm invested in several large tech companies. My grandfather had been a little more old-school but still learned what was popular to keep up with current demand.

On the other hand, Nana had an email address but never checked it. She also hated texting but finally realized that was the only way she'd get ahold of Gregory and me.

"If you want to get rid of me, just say so, Nana."

"That's not what..." she trailed off, blushing as she glanced at Pietro. "That's not what I said. I was just making sure you had what you needed to get your work done."

"I downloaded some files from the server on my way here, so I planned to sit outside and work a little today. That's not interfering with *your* plans for today, is it, Nana?"

"No, Chicklet." I cringed at the nickname, but I was fairly certain that was why she kept using it. I'd obviously gotten my irritating habit of using ridiculous nicknames from her. Now I knew why Sam hated it so much when I called him Spamela. *Chicklet* made my eyelid twitch.

"Pietro was going to teach me how to prune the rose bushes, so they'd flower more next year."

"Really?" I frowned. Despite hating the trappings of the size of her bank account, Nana had never been a fan of outdoor work. She didn't think it was beneath her, but I'd never seen my grandmother excited at the prospect of gardening. "Since when do you care about your rose bushes flowering? Don't you have a company that cares for the grounds here?"

"Well, yes, but Pietro is a master gardener, and he's done wonders with the landscaping at his place. It was in shambles when he moved in, and now it's a veritable oasis."

"Hmm." I tried to hide my smirk but failed, glancing briefly at Pietro, who was nursing a freshly squeezed orange juice with reddened cheeks. Maybe I would hit up one of those Internet cafés and give the two of them some privacy. "Which one of those cafes serves the best lobster rolls? Bonus points if they have fried clam strips."

The beaming, semi-grateful smile my grandmother graced me with was worth spending a few hours away from the house to give them some privacy.

Luckily, the restaurant she recommended was only a short walk down the beach. It felt good to breathe in the fresh sea air, have the wind whipping at my ponytail, and the soft sand beneath my feet. It made the world seem less hectic, and my mind already felt clearer. I had a feeling Nana was sitting on the Sam bomb to diffuse when I least expected it. She never forgot anything, so I knew from her hinting over the phone the subject was far from over.

MY ASSESSMENT WAS CORRECT. Nana was waiting on the back patio of her cottage—read: Cape Cod mini mansion—when I walked back after getting in a few solid hours of editing in the seaside café she'd recommended. My stomach was pleasantly full of carbs and local seafood, making me miss the summers I spent here as a teenager.

Maybe I needed to make time for that to start happening again. The promotion would come with two weeks of paid vacation every year, and while most editors failed to take advantage of it, I could see myself planning a working vacation from now on to spend time with Nana. Who knew how many years I'd have left with her? I already regretted enough things in my life. I didn't want to add neglecting the only person who gave a damn about me in my family to the list.

"You get all your work done with the free Fi-Wi?"

Rolling my eyes, I settled into one of the plush cushions on the rattan lounger next to the one she was stretched out on and dropped my bag to the flagstone. "You know it's called Wi-Fi, Nana. You aren't that old."

"Yeah, yeah, Chicklet, I know. But it's still fun for me to tease you youngsters about your obsessive need for technology. I get it with your brother working in marketing, but book editors in my day did just fine with pen and paper."

"Publishing is very much in the digital age, Nana. You have to keep up with the times, or you'll get left behind. The part-time interns in the office already make fun of me for doing a paper edit on the final draft of most books I work on."

"Not this one? I haven't seen you with your trusty red pen. Why is that?"

Laying back against the cushion behind me, I stared up at the clear blue sky with scattered, fluffy, white clouds. "It's different for this one. I'm working with someone. He needs to be able to see my notes."

"How's that going? I can't see you giving up the reins all that easily. Doesn't Isobel let you have quite a bit of freedom?"

"She does, but two authors co-wrote this book. Only one of them works with Isobel. I've been doing edits with the other author's editing team."

She pursed her lips, nodding as she pulled her sunglasses to the tip of her nose. "Sometimes, it's not such a terrible thing to be part of a team."

"It's not the team that I'm a part of. I work well with Sam, but..."

"Oh, so this is the infamous Sam?" Her eyes lit up with this added information, and I knew my avoidance of mentioning him hadn't gotten me out of the inevitable conversation.

Groaning quietly, I threw my forearm over my eyes, preparing myself for her interrogation. "It's not like that, Nana."

"You sure about that? You're being awfully dramatic for someone who just has a professional working relationship with someone."

Damn my brother for telling her all my secrets. Thank God he didn't know what was really going on with Sam. He'd have had a field day teasing me about dipping my quill in the company ink pot, even if I didn't technically have the quill in the relationship.

"What's the problem, Chicklet? It sounds like he's your age, understands the stresses of your job, and if Gregory is talking about setting him up with that fancy pants PA of his, he must be handsome."

"We both want the same job, Nana. It's...it's complicated."

"So un-complicate it. Is this job more important to you than finding someone to love? Someone to share your life with? I'm not going to be around forever, and I know you don't like to let people close enough to see you vulnerable."

"What would anyone in this family know about love?"

At her sharp intake of air, I knew I'd hit a nerve. She'd been coaxed into marriage with an older man at nineteen, one I knew she didn't love romantically. She was fond of my grandfather, but they never acted like they were in love. Not that I had any clue what love looked like outside the books I edited.

"I know none of us have set the best example for you or your brother on what true affection looks like, but I did love your grandfather. It was a different kind of love, but he was a good companion to me for many years." She paused, turning her head toward the house slightly up the beach, which I assumed was owned by Pietro. She seemed different around him. Maybe Nana knew more about love than I thought.

"Learn from my mistakes, Kristine," she sighed. "When you find love, don't let anything hold you back."

"Is that what you're doing?"

I was sure she would've been if she could blush, but she turned back toward me with an indulgent smile. "Don't try to turn this back on me. Let that young man know how you feel about him. You never know when you'll reflect on a missed opportunity and regret it for the rest of your life."

Before I could bombard her with questions about what that meant, she slowly eased herself out of the chair, pulling on the gardening gloves she'd been holding in her lap and turning toward Pietro's house. "You work on getting your head out of your ass. I've got a date with some hydrangeas."

"I thought it was roses, Nana?" I teased, laughing as she waved her hand at me dismissively over her shoulder.

"Whatever, Chicklet. Quit ruining my dramatic exit."

It seemed I wasn't getting any sympathy for my conflicted feelings from Nana. Maybe it was time to embrace them instead of running from them. The only catch was I didn't know if I could love someone, much less let Sam in close enough to try.

SAM

BOSTON

WHEN I ARRIVED AT the office on Monday, the little colored dot next to Kristine's name on the intraoffice messenger was still red. It wasn't like her to remain offline for this long. If she were logged on remotely, it would still show her as online, but I hadn't seen the little green dot next to her name since last Tuesday. I was starting to worry that she would do something stupid like drop out of the running for the promotion. I knew it was causing her stress if her interactions with me as of late were any indication, but it wasn't like her to back down from a challenge.

She also hadn't responded to my epically bad idea to Super Like her on Tinder while I was drunk. I knew she checked her email obsessively, so she should have gotten a notification of my drunken proclamation. If she was like me, she probably had the notifications turned off on the app, but I was anxious to see her reaction. I couldn't take it back now, and I was sure it made me look like a desperate loser, but I was letting it ride. She couldn't avoid me forever.

"Hey," Adrian greeted from the doorway, hanging his bag up on a hook next to the doorframe in his office. He had an oversized travel mug in one hand and a stack of papers in the other. "Thought you might want to look these over. It's the schedule from the last tour I managed."

"We don't know if Evan will agree to go yet." I frowned as I watched apprehension roll through Adrian's shoulders, but his smile was calculating.

"Chase has got him so pussy-whipped I bet he caves. I'm not worried about it."

"I highly doubt she's going to manipulate him into doing something he doesn't want to do."

"Wouldn't be the first time a woman manipulated Evan," he scoffed, sitting behind his desk and pulling open the laptop he kept in his office. Kristine had given me a hard time about my company-issued laptop, but his was like mine on steroids. Kind of like his shoulders.

"Is that what happened before he..." I'd just started at Vivid when Evan mysteriously packed up and left the city without warning. I knew he'd been tense around that time because of a book release, but it sounded like a woman was involved in his sudden need for seclusion.

"Yeah, his psycho ex was a piece of work. Total head case, super jealous. She didn't like the idea of him traveling around the country and meeting fans without her. He's always been a little shy, but that viper had him scared of his own shadow by the time they split up."

It also explained a little about the absence of any romantic subplots in his novels during that time. I couldn't imagine trying to focus on writing about two people being romantically involved if my own love life was falling apart. It was hard enough to focus on editing the scenes with Frances and Dominic toward the end of Chase and Evan's current novel while things were unsettled with Kristine.

"Well, I hope Chase doesn't manipulate him, but thanks for the information in case I need it." I awkwardly lifted the folder and nodded before shoving it into my messenger bag. I'd have to look at it when I got home later. It wasn't like I had anything else going on in my evenings anymore. Taylor and Caleb had asked me last night if we'd broken up since Kris hadn't been at the apartment much lately, but that would have involved us dating.

This book tour was going to complicate things even further. She couldn't hide from me if we were together every day. I knew there would be days of traveling and some downtime between events, and it wasn't like I could confront her while we were working. But it would be easier to corner her if there wasn't anywhere for her to escape. It seemed like a dick move to ambush her, but waiting patiently wasn't getting me anywhere. Being the youngest child, I knew I'd been a little more spoiled than my sisters, and I wasn't a fan of delayed gratification.

It wasn't just about the sex anymore, although my dick had been quite disappointed in the last few weeks that my hand was the only attention he was getting. Kristine had brought something into my life I hadn't had before. Someone who challenged me and didn't put up with my shit. I also didn't feel like I had to censor any part of my personality or put on the façade of a dumb jock around her. That act may have worked for Adrian, but I hated it in college when girls assumed I was just a pretty face who knew how to handle a stick—in more ways than one.

"Where's the dragon been this week?" Adrian asked after a few minutes of typing, leaning back in his desk chair. "Don't you two usually work together more now?"

"I'd have thought Isobel would have told you," I tried not to smirk, but I wasn't sure I was successful when I saw his jaw clench and his eye twitch.

"Why would she tell me? We don't spend that much time together." His eyes darted everywhere but my face, his jaw clenching again. Yeah right. They spent quite a bit of their time together lately, in and out of the office, but I wouldn't burst his little bubble if he thought they were being discreet.

"She's out of the office for a few days, using her vacation days or something. I think she's supposed to be back today or tomorrow. I'm not sure." It wasn't like she'd responded to my one piss poor attempt at communication to tell me herself.

"Well, I guess you'd better enjoy the reprieve while you've got it. She'll be back in here making her little snide comments soon enough. If you're stuck with her on this book tour, you might want to invest in noise-canceling earbuds."

"She's not that bad. I know she can be a little—"

"Bit of a bitch," he interrupted, and I felt my temper swell. Kristine wasn't the easiest person to interact with sometimes, but underneath all that snark, she was a good person.

"Knock it off."

"Excuse me?"

"How would you like it if I started calling Isobel a bitch?"

Rolling his eyes, he sat back in his chair, but I could see the muscles in his neck flex as his jaw clenched. He was trying to appear unaffected, but my question had hit a nerve.

"She's your superior, Mr. Langley. I'd advise you to be respectful in this office."

"Pot meet kettle, Adrian. You can't go around calling people bitchy, no matter how much they irritate you."

"She calls me Dickhead." He had a point, but he *was* a dickhead, so... "Whatever, Sam. Just make sure you pack your cup."

BY THE END OF the day, Adrian still hadn't reappeared after another 'business lunch,' and I was antsy. I'd gone through the packet Adrian had given me and had a fairly good idea of what would be expected of me during this book tour. It was a lot of verifying information with the different venues, ensuring copies of the books were on hand, and arranging for the marketing materials to be transferred from city to city.

We'd also be responsible for ensuring the daily schedule the PR department set out was followed. Signings could last for hours in some larger cities, depending on their popularity. It was a lot for a typical author, but I wasn't sure how he would handle crowds considering Evan's aversion to social interaction.

Typically, in the weeks or months leading up to a tour, our team would be responsible for pulling passages from the final manuscript for the marketing team, but all of that had already been done. Even though he was a colossal jackass, Gregory's software program made our lives easier. As we'd edited, we could highlight passages and mark them to be pulled up later. Kristine grumbled every time I suggested we flag something, but I think even she saw the time it saved us down the road.

Deciding I wasn't in the mood to deal with public transportation, I walked home, stopping to pick up Thai food. Taylor and Caleb were playing video games when I got in, cursing at each other through their headsets. Normally, I would have joined them, but I wasn't in the mood to try to be social right now.

After I'd polished off my Thai noodles, I opened my laptop and reviewed the edits I'd done since last week, noting that a few things had popped up on the file over the weekend. Despite avoiding me, Kristine had been working over the weekend, wherever she was.

Closing my eyes, I tried to sort through the mess in my head, hating that I'd let myself get attached to her. She'd told me from the start this was just a fling, but I'd gone and caught feelings for someone emotionally unavailable. Go figure that the first girl I was interested in doing more than just fooling around with wouldn't be on board. Maybe Kent was right. The prospect of getting married someday didn't seem horrible. Most of my friends who had stayed back home were already on the family plan, starting their homemaking lives, while I tried to get a promotion that made my life difficult.

Despite my mother's assumptions, it was hard for me to be away from my family. Maybe after the book tour, I'd look for editing positions closer to home if this fantasy position didn't pan out. I knew my feelings for Kristine were dangerously close to developing into something real and substantial, but it still felt like it had an expiration date surrounding this promotion.

A loud chirp from my phone startled me. I must have fallen asleep, but my alarm clock said it was only a little after 10:00.

Groaning at the stiffness in my shoulders, I unlocked the screen, almost dropping it when I noticed a little red bubble on the Tinder icon. Either someone else had messaged me, or Kristine had finally responded.

My palms were sweaty as I opened the app and clicked on the chat feature, my direct message with Kristine showing it'd received a response.

> *Kris: I said himbos need not apply.*

I laughed at her snarky response; glad she didn't seem angry that I'd been on the app and found her profile. Trying to text her directly probably would have been easier, but I wasn't convinced she'd respond after last week. This got her attention and left the ball in her court. Now I just had to figure out how to respond in a way that wouldn't scare her off.

> Sam: I'm a reformed himbo, tyvm.

> Kris: If that's what you've gotta tell yourself.

> Sam: You don't seem to mind.

When her response wasn't immediate, I wondered if I'd pushed it too far. Unintentionally stalking her on a dating app wasn't exactly giving her space, but I couldn't seem to help myself.

> Kris: Adrian not keeping you entertained this week?

> Sam: I miss your insults more. It was quiet in the office without you this week.

> Kris: Such a sweet talker.

> Sam: Would you make fun of me if I told you I missed you, not just your scathing remarks on my character?

> Kris: Yes...

I waited as I watched the little dots move that indicated she was typing. My last comment had bordered on the desperate side, but I did miss her. Being dismissive and not telling her how I really felt had left things up in the air up to this point. Maybe a little transparency would eventually be reciprocated—or she'd break things off for good, but I was hoping for the former.

> Kris: I may have missed you too.

> Kris: Not just for what's hidden under those work clothes, either.

> Sam: My forearms?

> Kristine: Maybe those too.

She missed me too. I could live with that.

> Sam: Are you back in the office tomorrow?

> Kris: You sound a little needy again, Sam.

Yeah, I know.

Sam: Where are you hiding out?

Kris: I'm not hiding.

Sam: Mmhmm.

Kris: I'm not. I'm visiting family.

Sam: You're in NY?

Somehow, I had a feeling that wasn't where she was, knowing she'd rather spend time with Adrian before she went to see her parents.

Kris: Ew. No. Visiting Nana at the Cape.

Sam: How very bourgeois of you.

Kris: Don't make me spank you.

Sam: Is that supposed to be a deterrent?

Kris: There might be a paddle in that black box you keep trying to spy inside.

Sam: Sounds fun. ;)

The meeting with Chase and Evan was on Thursday, but I was meeting with a new author that Adrian had just signed tomorrow. She'd been hesitant to work with a traditional publisher, having self-published her first series of books, but we were hoping to take her work wider and expand her audience. Adrian wanted me to watch the process, certain that I'd get the promotion, and this would soon be part of my job duties.

I was still uncertain, knowing that as soon as I received the excerpt for the manuscript trials, I'd need to bring my A-game. The field was still wide open. Kristine and I were not the only copy-editing interns still in the running. We may have been a couple of stronger candidates, but we were out if the panel didn't like our work.

Kris: I should be back home Wednesday. I'm sorry I've been quiet lately. It's nothing you've done. I'm just working through some things.

I probably shouldn't tell her I would anxiously await her return, but I knew I'd be watching that little red dot on the intraoffice messenger as I had been since last week. As soon as it was green, I wasn't sure if I had enough self-control to stay away from her.

> *Sam: Enjoy the rest of your visit. I'm sure I'll see you around the office this week. As long as you're not still hiding from me.*

My phone almost slipped through my hands when a text message notification from Kristine scrolled across the top of the screen.

> *Kristine: No more hiding. I'm trying.*

I hoped that was true because I wasn't sure how much more of this back-and-forth I could take before I cut my losses and walked away. My attraction to her was already making me do things out of character, trying to figure her out, but even I knew there was no way to force someone to love you if they didn't.

TWENTY-ONE

KRISTINE

CAPE COD

THE FERRY WAS RUNNING behind—something about scheduled maintenance at the main dock in Boston Harbor taking longer than usual—which spelled disaster for returning to Boston in time for work today. I should have left on Tuesday night's last ferry, but Nana had purposely misplaced her keys to keep me here longer. I felt terrible she was so desperate for company that she was lying to hold me captive, but I also knew Pietro would keep her plenty occupied.

He'd been seated at the breakfast bar again this morning, eating a freshly baked blueberry muffin, a robe pulled on over his pajamas. They hadn't even tried to hide that he'd spent the night again, and while disturbing, I was glad that Nana had someone worth traumatizing her grandchild over.

Chase and Evan were making an appearance at the office this week, and with me being on *forced* vacation, it meant I needed to get back to the office to catch up. As far as I knew, Isobel still hadn't managed to get Chase to agree to the book tour, but once Chase was trapped in her office, it was only a matter of time until Isobel coerced her into doing what she thought was best.

I still hadn't interacted with Evan—other than when I'd unknowingly caught him in the city with Chase—so I was curious what he was like beyond what little information Dickhead and Sam had divulged about him. Although if the book tour went ahead, I'd be spending plenty of time with Chase, Evan...and Sam by default.

He hadn't called after our little Tinder conversation, but I wasn't sure what I expected. I wasn't sure how to take his silence after I told him I was trying. Nana had convinced me I might not need to avoid getting attached to Sam. Our future beyond the next few months was still uncertain, but I didn't want to push him away anymore intentionally. I was scared, though, and I knew I'd probably do something stupid instead of talking to him about my feelings. This whole relationship business didn't come easily to me.

Finally, after sitting in a café next to the dock for three hours staring at the cursor on my computer screen, lost in thought, the ferry pulled into position. I packed up my bags and headed down to board the boat.

The water was choppy, and a late spring storm was on the horizon in the forecast for the afternoon. I'd intended to go over my last set of edits using the free Wi-Fi on the boat, but the rocking forced me to close my laptop and settle in with a view out the windows. So, I spent the trip watching the landscape of the coastline gradually transition from quiet beaches to urban buildings and skyscrapers by the time we hit the harbor in Boston.

I was already running late for work, but Isobel's texts assured me I could take my time as long as I was at the office for our meetings with Chase tomorrow.

Not wanting to drag my luggage into the office, I took an Uber to my apartment building, changing into something more professional-looking before heading downtown. It took me way too long to decide what to wear, finally settling on a sheath dress, throwing on my raincoat, and grabbing my umbrella before I booked another ride on the app.

I TOLD MYSELF THAT the dress wasn't for Sam, but when the car dropped me off in front of the building, and I caught sight of him walking down the sidewalk outside the building, my heart started pounding. I thanked the driver and hustled down the pavement, grabbing the door right as he prepared to let it go.

"Hey," he greeted me with a smile as he glanced back and noticed my hand on the edge of the door.

"Hi."

His smile widened as he stepped to the side, grabbing my hand and tugging me inside as I tried to retract my umbrella. Sam's hair was wet, curling around his forehead and ears, moisture dripping from the light layer of scruff on his chin and his glasses, dropping onto his crisp dress shirt. He was wearing a lightweight jacket but still half-soaked from being out without an umbrella.

"Forget something at home today?" I teased as I shook my umbrella over the rug inside the door.

"Eh, a little rain never hurt anyone. You're late today. Trying to play hooky again?"

"No, the ferry was late," I scoffed as I carefully navigated across the wet marble tile toward the bank of elevators. My heels slipped slightly, and Sam's hand shot out, catching me by the elbow. "Thanks."

"Don't need you having to hobble around on a cast while we're traveling."

Frowning, I jabbed at the elevator button. "They still haven't agreed to anything. We may be stuck here for the next few months."

"Adrian is convinced it's a sure thing. Legal wants to reduce their royalties if they don't agree. Kind of a dick move, but I think they may go for it."

"I'm sure Dickhead didn't have anything to do with that being snuck into their contracts."

"Of course not," Sam laughed as the elevator doors opened, and he ushered me inside with a gentle press of his hand to my lower back. "He'd never do anything that unethical to one of his authors."

"I bet you can't wait to get away from him," I chuckled, making eye contact as he settled beside me at the back of the elevator after selecting the button for our floor. "I don't know how you've lasted this long."

"Nothing is a done deal yet," he smiled, his lips tight, obviously thinking of what'd kept me away from him lately. He still had to earn the promotion first if I didn't throw up roadblocks. The mature thing would be for me to drop out of the fantasy position, the position in New York was mine for the taking if I wanted it, but my pride and my need to stay independent made our lives difficult. I knew Sam would never say anything to persuade me, but I hurt both of us by holding onto the possibility of staying in Boston so tightly.

"Why were you out of the office this late?" It was already past 3:00 pm. He wasn't carrying anything besides his messenger bag, so it wasn't likely he was out in the rain doing an errand for Dickhead.

"Uh." He shifted awkwardly before glancing over nervously. "Client lunch ended up taking longer than we thought it would."

"Since when do you meet with the authors? And out of the office?"

Isobel regularly took some authors to lunch when they were in town, but she'd never invited me. Most of them knew who I was, but typically the copy-editing interns didn't meet with them outside the office. We were faceless names in the margins of their manuscripts.

"Uh, Adrian wanted me to come and observe. Jessica wanted to talk about the whole editing process, and you know how Adrian is hopeless when it comes to polite interaction with people."

Oh. Not only was he meeting with authors, but Adrian was already grooming him. Nice. Guess it didn't matter if the job was his yet or not. The good ol' boys' club seemed to be at work behind the scenes to give him an edge. My eyes narrowed as I gave him a pointed look.

"It's not like that, Jessica was just really chatty, and when Adrian needed to get back to the office for a meeting with the genre heads, I told him I could stay and fill her in."

Dig the hole deeper, Sam. I was assuming that the Jessica he was talking about was Jessica Prange. She was an up-and-coming mystery writer with a semi-successful series about a sexy female detective already self-published. I'd seen her headshots. Jessica was a tall, slender redhead with ample cleavage revealed in most of her author photos and dual dimples to set off her light blue eyes. And Sam had just spent several hours keeping her 'entertained.'

Unbidden feelings of jealousy for the experience and that he was out with a sexy, semi-successful author at a several-hour-long business lunch hit me like a freight train. But then, Sam didn't have any obligations to me, especially not with my behavior over the past several weeks.

Shit.

"Hey."

His fingers grazed against my palm as he clasped my hand, tugging me slightly toward his side. When the tips of the fingers of his other hand tilted my head toward him, I closed my eyes, letting out a harsh breath.

"It was just business. I was honestly anxious to get out of there and finally escaped when she had to take a call from her fiancé."

"You don't owe me any explanations, Sam." I'd been back for less than ten minutes, and I was already screwing this up. Nana would be disappointed. I truly did have my head lodged squarely up my ass.

"You aren't jealous, are you?" I could hear the amusement in his voice as he stepped in front of me, urging my chin up.

"Quit being so smug." I batted his hand away, pressing against his chest as I stepped around him when the elevator doors opened.

"Did someone miss me?" Sam teased as he followed me down the hallway toward Isobel's office.

"No, and don't you have your own office to go to?"

"Oh, come on, I'm just teasing," he laughed as he grasped my hand, stepping around me and glancing into Isobel's office before he pulled me inside and closed the door behind us. "How was your week?"

I ducked under his arm and tossed my bag into a chair at the table, reaching for the light switch next to the door. He watched with an indulgent smile, dropping his bag to the floor.

"It was fine. Nice to work in peace for once." I smirked. "It's been such a pain in the ass the last few months to have this annoying guy following me around the office all the time."

"Oh, I'm sure it has been," he laughed, stepping forward. I stumbled back, my thighs bumping into the chair behind me. I grasped the back of the seat before I did something stupid like pushing up onto my toes to kiss him as he stopped directly in front of me. "I'm the worst, remember?"

"Still self-aware, I see."

"I missed you," he confessed, dropping the smug façade and cupping my cheek with his warm palm.

"What are you doing, Sam?"

"Just saying hello," he murmured, leaning in to place a soft kiss against the side of my mouth, lingering as his fingers slid into the loose hair at the back of my head. His warm breath fanned over my face as his lips hovered near mine, hesitating. The anticipation of his next move caused my pulse to race and my patience to thin as I tried to play it cool. Letting out a stuttering breath, I closed my eyes, fighting the urge to lean in slightly as his lips grazed mine gently before he stepped back.

"But I should probably get back to work. Since not all of us get lengthy vacations away from the office." His voice was still teasing, but I could see the tension around his eyes as he reached to grab his bag.

"It was good to see you, Sam."

He nodded, pulling the strap over his shoulder as he reached back to open the door. "You too. I'll see you tomorrow?"

"Yeah, they're supposed to be here around 9:00."

One final nod, and he was gone. I collapsed into the chair behind me, and my fingers pressed to the place his lips had touched. The effect of his mouth pressing against my skin had lessened from the initial frenzy of the first few weeks, but it still made my head swim. I had no idea how to keep trying to resist him. Nana had told me to go for it, but something still held me back.

"GOD, THAT WAS BRUTAL," Sam sighed as he settled across from me at the table in the corner conference room.

I'd texted him to meet me in here after Chase and Evan had left, finally agreeing to the book tour, even though I could tell it was under duress on Evan's part. Chase had taken him on an extended lunch midday and convinced him they should do it. I don't want to know her motivational tactics, but it was clear that those two were goners for each other. It was disgusting, but I was envious of their relationship. They hadn't given two shits what Isobel and Adrian thought of their relationship, and I had a feeling Chase might be fleeing Boston for good to Evan's hideaway in the woods.

"Were you in there while Evan went off on Adrian?" I laughed. I'd caught Chase sneaking around in the hallway near his office, eavesdropping on her boy ripping into Adrian when he started questioning their relationship. He'd been gloriously pissed when Adrian tried to disparage Chase, standing up for her and claiming he wanted to marry her. She'd also caught me eavesdropping, trying to figure out what was happening between Sam and me. If I only had a clue.

He'd been flirty throughout the day, but I still wasn't sure how to act around him. I needed to apologize for my recent behavior toward him, but now we would be forced to go on this tour, and I didn't want Chase and Evan to figure out we were...doing whatever Sam and I were doing.

"Yeah, Adrian's face got so red when Evan was yelling at him. That was the first time I'd seen him worked up about anything. Cut twenty thousand words from a manuscript, no big deal. Tell him his sex scenes suck, and he needs to get a consultant, fine, whatever. But start talking shit about Chase, and Evan pulled out the alpha male."

"Chase thinks something is going on with us." That was why I needed to talk with him. While something was going on—maybe—we didn't need that getting back to either of our bosses, especially not with everything on the line. Not that they had any room to say anything. But the fact of the matter was, we'd been carrying on a physical relationship on company property. If that came out, we'd be lucky to keep our jobs, much less earn anything with more responsibility.

"Well. Something is going on...or at least there was. Am I supposed to pretend we aren't friends now?"

"Friends? That's the label you're going with? We need to subdue our *friendliness* around people from the office."

"If you hadn't noticed, things have been sufficiently subdued, Kris. You've barely spoken to me the last few weeks." He was right, but we would be spending lots of time together starting in a few weeks, and we needed to maintain our professionalism at least. Rumors had been flying around the office about Adrian and Isobel all day, and I didn't want to be the next hot topic of gossip.

"I know, but..." I didn't even know how to tell him exactly what I needed. "Chase will tell Isobel if she thinks we're involved, and I don't want it to..."

"Make you look bad? Are you ashamed of me now? Isobel is hardly going to tell the hiring team even if she did find out about the two of us."

"Sam, you know it's not like that."

"Isn't it? You plan to keep me your dirty little secret forever?"

"It's not like we're dating. It was never supposed to be anything serious. I keep telling you this, and you don't listen to me." Nana would kill me if she knew I was downplaying my feelings like I was.

Sam squinted, and for a moment, I thought he would call me out on my bullshit, but he nodded, crossing his arms over his chest. "Fine, you want to play it like that. I can be the best platonic coworker you've ever seen. I'll keep my hands to myself. Can you do the same?"

"God, how does your ego even fit in this room? Have you been taking notes on Adrian's personality *and* his job?"

Isobel had been too distracted to do anything other than relaying the information Sloane had been feeding her throughout the entire process. Sam was being groomed for the job, and Isobel was hardly in the office, having a very unsubtle affair with the office jackass and encouraging me to take vacation time.

I felt like the more I wanted it, the further the possibility of this job slipped beyond my grasp. Maybe I needed to talk to Sloane about New York. I didn't want to sit back and let Sam—or someone else—waltz right into the position while I left the other one on the table.

"Fine, you want space. I'll give you space...again." Sam stood from the table and grabbed his bag, not glancing back as he closed the door behind him. Once again, I was left feeling like an asshole while I pushed everyone away from me. Maybe I was a lost cause.

"COME ON IN, KRISTINE," Sloane greeted with a smile from the door to her office. I was low-key jealous of her floor-to-ceiling windows, a view of downtown Boston stretching out on the other side of the glass. The view from Isobel's office was nice, but this was something else.

She gestured for me to sit in one of the chairs across from her desk. I gingerly sat on the edge of the cushion, trying to remember all the lessons drilled into me during my teen years about maintaining posture and meaningful eye contact.

"Chloe left a note that you wanted to discuss something with me?"

Her assistant had tried to coerce me into divulging what I needed to talk to Sloane about, but I'd remained close-lipped, making the soonest appointment I could get into her office. Isobel had been back and forth with the formatters all day on the back matter for the book, and I hadn't been able to get her alone for a moment, much less to tell her that maybe she'd been right. She'd be rubbing it in my face if she knew I was even considering the position I'd denied wanting so adamantly.

"Isobel told me that you were putting my name forward for the position in New York?"

"Is that a problem?" Her expression was carefully neutral as she leaned back in her chair and scanned my face.

"No," I sighed, taking a deep breath. "That's why I wanted to talk to you. I know Isobel told you I wasn't interested in the position..."

"But you've changed your mind? Your brother told me it was best to let you come around to the possibility on your own."

I bristled at the mention of Gregory, but he was right. I wasn't the type to be told to do something. I needed to make my own decisions and not feel like I was being forced into something.

"I'm open to the possibility. I'd still like to be considered for the position in this office, but I'm eager to take on more responsibility."

"That's good to hear, Ms. Willard. The progress reports Adrian and Isobel have shared with me regarding your and Mr. Langley's performance in this collaboration have impressed the hiring panel. I'd love to see one or both of you taking on a more active role within Vivid. It was disappointing when you shied away from moving on in the same genre you already excel at, but you'd also be a good fit for the fantasy position."

"Thank you."

"I give credit where it's due. Adrian informed me Ms. Rodgers and Mr. Stineman have decided to participate in the book tour. Are you up for the challenge?"

"Yes, ma'am. I'm ready to see what a full-scale tour looks like behind the scenes." I'd hate every moment when I'd rather be here doing actual work as an editor. At least Chase wasn't as high maintenance as some of the other authors.

"Well, it's not exactly full scale, but it'll give you a good idea of what some of the responsibilities of the position entail. I'm sure it'll look slightly different within the fantasy department, but it'll be a beneficial experience for both of you."

"Yes, of course."

"Was there anything else you needed?"

Maybe some Prozac or Xanax to make it through the next few months, but I'd accomplished what I set out to do.

"No, thank you for considering me for these positions. I'll try my hardest to demonstrate my willingness to learn in the next few months."

"I'm sure you will," she said with a smile. "I'm looking forward to seeing what you do with the manuscript samples in the next few weeks."

As much as it pained me to do it, I wasn't throwing away the possibility of a promotion because of some family bullshit. Mason didn't deserve that kind of power over me anymore, and I would start living on my terms. Starting with figuring out how to keep my hands off Sam long enough to get through this tour. Then I needed to decide if what we'd started months ago could survive the outcome, whatever it may be.

SAM

BOSTON

I WAS MISTAKEN IF I'd thought our lives were complicated while navigating co-editing our last two projects with Evan and Chase.

Being dragged into Public Relations training was akin to torture. I'd honestly rather wax my chest hair than sit through more training modules with Diana. It wasn't that she was horrible to work with, quite the opposite, but it was so damn boring. It also didn't help that Chase and Evan barely attempted to keep their hands off each other. They were constantly touching and staring at each other, sneaking off for long lunches and coming back looking rumpled. It'd been a long week leading up to the book launch, and no end was in sight.

Kristine had been as snarky as usual but still pushed me away at every opportunity. Whatever fragile friendship we'd had before we started sleeping with each other had stagnated. I wasn't any closer to getting her to let me in emotionally, even without the physical side that I missed desperately.

I knew I could easily go out and get laid if I was that desperate; Blake was always up for having someone to bar-hop with, but it had lost its appeal entirely. The easy, no strings attached lifestyle I'd lived for six years held no draw. I wanted the inside jokes and the person who teased me relentlessly. I wanted more than the warm body in my bed for a few hours. I wanted a companion. As much as I hated that I did sometimes, I wanted Kristine.

"Only a few more hours," Kristine murmured as she shoved the itinerary folders Diana had given us into her bag. "Then the real torture begins."

"I'm looking forward to the next few months," I confessed. While I knew she liked an editor's behind-the-scenes work, I was anxious to expand my skill set. It also didn't hurt that we had a few days to explore each city. We'd traveled as much as having five kids allowed when I was younger, but it was different as an adult. During university, I was always training during school breaks or trying to make up the work I missed when the team traveled. I had no wild Spring Break vacations or trips to foreign countries during the summer.

Kristine may have taken her resources as a child for granted, but I wanted to travel a bit while I was still young and unattached. I also had a tough time believing she'd ever seen the places she visited with her family as a real tourist. There was something fun about doing the cliché tourist destinations and walking around a new city without a tour guide. There was only so much you could explore from your ivory tower.

"Of course you are," she sarcastically replied, rolling her eyes. "I bet you think living out of a suitcase is fun."

"Well…" I mused. I didn't need much, and most hotels had laundry service. I could make do for a few weeks with only what I could fit in a suitcase.

"Ugh, just kill me already. I'm going to get tired of the taste of vomit in my mouth with how those two are all over each other." She tilted her head toward Chase and Evan, clearly in their own little world.

"You're such a romantic," I teased, laughing at the full-body shudder and groan of disgust that she responded with.

"Don't accuse me of something so horrible, Sam."

"Did you actually call me by my real name? Gasp. Are you losing your touch?"

"Shut it, Spamela." She glared and huffed as she headed toward the door at the back of the conference room.

"There she is," I smirked, following her into the hallway. "I knew it wouldn't last long."

"You're leaving yourself wide open for insults with that one, Sammy."

Stepping closely behind her at the closed elevator door, I brushed her hair aside and whispered in her ear. "We both know my stamina is more than you can handle." Her mouth dropped open as I stepped back, heading toward the door to the stairwell. "Don't be late tonight."

The door closed behind me with a thud, muffling her caustic retort, but nothing she could say today would spoil my excitement. Now that the boring stuff was over, we could finally get this show on the road.

"Where's your shadow?" I asked Isobel as I joined her at the table next to the entry of the ballroom. I arrived at the hotel half an hour earlier than Adrian had told me to report, my luggage already stowed in our shared room for the night. Kristine would lose her shit when she discovered he'd booked us a shared two-bedroom suite for the first night. We were guaranteed private rooms for the rest of the book tour, but I didn't mind sharing for one night.

I'd claimed the smaller bedroom, moving the chocolates from my pillow to Kristine's. A little peace offering for poking fun at her this afternoon.

"Adrian is coordinating the schedule with the event planner." She continued verifying the name tags on the table with the sheet on her clipboard, straightening the rows on the table outside the ornate wooden doors.

"Not the shadow I was talking about, but good to know."

She tried not to look flustered as she looked up from her work, but I could see the tension around her mouth. Isobel hadn't meant to confirm something the entire office already assumed. She and my boss weren't exactly subtle.

"Kristine is with Diana in the conference room down the hallway from the main desk. They're sorting the PR packets and double-checking the advance print copies we're handing out tonight."

"Where do you need me?" I knew Is was running the show tonight, having dealt with all of Chase's book launches. Adrian may have boasted that Evan had more bestsellers, but he hadn't had more than a virtual launch for as long as I worked at Vivid.

"Can you check on them and make sure they have everything they need? I've got this handled, and I checked everything inside earlier. There's still a few hours before I need the two of you to start working the crowd."

"On it." I nodded, heading back into the lobby. There was a wall placard to direct me toward the conference rooms and business center, but Kristine's loud laughter guided me toward the correct one.

"Sounds like a party in here," I smiled, watching her talking animatedly to Diana about something across the room.

"Hardly." Her eyes twinkled as she glanced toward the door. She was bent over a table full of papers, quickly pulling a sheet from each stack and shoving them inside a black folder. "You can come help. Nice of you to finally get here."

"I'm here earlier than I was told."

"Let me guess. Adrian told you to show up a half-hour from now." Her head shook dismissively, rolling her eyes before returning to the task before her. "Nice to know you two read the itinerary."

"I'm here now. Put me to work." Joining her at the table, I took off my sport coat and unbuttoned my cuffs, rolling up my sleeves while she watched me out of the corner of her eye. I didn't say anything, but I could tell by the tense silence she was enjoying the show.

Baby steps.

"Now that you two have this handled, I'm going to check in on my team in the ballroom." Diana waved on her way out the door, and then it was just the two of us.

"You look nice," I murmured as I reached around her to grab a folder from the box on the floor at her side, my chest grazing her shoulder on the way back up.

"Uh." Her voice was husky as she cleared her throat. "You too. I didn't realize you owned more than one tie."

"I've got a whole box full of ties and belts under my bed. You've got an arsenal stored under yours. I've got other surprises."

"Is that where you store your big sticks and ball-handling equipment?" She laughed, stepping in front of me and reaching across the table to grab another sheet of paper.

My free hand dropped to her waist as I took a step forward, lightly pressing my hips into her before I reached around her for a paper from a different stack. "We both know that's not where I keep my big stick."

"Eh," she laughed, looking over her shoulder at me. "Your stick isn't that big."

"Big enough," I teased as I leaned over her, caging her against the table with an arm on either side of her. "You seem to be in a better mood than you were this afternoon."

She ducked under my arm, dropping her folder into the box at the end of the table. "Who needs other ways to relieve stress when a girl has an arsenal of mood enhancers under her bed."

Well, that backfired.

Despite their worries over the last several weeks that the book wouldn't perform well, Chase and Evan were wide-eyed as they took in the ballroom full of people packed inside, mingling and laughing as they waited for the event to start.

Kristine had been avoiding me, keeping busy with last-minute preparations Isobel threw at us as people started to arrive. That was how she'd spent the last several weeks. Alternating between poking at me to try to get a reaction and avoidance.

We'd passed each other a few times in the gym, but I didn't engage, giving her the space she'd asked me to give her. That didn't mean I played nicely, though. I may have strategically pulled my shirt off a few times when I knew she was unsubtly staring in my direction. The pink cheeks and darting eyes indicated I'd accomplished my goal, but I didn't confront her. And she usually retreated quickly after that, darting into the locker room while I finished using the treadmill or a piece of equipment on the weight floor.

She'd break eventually, and I would wait until Chicago to execute my plan. We just had to make it through the next few days, and she'd be mine for an entire day.

"You ready?" Adrian asked as he stopped where I'd been working, nodding toward the stage on the other side of the room. He'd already been networking with some executives holding court at the open bar. Sloane had stopped me to check in on her way through the door, but I hadn't seen her since.

"Yeah, I think we've got everything handled," I confirmed, following his lead as he approached where Isobel greeted Chase and Evan, Kristine close by.

"At least you two don't look like you've been screwing in the supply closet," Adrian laughed as we reached them, and I rolled my eyes as I stepped in next to Kristine.

Isobel and Chase both verbally jumped on him as Kristine sighed in disgust, glancing over her shoulder at me with an eye roll. "You put your foot in it again, Dickhead?"

"Sounds like he put his whole body in it," I chuckled as my boss narrowed his eyes at me.

"Hey," he pouted with a scowl. "I thought you were supposed to be on my side. Traitor."

Yeah, not defending you for being an idiot, Ad.

Kristine and Adrian bickered for a few minutes before she stomped off, leaving the rest of us behind.

"I'm just gonna…" I hooked my thumb over my shoulder in her direction, gesturing awkwardly that I would follow her as Isobel laid into him. Chase rolled her eyes as I walked away, leaving them to rein in Adrian's mouth.

Kristine angrily pulled paperback copies of the book from a box under the promotional table, slamming them down on the black tablecloth before repeating the process.

"What did those poor books do to you?" I almost stepped back at the glare she aimed in my direction, but I knew she wasn't mad at me. She knew I had no more control over Adrian's mouth than the rest of us.

"Fanny likes it rough," she huffed, wiping her hands on her dress pants and turning toward me. "Sorry," she sighed. "I didn't mean to snap at you. He gets under my skin. You'd think he was a grown adult by his looks, but nope. There's a perverted little asshole with the IQ of a toddler trapped inside all that bulk."

"Yeah, I don't think his filter is broken. He never had one to begin with."

"I just don't understand how Isobel can put up with that." She waved her hand angrily in his direction. "She's got to have more self-respect than that. He's horrible."

"Maybe she sees something in him no one else does," I said quietly, leaning to the side to make eye contact. "We both know that appearances can be deceiving."

Her eyes flashed something that looked like understanding, and she nodded tightly before she handed me a stack of books, pointing to the table by the door where Diana was set up with her team. "I think they're almost out."

She may have been dismissing me for the moment, but I knew my comment made her think about what people said about her outward impressions. The tough outer shell may have been in place around everyone else, but I'd seen the real woman behind her defenses.

I WATCHED FROM THE opposite side of the room as Kristine hugged a tall, dark-haired woman, talking animatedly before she shook hands with the man at her side. Chase was excited to see the couple as well, and they all chatted, surprisingly, Evan included, before Isobel grabbed the authors and steered them toward the stage.

My curiosity was piqued about who their guests were, but with the subtle choker around the woman's neck and the possessive hand on her back, I figured this was the Dominant and his submissive they'd worked with while writing. Kristine also knew them, and I realized she must be the blogger supplying her little black box. I wondered if it was inappropriate to thank her for the gifts she sent. What was the etiquette for showing appreciation to someone who supplied a toy that allowed you to give your not-a-girlfriend multiples?

"You can join them." Diana had been utilizing me at the check-in table, but now that things were getting started, arrivals had slowed.

"You sure you don't need me?"

"We've got this covered," she assured. "Not my first rodeo, remember? Thanks for the backup."

Kristine was standing by herself, nursing a drink, as she watched Chase and Evan get pulled up onto the stage with Isobel. Adrian still looked like a chastised puppy as he stood off to the side, waiting.

"Drinking on the job?" I teased, knowing that she likely had soda with a cherry inside her glass.

"Yup. I thought, since Adrian can get away with it, why the hell not?"

Leaning forward to sniff at her glass, my suspicions were confirmed. "Hitting the hard stuff, huh?"

"Stop it." She swatted at my shoulder half-heartedly as she looked everywhere but at me.

"How're you holding up?" I asked as I took in her tense posture.

"You act like I'm going to fall apart under the pressure. I can handle myself just fine at these things."

"I know you can." She was more than capable of handling tasks that would make most people balk. "I just know you don't like these things."

"Not like I have a choice," she commented, her head turning to follow Evan out the side door of the ballroom. "Where's he going?"

"Maybe to get some air?"

Her eyes flashed toward Chase, narrowing as she stood next to a tall guy who'd come in the same time as the Dom and the sex toy blogger. A tall, slender woman approached them, a calculated smile pulling at her overly filled lips.

"Why don't you check on your guy while I check in with Chase?" Kristine placed her now empty glass on the table to our side before she nodded toward the door Evan had escaped through. "Something doesn't feel right."

"On it." The hallway was quiet as I pushed the door open, Evan nowhere in sight. Hmm.

Following the hall to the left, there were two empty smaller meeting rooms, but no Evan. Turning around, I walked back toward the hotel lobby, checking the hallway with the conference rooms, but all the lights were turned off.

Something did feel off as I turned back, heading down the hallway toward the main entrance of the ballroom. Evan was releasing the door handle as he turned in my direction, his face drained of all color. He staggered toward the hotel entrance as I tried to cross the lobby quickly, dodging people here for the launch and hotel guests as he fled.

I watched as the tall woman Chase had been talking to staggered out the door behind him, framed by two security officers, a trickle of blood running from her nose. They disappeared out the front doors as I wove through the last of the crowd, yanking open the door and holding it for a couple coming in with suitcases.

The woman had cornered Evan outside the building, gesturing wildly as he backed away from her, shaking his head. Who the fuck was she?

"Wait!" I yelled as I pulled open the outside door, watching helplessly as Evan closed the door of a cab at the curb, slumping against the seat with his head in his hands.

Shit.

TWENTY-THREE

KRISTINE

BOSTON

GODDAMMIT. THIS WAS NOT how I planned on spending my evening. I just wanted to enjoy the open bar and talk to interesting people. I didn't want to deal with this whole soap opera bullshit.

None of us had expected Evan's old girlfriend, Simone, to show up tonight. Adrian filled us in on their fucked up prior relationship and how she was why he now lived in seclusion. Chase seemed to know more of the story, but she was close-lipped as she stood with an ice pack on her knuckles.

She'd punched the bitch in the face when Simone cornered Chase and her friend earlier. I felt something wasn't right when I saw Chase's body language while they were talking, but Sam and I were too late to stop the explosion. Evan had seen them talking and taken off, leaving us to deal with the aftermath.

"Chase? Are you okay?" She was staring off toward the doors to the ballroom, waiting for Evan to reappear magically. I hated to break it to her, but the dude had fled like a felon on the run from the police, which was why I'd sent Sam after him earlier—clearly to no avail.

"What?" Chase flexed her hand as she looked at me, but her eyes didn't quite focus. Her knuckles had started to swell a little, but I was proud of the punch she'd landed on that little twat waffle.

"Honey, maybe you need to sit down." I took her arm and steered her toward an open table, helping her sit in an empty chair.

"I'm okay. I'm just worried." She continued to stare at the doorway to the ballroom, but we both knew Evan wasn't walking back through those doors any time soon.

"Hey, slugger, I managed to get that shrew barred from the premises," Isobel said to Chase in a soft voice as she took the seat beside her.

"We also convinced her it was in her best interest not to file charges or write anything inflammatory because her boss might have to find out that she stole their pass to this event," Diana spoke up from behind me in her usual no-nonsense tone.

"Ugh. What a piece of trash," I sighed. That woman was just a nasty, entitled wannabe. I could smell the jealousy from a mile away.

"An expensive piece of trash," Sam added as he stepped in behind me, his chest heaving from his wild dash through the lobby moments earlier. He'd tried to chase Evan, but when he took off in a cab...

"What?" Was she a prostitute or something?

"Didn't you notice the designer labels she was wearing?"

I looked at him like he'd grown another head. "Okay, dude, I know we let my brother think you were gay, but you're a straight guy. What exactly do you know about labels?"

"I have older sisters, and she had those high heels that women like with the red soles." Wow, maybe his observational skills were more up to par than I'd given him credit. A man who could identify Louboutins was kinda hot. It was still weird as fuck, though. "Pretty sure she had a Birkin handbag too."

"I don't know who you are..." I stared back at him with wide eyes.

"Oh, come on. My sister told her husband she wanted a Birkin bag for her next birthday, and he told her when hell freezes over. I may have googled it because I wanted to see what the hype was about."

"You're seriously such a goober," I laughed as I saw his cheeks turn pink in embarrassment.

"So, what is that bitch doing with twenty thousand in accessories?" Isobel asked as she pulled out her phone. I had a feeling Simone Woods was about to get hardcore internet stalked. "Not exactly something her income could justify. You probably get advances larger than her annual salary."

"I think you can rule out a sugar daddy because it sure as hell isn't anything freaky in bed." Chase's quiet voice was full of venom, making me laugh a little.

"Damn...she did seem like there was a stick shoved up her ass, probably in between her cheek implants," I agreed.

Chase's friend, Talia, approached the table with a wide smile. She and her male companion, Emory, had missed all the commotion. "Did someone say freaky in bed?"

Talia settled behind Chase and began to massage her shoulders. I loved Tal. She was always fun to interact with. I'd met her at Chase's book release a few years ago, and she was my sex toy guru. She'd hooked me up with a few things I knew I'd never want to live without again, including the rabbit Sam had performed magic tricks with.

"Has he come back yet?" The new guy looked distraught. I hadn't met him before, but I knew he was a part of the scene.

"Not yet," Sam shook his head. "Want to come with me to check their room?"

"Sure, man. I'm so sorry, Chase. I didn't know she would go all psycho ex-girlfriend until it was too late," he apologized, looking down at his friend with sympathy.

"Nathan, there was no way for you to know," she sighed tiredly, and I could see the adrenaline wearing off from her confrontation. Chase was starting to deflate the longer she sat there.

"Still doesn't make me feel any less guilty." I felt bad for Nathan, but that woman would have found a way to cause trouble even without his accidental introduction.

"I'll check in at the desk and leave him a message should he come back here on his own," Emory told us as he stepped in next to his partner, who was still comforting Chase.

"That's probably smart. Maybe let them know we also have his cell phone," Diana agreed.

"Do you think they'd have security footage of the main entrance?" Talia asked, nodding at a camera mounted in the corner of the room.

"On it." That was a great idea. "Emory and I can talk to the concierge and see what we can find out."

He nodded, gesturing toward the door before he pulled Talia into his chest, whispering in her ear and kissing her cheek. "Let's see if we can figure out which cab company he used."

I followed Emory out of the ballroom and down a hallway toward the main lobby. A tall man in a suit was behind the computer at the check-in desk.

"May I help you?" he asked with a welcoming smile. "I'm the hotel manager."

"Hello, Sir. We're here with the party for the publishing house. We've got an issue with one of our writers. Do you, by chance, have security cameras?" I asked in a sweet voice. He didn't need to see the inner bitch come out to play yet.

"Of course, but usually, we don't share footage unless a law enforcement agency requests it."

He looked a little startled at the wide smile I gave him. "Well, you see, one of your employees gave someone entrance to the ballroom we believe was stalking one of our writers..."

He immediately straightened, nervously adjusting his tie.

Gotcha.

"I apologize, Miss...but..." he rambled.

I looked at his name and raised an eyebrow as I delivered what I hoped would be our ticket. "Mr. Blithe, I would hate to have to alert the press gathered in the ballroom to the hotel security's little mistake. It'd be a real shame for them to question the reputation of such a fine hotel chain."

He visibly swallowed as I saw Emory smirk out of the corner of my eye. I was glad he didn't try to shoulder me out of the way to take over. *Smart man.*

"Well. It couldn't hurt to take a peek and see if we can come to a quiet resolution." So, Mr. Blithe was a smart man too.

"That sounds like a wonderful idea."

"Let me get someone to cover the desk, and you can join me in the security office." He picked up a phone, and within minutes a young woman was able to take his place at the front desk.

"Right this way..." He gestured toward a door with an electronic pad on the wall next to it labeled 'authorized staff only.' A little green light appeared as he swept a card he pulled from his pocket over it. Emory held the door open for me, and we followed Mr. Blithe down a well-lit hallway.

"Here we go," he said, knocking on a door labeled 'Security Technology.'

A short man with dark hair and glasses answered the door and immediately straightened his posture as he saw the general manager standing there.

"Yes?" the man asked, pushing his glasses up his nose with a strategically placed finger on the bridge.

"These people need to access some of the security footage from the main entrance," Mr. Blithe told him.

"Do they have a warrant?" the younger man asked, giving Emory and me a skeptical once over.

"Howard." Mr. Blithe scolded, clearly irritated with his employee.

"I'm just shittin' you. Come on in." Howard laughed as his supervisor huffed from the doorway.

"You can sit there," he instructed as he lifted a box full of random cables off a chair and patted the seat.

"Sorry. I don't get many visitors, so I just have the one," he told Emory, who was standing behind me.

"That's fine. I think I'll manage." Emory's face was a blank mask of indifference. He was intimidating when he wanted to be.

Howard started typing something into his laptop and then turned a computer monitor on his desk to face us. "So, what kind of time frame are we looking at?"

Emory glanced at his watch. "About half an hour ago. The main entrance near the valet stand. We need the name of a taxi company."

"Male? female?" Howard inquired.

"Male, slim athletic build. Gray suit. Just over six feet. Fairly sure he was wearing glasses. Was probably freaking the fuck out." Sometimes having a photographic memory came in handy.

"White, in his late twenties. Brown hair," Emory chimed in over my shoulder.

"Okay. Let me pull up that segment, and we can go through in fast forward. Let me know when I need to stop," Howard instructed. The footage showed a split-screen of the main entrance and a direct view of the valet stand.

It began playing, and we watched people go in and out, dropping cars off. Taxis pulled up just past the valet podium.

"Stop!" Emory called out.

Howard slowed the feed and made it skip back about a minute. We watched Evan, visibly distressed—pulling on his hair—walk out the entrance and start pacing just to the side of the doors.

Moments later, *Cuntzilla* walked out the door and saw him pacing. The bitch smiled as she sidled up next to him and said something that made his entire body tense.

"Grr..." Howard looked over at me in surprise as I growled at the screen. I really did not like that woman.

"Calm down, killer." Emory placed a hand on my shoulder. "Do the exterior cameras have audio?"

"Unfortunately, no," the tech responded, shaking his head. "Not this set."

I watched as the she-devil on the screen pressed up against him, running her hand down his front. He grimaced and pushed her off. Guess bleeding psychos with the start of double black eyes didn't do it for him.

She started flailing her chicken arms around, and he looked at her in shock. He freaked out when she tried to touch him again, and a taxi pulled up simultaneously.

Evan looked toward the entrance, where Sam was barely visible coming into the frame inside the doors, back to the crazy *bunny-boiler*, and then turned and bolted for the cab.

"Shit." I sighed. No wonder he ran. Psycho ex-girlfriend came at him when he was alone.

"Pause it," Emory instructed as the exterior-facing camera caught the side of the cab at the curb. Howard paused the screen and zoomed in on the cab company logo and a strategically placed phone number.

"Got it." Emory was already typing it into his phone. "Can you zoom in on the car tag number?"

The screen zoomed in and then pixelated. You could make out the first four characters of an identification number.

"Let me see what I can find out," Emory told us before he stepped out into the hallway.

"Who is that lovely specimen?" Howard asked, pointing at the screen.

"Oh, you don't want to go there. Black-eyed pea brain is a legit psycho." Simone was seen yelling at the valet in the frozen frame.

"Not her. Him." Howard pointed at the screenshot of the front entrance, where Sam was mid-stride with a fierce look on his face.

"Mine." I arched an eyebrow, then immediately sobered as I realized what I said.

Shit.

"Damn, girl. Get it," he chuckled, winking at me. Great. At least Sam wasn't here to witness this. His ego would become even more inflated. And it wouldn't make the situation between us any easier.

"Okay, so good news and bad news." Emory returned to the office with a grimace, still looking at the phone in his hand.

"Go with the bad..."

"Evan had a panic attack in the cab, and the driver kicked him out."

"What the fuck? They kicked a guy having a panic attack out on the street?" What the hell kind of cab company did that?

"In fact, it was some kind of parking lot, apparently, but don't worry, I told the dispatcher that he would be dealt with later," Emory said with a wry grin.

"So, what's the good news?"

"I've got an address of where he was dropped off. Chances are that he'll probably still be in the vicinity," Emory said, holding up his phone with a map displayed on the screen. At least we had somewhere to start.

"Shit. Let's hope the poor dude didn't get jumped." I'd seen people mid-panic attack before; that was a vulnerable state to be in and then dumped on the street.

"I'm gonna call Nathan and see if he can come with me to look. You fly out in the morning, so you should probably go help with Chase," Emory said quietly, not leaving any room for argument.

"Are you sure?" I wanted to help and felt like I was getting thrown on babysitting duty.

"It's getting late. You know Isobel won't let you delay your travel plans. Someone should get some sleep tonight. We'll find him."

"Is there any other footage you guys need?" I'd almost forgotten Howard was still waiting for us.

"Can you email me the clip of that woman confronting the guy in the gray suit?" I wanted proof if we needed to go after her. Isobel may have been able to get rid of her temporarily, but if she came after Chase or Evan again, I wasn't above calling in someone to make it clear she was to keep her distance—permanently.

He started typing again and asked for my email. Seconds later, my phone vibrated with a message.

"I also included a gif of your man striding out that door." Howard winked. "He's hot AF."

"Your man?" Emory asked with wide eyes.

I shook my head and fought the urge to throw things at Howie's head. "Don't worry about it, Em."

We thanked Howard for his help and walked back down the hall to the front desk. The manager wasn't there, so we returned to check in with the others.

"Hey *mehr*, how is she?" Emory asked, putting his arm around Talia's back. Chase was seated at the table blankly, staring down at her hands.

It looked like most of the press had called it a night and left. Only a few stragglers at the bar and people from in-house at the publishing company remained.

"No luck?" Sam stepped in behind me with his hand touching my back. I managed to hold still despite the jolt I felt at the contact.

I couldn't believe what I'd said in that office because I didn't get attached. I didn't have a real claim on Sam, and I certainly didn't need to continue obsessing over this limbo we'd been in for the last several weeks. "We got a lead, but no. We don't know exactly where he is now."

Nathan joined us a few minutes later, and we quietly decided Talia, and I would get Chase to bed while the guys went to look for Evan.

"I've got an idea," Sam said suddenly.

"We're desperate enough. Let's hear it." He narrowed his eyes at me before looking back at the group.

"Evan's got an Apple Watch."

Shooting a skeptical look in his direction, I wasn't sure how that was helpful. "This is your brilliant idea?"

"Let him finish. I think I know where he's going with this," Em scolded, and I closed my mouth. The dude had the intimidating Dominant persona down pat.

"Chase, do you happen to know his passcode?" Sam pulled Evan's phone out of his pocket, where he'd put it after Evan had entrusted him with it earlier in the night, and slid it across the table. She picked it up slowly and let out a shuddering breath before she typed in a code.

"Nicely done." I looked back at Sam. His eyes met mine, and I found myself unable to look away from the intense blue.

"We can track his watch and maybe ping it. Hopefully, that'll help us track him down," Sam explained.

"You have to be on a plane first thing tomorrow," Isobel said as she pointed at the both of us. I guess Sam was out of the rescue squad.

"It's fine, Sam. Nathan and I got it from here. Thanks for helping us narrow the field."

"We'll let you know once we've got him," Nathan assured, casting another guilty smile at Chase.

"Please call and let me know he's alright." She sounded exhausted. It was time to get her to bed.

"Alright then. Up you go," Talia urged Chase with an arm around her waist. She leaned heavily on her, and I followed as they headed toward the elevator. She rambled a little as we rode the elevator up, clearly very concerned for her partner. Talia and I helped her into her suite and cringed when we saw the rose petals on the bed.

Dammit, Evan... Fucking romantic gestures.

"Okay. It's time for the bathroom." Talia led her through the suite toward the open bathroom door. Chase didn't fight her, aimlessly following. "Can you grab her something to slip into?"

I nodded and walked toward the two black suitcases in the open closet. Luckily, they were unlocked. So, I hoisted them both up on the bed and unzipped them.

The first bag had men's clothes, but I saw something pink sticking out of the corner of the stack of clothes. I looked to the bathroom quickly and then lifted the shirt covering it.

"Damn, dude," I breathed out as I took in the bright pink rabbit sitting in Evan's suitcase. That book really did bring him out of his shell.

The second bag was Chase's. I grabbed a pair of shorts and a tank before re-zipping it and heading to the bathroom. Chase was standing in her underwear, swaying slightly as she brushed her teeth. The shock of the evening had finally hit her. I just hoped she could hold herself together because our schedule for the next few days had extraordinarily little wiggle room.

"Thanks. I got it from here if you need to get some rest," Talia assured me, pulling the clothes out of my hands.

"You've got to see what's in Evan's suitcase," I whispered in her ear. She gave me a quizzical look. "Bright pink vibrator."

"Oh! I know which one you're talking about." Her eyes lit up. "Good for him. I'll send you the information about it. You'd like it. It's the updated version of that blue one I sent you last year."

"Alright. You know I'm up for your recommendations," I laughed, remembering the night that Sam had used that very model to make me come harder than I ever had in my life.

Quickly saying good night to Chase, I returned to my room down the hallway. Sam and I were sharing a two-bedroom suite. Adrian had done something nice for once, but it only made my resolve to avoid Sam crumble. It'd be easier to stop thinking about him with more locked doors in between us.

The lights were off when I returned to the room, so I thought he'd gone to bed. Boy, was I wrong. He came out of the bathroom shirtless right as I walked past his door. Water droplets dotted his chest and slowly ran down the exposed skin as they disappeared into the dark fabric of his low-slung pajama bottoms. His hair curled slightly at the ends, still damp from his shower.

My mouth went dry as I stared openly at the tan, muscular chest on display. I'd seen and touched that chest dozens of times over the last several months, but damn, that was a fine-looking man.

Fuck. I was screwed. I was never going to be able to resist Sam.

TWENTY-FOUR

SAM

BOSTON

SLEEP HAD BEEN ELUSIVE, especially knowing Kristine was in the next room. She'd seemed startled to see me standing in the doorway shirtless when she'd gotten back from dealing with Chase last night, but I wasn't sorry. She may be determined to put space between us, but I wouldn't make it easy. It was hard—so very hard—to go from constant sex to nothing in the span of a few weeks. She could suffer for a bit like I'd been suffering.

My dick was bound to start chafing if I had to keep whacking off to be able to stand in the same room with her. What drove me nuts was when she acted like we'd never been more than just colleagues. Besides the occasional lingering glance, she'd reverted to pre-collaboration Kristine, and I was left trying to keep up with these platonic interactions like I didn't actively imagine her naked.

It was even harder—yes, I was fixated on that word lately—with Chase and Evan mauling each other at every opportunity. I knew we'd thought his imagination had improved while they were collaborating but judging by how they behaved around each other while we were doing the press training, I was convinced those two had done some *very* hands-on research.

I wasn't sure what I expected last night when I'd been introduced to her friends Emory, Talia, and Nathan, but it was clear those three had imparted quite the kinky sexual education on Evan. He didn't seem like the same person from six months ago who'd come to the office to take care of his last set of contracts under major duress.

Until the party, he'd been funny and social—and completely smitten with Chase—until Simone had shown up. She'd pushed him right back to where he was when he went into hiding. He was nervous and shaky as I'd tried to catch him before he jumped in the cab, but he was too fast.

My phone was filled with text messages, a few from Isobel letting us know that he'd been found, but as far as I knew, he still hadn't shown up at the hotel, and we needed to leave shortly to head to the airport. This tour was waiting for no man, and I hoped Chase was up to the challenge of flying solo because all our futures depended on this tour going well.

It was already bound to be strained if Kristine and I continued to be forced to share hotel rooms. At least we were supposed to be in separate rooms for the rest of the tour. Knowing a thin wall was the only thing keeping me away from her last night was torture. I'd had to talk myself out of knocking on her door at least a dozen times.

"Hey, you awake?" Kristine's voice carried through the door, pulling my attention away from my messages. I'd packed last night, so all I needed to do was put on my shoes, and I'd be ready to go.

"Yeah, just give me a sex... I mean, sec." *God, Sam, could you be more obvious?*

"I'm going to pick up some coffee downstairs. Isobel still hasn't heard from Chase, and they'll be here in a half hour to take us to the airport."

"Okay, I'll head down after I'm done here. Just need to pack up my laptop."

She was still standing in the little sitting area in the middle of our small suite when I left my room, sliding her tablet into her bag.

"Do you want me to grab you something, or...?" She trailed off, shifting her hair behind her shoulders after she pulled on her bag.

"Nah, you go on ahead. I can head down there and meet Adrian while you're retrieving Chase. Have you heard anything more about Evan's whereabouts?"

"No. Should we be worried? Chase struggled last night, and if he doesn't show up, we'll all be fricking screwed. Do you think she can pull this tour off by herself? Sloane still doesn't know what's happening, but it's only a matter of time, right?"

"Take a breath." It was clear Kristine was getting herself a little worked up about it. But we had to try to make do with what we had right now and keep the one writer we had on track. "Just go sort out Chase. I'm sure Diana will have a plan." That was her job. The public relations department's entire job was to manage situations like this. She'd know what we needed to do until we determined whether Evan was joining us. "We can still pull this off. I know we can. Let's focus on what we can control and try to keep up with the schedule as planned."

"Really? You're trying to pep talk me right now?"

"We don't have a choice right now. We either fake it until we make it or return to the office and turn in our resignations now."

"That's a little too fricking dramatic, Sam. Even for you." A hint of a smile pulled at the corner of her mouth, and I could tell she was calming down a little.

"Yes, because I'm the one who has trouble with dramatics."

She narrowed her eyes, took a deep breath, and pulled up the handle on her rolling luggage, giving me one last skeptical glance before she was out the door.

At least she was still talking to me, even if she pretended we didn't mean more to each other.

"Hey, Sammy boy, where's everyone else?" Adrian was still in one of the chairs in the lobby, feet up on the coffee table, while Isobel stood off to the side of the main entrance on her cell phone. She didn't look particularly happy about her conversation, so I anticipated she either had no news about Evan or news none of us wanted to hear.

"Kristine went to check on Chase. Any word yet?"

"Isobel took a call a few minutes ago. I think it was from one of Chase's kinky friends. Hopefully, they managed to track him down because we're cutting it close on the schedule as it is."

"You're worried about the schedule right now, really?"

"What?"

"One of your authors had a panic attack and went missing overnight, and all you care about is the damn schedule for the tour? You're unbelievable sometimes." He could at least pretend to give a shit about Evan.

"Hey, you're twisting my words. Of course, I care about Evan, but I can't change the fact he isn't here."

Isobel was only a few steps away, angrily jabbing at her smartphone as she joined us. "He's safe," she sighed as she paced back and forth behind Adrian's chair. "But he's still asleep and was sick half the night. We don't have time to wait for him to get cleaned up. He's never going to make it on the flight to Chicago. I'm trying to secure him a seat on a later flight, but I can't promise anything."

"Fuck," Adrian muttered.

"What do you need from us? Have you talked to Diana yet?" I asked as Isobel continued to look down at the screen on her phone.

"She said you can stick to the schedule as planned. Obviously, she'll be there to facilitate, but it all depends on what state Chase is in. She's usually rather good at rolling with the punches when things change at the last minute, but this is a pretty big punch."

A few moments later, Kristine stepped out of the elevator with a slightly disheveled Chase in tow. She looked like she'd slept better than I had, but there was a tightness in her mouth I wasn't used to seeing. She was typically a vibrant, sarcastic force to be reckoned with, but right now, she looked vulnerable.

KRISTINE WAS IN A foul mood, snapping at everyone once we got to the airport. I helped Chase find a charger for her dead battery in the gift shop. Then, I tried to keep her occupied while Diana spent half the morning talking on her phone, and Kristine glared at everyone.

The Chicago leg of the tour was starting off great.

Chase got confirmation from Nathan that Evan was on his way, but we still had no idea when he'd join us when our flight took off.

I tried to initiate some small talk on the plane to distract her, but it was clear no one was in the mood to chat. Kristine put in her earbuds and ignored me the entire flight, so I opened my tablet and worked on edits to the fantasy manuscript.

We were all on edge with Evan absent, going through the motions as we landed and retrieved our luggage. Chase was upset they had no way to contact Evan after Kristine discovered he'd lost his phone down a sewer grate when Emory and Nathan tracked him down. They'd used it to ping his location, but he'd somehow dropped it outside the bar they found him in.

He was supposedly headed toward the hotel, and then the airport, but no one had heard from him directly.

KRISTINE AND I HAD adjoining rooms on a different floor than everyone else's at the hotel, so we parted at the elevator with instructions from Diana to meet up with her later to head to the first venue.

I spent the next several hours working on the manuscript, making some good headway and wondering what Kristine thought as she looked through the same pages. Her style was completely different than mine, but I knew she'd have some clever suggestions for the few plot holes I'd picked up as I read through.

The shower had turned on briefly in her room, but she was otherwise silent as I continued to work. After this morning, I knew she wouldn't answer if I knocked on the door, but she had a few days to cool off. I wasn't giving her the option to back out of our plans at the end of the week.

Thankfully our incomplete team was able to get to the book reading and keep to the schedule even if we were down an author. At least Evan already had a reputation for being reclusive to pass off as a temporary excuse for his absence.

"She's doing amazing," Kristine whispered as we watched from our spots at the side of the room during Chase's reading. You'd never have guessed the events of the last twelve hours as her confident voice rang out, flawlessly reading the passage I'd picked out for today. Knowing you'd helped an author polish a powerful passage in their book was a heady feeling.

Chase and Evan's styles complemented one another; this book was the best of their strengths, her descriptive language combined with his ability to weave a plot.

"She's got this," I smiled, oddly proud that we got to be an integral part of this process.

When she finished reading, and Diana opened the floor for questions, I cringed when Kristine's hand shot up.

"I've got a question..."

"Go ahead," Chase nodded.

"So, when developing a book like this, a certain amount of research goes into making sure things seem believable." Kristine paused, her eyes scanning the room and her body tensing as she spotted something across the room. I followed her gaze, and my eyes widened as I watched Evan sit in a seat toward the back.

"Go on," Chase's voice rang out over the microphone, and my eyes returned to her as Kristine finished asking her question.

My attention was split, half-listening to Chase's answer and watching Evan. A small hand clasped mine, and I glanced down at Kristine, our eyes meeting for a loaded moment as we watched everything unfold.

Evan's hand shot up, causing Kristine to squeeze my hand as he stepped into view. My pulse raced as we watched them meet in the center of the aisle, Evan pulling Chase in for a passionate kiss.

"Get a room!" Kristine yelled, but when she looked back at me, her eyes were full of something other than hostility for once. Maybe she wasn't as far away as she seemed sometimes.

"So, YOU TWO ARE the brains of the operation?" Kelly, Evan's elder sister, joked from her seat down the bar where we'd escaped after our professional obligations were fulfilled.

"I'm more of an editing ninja. Get in there, fix the chaos, and move on," Kristine tittered. Of course, she would downplay her skills. She avoided outright boasting in the office but was more than competent at her job.

I'd been dragged out to a local restaurant a few blocks away from our hotel with Kelly and Kristine after the two lovebirds had disappeared for the night at the end of the book signing. The three of us were seated at the bar, the two women bantering like they were the best of friends. Kelly was curious about our jobs, but Kristine was playing down her part in the editing process.

"But you could be an editorial samurai," I smirked as I tilted my bottle back and winked at her.

"I generally try to avoid swords," Kristine laughed, making eye contact with me behind Kelly's back.

"Oh, I didn't realize you were a lesbian." Kelly's comment caused me to sputter loudly, choking down my beer as she swiveled on her barstool to face me. "You alright there, Sam?"

"Yup," I breathed heavily before I took another sip, trying to cool the burning in my throat. "I'm good."

Kristine still smirked at me, enjoying my discomfort at Kelly's comment. I could vouch firsthand that Kristine was definitely not a lesbian. Bi, maybe—we hadn't exchanged our complete partner history—but she most certainly liked dick. I knew that much. And given the twitch in my pants, my dick hadn't forgotten how much it liked her, either.

At least I didn't have to feel guilty about whacking off in my shower tomorrow morning since we were in separate rooms. This entire book tour would be a lengthy test of self-restraint and patience. The proximity was good for forcing Kristine to spend time with me because she had nowhere to hide, but I couldn't push her too hard. Her mood was already precarious.

"It's alright if you are," Kelly assured Kristine as she glanced in my direction with a wide smile. "There's nothing wrong with appreciating a beautiful woman."

Before Kristine, I may have given her a second glance or even tried to take her back to my room, but as of late, I only had eyes for the sassy woman on her other side. And going after my author's sister had to violate all kinds of ethics guidelines. Not that starting an office affair was much better. At least I hadn't been the only instigator in that. She pursued me as much as I did her in the beginning, the feel of her underneath me proving addicting.

And here I was weeks later, still twitching for a fix.

"Sorry to disappoint," Kristine smirked, licking her lips before she drained her beer. "I'm very much a fan of the masculine touch."

"Same, girl. Same," Kelly laughed as she looked over toward me again.

Kristine was drunk by the time we left the bar, clinging to my arm as we poured an equally drunk Kelly into an Uber before we walked back toward the hotel a few blocks away.

"She kept staring at you," Kristine pouted, her voice slurring subtly. "I didn't like it."

"Hmm," I hummed, refraining from fueling her spark of misplaced, intoxicated jealousy.

"She was hot," she giggled. "If I liked women, I'd tap that. I bet you'd like to watch that, Sam."

Nope. Not commenting on that one.

"Have you ever watched two women kiss?" she asked as she snuggled closer to my side. She wasn't seeking warmth; the summer heat had barely faded when the sun went down. I caught her hand as she reached for my belt loop, holding it tightly to my chest as I guided her down the sidewalk. "Oh, come on, you're no fun. Aren't you going to answer my question?"

"No."

"No, you've never watched, or no, you're not answering?"

I had—much more than that, in fact—but it felt like a lifetime ago since I'd spent the night with two eager university cheerleaders who liked to share. I wasn't that person anymore.

"We need to get you to bed," I changed the subject as I led her toward the entrance, pulling open the door as the valet shot me an amused look.

"Hmmm. Yes, please," she hummed as she dug her fingernails into my chest through my shirt. "Tuck me in, Spammy."

"Where's your room key?" I asked as I guided her inside the first open elevator, pressing the button for our floor before I disentangled her from me and leaned against the opposite side of the elevator.

"In my bra," she giggled, unbuttoning the top button on her blouse and pulling out the little piece of plastic. "Or did you want to look for it?" she teased, her fingers fumbling as she tried to put it back in her hiding place. She was hammered, and I was thankful she had me to put her into bed and not a random stranger.

"I'm good. You hold onto that."

"Geez," she sighed. "For someone so desperate to get into my pants a few weeks ago, you sure have changed your mind."

Knowing that she was trying to get a reaction, I took a step toward her, leaning over her as I brushed her hair aside. Her eyes closed, and her soft mouth dropped open as I whispered in her ear.

"We both know if I took advantage of you tonight, you'd never forgive me for exploiting a moment of weakness. I want you sober when you beg me to kiss you again."

"Pffft," she scoffed, pushing me away with a hand in the center of my chest. "Don't hold your breath."

"Don't worry," I laughed as the elevator stopped on our floor, and I led her down the hallway to our rooms a few doors down. Taking the key card out of her hand, I opened her door and steered her inside. "I won't be holding my breath for long."

Her eyes flashed with surprise as I let the door swing closed in her face, quickly escaping inside my room with a shake of my head.

Chapter
TWENTY-FIVE

KRISTINE

CHICAGO

Sam was quiet the next morning, meeting me at the elevator with a steaming coffee cup and a frown. "You feeling alright?"

I nodded, taking it from him and raising my cup up to my lips, inhaling the rich aroma of dark roast coffee before I took a hesitant sip. My recollection of the events of the previous evening was blurry, but I knew I'd made an ass of myself. Acting jealous of Kelly, practically throwing myself at Sam on the sidewalk and again in the elevator.

My fuzzy brain couldn't remember everything he'd said at my door, but I knew he'd said something about not holding his breath for long and me begging him to kiss me. He'd likely be asphyxiating before that happened.

"I'm fine. Just a little tired. Nothing a gallon of coffee and some water won't fix," I shrugged as I avoided eye contact. We both knew I was the source of the tension between us, but I wasn't sure how to ease up and maintain the distance I knew I needed to protect myself.

Sam had already worked his way past my defenses more than once, and every time he smiled at me, I lost more and more control of my determination to keep him away. He'd already made me feel more needy and desperate than I liked, and it wasn't purely for his physical touch.

He understood me in a way that terrified and pissed me off equally.

"Do you have plans tomorrow?" he asked casually as he leaned into the corner of the elevator. I knew we had tomorrow off. Chase and Evan were heading to see his family after their signing in the morning. Diana assured us she had it handled, so she'd told us to take the day off while we could get it. The smart thing would be to buckle down and get more work done on my manuscript edits, but I hadn't made the smartest choices lately.

"What do you have in mind?"

He paused, cup midway to his mouth as he looked over at me, clearly not expecting me to agree to spend time with him.

"You've never been to Chicago before, right?"

I shook my head, refraining from telling him that domestic tourism was beneath Melissa Willard's standards. She'd prefer to take the corporate jet to Paris or Barcelona than to Chicago.

"Perfect. Let me take care of everything. I promise I'll show you an enjoyable time in the windy city."

Sam's good mood was oddly infectious for the rest of the day, and we easily worked side by side as Chase and Evan did their thing, my frame of mind lightening from my dark mood this morning. He hadn't brought up last night, clearly giving me a pass for acting like an asshole in front of him.

"You ready? Diana said we can take off." He pulled his messenger bag over his shoulder, gesturing for me to walk in front of him as I grabbed my bag. "I ordered an Uber already if you want to share. It's too hot to hike across the city in work clothes."

Sam had already ditched his suit jacket; his sleeves rolled up to his elbows. Forcing myself not to stare at the arm porn, I kept my eyes forward until we were outside on the sidewalk. Then I was hungrily taking in his muscles' strong play beneath all that tan skin as he opened the car door and held my hand to help me inside.

I clutched my bag in my lap as he placed his at his feet, using both hands to scroll through and answer the emails on his phone, the muscles flexing as his fingers flew across the screen. The humidity had caused his hair to curl lightly around the edges of his face, and I was practically panting as I watched a bead of sweat track down his neck and under his collar. There was clearly something wrong with me finding sweat sexy, but it made me recall how he looked sweaty and rumpled from other exertions.

My self-imposed chastity was backfiring the more time I spent with him. Maybe I *would* be begging him to kiss me. I was already imagining it. The soft feel of his lips on mine and how he sucked on my lower lip which made my toes curl. The feeling of his fingers in my hair or grasping my neck as he coaxed my lips apart with his tongue and...

"You coming?" Sam asked as he pushed the door open on his side of the car.

Not yet, Sam. Not yet.

"Yup." He hesitated at the squeak in my voice, searching my face as I tried to remain impassive. My neck felt hot as I placed my hand in his outstretched palm, letting him lead me inside the hotel. Tomorrow was going to be interesting.

My PHONE CHIRPED FROM my nightstand the next morning, earlier than I would have liked on a day I could have been sleeping in, but I'd already been awake for a few hours trying to get some work done. If I was going to lose a full day, I had to take time where I could get it, even if it meant sacrificing sleep.

> Sam: Whenever you're ready, I've got breakfast. Come get the sausage while it's hot.

Somehow, I doubted he was offering the kind of sausage I had been craving lately.

> Kristine: Let me throw on some shorts, and I'll be ready in 5 minutes.

> Sam: You don't need to get dressed for me. Come on over without pants. I won't judge.

Laughing, I sent him back an emoji with its eyebrow raised, receiving a crying laughing emoji in response.

> Sam: Worth a shot. I'll take off my pants if it helps you feel more comfortable.

> Kristine: Tease.

> Sam: Who said I'm teasing? I'll gladly walk around without pants for you.

> Kristine: Just walking around?

> Sam: Well, I can think of something more fun to do without our pants on, but I'll let you decide.

My heart fluttered as I rushed into the bathroom, checking the light makeup I'd put on after my shower early this morning. I'd let my hair dry in its natural waves, a ponytail holder on my wrist for when it inevitably got too hot to keep it down.

I'd spent more time than I wanted to admit rifling through my suitcase this morning for something casual, settling on a fitted tank top and a pair of high-waisted denim shorts. They were a little on the tight side, so I'd left them off while I worked, but I turned to check the fit in the mirror as I shimmied them over my hips, hoping it didn't look like I was trying too hard.

My phone buzzed again as I applied another coat of lip gloss, rubbing my lips together before I picked it up and glanced at Sam's text.

> *Sam: Your food is getting cold. I'm sure you look gorgeous.*

Those annoying butterflies were back as I crossed the room, grabbing my small purse before I knocked on the door to his room.

"I was right," he smiled as he opened the door, his fingers lingering on my hand as he pulled me inside his room. "Mmm. You smell good too."

I blushed as I focused on the tray on his made bed, two silver domes concealing the contents of both plates.

"Someone promised me food," I deflected as he sat down on one side, gesturing for me to sit across from him.

"I wasn't sure what you'd be in the mood for," he confessed, grasping the handles on the top of both domes. "So, we have carb overload and more meat than anyone should probably eat in one sitting."

The plate on the left had a steaming pile of pancakes on one side and a few slices of French toast with a generous dusting of powdered sugar on the other. He was right about the other plate. Crispy bacon pieces were piled high next to an equally impressive stack of sausage links.

"That's quite a lot of meat you've got there, Sam," I giggled, my eyes widening before I realized the joke I'd walked into.

"Nothing you can't handle, Kristine," he winked before picking up a piece of bacon and biting it. Maybe today would be more fun than I was expecting.

The next ten minutes had me practically squirming against his sheets as we ate companionably side by side. Sam offered me bites of rich, eggy, sweet French toast on his fork, dripping in syrup in between, practically devouring the entire pile of bacon.

I slapped his hand as he reached for the last piece, pointing the end of my fork at his face. "Hands off. That's my meat."

"So possessive," he laughed as he reached for it again, ignoring my glare and pushing my fork down with his other hand before he lifted the piece to my lips. "Don't worry. I'll share my meat with you anytime."

"Freak," I giggled, taking an overly large bite and fake moaning as I chewed, enjoying the predatory look in his eyes as he watched me lick my lips.

"You seem to like it." His voice was low as he popped the rest of the piece into his mouth, winking as my eyes widened when I realized he'd stolen the rest of it.

"You'll pay for that," I warned, jabbing my fork into the last breakfast sausage and turning away from his grabby hands.

"Bring it on," he laughed, watching me take a bite with rapt attention.

After our breakfast of foreplay, Sam requested an Uber and wouldn't tell me what our first destination would be. I tried to peek at his phone as we waited at the curb, but he shoved it into his pocket before I could wrestle it out of his hand as if that'd stop me.

"Chill. You'll like it, but you do need this," he laughed as he pressed a small plastic package into my hand. "Wait to open it until we get there."

Sam pointed out landmarks as we rode across the city. The traffic was busy but steadily moving as we worked toward Lake Michigan. I had a feeling I knew what we were doing when I saw the iconic Ferris wheel of Navy Pier come into view, but Sam was still tight-lipped.

"Boat tour?" I guessed as he tugged me out of the car and checked his watch, grasping my hand and weaving through the crowd toward the sidewalk to the right of the long pier.

"You'll see," he smiled as he looked back, squeezing my hand and tugging me along.

There were a few ferry boats moored at the dock, and I paused, watching the people file onto their berths. They were smaller than the ferries out of Boston Harbor to get to Nana's, but they looked fun enough.

"Come on," Sam tugged, gesturing with his head further down the pier. Once we passed the crowd, a smaller red boat sitting docked beside the larger ones became visible, a line of people chatting excitedly as a crew member unhooked the rope and waved the first few passengers forward. Sam pulled me after him, holding his phone out for them to scan his tickets before he grasped my hips and urged me onto the metal gangplank.

I glanced over my shoulder at him, laughing as he wiggled his eyebrows at me, nodding forward. He steered me to an empty row of seats toward the front, sliding in after me and throwing his arm over my shoulders as he leaned in close. "This work for you? Thought you might get bored on one of the other, more sedate, tours."

Before I could respond, a man with a megaphone stepped up in the front of the boat, and the crowd quieted down.

"Welcome aboard the extreme thrill sea dog ride of the Chicago lakefront. Are we ready to get wet?"

My eyes widened as I looked at Sam and down at the small package in my hand. Tearing it open, I saw a waterproof bag, the perfect size for slipping my purse and sweatshirt. "You planned this."

"Wouldn't want you to get too wet," he laughed, holding the bag open as I shoved my things inside, rolling the top and stowing it in the mesh pocket of the seat in front of me. He sat back and fastened his seat belt, and I followed suit, pulling the belt tight across my lap.

"We both know that's a lie," I chuckled as I leaned into his shoulder, not hesitating when he placed his hand palm-side-up on his thigh.

Grasping his hand, I smiled up at him, unable to resist his infectious good mood.

"YOU'VE GOT A LITTLE something..." I giggled as I gestured to the wet spot on the front of Sam's shorts. We'd both gotten soaked as the boat twisted and spun, picking up speed across the lake and spraying water all over the passengers. I had to admit, it was fun, and Sam didn't mind as I screamed, loving the way he kept pulling me into his side.

"Yeah..." he laughed, awkwardly pulling at the soaked material. "Didn't help that you were climbing in my lap and dripping your hair all over me when he started spinning the boat."

"You've never argued with me climbing into your lap before."

"Wasn't arguing this time either. Just looks like I can't control myself now," he laughed, pulling me in front of him and wrapping his arms around my waist, the tips of his wet hair tickling my cheek. "You'll just have to walk in front of me to hide my embarrassing wet spot."

"You just want to stare at my ass," I laughed and jumped forward when he mimed grabbing it and growled at me. "Pervert!"

"You like it," he smiled, taking my hand and pulling me back down the sidewalk toward the entrance to Navy Pier. "Let's go. We've got places to go and people to do."

"I think it's supposed to be people to see, Sam."

"Eh, I like my version better," he smirked, tugging me behind him again. Every time he reached for my hand, I found myself resisting less and less, enjoying that he'd planned this entire day for us to do something fun. His comments about me relaxing and letting my hair down had hit a sore spot with me before the tour had begun, but he was right. Sam away from the office, was funny and charming, relaxed in a way that I craved. He'd even played amateur tour guide on our walk north from the pier, pointing this way and that as he talked about nearby places.

A half-hour later, I followed Sam into yet another elevator, relaxed and content, forgetting that I was supposed to be keeping my distance from him. The reasons I'd given myself weeks ago didn't matter anymore. I liked spending time with him; he made me laugh, teasing me when I started taking things too seriously. Outside the pressure of the office, I craved Sam's attention, and when I wasn't afraid of someone from the office seeing us together it was easy to forget my reasons for pushing him away.

"You're not afraid of heights, are you?" he asked as he pulled my back into his chest in the corner of the crowded elevator. I'd seen the signs when we were entering the doors to the old Hancock Center for the Chicago 360 observation deck.

"Little too late for that now," I laughed as I watched the numbers rise rapidly on the panel next to the elevator doors.

"Just making sure," he whispered as his fingers brushed my sweaty hair off my shoulders. His lips traced the curve of my shoulder, and I closed my eyes, leaning back into him as his hands settled possessively on my stomach. "I should already know you're not afraid of anything."

He was wrong, though. I may not have been afraid of heights, but I was acutely terrified of falling for *him*. Every kind action, every patient smile, every time he did something goofy to make me laugh, and every sarcastic comment drew me in, reminding me that all I had to do was let him in, and he could be mine.

"It's even more impressive in the dark," Sam smiled as his long fingers traced my palm in line for Tilt, the ride that featured a movable bank of windows that leaned forward over the city.

"I bet you say that to all the girls," I laughed, shaking my head.

"You're the only girl I'm interested in impressing, in the dark or otherwise."

Warmth spread through me at his low chuckle, and I bit my tongue, afraid I'd confess how impressed I already was with him.

As I looked out at the bustling city moments later, adrenaline coursing through my system as the glass tilted forward, I tried to catalog this feeling. So, I could look back on it when I inevitably fucked up again. Sam's companionship already meant more to me than any promotion, but I'd never tell him that. How could I explain that he made me the person I wanted to be and keep my distance at the same time?

After this book tour, I knew I would either love or hate him, and I wasn't sure which possibility was more terrifying.

"Oh, come on. Just try it. I promise it's good," Sam laughed as I held up the piece of food he'd called a pizza in front of my face, studying the thick dough piled high with toppings.

"This is not pizza," I frowned, sniffing it experimentally. It smelled alright, but I was a New Yorker. Our pizza was thin and crispy, not whatever this was.

"Open your mouth," he urged, pressing his thumb in the center of my bottom lip. "You know you want to try it. Just a little. You can do it. I know you can. Just slide those sexy lips open for me, baby."

Heat flared through me at how he was staring at me and the deep voice he was using to coax me into doing what he wanted. A man trying to force-feed me shouldn't be sexy, but with Sam…everything made me think of sex. Especially when what he said would get me hot in another context.

"Fine," I sighed, covering his hand with mine and opening my mouth.

"That's it," he whispered, leaning close, his hot breath on my neck. "Take it. Just a little more."

"Mmm." I hummed as I bit down, and the flavors rushed along my tongue. It still wasn't what I was used to, but it was good. The spicy sausage and rich tomato sauce teased my taste buds for another bite.

"Good girl," he hummed, laughing when I took another bite and pushed my palm into his forehead as I pried the slice out of his hands. Narrowing my eyes, I finished the whole piece, enjoying his loud laughter as I grabbed another. "What did I tell you?" His voice was so smug, but he was right. Chicago-style pizza was better than I expected.

Instead of responding, I grabbed a large piece of pepperoni off his abandoned pizza, quickly shoving it in my mouth as I turned and flipped him off.

"Hurry up," he chuckled, watching me chew. "We've still got places to be."

"No," I shook my head as Sam grasped my hand, pulling me back toward him.

"Oh, come on, I won't show anyone. Please," he pouted as he wrapped his arm around my waist and held me against his chest. "Just for me. I won't post it anywhere."

"This is a little too touristy."

He tucked his face into my neck, rubbing his stubble against my cheek. "I hate to break it to you, but you've been doing touristy things all day."

"Yeah, but there's no evidence."

"I know," he laughed, tightening his grip on my waist and holding me in place as he quickly stretched out his arm, his phone aimed at where we were standing in front of the cloud gate in Millennium Park. "But humor me."

"You suck," I pouted as he rested his chin on my shoulder, gripping me tightly to his chest.

"You like me anyway," he whispered as he quickly snapped the picture, the sun glinting off the huge metal sculpture at his back. "Let's go. Only a few more hours until the sun starts to set."

Sam didn't let go of my hand once as he dragged me through lush park after lush park along the edge of Lake Michigan. Past fountains and playgrounds, the heat drew out the city's residents, enjoying the sunshine and the gorgeous weather. By the time he led me up to the Field Museum of Natural History front steps, I was hot and sweaty, but I didn't even notice as he dragged me through security and showed me his favorite exhibits.

We made our way through the museum campus, watching the sea turtle in the main tank at Shedd Aquarium, his hands tucked into my front pockets as I leaned back against his strong chest. He teased me later, whispering useless space facts in my ear as I tried to listen to the tour guide at the Adler Planetarium.

He held me close as I stood in the grass outside, watching the sun set behind the lake, having kicked off my shoes. I hadn't felt so relaxed in as long as I could remember, and when he kissed my neck, reminding me that we should grab a quick dinner and head back to the hotel soon, I closed my eyes and tried to remember the moment I knew I was likely in love with him.

"Did you get the updates to the schedule that Diana sent for tomorrow?" he asked as I leaned against his shoulder on the ride back to our hotel after stopping at a local burger restaurant for dinner and eating outside on their patio.

"No." To be honest, I hadn't checked my phone since this morning. Spending the day with Sam had been an escape from reality that I needed, but our lives would be thrown into chaos again tomorrow.

"It should be in your inbox. She just sent it over."

"Hmm." I didn't want to think about work. Today was perfect, and I was anxious about what it meant once we returned to the hotel. Sam had been affectionate all day, but besides suggestive, flirtatious comments and a few fleeting kisses to my neck and shoulders, he'd been the epitome of restraint. He'd teased me about begging for a kiss, but if he didn't kiss me soon, I might actually combust from pent-up sexual tension. It was taking all my self-restraint to keep from touching him.

"Are you alright?" His voice was low, his warm breath fanning through my hair as he hugged me to his side. The phone in his hand was open to his email client, showing multiple emails from Adrian and one from Sloane. She was confirming his virtual interview a week and a half from now.

"Fine," I whispered back, feeling the anxiety I'd been holding at bay start to creep back in now that we were headed back to reality.

"Come on, we've got an early start tomorrow," he smiled as he pulled the door open to the Uber moments later, helping me out of the car and ushering me through our hotel lobby and into the elevator. My hands were clenched into fists, trying to keep myself in the moment. I needed his presence to forget everything that was at stake. And how behind I already felt as the commitments of the tour kept me from working on my manuscript edits.

By the time we reached our rooms, I was on the verge of a panic attack, not wanting to return to how things were but helpless to stop it.

"Hey," Sam grasped my hand as I stepped in front of my door, pulling me toward him with a gentle smile as he shoved his phone into his back pocket. He leaned in, and I closed my eyes, my hands clenching the material of his warm shirt, waiting for him to kiss me. Warm breath fanned over my cheek, his fingers pressing into my back as he drew me into his chest. "Thank you for spending the day with me. I enjoyed spending time alone with you."

His lips grazed my cheek, pressing lightly as he leaned in, inhaling deeply while one of his hands tangled in my loose hair. I soaked up his calming presence, laying my forehead against his strong chest before I tilted my face toward his.

My heart was hammering in my chest as I turned, his full lips grazing my cheek. He lingered for a moment and then leaned back, my eyes opening as he released me and took a step back.

"What are you...?"

He leaned back in quickly, kissing my cheek softly before pulling my hands from his shirt. "Go to bed, Kristine."

"But?" He was supposed to kiss me. Not just hug me like that and walk away.

"Goodnight, get some sleep," he winked as he took a few more steps and swiped his keycard on his door. "We've got another early morning."

My mouth dropped open as he stepped inside his room, the snick of the door lock almost as loud as my heartbeat in the empty hallway.

Waiting for a moment, I realized he wasn't coming back as I heard the water turn on in his room.

What the hell? Did he just walk away?

Fuck.

SAM

CHICAGO

THE LOOK ON HER face as I escaped back to my room was almost comical. I knew she wanted me to kiss her. It was obvious by how she'd been staring at my mouth for the last several hours. But I meant what I'd told her. I wanted her to beg me to kiss her, not just comply because I initiated things between us again. She would continue pulling away from me whenever she got scared if I took the lead again. It was time for her to take what she wanted and own it for once.

A hot shower had helped clear my head, and the other side of the wall was quiet as I got ready for bed and repacked my suitcase. I'd considered making reservations somewhere flashy instead of taking her for a burger, knowing she'd been wined and dined before. There wasn't any restaurant I could have taken her to that would've impressed her. I could tell by her reactions that no one had ever played tourist with her in an unfamiliar city and just enjoyed spending the day in her company without any distractions or ulterior motives.

Seeing Chicago through her eyes had been a new experience for me too. My parents had brought my sisters and me on day trips when we were younger, exploring all the museums, and my dad had even taken me to a few Cubs games when I still played little league. It had seemed so big and filled with so many impressive sights when I was young. I wanted to share that feeling with Kristine.

I knew she'd kill me, but I emailed the photo of us at the Cloud Gate to myself and quickly assigned it as the screensaver on my personal tablet. She hadn't wanted to take the picture, but the genuine smile on her lips, her cheeks glowing, had been the best part of my day. She'd put her armor away, trusting me. It may have only been for a few fleeting hours, but she'd let me in and enjoyed herself.

That spark of connection was still there, burning brightly beneath the surface. It would have been so easy to take advantage of it, stoking the fire and taking her back into my bed—showing her with my body how much her company affected me. But I could wait. It might kill me, but I could wait for her to acknowledge her feelings for me. The time and the distance she'd put between us since our intense affair in Boston hadn't diminished the heat between us.

"GOOD MORNING," I SMILED as I joined Kristine on a bench in the lobby the following morning. Diana was sitting across the small seating area, rapidly texting as she glanced up toward the elevators.

"Hm," Kristine hummed, picking up her travel mug of coffee from the table before her and moving to sit next to Di.

She refused to look up as she pulled out her phone and angrily stabbed at the screen. It was clear from her body language she'd stewed on last night and decided that she was angry with me. I'd expected it, but we had to stop this cycle of me pursuing her and then her running away. The only way she'd see how I felt about more than just her body would be to spend time with me outside a hotel room. I could take a bit of her ire as long as it ended up with her seeking me out for more than the orgasms I could give her.

"Morning, party people." Chase was in a good mood as she wrestled her black suitcase into our small seating area, dropping into the couch next to me with Evan only a few steps behind. He looked relatively relaxed, watching the blonde to my right with a quiet intensity.

"Morning, Chase. How was your evening?"

"It was spectacular," she laughed as she turned and grasped Evan's hand, kissing his palm and tugging him to sit on the arm of the couch next to her. "Good food, good company, seeing my family, baby snuggles. What more could a girl want?"

Kristine glanced up, narrowing her eyes at me before she resumed glaring at her phone.

A kiss, I wanted to say, just to tease her, but she'd kill me if I outed us to Chase and Evan. She'd already told me Chase had suspicions of our relationship being more than professional. Obviously, I could not care less if they found out about it. But I still didn't know how Kristine would react to people knowing about us.

"How was your day, Sam? Did you enjoy some downtime?" Evan asked as his fingers played with the end of Chase's loose ponytail.

"It was better than I was expecting," I admitted. "There's just something about Chicago that Boston can't touch."

"I know what you mean," he smiled. "It's a good place for new beginnings."

As Chase smiled warmly at him, covering his hand with her own, I realized that while Kristine may have been mad at me right now, our time in Chicago did feel like the start of something new.

"No." Kristine's arms crossed her chest, and she glared at me from her spot to my right. "Not going to happen. You can share with Evan."

There hadn't been a large enough Uber available at the Denver airport for all five of us to ride together, so Kristine and I had gone ahead to our hotel while Chase, Evan, and Diana waited for our luggage to arrive.

The only hitch in our plan—to get the room keys for our party—was the hotel had overbooked the rooms. Only three were available instead of four, and two had king-sized beds. The third had two double beds, so we had enough places for everyone to sleep comfortably, but Kristine refused to share a room with me.

"It's only a few nights. We'll each have separate beds. I'll let you have the first dibs in the bathroom. This isn't a big deal."

"You're right," she huffed, her fingers flying across the screen of her phone. "It's not a big deal because you and Evan are sharing one of those king-sized beds. As you said, it's only for a few nights. You'll be fine."

The desk clerk looked at me apologetically as she tried to provide us with the only alternative she could manage with a fully booked hotel. "If you'd like, I can send a single cot to the king suite. There may be enough room to set it up next to the bed, and then there wouldn't be the need for anyone in your party to share beds."

"Can you give us a moment?" I asked calmly as I grasped Kristine by the elbow and looked for somewhere to steer her off to the side, hopefully out of earshot of the clerk.

"Yes, of course. I'll work on getting breakfast vouchers together for all of you to thank you for accommodating the reservation change."

"There wouldn't be a need for you to thank us if you'd gotten the damn reservations correct," Kristine hissed as I dragged her away from the desk.

"Would you quit it?" She slapped my hands away as we stood off to the side of the reception area outside the closed restaurant. "Stop pretending you have any say in this."

"I'm not the one who needs to quit having a tantrum," I sighed, pulling open my phone contacts and hitting the green button to connect the call I needed to make.

The phone rang twice before a deep voice picked up, a familiar laugh sounding through the phone in the background, along with the hum of activity you'd hear if you were out somewhere crowded. Good, at least he was with Isobel.

"What's up, Langley?" Adrian asked cheerfully. He'd obviously avoided reading the text I'd sent him, or he wouldn't sound so chipper.

"The reservations in Denver were fucked up." No point in sugar-coating the situation.

"By whom?" he asked, his voice getting louder as the background noise faded. I could hear Isobel asking what was happening in the background, and then a quiet curse as a text alert chimed.

"I don't know, but they're fully booked, as is every other hotel in this part of the city. We've only got three rooms. Kristine is losing her shit."

He leaned away from the phone, and I could hear his muffled voice as he talked to Isobel, trying to troubleshoot.

"Vivid will cover something special for you guys if you can make this work," he sighed loudly. "There's nothing we can do from here. The hotel can't accommodate another room."

"We don't want anything special," Kristine hissed, obviously hearing Adrian's solution. "We want our damn privacy."

"I don't know what she expects me to do," he growled, "The hotel is booked solid, and Isobel checked with travel. There isn't anything else available. There's some conference going on. The closest place with rooms is some three-star residence suites thirty minutes away."

"Sam will take it," Kristine chimed, trying to pull my phone from my ear.

"Sam will not take it," I frowned, prying her fingers from my phone and switching to speakerphone.

"Of course, she'd be throwing a fit. Can't fucking agree to anything," Adrian sighed loudly, and I saw a flash of annoyance as Kristine opened her mouth to respond. I quickly reached over and put my hand over her lips.

"You're on speaker."

"Yeah, Dickhead, you're on speaker," she said angrily, peeling my hand away.

"Whatever, dragon lady. You're the one causing the problem here."

"How am I causing the problem? I'm not the one who made the hotel reservations. I shouldn't be forced to sleep with your intern because you're too stupid to confirm a reservation correctly."

"No one's forcing you to sleep *with him*, Kris. You only need to share the same room with him for a few nights. I'll take care of making sure the reservations in LA are correct. You won't even be in your room most of the day, so I'm sure you two can manage to be civil with each other." Isobel's authoritative voice left no room for argument. I could see how she was easily able to keep Adrian in line.

"But Evan and Chase..." Kristine sputtered.

"Are staying in the king suite because they're the reason you two are even on this tour. Or have you forgotten that you have this opportunity because of the book *they wrote*?"

"But..." Kristine sighed, but I could see the resignation in her eyes.

"It's a professional arrangement. I expect you two can behave like grown professionals," Isobel spat out before she hung up.

And that, ladies and gentlemen, was why they paid Isobel the big bucks. She was an expert at diffusing unruly talent. Even when they were her subordinates and not an author with a penchant for dramatics.

"So..." I nodded as I held out my hand in her direction, using my other to tuck my phone back into my pocket. "Want to go tell me which bed you want?"

"This isn't some free pass to..."

Sighing, I shouldered my bag and grabbed the handle of her small tote. "We've slept in the same room before, and I've managed to keep my hands to myself. I think I can exert a little bit of self-control."

"I know, but..."

"At some point, you'll have to start trusting me." It wasn't like I was going to attack her in her sleep. I'd made it clear I was waiting for her to initiate things.

"It's not that..." she sighed as she followed me toward the bank of elevators.

Lowering my voice, I leaned in toward her ear. "I told you before that if you wanted me, you needed to..."

"*Please*. I'm *not* going to beg you to kiss me," she scoffed, irritation flaring through her eyes.

"Let's go drop off our carry-ons before they get here." I nodded as I motioned for her to board the elevator car before me.

"Fine. But you're the one getting up early to get ready first. And you can't use all the hot water while in there..." She was grasping at straws to remain irritated, and I found it oddly charming. The reasons for arguing this were slipping, and I knew she didn't want me in the same room because of the temptation. Or being forced to decide about us.

"Well, you could always join me and solve both problems." I knew I was riling her up, but I couldn't resist.

"Fuck off, Sam."

"I thought we'd established that's what I'd be doing with all the hot water," I laughed, but I could tell from the way high spots of pink appeared on her cheeks that she was thinking about what that meant.

"I hate you."

"Pretty sure you don't, but whatever you need to tell yourself," I winked as the elevator stopped and I stepped out, leading the way to the room she was being forced to share with me. Things were bound to be interesting over the next few days. She could play hot and cold all she wanted, but I knew it was only a matter of time before she caved and came begging. I might get kneed in the nuts first, but I was betting on her kissing me before we left Denver.

KRISTINE WAS CRANKY, TO say the least, the full day we were in Denver, refusing to talk to me any more than was necessary, insulting me when she did, and remaining silent at night once we settled back into our room. But cold showers weren't necessary because the glares she aimed in my direction were enough to shrivel any reactions I may have had to her. It was clear that I'd hurt her feelings the last night in Chicago. But I wasn't backing down.

I'd taken the chance and initiated everything between us. It was time for her to make the first move. I wasn't kissing her and making it easy. Especially not now that she was throwing a hissy fit that I'd left the ball in her court, and she'd hesitated. She could have easily come to me, but she chose to pout.

"Do you need the bathroom?" I asked as I dropped my messenger bag to my mattress, breaking the tense silence.

"Well, I need to brush my teeth, but I guess you can go first as long as you're not going to take a dump or whack off in there."

"Wow," I laughed, moving over to my suitcase and pulling out my flannel pajama pants. "I was going to remove my contacts, brush my teeth and change quickly, although your suggestions sound so appealing."

"Don't pretend you haven't done both in there before."

"Yes," I teased as I headed toward the door, leaning against the frame as I watched her start to pull out her pajamas. "You caught me. Knowing you're out here listening, how will I ever resist whacking off in here? Should I leave the door open so you can watch this time?"

"Oh, go frick yourself."

"Yes? No? Just leave it open a crack so you can pretend you aren't peeking?"

She turned and glared at me, throwing her pillow in my direction before I disappeared behind the door with a laugh.

Unable to resist her ire, I fake moaned while brushing my teeth, almost spitting my toothpaste all over the counter when I heard a loud thump against the door. It appeared my humor was not appreciated.

"It's all yours." I gestured dramatically toward the bathroom as I sat on the edge of my bed. "Don't worry. I kept the penis touching to a minimum."

"You're so hilarious," she said, rolling her eyes as she glared at me on her way across the room.

"Why, thank you," I chuckled as I scooted back, pulling my comforter over my lap as I lay down.

Her eyes were on me as she stood in the open door, widening as she watched me pull my shirt off and lean back against my pillows.

The door slammed shut, and I found myself laughing. She'd crack eventually. She couldn't stay mad at me forever.

As it turned out, she lasted approximately four hours.

A QUIET MOAN AWAKENED me a few hours later, the room dark, the faint glow of the clock on the nightstand separating our beds the only thing I could make out. 2:07 am barely visible as I squinted to read the numbers.

Fingers twitched against my bare stomach as warm breath fanned across my shoulder. Kristine—well, I assumed it was her—was under the covers of my bed, her head resting on the pillow next to mine, her lips pressed against my shoulder as she lay with her arm draped across my torso. One of her legs was thrown over mine, her body half lying across me.

So much for not wanting anything to do with me.

I reached up, slowly pushing the hair away from her face as I tried to make out her features in the dark. Her dark lashes fanned against her fair cheeks; her face more relaxed than I'd seen it in weeks.

Turning slowly, as not to wake her, I carefully pulled her closer, tucking her against my chest as I ran my fingers through her soft hair, closing my eyes.

I was sure she'd freak out in the morning, but I'd enjoy the nocturnal snuggles while I could.

When I woke up a few hours later, she was already gone, the bathroom dark, and her laptop case missing. Part of me wondered if I'd dreamed her climbing into bed with me, but the lingering scent of her shampoo and the warm travel cup of coffee she'd left on the nightstand beside the bed indicated otherwise.

"I DON'T UNDERSTAND WHY we have to do this," she sighed as she closed her laptop and shoved it into her bag. "I have things I need to work on, and going out to some stupid brewery tour isn't on my list of things I'd like to do right now."

Not wanting to break our temporary truce, I didn't say anything to Kristine about our sleeping arrangement the previous night, working quietly with her on the last morning of the tour in Denver. We'd packed up everything early, ready to head to Seattle, but this afternoon we were scheduled to tour some local breweries with Chase and Evan.

"Adrian is trying to make up for the room situation. I think you can afford to relax for a few hours. It might be good for you."

"Relaxing for a few hours is why I'm behind. If you hadn't noticed, we've been a little busy during the day, and you monopolized my only day of freedom."

Wow. "It's nice to know that spending an entire day with me was so horrible for you."

"That's not what I..." she sat on the edge of her bed and leaned forward, clenching her eyes shut and rubbing her temples. "I'm sorry. I know I'm not the best company, but you're almost done, and I still have a full set of chapters to complete. It's a nightmare, and I've been distracted for days. We're leaving again tomorrow and..."

"Breathe." I crouched in front of her, placing my hands on her knees. Her whole body was a live wire of tension, and I felt bad that I was part of the cause of her little meltdown. "Just a few hours, and we can devise an excuse to leave."

"Quit being so nice to me," she pouted, looking down at me.

Using my thumb, I reached up and smoothed the wrinkle between her eyebrows. "You need to relax. Please come with us?"

"No flirting."

"Fingers crossed," I laughed, pulling her hands away and cupping her cheeks. Leaning in slowly, I kissed her forehead. "I'll be on my best behavior."

"I'm serious. Chase is way too observant. She's been watching us."

"All she's seen in the last few days is you snapping at me and ignoring me." If she wasn't giving me a death glare, she'd been taking over and telling me I'd been doing things wrong for the last two days. I knew it was because she was stressed, but I doubted Chase thought it was Kristine showing affection toward me.

"Then we should keep it that way. Throw her off the scent."

"Should I start insulting you now?" I teased, rubbing my thumb along her cheekbone. "It'd really confuse them if I came up with some obnoxious nicknames and poked at your work ethic."

"Yeah, yeah," she sighed, laughing a little. "I get it. I'm a horrendous bitch."

"As long as you're self-aware." She took my teasing in her stride, and I could see from the contrite look in her eyes that she'd only been reactionary for the last few days from stress and a bruised ego. I could tell when she was invested in hating someone, and even at her crankiest, she lacked that conviction with me.

"You should be mad at me."

She was right. I should be mad at her, but I also understood her. She didn't want to be vulnerable, and here I was, poking holes in her defenses left and right. "I should be, but I'm not. This is who you are. If I didn't like it, I would have walked away already. But I happen to like you, even when you're a hell beast intent on my destruction."

"You've got issues," she laughed as she shook her head.

"No more than anyone else," I smiled. The arched eyebrow she aimed in my direction made me laugh, pulling her up as I stood. "Except maybe you."

"Watch it, Sam," she growled, but there wasn't any bite to it.

"TELL ME AGAIN WHY I agreed to this?" Kristine sighed dramatically, laying it on thick for Chase's benefit, I was sure.

"Because we're awesome, you would have just spent the day inside your room, and we get to drink beer paid for by the publishing house," Chase shrugged in response.

"Sounds like a win to me. Come on, Kris, live a little," I teased with a wink. I expected the eye roll I received.

"I'm looking forward to a little bit of a break," Evan nodded.

"But we have to be on a plane at the ass crack of dawn tomorrow," Kristine whined. I would have laughed at her dramatic delivery if I didn't know she was acting.

"Since when have you gone to bed before midnight?"

She narrowed her eyes at me, not expecting me to play along so well, but she told me to make it sound believable. "Have you been monitoring my sleeping habits?"

"I am sleeping a few feet away from you, and the glow of your phone makes it hard to sleep." She crossed her arms over her chest, trying to look intimidating, so I laid it on even thicker. "God, I hope the hotel in Seattle doesn't fuck up the reservations."

I secretly hoped they did, but I wasn't telling her that.

"Oh," she snarked. "Cause it's so impossible to spend time with me."

"Because I'd like to be able to go to sleep without worrying that I'm going to get glared at for every move I make," I growled. I saw the corner of her lip twitch and could tell she was fighting to smother a laugh.

We'd stepped closer to each other, spouting faux—mostly—grievances at one another as Chase leaned in to whisper in Evan's ear. I could tell they were still watching us, but our public spat had thrown them off the trail for now.

"Alright," Chase interrupted, gesturing to the door. "Break it up. Our ride is here. Get your asses out that door."

I slowed down as Chase and Evan walked out the door, grasping Kristine's elbow as I leaned toward her. "Happy now?" I laughed.

Her answering grin was adorable, her eyes bright. She'd enjoyed fake fighting with me. "It'll work."

She smirked and turned her nose up once we got to the Uber van, glaring at me as she climbed into the front seat.

Chase and I chatted as we headed toward the first brewery where the tour Adrian and Isobel had booked for us would begin. It was the least he could do for all the drama our arrival in Denver had caused. Kristine had calmed down, but no one else needed to know that being roommates wasn't quite the ordeal she'd played it out to be initially.

The tour kept Chase and Evan occupied, their flirtations distracting Chase from her fixation on Kristine and me. When we got to the last brewery, the four of us grabbed a table, and the conversation was much less stilted than before.

"Oh, come on," Kristine laughed loudly as she set her sights on Evan. "You're telling me that you'd never used sex toys until you met Chase? I find that hard to believe."

I didn't find it hard to believe. She'd only interacted with Evan once he was dating Chase. The timid man I'd met a few years ago was a shadow of who he was now. After hearing about his history from Adrian, I could see that Chase had completely shaken up his world.

"It's always the quiet ones that are really freaks behind closed doors," I teased, squeezing the hand that'd ended up on my knee underneath the table.

"You speak from experience, Spammy?" Kristine's eyebrows rose, a challenge in her eyes as she ran her foot up the back of my calf. My cheeks heated a little at the blatant look of lust, and I leaned across the table, licking my lips.

"Wouldn't you like to know?"

"In your dreams, pretty boy," she breathed, grabbing my hand and pulling it into her lap, forcing me to scoot closer to the table. The heat coming from between her legs was overwhelming, and I had a feeling if I pressed my fingers closer, I could feel how wet she was beneath her thin leggings.

Chase and Evan talked about taking a tour at a hotel nearby as Kristine released my hand, groaning dramatically as she pulled out her phone. "Ugh. Actually, Is just filled my inbox with pages to proof."

My lips pinched shut as I fought the urge to blurt out that I would be happy to fill her box with something. She angrily tapped at the screen of her phone, and mine vibrated in my pocket as she made her excuses to head back to the hotel.

Standing from the booth, I placed my hand on Kristine's back, enjoying how she leaned toward me. "Want some help? Two sets of eyes might help you get through it faster."

"We'll see you two nauseating lovebirds later," Kristine sighed loudly and stood from the table.

When we reached the sidewalk outside the brewery, Kristine giggled, looking over at me as she bumped her shoulder into mine. "Not bad, Sam. I think they bought it."

"What can I say?" I chuckled. "You make it easy to pretend to be irritated."

"Well, thank you. I appreciate the assist. If they got any touchier in there, I may have vomited in my mouth."

The hand resting on her back slipped around her waist, pulling her into my side as we quickly walked down the street toward our waiting Uber. "They weren't the only ones getting touchy in there."

"Shut it," she growled, placing her hand in the center of my chest. She'd never admit it, but she'd been the one who'd initiated touching me under the table, only a foot away from the people we were supposedly hiding our relationship from.

KRISTINE

DENVER

"Ugh."

Sam's head immediately swiveled in my direction as I groaned. I knew he'd been watching me out of the corner of his eye after we returned to the room, waiting for me to talk to him. The mixed signals I was throwing out left and right had been giving me whiplash, but I really did need to get work done tonight. Our flirtation from earlier was pushed to the back burner as soon as we got back. I'd pulled out my laptop and tried to get back to work, my slightly intoxicated brain having difficulty focusing.

This manuscript sample was ridiculous. He had no idea how easy he had it with the other sample we'd been given from the fantasy editors. The one they'd sent me from romance was...rough.

I understood that they were using the samples to gauge our editing skills, no matter the quality of the work, but who came up with this shit? It was dreadful. There was absolutely no way this was from a book that Isobel was considering.

Adrian probably could have written something better in terms of smuttiness, even with his chauvinistic views of the world. That in itself was a terrifying thought.

I scanned the passage again, trying to ignore Sam's staring, but I couldn't help cringing as I read some of the more...descriptive...language.

He plunged his love lance into the depths of her cavernous pleasure pool.

Seriously? *Love lance...* What in the fuck was that shit? Was this dick jousting now? And cavernous? Did she have the world's roomiest vagina? Ew. This passage was more likely to make me vomit than turn anyone on, myself included.

"What's wrong? You look like someone told you to throw away all your red Acroball pens."

"You shut it. That's blasphemy!"

A warm flush started in my cheeks as I glanced over where he was perched on the edge of his bed, an amused grin firmly in place. It was the same bed I'd slept in last night, despite my protests that we needed to remain strictly professional with each other. I wasn't doing a particularly good job controlling my behavior around Sam. The soft sighs he made in his sleep and all that warm exposed skin had proved irresistible.

"A bit creepy that's where your brain goes when you think of things that'd annoy me. I'm not sure if I should be concerned or flattered that you know the specific brand of pen I like." Raising an eyebrow, I glanced at him, watching that cocky smirk grow as he continued watching me, knowing it unsettled me when he wasn't talking.

"A bit creepy that you spent half last night glaring at me from across the room, yet I found you under my covers at 2:00 am clinging to me like a koala bear."

"Koala bears bite, you know," I snapped back, my fingers clenching on my stylus. I was being overly defensive again, but being that way was ingrained in me. It was second nature. "Whatever, Sam. Just let me get through this horrendous edit. I can't deal with your smug face and try to sort through the mess of this fricking train wreck."

"Is it really that bad? The fantasy pages haven't been anything too terrible. Ellipsis and spelling discrepancies all over the place, but those are easily fixed."

"Yeah, well, they're obviously punishing my eyes with this shit. I wish it were just continuity issues. Sloane and Isobel kept poking me to stay in the running, but they are pushing my boundaries with this garbage."

"I'm sure you've seen plenty of gratuitous smut in your tenure under Isobel."

The corner of his mouth quirked as he obviously recalled what he'd just said, but I was too upset to make the easy joke about me being under Isobel.

"Oh, no." I shook my head. "This isn't smut. This isn't even erotica. This is just painful to read, and I wonder if this author has even had sex before. They certainly haven't been having good sex, that's for sure. And the pen name is cringy as fuck."

He placed his tablet on his nightstand and took a few steps toward me, hesitating before taking the seat next to me and holding out his hand. "Let me see."

"Don't say I didn't warn you."

Sam's fingers brushed mine as he grasped my laptop. He was close, the side of his arm brushing against mine as I fruitlessly tried to tamp down my physical response to his solid presence. He smelled faintly of a brewery, which made sense since we'd been in half a dozen, but the underlying masculine smell that was uniquely him had my pulse racing. I'd been as close to him as a person could get, but I felt like it would never be enough with him. I couldn't get him out of my system because he'd gotten under my skin. If I was completely honest with myself, I didn't want to either.

"Okay, you were right."

Snapping out of my daze, I pulled my leg onto the mattress and turned to face him. "Excuse me? What was that?"

"I'm not repeating it," he said with a smile, tapping his fingers on the edge of the screen. "But this is bad. And exactly why I don't edit romance novels. I wouldn't get through this without laughing my ass off."

"Laugh it up, jackass. Don't think I've forgotten your responses to the first smut we read together. You were like a little blushing virgin when we read about the prostitute and that detective."

"Yeah, yeah, hold that over my head again. What's wrong with the pen name?" he frowned as he looked down at the title page, the name *Cleopatra Torres* emblazoned in all caps.

"Seriously? You don't get it?"

"What am I supposed to be getting?"

Holding in my laughter, I almost choked as I giggled out. "If I didn't know better about you, I'd say it was fitting that a straight male editor couldn't figure out that name." He didn't respond, clearing his throat as he sat up straight next to me and held his neck high. "Still?"

"Fine, explain it to me," he sighed, pretending to be annoyed, but I could see his lips twitch.

"Cleopatra Torres...*Cle Torres*." Pausing, my eyes widened as I could tell from his blank expression, he still didn't get it. Geez. "Clitoris, Sam! Their pen name is clitoris!"

"No..."

"Yes," I sighed dramatically, smothering my laughter. "My God, men really do have a challenging time figuring it out. At least their pen name didn't have something to do with the G-spot, or you'd never find it."

"Found yours pretty easily." The pink in his cheeks made me think he was embarrassed to miss the fairly obvious innuendo, but he'd never admit it.

"Yeah, well, at least you've got that going for you—certainly isn't your ability to pick up on dirty jokes."

"Alright, let's see what we've got here." He cleared his throat before he looked back down at the screen.

"Liza gasped out to the heavens as Darcy's long fingers penetrated her crevasse with aching slowness."

"This author loves to refer to rock formations to describe lady parts. Not exactly enticing, but let's keep going..."

"He moaned against her brow as her silken folds clamped down on his hand like a vice, grasping and releasing as she spasmed against the sheets."

"That part isn't terrible, but it sounds more like his fingers induced a seizure, not an orgasm..."

I fought back a laugh as he continued.

"Liza lay spent against the virginal white sheets as he climbed between her outstretched legs and plunged into her depths. He fought against the current of her contractions, his sword sinking into her flesh, over and over until he found his completion buried in her firmly."

"His sword?" Sam laughed as he bumped his shoulder against mine. "I thought it was a lance, but at least she didn't call it a seminal sword."

"Oh, my God," I giggled as he circled a few words on the screen with my stylus, writing little notes in the margin. I was sure they were profound observations of this clearly superior work of literature.

"Oh, look, Kris, he's got quick recovery," he continued, his voice amused as he scanned further down the page. "They're going at it again, but it looks like she's performing her starfish routine face down this time *while he mounts her like the stallion in her father's stables.* Should I keep going?"

"No!" I laughed as I swatted his arm. "Stop, stop. You've ruined *Sam's Sexy Storytime* for me forever."

"Oh really?" he smirked, placing the laptop down as he turned in my direction, his fingertips skating along the edge of my knee as he scooted closer. "Sam's sexy story time, huh?" He leaned in, his nose barely touching my cheek as his lips grazed my ear. "You like it when I read to you?"

My mouth opened to respond, a choked gasp slipping out before I clamped my lips shut, terrified another embarrassing 'wha' noise would slip out. It'd always turned me on when he'd read to me in our conference room, but I'd never outright confessed that to him. Now he'd never let it go.

"I bet I could get you excited with this terrible *Pride and Prejudice* knock-off." His voice was low and rumbly, the combination of it and his warm breath on my cheek working to drive the terrible words I'd been forced to edit from my brain. "Or should I make up my own story to see if I can get a reaction from you?"

"Sam," I whined. He was crossing the boundaries again. He was making it hard to justify staying away from him when our attraction burned so brightly.

"You ready to tell me something?" he breathed, his fingers burrowing under the hem of my loose sweatshirt. "All you have to do is ask…"

The problem was that I couldn't justify my stubborn refusal to beg him to kiss me any longer. I wanted him to keep going. To lay us both bare against the sheets and make me forget all the reasons I'd convinced myself to stay away from him.

"Don't stop," I whispered as I turned my head, grazing my lips against his as I grasped the front of his T-shirt. I knew what he wanted from me, and I was too weak to keep fighting it. "Kiss me. Please."

He didn't hesitate as his lips captured mine possessively, his tongue slipping inside, reminding me of all the things he could do with that mouth of his. My skin prickled with awareness of how I continued to react to his touch.

"Sexy Sam fought to catch his breath, leaning into the warmth of curvaceous Kristine's neck, his lips trailing along the delicate shell of her ear," he whispered, his lips tracing the path he'd described with his words. I was too turned on to laugh at his ridiculous narration. "She squirmed against the sheets beneath him, the heat of her almost unbearable against his thigh. He found himself imagining how the skin of her chest flushed as her arousal built, the sight always making him desperate to lay his hands upon every inch of her sexy body."

I was panting underneath him as he leaned away, his long fingers peeling my sweatshirt from my torso, my nipples pebbling as they were exposed to the cool air of the hotel room. Sitting up, I helped free my arms, watching as he stared at my exposed skin with a heated gaze.

Sam carefully secured my discarded laptop on the nightstand next to his tablet. His shirt followed mine to the floor, and my fingers immediately sought out the warm skin of his chest. I traced the lines of the taut muscles on his stomach, watching his eyes dilate as his breath caught in his chest before he continued, his voice deeper than previously.

"Sam's lips ached with the thought of caressing every bit of her soft skin with them. Exploring the pale expanse of her loveliness before moving to where she was warmest. He'd imagined placing his mouth on her constantly over the last several weeks. He dreamed of making her moan his name, the way it felt when she drove her fingers into his hair, the exquisite pain mixed with the pleasure he felt as he brought her to release with languid flicks of his tongue against her wet flesh."

Those words spoken aloud in his deep voice made my pulse race as his strong fingers pulled down my leggings, tugging them free from my legs and discarding them onto the growing pile of clothing on the floor. He stood beside the bed and hastily shoved down his jeans before urging me back into the pillows with a firm hand.

"Sam loved the little gasping noises she made as she came against his fingers, as she pulsed against his tongue, and especially when he slipped inside her and made her body sing with his cock."

Sexy story time would push me over the edge before he even had my panties off.

"Keep going," I urged as I fingered the waistband of his boxers, my mouth watering as the dark material of them pulled snug against the hard outline of his cock.

"He fought with his thinly stretched control as his fingers traced her heaving breasts, watching her nipples darken and pebble against them." Sam's hands were cupping my breasts, using his thumbs to tease my nipples as his words described. His voice was low and rough; each syllable laced with arousal.

"Please," I begged, no longer caring I was giving him what he wanted. His strong fingers traced down my pelvis and cupped me possessively, pressing my drenched panties into where I wanted his attention the most.

"His cock was aching as he continued to press the wet material into her, enjoying the way her hips shifted restlessly against the sheets, wanting nothing more than to push the lace aside quickly and plunge his fingers inside her."

"Fuck, yes," I panted, wanting exactly that.

"But he was enjoying the tease, using soft touches and barely-there caresses against her nipples, enjoying the sight of her frustration building, knowing that the release would be much more intense when he got her there."

I narrowed my eyes and gripped his wrist, pressing his hand firmly where I wanted him.

"She was getting impatient. He could tell from the quick breaths that made her chest heave and how she tried to force his hand..."

"Shut the fuck up, Sam, and quit talking. I can think of better things for you to do with that sexy mouth..."

He chuckled, leaning over me, his hand pressed into the thin material of my panties, my clit throbbing against the tips of his fingers.

"Story time over now?"

"Ya think?" I raised an eyebrow as I leaned onto my elbow, pressing my bare chest against his. I was about to explode...or push his smug ass to the floor and take care of things myself while he watched. That line of thought had merit, but I needed him inside of me right now. However I could get it. It'd been too long.

"How do you want me?" he whispered in my ear as he pressed me back against the bed, one of his hands gripping the hair at the back of my head as his other nudged one of my thighs over so he could settle between my legs.

"I want you to stop talking," I growled as I nipped at his neck, thrusting my hips up toward his.

"Do you want me to make you come?" His voice was low as he ground against me, the hard bar of his cock pressing against my clit with the movement.

"I'll do it myself if you won't," I challenged, my hand pressing in between our bodies and dipping beneath the waistband of my panties.

He gripped my wrist and pulled my wandering fingers away, pressing them back against the mattress.

"Someone is a little impatient right now," he chuckled into my skin as his lips teased along my neck, his movements unhurried.

"Someone is being a tease right now," I growled, bucking my hips into his.

"I thought we weren't supposed to be sleeping together. What happened to keeping things professional?"

He was being deliberately difficult, but he knew I loved it when he wound me up, took my obsessive need for control, and turned it back on me. It'd been so long since he'd been pressed against me like this. Since he'd been inside of me. Since he'd made me come and kept right on fucking me until I couldn't breathe anymore. Maybe I'd been incredibly stupid to fight him about what was happening between us, but as he touched me, I found my walls crumbling again. I was defenseless against the depths of my feelings for him, which terrified me more than anything.

"I'm wide awake," I panted. "We don't need to sleep together later. I want you to fuck me. Make me come...please."

No more words were exchanged as he leaned back, pulling my panties from my legs before he buried his face between my thighs. He licked me like a man possessed, growling into my skin as he sucked hard on my clit, flicking it with the tip of his tongue until I was free-falling into an intense orgasm, clenching hard against the fingers he'd slipped inside me to push me over the edge.

"God, that was sexy," he growled, kissing a wet path up my chest, pausing to flick my nipples with his wicked tongue, then snaking a trail up the side of my neck. "You make me so hard. Watching you like that, feeling you against me..."

The hand holding mine to the bed guided my fingers between us, pressing into the unrelenting hardness barely concealed by the material of his boxers.

My fingers wiggled free of his, and I slipped them through the little flap in the front, grasping his hard length and squeezing.

It was my turn.

"She grasped his heavy weight in her hand, enjoying the way his flesh throbbed against her fingers, his hot breath stuttering in her ear. She knew how it felt to have him surging into her, and the ache between her thighs intensified as she imagined him thrusting into her warmth."

Sam growled into my ear as I started to move, rhythmically pulling his length between my fingers, enjoying the solid weight of him above me. I'd never admit aloud how much I'd missed him over the last several weeks. How it physically hurt to be with him most days and deny myself the pleasure of touching him, even if it was simply to hold his hand.

"Her thoughts as she touched him were wild, thinking about how he felt in her hands, warm and hard like satin stretched over steel. Her mouth watered at the memories of how he felt in her mouth, against her tongue, thrusting as he came down her throat, grunting her name as his hips surged the solid length of his cock between her lips."

Sam groaned lightly in my ear as he thrust into my hand, my whispered words causing him to swell and harden against my palm. My words were affecting him as much as he had affected me.

"She imagined his big cock inside her, reaching places her fingers, or toys could never touch. Nothing felt as good as he did inside of her. Nothing could replace how his warm body covered hers or how he moved. How he made her feel things she didn't know she could feel."

"Fuck, keep going," he panted as one of his hands grasped my breast, his thumb roughly brushing against my overly sensitive nipple.

"She recalled all the nasty fantasies she'd had about him over the last several weeks as they sat beside each other in endless meetings. About him pulling her into an empty conference room, bending her over a table, and making her cry out his name for everyone in the office to hear."

"I'm so close," he panted as his hips pressed into every slick pull of my palm against his cock.

"She even imagined pushing the emergency stop in the elevator, getting on her knees, and peeling down his pants. Sucking on his dick so hard as he held her in place with his big hands, erupting in her mouth before turning her against the elevator wall and making her come until she couldn't walk."

Sam's hips jerked, and his release spilled over my fingers as I kept a firm grasp, milking every last drop from him.

"Fuck. That was intense," he panted, rolling to the side, pulling my hand from his boxers, and gathering my naked body against his warm chest.

"You could say that," I giggled, my voice sounding light, even to my ears.

He turned to face me, tracing his fingers on my lips, his eyes soft. How I ever thought I could resist him was still a mystery, but he'd given me space to figure that out, and I appreciated that more than he knew.

"I don't think I can continue to stay away, Kris..."

"I..." my throat cracked as I tried to find the words I knew he deserved to hear from me. "I'm sorry."

"You don't need to apologize," he whispered, cupping my cheek.

"No." I held his hand to my cheek as I shook my head. "I do. I was terrible to you because I was afraid. Because I *am* afraid."

"You don't need to be." His voice was soft, and I hated that he was still so understanding, even after I'd been a bitch in every conceivable way.

"The way you make me feel terrifies me sometimes."

"You terrify me sometimes, too." He smiled, pulling me against his chest and sliding one of his legs between mine.

"This isn't funny," I frowned.

"Don't be so serious all the time," he teased as he brushed his mouth against mine. Just a fleeting press of his lips before leaning in and pressing me into the pillow, his large body following as he nestled between the cradle of my thighs.

He kissed me without hurry, slowly feeding kindling into the fire burning between us, driving away the worrying thoughts in my head and making me forget everything except for the feel of his skin.

"Sam," I whined as he ground against me—hard again.

"Stop thinking. Just be with me. Please," he pleaded as he reached down and pulled at the waist of his briefs, sliding them down his legs. "Stay with me in this moment. Let me show you how I feel."

He left me briefly, pulling a condom out of his bag and sheathing himself before he laid back down, kissing me passionately as he settled between my thighs.

"Oh God," I moaned, my back arching as he slipped inside me, slowly rocking his hips until he was seated as far as he could go. "Don't stop," I panted as I met his slow thrusts with eager desperation that had nothing to do with chasing down an orgasm. "Don't ever stop."

"I won't," he whispered as he groaned into my neck, holding me tightly. "I won't ever stop."

And I had a feeling that neither of us was referring to the physical attraction between us anymore.

TWENTY-EIGHT

SAM

SEATTLE

A LOUD THUMP SOUNDED from the door that connected my hotel room to Kristine's. We hadn't requested adjoining rooms, but I wasn't complaining when the hotel desk clerk informed our group that we had three rooms together. Chase and Evan were in a small corner mini-suite, and we were in two standard adjoining rooms along the same hallway. Kristine pretended to be relieved that we weren't forced to share a room, but I knew better. We may not have been sleeping in the same room, but I knew she'd end up in my bed again. She just wasn't admitting it yet.

I'd laughed when she made a big deal over checking the lock on her side of the adjoining door when I'd helped her with her luggage earlier, but as another reluctant knock sounded, I knew she'd seek me out. We'd been playing this game of cat and mouse, and I was content to let her lead. She couldn't stay away from me any more than I could stay away from her. If anything, the forbidden nature of sneaking around in hotel rooms and trying to keep Chase and Evan from discovering what was happening between us only added to the heat.

We had kept our hands to ourselves on the short plane ride from Denver, but she'd unsuccessfully tried to get away with sneaking looks at me all day. I'd held in my laughter several times when she realized I'd caught her staring again. It was adorable how she couldn't keep her blushing at bay.

"Come on." Her voice was muffled as I ran the towel over my head, drying my hair after getting out of the shower. It would have been better if she was in there with me, but I could try to coax her in there later.

"Give me a minute," I shouted back, crossing the room and pulling open my suitcase, quickly pulling on a pair of boxer briefs. My chest was still wet, so I didn't bother with a shirt, but it wasn't like it would be new for her to see me shirtless. The fingernail marks on my back spoke otherwise. "I'm naked."

"Hurry up, you jackass!"

I'd been in a good mood since our flight landed because she'd finally stopped trying to pick fights with me in front of Chase and Evan. She'd been quiet since we'd finally relieved some of the tension between us, but I knew it was only a matter of time before she started panicking again. I only hoped she'd let me give her more orgasms to stave off a meltdown. While our verbal communication still lacked clarity, our bodies always knew exactly how to speak to one another. And she seemed to be using my cock like an emotional support animal. An emotional support cock, if you will.

"Geez, keep your pants on," I laughed as I flicked the deadbolt, pulling open the door. I knew it was a dick move to open the door, barely clothed, but we were alone. She didn't need to freak out seeing a little of the skin she'd been licking the night before.

"Seriously?" She rolled her eyes as the door swung open, huffing, but I saw her eyes widen before she schooled her features to indifference. Kristine could play hard to get all she wanted, but we both knew otherwise.

"What? I wanted to take a shower. I don't happen to enjoy smelling like an airplane."

"Put on a damn shirt," she laughed, but her hand lingered as she pushed against the middle of my chest and shouldered her way into my room. "Isobel sent me an email, and the desk just called to let me know we have a package from Adrian. Evan will probably lose his shit, but they've sent some outfits for their reading in the morning."

"Like what kind of outfits?" I frowned. They were booked to do an erotic reading at a high-end erotic art gallery in the morning, and if Adrian bought Evan a gimp suit or something, we'd never finish this book tour. It would be just his humor to send him something ridiculous that he knew would push Evan's boundaries, but I also didn't want to deal with the hissy fit if Adrian found out Evan refused to wear whatever he sent.

"This is why you need to get dressed so we can find out."

"Are you sure you want me to get dressed? I'm sure the desk can hold the package for a little longer."

Her eyes widened, a flash of irritation mixed with interest clearly visible before she schooled her features and pointed toward my luggage. So bossy and so easy to rile up. I was enjoying this change to our dynamic immensely.

Kristine watched me as I crossed to my suitcase, taking out a pair of worn jeans and pulling them on slowly. She shifted nervously, rubbing her palms on the sides of her black leggings, but she didn't look away, watching me pull out my stack of shirts and place them on the bed, finding a worn black t-shirt.

"Sam," she sighed, taking a step toward me, her fingers flexing.

"Hmm?"

"We really need to stop doing this."

And there it was. Her nerves were making her pull away again. Closing the distance between us with a few steps, I leaned in, grazing my nose along the side of her cheek. "Sometimes," I whispered, enjoying the way her breath caught at my proximity, "heading down the path you think is the wrong choice can be the one you were meant to follow all along."

Her body trembled as she stood completely still before me, her shallow breaths the only sound in the room. I could keep coming after her. It'd be easy to kiss her again, fall into the bed on the other side of the room, and show her how good we were together. But it wouldn't help the distance she kept between us in every other aspect of our relationship.

It appeared we were at an impasse again.

The small hand pressing into the middle of my chest wasn't a surprise, and neither were the two steps she staggered backward as she ran a nervous palm down her loose hair.

"How profound of you, Langley. Have you sold that one to Hallmark yet?"

"We're reverting to last names now?"

She huffed, crossing her arms over her chest. My smile grew when it only served to push her tits together, the soft swells nearly spilling right out the neckline of her form-fitting tank. Kristine's traveling clothes were the most casual I'd ever seen her, and I liked seeing her clean-faced and soft-looking in a pair of sweats. "You didn't like it when I called you Spamela."

"Touché."

"Although I think Langley fits in lieu of an alternate nickname." She made a pointed glance at my lower half.

"Well," I laughed, pulling my shirt over my head. "I think we could brainstorm a fitting name for you to yell out later."

"Keep it in your pants, Langley. Let's get this over with," she frowned, pulling her hoodie closed and securing the zipper as she noticed where I was staring.

"Well, which one do you want? Do you want me to keep it in my pants? Or do you want to get this over with?"

"Leaving now," she called over her shoulder, heading toward the door separating our rooms. "Or I'll take care of it without you."

"Can I watch?" I laughed as I sat on the end of my bed to pull on my socks and shoes.

Her middle finger was the last thing I saw as she slammed the door closed, but I smiled when I heard her muffled laughter through the wall. She didn't say no.

> *Sam: This isn't some spy movie.*

> *Adrian: What's the target's location?*

UP YOUR ASS.

> *Adrian: ETA on package drop?*

"What the hell are you texting over there?"

"Adrian is being a dumbass." I rolled my eyes as my phone pinged with another text. "Big surprise."

> *Adrian: I need visual confirmation you have eyes on the target.*

Kristine pulled my phone out of my hand, quickly responding to his text as we waited for Evan and Chase to climb out of the car Diana had arranged to take us to the venue for the book reading. He was visibly nervous, unaware it wasn't a traditional bookstore. Our official itineraries had only listed today's event as an author reading followed by the book signing with a question-and-answer session.

The nondescript brick building with thick burgundy curtains hanging in the storefront window didn't reveal what was inside, but I'd googled the name Diana shared with us on the ride over, and I was intrigued. Their website showed it was an erotic art gallery, housing a complete library of erotic literature—both fictional and non-fiction—and it regularly held educational classes as well as gatherings for the local kink community.

Chase was reveling in the outfits as she joined us on the sidewalk, laughing as she adjusted her black leather skirt. "I feel like a naughty librarian."

Evan was transfixed, watching Chase with a hungry look while anxiously plucking at the side seams of his tight leather pants.

Kristine loved it, smacking Evan on the ass, which only caused a small jolt of jealousy to flare through me before he started pulling off the accessories to his outfit and shoving them into my hands. The women continued to laugh as I stowed away all the leather and chains inside my messenger bag. While ridiculous, Evan's outfit wasn't nearly as bad as we'd expected, and he was carrying off the leather pants well. I think it helped that Chase seemed to enjoy them.

Chase distracted Evan by kissing him and whispering something suggestive in his ear. At least, I assumed it was suggestive by how he cleared his throat, clearly looking flustered as we all followed Diana through the front door to the gallery.

"Damn." Kristine laughed, drawing my eye to the sign she was studying inside the entryway. "It's too bad we won't be here tomorrow. They're having a class on squirting."

Her expression was one of curiosity and humor, but the loaded look she sent in my direction had me adjusting myself and clearing my throat as I stared back.

"Let's get set up. You're scheduled to start in a half-hour." Diana steered Chase and Evan toward a reception desk off to the side.

Kristine stepped back toward me, linking her arm with mine briefly as she looked back at the area where the art gallery was set up. "Want to go take a look around?"

My head was nodding—almost frantically—as I placed my arm around her back, turning her toward the entry and clearing my throat. "Absolutely. Lead the way."

While I'd appreciated the local art scene at Duke and after I'd relocated to Boston, I had to admit, I'd never been to a gallery that so openly displayed explicit images and never so many in one location. Everywhere you looked, there were erotic scenes depicted in a range of styles, mediums, and intensity. Even the more abstract pieces had a quality that drew your eye to the sensual poses and seductive lines of color.

Kristine paused, lingering in front of a piece done in various shades of black and gray hatch marks—the shadowy, fragmented figure of a woman lying face down with her neck arched in the lower portion of the frame. Her back was a harsh curve, a man's hand holding down the base of her neck as his other hand pressed into the area beneath her shoulder blade with his fingers splayed and grasping her skin. Her hips arched back into his in the center of the piece, and his legs splayed open as he clearly penetrated her, his calves straining with his implied thrusts. The top of his head and the shadowy impression of his downturned face were visible in the top corner of the frame, his gaze falling toward where she was captive beneath him, his shoulders strained with the effort to maintain their intense coupling.

"Why'd you stop?" I whispered, stepping in behind her as she quietly studied the piece, her bottom lip pulled taut underneath her top teeth, her breaths shallow. "Do you like this one?"

Kristine nodded, leaning back into my chest, her fingers reaching down to dig into the material covering my thigh as she stared at the erotic scene inside the ornate gilded frame.

"What do you like about it? Does the thought of being dominated like that turn you on?" A shiver radiated from her shoulders down to where I was pressed into her, her breath catching as I gently rubbed my nose into the soft skin behind her ear. She smelled intoxicating, all smooth skin and gentle florals, part of it her natural scent intermingled with her shampoo. I'd heard the shower in her room turn on early this morning and stroked away my morning arousal in the rumpled sheets of my lonely bed as I imagined her touching herself under the warm spray.

I'd assumed she'd join me last night, but I'd fallen asleep alone in my bed, her room silent on the other side of the wall. It would have been easy to knock on the door and insist she join me or follow her into her room, but I wouldn't force her to decide with my constant presence. If she genuinely wanted me, she needed to show me with more than just her body.

"Who would you imagine doing this to you, Kristine?" A small moan escaped her mouth as I reached around and cupped her throat loosely in my hand. Her pulse raced wildly beneath my palm, and she whimpered as I pressed my hips into her back, already hard as a rock. "Do you wish I was holding you down and making you take my cock as you grasped my soft sheets? Does it make you wet picturing me grasping your neck as I give you all of me, as hard as I can manage, our skin slapping together?"

"Fuck," she exhaled as she closed her eyes, her face tilted toward me, her soft mouth falling open as I increased the pressure on her neck. We'd had some intense sex in the last few months, but the thought of holding her down, her hips thrust into the air as she took my cock, was one fantasy I was desperate to fulfill.

"Tonight," I promised as I released her, stepping back and grasping her hand as she followed me to the next piece with a dazed look. Her reactions told me she was picturing the same thing, and I wouldn't bother hiding that I wanted her in my bed later.

We walked quietly, hand in hand, as we wandered between the gallery walls, occasionally pausing to study one enticing piece or another. My hard cock pressed into her as she leaned against me at every opportunity.

I was almost desperate to be done when Chase and Evan finished the reading and the signing, patiently answering the questions during the Q&A with the attendees. They'd fallen into a comfortable banter with each other during their time in front of the crowd, and everyone was eating it up, utterly entranced by their obvious chemistry.

"Would you like to join me for dinner?" I asked Kristine, glancing toward where Diana was talking to the gallery owner.

We were almost done packing up all the promotional materials, ready to send them ahead of us to Los Angeles and the next leg of the book tour. It was almost half over, and Kristine and I were still locked in this battle of wills, neither of us willing to admit the depth of our feelings.

I submitted my manuscript trial to the hiring committee this morning, and I should have felt relief at finishing the work, but I wanted to ask Kristine how she was progressing. She'd changed the subject every time I'd brought it up, continuing to distance herself from me professionally. I knew we were each other's competition, but I'd never use that to manipulate her. I was proud of her tenacity, no matter the outcome, fighting to earn what she wanted. It was the part of her I loved the most—her independent spirit—even if it was also the cause of the emotional distance she forced between us.

"You know what happened the last time we went out to dinner," she said dismissively, turning away as she yanked the vertical banner from the hanging stand and angrily rolled it up before dropping it into the storage bag.

"No one in Seattle gives a shit who we are, Kris," I smiled, loving that a simple request was getting her skittish again. The loaded looks, and the way she'd pressed against me earlier told me everything I needed to know. She wanted me, but she was scared to see things through again. Sleeping together in Denver hadn't cooled things off. It'd just made the desperation more bearable.

"I've heard the restaurant in the hotel has good reviews. I may order something and take it back to my room."

"Would you like some company?" Eating alone didn't appeal to me, and she hadn't argued when I'd promised her I'd have her underneath me tonight.

"Fine," she sighed, nodding her head. "But you're not eating in my bed. I don't like crumbs in the sheets."

"We both know you'd love it if I ate my dessert in your bed," I smirked, laughing as her eyes widened. "But I promise I won't leave behind any crumbs."

"You and your dirty promises."

Chapter
TWENTY-NINE

SAM

SEATTLE

Kristine had been quiet as we submitted a carryout order on the restaurant's website using my phone, shared an Uber back to the hotel, and stopped to pick it up before heading to her hotel room.

"I'm serious," she warned as she stopped at her room, angrily swiping the keycard across the reader and pushing open the door. "You're not making a mess in my bed with that." The pointed look she gave the carryout bag in my hands was comical. The mess I'd leave in her sheets shortly had nothing to do with our dinner.

"Don't worry. The only mess in that bed tonight will be coming from you."

She stumbled as she crossed the threshold, using the wall to stabilize herself as I stepped through the doorway behind her. When she'd been helping Diana set up earlier, I'd snuck back to the library portion of the gallery and purchased the guide accompanying the squirting workshop she'd commented on. It was a quick read, giving me all the information I needed before it'd been shoved back into my messenger bag.

"You wish," she said haughtily, marching toward the sliding glass door to her balcony and pulling the door open. The cool night air rushed in. The city lights visible across the horizon with the Space Needle at the apex, and the city sounds around us.

"I don't need to wish." I followed her out, placing our dinner on the small table outside, pulling her chair out before I settled into mine next to her, and took out our warm containers. We sat in loaded silence as we ate our food, Kristine occasionally making eye contact as she took a bite or licked something from one of her fingers. It wasn't an outright erotic display, but as she pulled out her slice of cheesecake, I imagined smearing it across her chest and sucking it from her nipples.

"Stop looking at me like that," she whispered as she licked the fork poised at her lips.

Smirking at her frazzled expression, I knew it wouldn't take much to get her to abandon the cake for a more *filling* dessert. "No."

"Sam," she whined, pointing the empty plastic implement in my direction and opening her mouth.

Before she could lay into me, a loud feminine moan broke the silence between us, drawing our attention to the balcony to our right. A grunt followed by a low masculine voice moaning, *"Is that what you want?"*

My pulse pounded in my ears as I returned my empty container to the bag on the floor, holding my finger in front of my lips as I took the fork out of Kristine's hand, pointing over her shoulder. The moaning had come from the direction of Chase and Evan's suite, and after a few more muffled declarations, I heard Chase moan out, *"Oh God, yes!"*

"Holy shit, are they fucking?" Kristine whispered as I rose from my chair, pulling her up with me and creeping to the edge of the wall that separated our balconies. If we leaned around it, we could easily see what was happening on the other side, but I stepped into the shadows, pulling Kristine into my chest as I leaned back against it.

With my back pressed against the wall, I caged Kristine against my chest, my hands possessively gripping her hips. My ears strained to hear the gasps of pleasure from behind us as Kristine wiggled anxiously, the feeling of her ass causing me to harden.

There was something desperate and forbidden about listening to Chase and Evan, but neither of us moved. The curiosity of this voyeuristic act sparked my intense reaction to Kristine, and hyper-awareness of her every move against me amplified.

"Oh, fuck me!" the feminine voice moaned again as I slipped my fingers underneath the hem of Kristine's blouse, pushing my fingers underneath the cup of her lacy bra and cupping her breast in my hand. Her nipple was hard against my palm as I ground my hips into her from behind.

"Are you wet?" I whispered into her hair, my ears straining to hear the sounds of smacking flesh behind us.

The groan of, *"That's it, baby,"* followed by a masculine moan, was almost drowned out by Kristine's more delicate noises as her head pressed back into my chest.

Her hand found my zipper and pulled it down roughly between us as she grasped my cock, squeezing as, *"Fuck yes. Come on me, baby,"* was practically shouted from the man on the balcony.

My other hand pressed down the front of Kristine's slacks and found her wet and wanting as the feminine cry of, *"Oh God, I'm coming. Fuck, fuck, fuck,"* sounded out.

A loud groan of satisfaction came from behind the wall, almost matched by my moan as Kristine's bare hand slipped beneath the fabric of my boxers and gripped my cock with desperation.

"Oh fuck, Evan, it feels so good." At Chase's loud declaration, Kristine turned her face into my bicep and moaned as I played with her slick clit frantically, the heat coming from her wet skin making me desperate.

We heard a few more moans followed by indiscriminate whispers and feminine giggles before the door to the other balcony closed, leaving us outside alone, desperately pawing at each other as we sought release. Kristine was writhing against me as I pushed her over the edge, the bite of her teeth on my arm almost pulling me over with her.

I didn't give her any time to come down as I pried her hand from me and spun her around. Pulling her up against my chest, I strode toward her open door, not bothering to close it. I lowered her to the bed and pressed her into the soft white sheets.

Our mouths were frantic against each other as I plunged my tongue into her mouth, yanking at her button and zipper before peeling her pants and panties down her legs. She was soaked against my fingers, soft and warm as she pressed her hips into my touch, clearly desperate for more despite already coming on my fingers on the balcony.

"Scoot back," I demanded as I leaned away from her, quickly undoing the top buttons of my shirt and yanking it over my head. Pushing my pants to the floor, I stepped out of them, climbing back onto the bed naked as I helped her pull the rest of her clothing out of the way.

"So bossy," she laughed, her voice husky, but I didn't respond as I lightly grasped her throat and pressed her head into the pillow.

"Stay here," I commanded, roughly pressing one of her thighs into the mattress with my other hand. She nodded, her fingers clenching the sheets on either side of her hips as she tried to remain still below me.

Releasing her momentarily, I grabbed the other pillow from the bed, shoving it under her hips before I scooted back, lying in the cradle of her thighs on my stomach. She pressed her hips toward me before I pushed them back into the bed with my palms, leaning in to take a long lick of her pussy. She squirmed underneath me, reaching for my hair and tugging. Carefully pulling her fingers loose, I pressed her hand into the bed again, using my other thumb to roughly press against her clit. "Don't touch."

"Fuck," she groaned, nodding as her fingers clasped the sheets again, hips arching toward my mouth. She watched me with hooded eyes, moaning again as I tilted her hips upward and slipped my middle finger inside her. I used the fingers on my other hand to pull the hood of her clit up and leaned forward to suck on the hard nub as I added another finger and curled.

I'd gone down on her before, and she was responsive, but now that I'd read the instructions in that guide, I pressed in farther, seeking out the rough patch of flesh inside of her and pressing into it firmly with my fingertips.

"Oh God, too much," she moaned as she squirmed against my face, her hips trying to skate across the pillow.

"You can take it," I coaxed as I pressed harder with my fingertips, curling my fingers insistently as I felt her walls clench me sporadically.

Returning my mouth to her clit, I sucked and licked at her as I pushed her closer and closer to release, her desperate cries loud in the quiet room. I absently wondered if another couple could hear her cries on their balcony, continuing the cycle that Chase and Evan had triggered.

"Oh fuck. Oh fuck," she chanted as my fingers moved faster, my tongue never letting up against her clit. I could tell she was trying to fight it, telling me to slow down and grabbing the hair on the back of my head again with both hands. Determined to succeed, I nipped at her clit, adding another finger as I pressed against her G-spot with determined strokes of my fingertips.

A choked cry rang out, followed by a long desperate moan as her hips shot up from the pillow, and a small gush of fluid followed the clenching of her muscles against my hand. "Oh fuck, Sam!"

"That's it," I panted as I pulled my fingers from her sated body, impressed at the wet stain on the pillowcase beneath her.

Her eyes were tightly closed as I pulled it from under her hips, tossing it to the floor before I grabbed a condom from my pants on the floor. Unable to resist her any longer, I covered her body with mine, the head of my cock sliding in the wetness between her legs.

She still had the sheets clasped tightly in her fingers, panting as I shallowly slipped inside her, moving to kiss the skin beneath her ear as I easily pushed the rest of the way inside. She wrapped her arms around me, clinging to my shoulders as I set a languid rhythm, enjoying the little breathy moans she was panting into my neck.

"Fuck," she panted, nipping at my collarbone breathlessly. "I think you're trying to kill me."

"Definitely wouldn't want to do that," I laughed as I slipped my hand beneath her ass, pulling her hips up into each of my thrusts. She was tight but so wet after her orgasm, her walls clinging to my cock in a way that made me want to surrender myself to her warm body.

"I want you to take me like the drawing," she whispered into my ear as she pressed her hand against my shoulder, urging me to lean back.

"Fuck," I grunted as I lifted myself off her, grasping her hips and turning her over before I pulled them into the air. The bed shifted as I stood on the mattress, leaning over her and bracing my hand on her back while I pressed myself against her. As my cock slipped back inside, I leaned forward, my other palm gripping the base of her neck, holding her head down as she grasped the sheets on the bed in front of her. She moaned as I seated myself fully, the angle making her feel tighter than usual. My hips sought a quick rhythm as my muscles strained, the fit pushing me toward release quickly.

Kristine cried out with each thrust as I slammed my hips into hers, my fingers digging into her back. My eyes watched where we were joined, entranced by how her ass jiggled with each thrust and reveling in how hot it looked as her body grasped mine. Long before I was ready, her body stiffened, clenching mine tightly as she gasped against the sheets, her release trailing down the front of my thighs. It forced an almost violent release of my own a moment later.

We were both panting hard as I pulled out and collapsed to the bed, pulling her into my arms and burying my face into her sweaty neck as I curled my body around hers.

"See, I promised no crumbs. But someone did leave an impressive wet spot," I whispered once I could speak, and my heart warmed as she laughed, pulling my arms tightly around her while pressing back into me as tightly as she could.

"Eh, it was okay," she panted, her voice hoarse. "You make a girl squirt, and suddenly you're a sex god."

"Mmmhmm," I hummed, my lips pressed against her shoulder.

She may not be ready to admit it with words, but she was just as desperate for me as I was for her. And chemistry like ours couldn't be stifled forever.

THIRTY

KRISTINE

SEATTLE to LOS ANGELES

SAM AND I HAD barely been able to keep our hands off each other all night, both showing up in the hotel lobby this morning—carefully timed to arrive separately—with matching tired smiles and hickeys in various places under our clothes. Chase was too busy staring at Evan to notice, her own sleep-deprived grin firmly in place. I'd been surprised at their exhibitionist display the previous evening, but it'd led to the most intense night I'd ever had in my life. They'd never know the events their rendezvous had triggered, but it was something I'd never forget.

The ride to the airport was quiet, Diana prepping us for the next city, Los Angeles, and the back-to-back appearances over the next three days before a much-needed day off.

"You're coming to Disneyland with us, right?" Chase whispered as she leaned her head over the middle seat of the hotel's airport shuttle, leaning into Evan's side.

Glancing over at Sam, who was pretending to be reading his text messages while the toe of his shoe was rubbing up against my calf suggestively, I shrugged, unsure what we were doing on our day off. He'd dragged me out of my hotel under duress in Chicago, but I was much less hesitant to spend my downtime with him after the last few weeks. If I could concentrate long enough to submit my manuscripts, I'd gladly spend every waking moment with him.

"Sam?"

Chase smirked as I looked at him askance, her eyes bouncing between us before she laughed. "Well, I was asking you, Kristine, but we've got four tickets, so Sam is welcome too. This is supposed to be part of Adrian sucking up for the hotel mishap."

"Nice to know you're all thinking of me," Sam said, the sarcasm clear in his voice.

"You know you're not the hard sell. I figured you'd want to join us. It is the second happiest place on Earth, you know."

"Ew," I cringed, not wanting to know what she considered the first as I saw the back of Evan's neck slowly turn red. He avoided eye contact with all of us, pretending to read a book, but I could tell from his rigid posture that Chase's hands were busy in their seat.

"Disney *World*, you pervert. Disney World is the first," she giggled, but Evan's posture was still tight as she leaned over to kiss him on the cheek and whisper something in his ear.

"Sure, whatever you say," Sam laughed as he shook his head.

"Fine," I sighed, knowing I'd agree to go too. My secret love affair with roller coasters would cement it if my growing addiction to Sam's presence didn't. I was interested to see if Sam would join me on them, knowing I'd be hardcore judging him if he didn't share the same passion for adrenaline at a theme park. "If it makes you happy, I'll fricking go."

My phone buzzed in my hand, Sam's name flashing across the screen as Chase turned back around.

> Sam: Faker. I bet you secretly dressed up as all the Disney princesses as a little girl.

Biting my lip to hold back my smile, I responded without looking in his direction.

> Kristine: The only princess I ever dressed up as was Princess Leia. I didn't need a prince to rescue me.

> Sam: She had Han.

> Kristine: She also had a blaster and a kick-ass blue lightsaber. She didn't need a grabby old pervert to rescue her. And he most certainly wasn't a prince. I bet you dressed up as Superman more times than you care to admit.

His lips twitched as he tried to hold in a laugh, my comment hitting the mark. I could picture a tiny, messy-haired, bespectacled Sam pulling off the perfect Clark Kent.

> Sam: Cavill's got nothing on me.

> Kristine: You keep thinking that, oh, delusional one. I reserve my right to make a judgment until I see you in spandex from the neck down.

> Sam: All you had to do was ask.

He couldn't hold in his laugh, looking over at me with an amused grin, a challenging eyebrow arched in my direction.

"I THINK THEY'RE FINALLY asleep." The stubble on Sam's chin tickled my neck as he whispered in my ear from across the armrest between our seats on the airplane.

"Good for them," I murmured as I tried to focus on reading through the notes I'd left in the mark-up of my finished manuscript edit. I knew Sam had already sent his back, but I was a little behind with twice the work and him distracting me most evenings over the last week. I still had a few days until the submission deadline, but it wasn't like me to be working on an assignment down to the wire.

"Have you ever gotten off in an airplane?"

My nipples responded like the greedy whores they were at his question, stiffening at the suggestion in Sam's rich voice.

"As a matter of fact, I've gotten off quite a few airplanes. That is how transportation usually works. You get on, and then you get off at your destination."

"That shouldn't have sounded as dirty as it did," he chuckled, pulling me toward him with the arm he'd had wrapped around my back. "But you know that wasn't my question."

"No," I sighed, closing my laptop and reaching down to push up my tray table.

"Leave it," Sam whispered, adjusting the blanket I'd stretched across my lap to cover his legs.

"What are you doing?"

He angled sideways, leaning into the seat as he turned my body toward the window. His seat was in the middle, the empty aisle seat behind him. The plane we'd boarded in Seattle was half empty, the row behind us unoccupied, Chase and Evan in the row ahead of us.

"Relax," he whispered as his hand crept under the blanket, slipping beneath the waistband of my leggings.

He didn't leave me much room to move, gripping my other hip tightly as his wandering fingers pulled my panties to the side. I was trying to hold still, my closed laptop still awkwardly perched on the edge of my tray table. If I squirmed, it'd be easy for any passing flight attendant to figure out what we were doing.

"Fuck," Sam grunted as his fingers slipped effortlessly against my clit, causing heat to flare through my body.

Harsh, low pants escaped my lips as he quickly manipulated my overheated skin, pushing me to the edge. He knew exactly how to touch me. Stars danced behind my eyelids as I clenched my eyes shut, trying not to moan as I started to pulse against his fingers moments later.

"Such a good girl," he whispered, his nose pressed into my cheek. "I love it when you come all over my hand."

Part of me wanted to tell him to fuck off at the smugness in his voice, but the other part wanted to reach under the blanket and make him come all over *my* hand.

"You really are the man of steel," I teased as I reached beneath the soft flannel and cupped his rigid length, but he caught my wrist, his fingers still damp. He placed my hand back in my covered lap and kissed the skin beneath my ear before facing forward in his seat again.

"Was that fast enough for you?"

Oh, that cocky bastard. It was on.

THE SCHEDULE IN LOS ANGELES was brutal, with back-to-back signings mixed in with a radio appearance and enough readings for us to be worried Chase would lose her voice by the time we left.

When we finally arrived at the gates of Disneyland, I was amped up and ready to blow off some steam.

Evan was twitchy and having trouble with the crowd surrounding us, but Chase did an impressive job calming him down. It was oddly endearing to watch her whisper to him quietly as Sam tried to get me riled up with suggestive comments that he knew would ensure that I had to censor my responses.

By the time the gates opened, I was a squirmy mess and relieved that Chase and Evan were doing their own thing for the morning. I wasn't sure how I would exact my revenge against Sam without getting arrested, but he had it coming with his little performance on the airplane.

"Make a run for Adventureland or Tomorrowland?"

"Rookie," I laughed as I reached back and grasped his hand. "Try to stay close."

I hadn't been to Disneyland since it'd opened, but I knew if we didn't make a break for Galaxy's Edge that we'd never get on any of the rides back there. The new Star Wars attractions were a hot commodity for park-goers.

Sam clung to my hand, his chest close to my back as we wove through the crowds on Main Street, taking the quickest route through Frontierland and ducking under the bridge that led to the newest section of Disneyland. I'd been up early, securing our places in the virtual queue before leaving the hotel. It paid to be overly prepared because I was able to get us slotted into the earliest time available.

While he'd been flirting with me at the main gate, I'd gotten the push alert on my phone that our boarding group was open for the next hour.

"Hold on," he tugged at my hand to slow down as I speed-walked through the crowds, the ride entrance off to our left down the path. "You're missing it."

"Let's go," I laughed as I yanked against his hand, "If we hurry, we can avoid the line."

"But..."

"Now, Sam. I don't want to miss our time slot because they won't let us on otherwise."

"But..."

"Put your lightsaber back in your pants and move it, Langley." His eyes widened as he nodded and followed close, his hand gripping my hip as I darted between people. It'd been a few years since I'd been in a theme park and almost a decade since I'd been to Disneyland, but I wasn't wasting time gawking at some cool spaceship replicas when I could be enjoying what we came here for. The rides.

We were panting as I pulled up the virtual queue on my phone, heading toward the entrance.

The setup reminded me of the old Great Movie Ride—sadly closed since I'd ridden it as a child—at Disney World's Hollywood Studios, but as we entered the immersive environment of the ride, I grasped Sam's hand tightly, reveling in the way he quietly took it all in. I should have known he'd be a Star Wars nerd but seeing him enjoying the same things I did pleased me.

"What's next, fearless leader?" he laughed as we spilled out the exit, heading back into Galaxy's Edge.

"Stick with me, kid," I winked as I tugged him behind me, ready to cram in all the thrill-seeking we could for the next several hours.

"Wow," Chase laughed as she watched Sam follow me into the restaurant where we'd agreed to reconvene before returning to our hotel. "I didn't expect to see you two here on time."

Sam stepped forward, dropping into a seat next to Evan, leaving me with two options—sit on his lap or stand awkwardly beside the table. Unfortunately, my stubborn ass chose the latter, watching Sam stare at me expectantly, daring me to make a move.

The next few hours were torturous, watching Chase and Evan flirt with Sam only a few paces behind me. They were shameless as she took every opportunity to engage in PDA she could get, Evan looking flustered as a result.

Sam kept a carefully calculated distance, innocently brushing against me or tracing the outside of my hand as we sat beside each other on rides, purposely not touching. A quiet resentment of myself built as the night went on, wishing I were brave enough to reach out and grasp his hand.

When we finally decided to head back to the hotel, it was dark, and my avoidant behavior had trampled my excitement from earlier in the day. I could see why Sam was so frustrated with me. I didn't even like myself half the time.

"Oh, look!" Chase clapped as we paused near Sleeping Beauty's castle, pointing toward the walkway.

Sam stepped in behind me, close enough that his chest was brushing my back, but he kept his hands to himself as we watched the scene unfold. "What's going on...oh! Well, that's public!"

The hairs on my neck stood on end as we watched the marriage proposal unfold.

"I wonder what he's saying," Sam mused quietly behind me. I could feel his eyes on me, but I refused to look back, opting for snark instead.

"Probably something super cheesy and romantic."

Chase and Evan were in their own little world, wrapped up in each other as I stubbornly refused to lean back into Sam. I could tell they weren't listening as he leaned toward my ear.

"If you'd let your guard down a little, you'd see sometimes a little romance isn't such a terrible thing." His fingers grazed my palm before he stepped back, putting distance between our bodies. My hands clenched into fists as I forced myself not to react, knowing he was right.

The following evening, my manuscripts were submitted, and I was about to explode if I had to spend the night alone in a hotel room.

My anxiety had been building the longer the tour went on, and my resistance to Sam was starting to crumble before my eyes.

When my phone vibrated with a text message, I jumped on it like a rabid animal, unlocking it and sighing with relief when I saw Chase's text message.

> Chase: You up for a night out? Diana was offered passes to a new club at our signing today.

> Kristine: I'm in. What time?

> Chase: Really?

> Kristine: Don't act so surprised. I'll go ask Sam.

> Chase: Yay! Meet us downstairs in an hour, and we can ride together.

> Kristine: Evan alright with this?

I knew he'd been anxious about the crowds at Disney, so I didn't know how he'd handle a crowded club.

> Chase: VIP passes. Sometimes it pays to be important-ish.

Sam was in a towel again when he opened the door between our rooms in answer to my knock, water dripping from his dark hair and making its way down his sculpted chest.

"Yes?" he asked slowly, an amused grin pulling at his lips as I tried to fight through my stunned silence. He was too attractive for his own good.

"Get your pants on. We're going out."

"You sure that's what you want?" He laughed, taking a step forward and hooking his finger underneath the thin strap of my tank top. "We can find something to keep ourselves entertained here if you'd like. Our flight leaves early tomorrow."

His skin was warm as I placed my palm in the center of his chest, afraid if he touched me, I'd end up in bed with him again. Realistically, I knew that would happen later tonight anyway, but I wasn't ready to give in yet.

"Chase invited us out. Try to clean yourself up a little. VIP lounge passes."

"I thought you liked me dirty," he chuckled as he leaned in, his wet hair sliding along my cheek as he whispered into my ear. "You wearing a dress?"

"I can." My voice was rough as I held back a moan, his lips tracing a wet path down my neck. I'd packed several dresses in my suitcase, knowing that after the signings in New York, I'd be attending Nana's birthday party in the city.

One of them was dark blue with thin crossing straps across the back, a matching shrug keeping it from being too revealing for a family function, but for tonight, I could ditch the covering and see what kind of reaction I could get out of Sam.

"Leave your panties off," he whispered as he sucked on my collarbone, his warm chest pressing into me as his hand settled on my lower back.

"Why should I?" I moaned as he pulled me forward, the distinct press of his erection against my stomach making my stomach flutter.

"Because they'll be soaked by the end of the night anyway," he whispered, grinding into me as he sucked on the skin just above my neckline hard enough to leave behind a mark. The others had faded, our intense night in Seattle only a memory.

"That sure of yourself?" I laughed, my back arching as he scraped his teeth against my nipple through the thin fabric.

"Yes," he laughed, leaning back and holding me upright before kissing me softly. "Come on over once you're ready."

He disappeared through the open door, the towel dropping to the floor before he walked out of sight.

Fuck.

THE MUSIC WAS LOUD enough to shake the windows in our Uber, and the line was wrapped around the building, but as promised, Chase and Evan's names at the door had us skipping the queue and heading up a long staircase before the doors even opened to the public.

It turned out the club's owner was a not-so-secret mystery reader who'd been thoroughly impressed by this new collaboration between authors. He'd cornered Diana while we were busy at a book signing, offering admittance to his new club and promising privacy in his VIP lounge.

"Man, if you don't offer to blow Evan tonight, I'm sure this guy will," I laughed as Chase and I sat wide-eyed across from the club owner, Jayce, and Evan. Sam was scrolling through his phone to their right, ignoring the fanboy asking Evan question after question. But as my phone kept vibrating in my hand, I knew he was texting me while I sipped on my drink. His hand had been practically glued to my thigh in the Uber on the way here, his fingers only straying to check for my panties once.

He was doing an excellent job of pretending to be indifferent to my presence in front of Chase and Evan, but I knew from the dark looks he kept shooting in my direction that I was in trouble.

"I know, right?" she giggled, leaning her head against my shoulder. "It's kinda hot to watch this guy get all worked up over him." I had to admit she was right. Jayce was attractive, and watching them sit side by side, lost in conversation, was oddly appealing. "I wonder if they'd kiss if I asked them to."

Almost choking on my drink, I waved my hand in front of my face with a giggle, my eyes watering as Chase broke into loud laughter. We were well on our way to drunk, which meant Evan would have his hands full with her tonight.

My phone vibrated again, and I looked down, unsurprised when Sam's name flashed across the screen.

> *Sam: Want to dance?*

Making eye contact across the table, I nodded once, carefully disentangling myself from Chase before making excuses to leave.

Luckily, her eyes were still riveted to Evan as I headed toward the stairs, Sam joining me a few moments later, his hand grasping my waist as he led me down.

"I had to get out of there," he shouted directly into my ear as he grasped my hand and stepped around me once we reached the ground floor. The sound was almost deafening, the bodies on the dance floor pulsing to the bass of the music pouring out of the speakers.

I let Sam lead as he pulled me through the crowd of writhing bodies, slipping my phone into his pocket before he grasped my hips and turned me to face him.

"Finally," he sighed as he pulled me close, his thigh pressing the tight material of my dress taut as his hands spread across my shoulder blades. His hips rolled to the beat as he held me tightly, grinding into the space I was needy for him with sensual movements.

His eyes were dark as he watched me, my mouth dropping open as my fingers grasped at his shoulders. I should have known he'd be like this, his movements fluid and sensual as our bodies pressed against each other. He'd shown me time and time again that his rhythm was flawless, but I hadn't expected him to be quite like this on a crowded dance floor.

As the songs transitioned from fast to slow and back again, I was lost in him, our bodies swaying together and sweat sliding down our necks as our connection never broke, lost in each other as the darkness hid our bodies in the crowd.

It was addicting to be the center of his universe, his eyes only leaving mine to watch how my body moved against his, responding to his touch in a way only he could control.

As a particularly suggestive song blared through the speakers, he turned me in his arms, his hand clasping my throat as he ground into me, using the fingers on his other hand to anchor my hips in place. "You're fucking sin incarnate," he growled into my ear, grinding into me, making me feel wanton in his arms.

"Please," I panted in his ear, leaning my head back into his shoulder. My hand gripped the outside of his thigh, my nails biting into the fabric of his pants as I writhed against him.

"What do you want?" he groaned into my skin as I gasped with the force of his hold on me.

Knowing he couldn't hear me over the crowd, I peeled his fingers from my neck, grasping his hand and pulling him behind me as I wove back through the crowd. My eyes darted back toward the VIP staircase, remembering the private powder rooms tucked down a dark hallway at the top of the stairs.

He was close behind me as we ascended the steps, his hand tightly clasped inside mine.

"Inside," I growled as I pushed him through the door, yanking at his belt as I backed him against the closed door once we were inside.

"What are you doing?" he laughed as he cupped my cheek, his other hand stilling the one on my belt.

"Whatever I want," I growled as I dropped to my knees, pushing his hand out of the way as I unclasped the belt and yanked his pants down his thighs. He was hard and throbbing in my hand as I pulled him free from his boxer briefs, pressing my other hand against the center of his chest as I lowered my head.

His skin was warm against my lips, and the desperate moan he let out as I pulled him inside my mouth with my tongue was worth the hard bite of the tile against my knees.

Sam anchored his hands in my hair, his fingertips digging into my scalp as I enveloped his cock in my mouth, sucking and licking as I reached up to roll his balls between my fingertips. I knew what made him needy, every quiet groan making me frantic as I sucked harder, bobbing my head and gasping as his shallow thrusts forced him toward my throat.

My lungs burned as I refused to let up, working him closer and closer to release, reveling in the way his legs started to shake and the low grunts in his throat as I swallowed hard against the head of him in my throat.

"Fuck," he moaned as I grazed my teeth against him lightly on the way up before sucking him back into my mouth, greedily rubbing my tongue against the underside of the head in a way that drove him wild. Sam may have made me come quickly with his nimble fingers, but as he moaned and released in my mouth a few moments later, I knew I had just as much power over his body as he did mine.

His eyes were glazed as I stood up, wiping my lips before I leaned in toward where he was braced against the door panting.

"Was that fast enough for you?"

The amused chuckle as he pulled me against his sated body and kissed my forehead had made every previous moment worth it.

"My turn," he chuckled against my ear as his hand slipped between my legs and across my bare flesh. "I think someone enjoyed themselves. Does having my cock in your mouth make you wet?"

"Don't sound so smug. You still have a job to do."

"Yes, ma'am," he murmured as he twisted us, so my back was against the door and dropped to his knees.

While my delayed retaliation for the airplane had caught him by surprise, I had a feeling he wasn't upset in the least.

And neither was I, to be honest.

Chapter
THIRTY-ONE

SAM

NEW YORK

"Sam," Evan's hesitant voice caught my attention as he stood off to the side of baggage claim, Chase and Kristine sitting on a bench off to the side, leaning against each other. Chase may have been battling the hangover from hell, but I knew the marathon of sex against every surface of my hotel room had burned off any alcohol left in Kristine's system, leaving satisfied exhaustion behind. My girl was sleep-deprived and joked that she'd been dicked half to death, but I wouldn't take back a moment of it.

"What's up?" I asked as we waited for our bags to make it off the plane and to where we were waiting. Diana had already headed to the hotel, meeting with Isobel and Adrian to discuss the schedule for the next few days.

"Can you meet me in the hotel bar after dinner?" He looked nervous as he glanced toward our drowsy girlfriends, his hand fingering something in his pocket.

"Sure, what's going on?" Kristine was sure to crash as soon as we were done for the evening, so I knew I'd have a little time to slip away without her noticing.

"I need your help with something. Adrian has gotten most of it arranged, but I need someone to help me with a project during the day before the dinner he coordinated with Isobel."

"Something in particular, or is it a secret?"

"You can't tell Kristine," he warned as he stepped toward me, his gaze going over my shoulder again.

"Why would I tell her?"

He laughed as he shook his head. "You two aren't that subtle. Something is going on between the two of you. Chase knew it as soon as press training started."

"Gotcha," I nodded, not confirming things, but I was smart enough to know it was a confirmation by omission in his eyes. He may have been socially awkward, but he wasn't an idiot. And part of his job was to observe the way people interacted with each other. I hadn't been hiding my behavior, and I knew Kristine had tells they'd probably picked up on weeks ago.

"I'm proposing to Chase."

My eyes widened as he nervously shifted from foot to foot, his body a live wire of nerves. "Congrats. That's awesome. I didn't realize things were that serious already."

I knew he'd—very publicly—asked her to move in with him in Chicago, and it was clear he was enamored with her. She was just as besotted with him, so I had no doubt she'd accept, and part of me was resentful of their easy coupling.

"What do you need me to do?" I asked, trying to concentrate on listening to his plans without my mind drifting.

"Are you coming to my room later?" Kristine asked as we shared the elevator up to our floor. The rest of our party had crammed into the previous elevator, Isobel and Chase chatting animatedly about the progress of her next project.

We were in separate rooms again, but they weren't adjoining.

"Why would I do that?" I teased as I leaned against the side of the elevator.

"Oh." She averted her eyes, staring down at her shoes, and I momentarily felt bad that she thought I was rejecting her.

"Is that what you want?" I asked, placing my hand in the middle of her back as I stepped closer. "What if someone comes looking for you?"

"Then I'll hide you in the bathroom," she laughed, leaning into my touch. "Please."

"You know I'll follow your lead," I sighed, hating that her first instinct would be to hide me, but of course, it would be.

She nodded, watching the numbers rise on the elevator, exhaling loudly as the doors opened. I let her walk out first, turning toward the left before she stopped. My door was down the opposite hallway, and I waited to see if she asked me to follow her.

"I'll text you." She shifted nervously, adjusting the strap of her bag on her shoulder.

"I'm meeting Evan and Adrian downstairs for a little while later on. I'll let you know when we're done."

"Oh, okay." The small frown on her lips made me want to fill her in, but it wasn't my news to share, and I wasn't in the mood to listen to her talk about how crazy he was for moving so fast. Just because she was terrified of commitment and letting someone in didn't mean others were.

I nodded, turning around, but her quiet voice stopped me. "Sam?"

"Hmm?" I glanced back.

"Do you need to go back to Boston right away?"

I pulled my bag off my shoulder, sliding the handle through the strap on the back of my laptop bag. "Not that I know of. Why?"

"Would you stay an extra night in the city with me?"

The open look of vulnerability on her features made me pause, holding in the joke I'd normally lob back in her direction. "If that's what you want. Any reason in particular?"

She sighed, closing her eyes before she pulled up the handle on her suitcase, her knuckles white with her firm grip. "My parents are hosting Nana's birthday party at their apartment in Manhattan. It's probably not going to be fun, but I don't want to go alone, and..."

I stepped forward, closing the distance between us and cupping her jaw, tilting her face toward me as I leaned in. She relaxed at my touch, sagging against my chest with her fingers tangled in my shirt as she blinked at me with those expressive hazel eyes. "If you need me, I'll be there."

"I do," she nodded. "I don't know how I'll ever return the favor, but..."

"Come to my friend's wedding with me in a few months. Be my date," I whispered, knowing it was too far away to have asked her, but I didn't want to take anyone else.

She nodded, pushing up to her toes as I gently kissed her lips, knowing that asking me to accompany her was a huge step toward her letting me in. I had no doubt she could plaster on a fake smile and a designer dress, faking her way through the party without assistance, but she wanted me there. And that meant more than any public declaration of affection.

SITTING AT THE DESK in my hotel room the next afternoon, I was nervous as I waited for the video call with Sloane to connect. This was the last step before the hiring panel would make their decisions, and I knew life was about to change no matter the outcome.

"Sam," Sloane's perfectly made-up face filled the screen as she sat at her desk in Boston, the skyline visible beyond her shoulders. "It's nice to see you looking relaxed. How's the tour going?"

"It's been good," I confirmed with a smile, easily slipping into small talk about the cities we'd been to, talking about how well their readers had received Chase and Evan's book.

"Well," she cut me off a few moments later. "I know you've got a dinner to attend in a few hours, but I wanted to take this last opportunity to talk to you about the positions. You and Miss Willard are the final candidates for the fantasy placement, but some last-minute developments while you two were out of the office have changed things."

I tried to school my features as she went on to tell me that they'd offered the non-fiction job to another candidate from the New York office.

"Unfortunately for Kristine, the position for the romance placement in New York is probably no longer an option," she continued.

"What?" I frowned. "I thought she was still being considered for that position?"

"She is, and after our talk before the tour, I was ready to consider her transfer seriously, but the copy editor who currently holds the position has likely decided not to transfer."

"Oh."

"It has thrown the hiring committee into a heated debate over which one of you to keep here in Boston, but I think we've come to a tentative agreement as to who to offer the position to."

I nodded, knowing they likely wouldn't tell either of us until they announced their final decision, but the outcome no longer worried me. I'd be fine either way. I was just worried about Kristine's reaction. This had been holding her back all along, making her keep me at a distance, and I hoped the outcome didn't negate all the progress we'd made in the last few weeks.

"We've also had a vacancy open up in another office that we think you would be perfect to fill." Sloane's voice was hesitant, almost like she shouldn't be telling me this, but my interest was piqued by how she stared at me intently through the screen. "Have you ever considered relocating to the Midwest? We don't need an answer immediately, but if you could think about it, we could offer equivalent positions to both of you..."

I WAS DISTRACTED AS Kristine, and I slid into the waiting cab in front of our hotel. My day had been frantic, spending the morning at the venue for our dinner and then coming back to get cleaned up for my video interview with Sloane. Then I'd spent another hour in a three-way video conference with the head of publishing in the Chicago office, talking to them about the available position.

It was an attractive possibility, but Sloane had disclosed she wouldn't move forward with their decision regarding the Boston office until she'd had her interview with Kristine. I'd spent the afternoon pacing my hotel room, trying to figure out if I'd even take a transfer if it were offered.

The only thing anchoring me to Boston was Kristine, and I knew she wouldn't hesitate to jump if they offered her the promotion, regardless of the location.

"Are you alright?" she asked as she reached between us and clasped my hand resting on the seat between us.

"Yeah, sorry," I apologized, turning my hand to interlock our fingers, knowing nothing would be decided tonight. There were some big decisions to be made in the next week that could change things irreversibly for both of us, and I honestly had no idea what I wanted.

Moving to the Chicago office would have been a no-brainer four months ago, but now I wasn't so sure. It'd be closer to my family, but it meant starting over. And if I left Boston, I'd likely be leaving my heart behind as well.

There was no easy answer.

THE MET CLOISTERS NEAR the Hudson River was surprisingly beautiful. The main courtyard had been transformed into an intimate setting to celebrate the last leg of the book tour. We'd all been so stressed over the last few months; it was nice to sit and enjoy the company of the people I'd come to regard as more than simply coworkers.

"Sit with me?" Kristine asked as she tugged me toward the table, a few familiar faces amongst the crowd. Adrian and Isobel were talking to an older couple, a striking redhead and a tall blond man who startlingly resembled Chase. The rest of that half of the table was filled with a few young couples and another older couple I didn't recognize. I knew Evan had invited their families tonight, so I was sure I'd meet them all later.

As Kristine tugged me toward the table, a familiar brunette turned the corner, her eyes widening as she turned toward us. "You guys are here too!" Kelly bounced in place before she sprang forward, hugging Kristine and me and tugging us toward the long table. "I'm so glad you were invited too. I was starting to feel like the thirteenth wheel, although now I'm just the fifteenth wheel instead."

Kelly chatted animatedly with Kristine as I watched, both barely coming up for air as she asked about our travels since we'd seen her in Chicago. Kristine left out all the hot sex we'd had, but Kelly kept glancing at our joined hands and smirking.

"Whoa," Kelly stopped talking abruptly, her eyes widening as she looked toward the door leading into the courtyard. "Who is that?"

Looking over my shoulder, I saw a familiar figure hesitantly headed in our direction, wondering if he'd brought his friends with him, but it appeared he was alone.

"Oh," Kristine laughed, smacking the back of her hand into my shoulder. "Crap, what's his name again?"

"Nathan," I sighed, rolling my eyes at her. I knew we'd only met the guy for a few hours at the book launch, but she rarely forgot anyone's name. It was clear I'd be carrying her out of here later if these two kept up with the wine consumption.

"Dayum," Kelly whistled, "Is he for me? Please say he's for me... I'd climb that mountain of a man like I was an explorer and mount his peak."

"Oh God," I sputtered, trying not to laugh at her antics. Her filter was almost as non-existent as Chase's. I wondered if Evan realized he was marrying his sister's fairer-haired clone.

Nathan hesitated, scanning the group seated at the table, clearly feeling out of place.

Kissing Kristine on the cheek, I let go of her hand and stood up, taking a few steps in Nathan's direction, holding my hand out in greeting. I was sure Chase or Evan had invited him, but they were still coming from the hotel. "Good to see you, man. Come sit with us."

"Sam, hey." He smiled hesitantly. "Chase found out I'd be in the city and invited me to dinner, but I didn't realize there would be so many other people here."

"Yeah. It's supposed to be a work thing to celebrate the end of the tour, but Evan flew in their families too. Chase and Evan aren't here yet." Kelly and Kristine's intoxicated laughter drew my attention back to the table. "There's someone you should meet."

Chase and Evan arrived shortly afterward. I sat back and quietly thought about what awaited us all when we returned home as Adrian toasted their hard work and dinner got underway.

Kristine and Kelly continued to bond over their Pinot noir, Nathan taking their antics in his stride, clearly intrigued by the elder Stineman sibling. He talked about his consultation project in Manhattan, keeping them both entertained with his story of the demanding architect he'd be working with for the next few months.

By the time Chase and Evan left, I was ready to return to the hotel, but I dutifully followed along as the table emptied after they disappeared.

"What's going on?" Kristine asked as she clung to my arm toward the back of the crowd.

"You'll see," I whispered back as we all filed into the small hallway overlooking the lower courtyard, watching through the large stone-encased windows as Evan dropped to one knee.

"Oh shit, not them, too!" she whispered as he held her hand over her mouth. "Is this where you were this afternoon?"

"Yeah." I nodded, holding my finger over my lips to quiet her so the group could hear Evan's proposal. It was oddly awkward but heartfelt, and Chase was practically in tears as she dropped to her knees in front of him on the stone path covered in rose petals. It'd taken hours for us to string all the lights, but I had to admit, it was the perfect setting for his proposal.

I felt a bit like we were intruding on a special moment as we watched it all play out, my heart clenching as I surreptitiously monitored Kristine's reaction. She looked half intrigued and half disgusted with the public display, leaning against my arm as she watched the happy couple's families fawn over them.

"God, I don't know why they're so eager to tie themselves down, but whatever floats their boat."

"What's so wrong with knowing who you want to spend your life with?" I asked, curious as to why the thought of such a serious commitment had brought out her snarky comments. She'd balked at the proposal we'd witnessed in Disneyland, but I hadn't expected this reaction after her more relaxed demeanor the last few days.

"Because it never lasts." She frowned, glancing up at me and then back to the glass in her hand, draining the contents. "And then what are you left with? Someone who resents you for the rest of your life? Excuse me if I'll pass on that kind of mistake."

And suddenly, with one comment, I realized while I was holding back decisions about my future because I wasn't sure where I stood with her, Kristine wasn't in the same position. She knew all along we didn't want the same things. She may have been letting her guard down, but she'd never want forever with me.

I'd just been the deluded idiot that assumed she needed time to open her heart and see how good we could be together. She was never going to want the future I did, and as I watched her reaction to the night's events, I knew that I needed to let go of my blind idealism and see things for how they really were.

THIRTY-TWO

KRISTINE

NEW YORK

Things had been awkward all morning. Sam disappeared out the door to my hotel room early with a stilted promise to return once he'd talked to Adrian about a few things going on at the office in our absence. He'd put the brakes on last night, just holding me in the darkness of my quiet room until the gentle caresses of his hand on the back of my head had lulled me into a partially intoxicated sleep.

He'd seemed amused by my drunken commentary most of the night, but something had changed on our ride back to the hotel. There was unspoken tension in our quiet trek across the city, and I didn't know what to say to break it. My track record with words wasn't the best, and I didn't want to blurt out the wrong thing and push him away.

Adrian and Isobel were taking on the remaining few book signings and readings back in Boston, gladly granting us a few days of paid vacation before we were expected to report back to them.

I was relieved Sam was accompanying me to Nana's party, knowing she'd be delighted that I was bringing him along. I wasn't sure how to introduce him to the rest of my family because the term boyfriend seemed a little infantile.

All I knew was that he'd finally worn down my defenses, not letting me escape when my fear of commitment reared its ugly head. Sam had metaphorically tamed the beast that was the mess inside my head.

My video interview with Sloane had gone well enough. Her focus clearly on the position in Boston. She'd seemed almost hesitant to answer my questions about the New York office, carefully steering my questions back to the fantasy position.

She'd told me they'd reach out to the final candidates as soon as we arrived back in Boston, congratulating me on a job well done on the tour and thanking me for my time. I wasn't sure if they'd be offering me the position, but I seriously considered turning down the New York position if they offered it and staying with Isobel. My family wasn't the driving force behind my decision any longer, but staying close to Sam might have been.

A hesitant knock pulled me from my chaotic thoughts, and I smiled as I opened the door to a rumpled-looking Sam.

"Hey," I smiled, opening the door wider. He'd checked out of his room, agreeing to stay with me for our last night here. "You get everything taken care of?"

"Yeah," he sighed, wheeling his suitcase inside and dropping into the armchair by the floor-to-ceiling windows, his head falling into his hands. "It's done."

"Are you okay?" I asked, crossing the room and running my hands through his soft hair.

He captured my hand in his, interlocking his fingers with mine and kissing my palm. "I'll get cleaned up in a moment. Just sit with me?"

He pulled me into his lap, tucking his face into my neck and clinging to me as I looked at the sun setting over the city, soaking up his undivided attention. Things were changing between us, and my heart warmed as he let me see his more vulnerable side. But then again, he'd never been the one who had trouble expressing their emotions.

"JUST STICK CLOSE TO me. They'll try to separate us if they can. I'm sure Gregory has told my parents about you. They'll look to corner us to poke holes in our story."

"Which is what?" Sam smiled as he sat on the edge of the bed, quickly tying an expert knot in his tie.

He'd come out of the bathroom much more relaxed, a small grin plastered across his face as he watched where I sat at the desk doing my makeup.

"What do you want it to be?" I asked, unsure of how he saw our changing relationship.

He stared at me for a few moments, his intense gaze a little unnerving, but I returned it, finally feeling like I'd turned a corner with my feelings toward him.

"I want you to be mine," he said quietly, causing my pulse to pound. "Even if it's only for tonight."

My throat was tight as I looked over my shoulder at him, nodding as I tried to decipher his suddenly serious demeanor. He could have my heart for more than tonight. It'd already been in his care for months without me realizing it. He'd been much gentler with mine than I'd been with his, and I knew that needed to change.

"I'm yours," I confessed quietly, realizing I meant it.

I'd been lying to myself the night before, letting my issues with my parent's marriage bleed into my reaction to Chase and Evan's engagement. The comments had been out of my mouth before I could contain them. Maybe the right kind of love could last without resentment.

And I wasn't going to hold myself back from the possibility anymore. It was time to let Sam see the real me, the one I'd kept under lock and key for years. Fuck my family and their broken relationships.

Maybe it wasn't too late to change. Nana had done it at eighty after staying in an arranged marriage for almost sixty years. I didn't want to waste that much of my life being afraid to love someone wholeheartedly.

"If only that were true," Sam muttered under his breath, but I heard him.

Staring critically at my reflection in the mirror on the desk in front of me, I vowed to let him past my defenses. It was time I stopped letting the fear of feeling like I wasn't enough rule my life.

"You're stunning," Sam whispered in my ear as I placed my hand in his, stepping out onto the curb in front of the imposing apartment building in uptown Manhattan.

"Thank you, but I'm a sure thing, Sam."

"And you're still stunning, regardless of your eagerness to get me naked."

Laughing, I tugged him toward the large glass doors, a familiar doorman holding one open for us.

"Nice to see you again, Ms. Willard."

I smiled, greeting the man who'd been stationed at the door for most of my life.

Nana had moved into a smaller unit in my parent's building, opting to rent out her large multi-level townhome once my grandfather passed away. She said it was too much for just her, and with how little time she spent in the city nowadays, it made sense to let another family use the space while she was on the Cape.

If it wasn't for my father and maybe Gregory, she'd probably relocate there permanently, but Nana was nothing if not loyal to her family. They just didn't always deserve it.

I probably also fell into that category, neglecting her to avoid confronting my father. At least I knew her door in the cottage was always open. But I probably needed to call first; I didn't want to walk in on anything that would scar me for life. Nana and Pietro seemed to be making up for lost time.

"You alright?" The firm grip of Sam's hand was a source of strength as we boarded the sleek elevator, the attendant greeting us before he pressed the button for the penthouse.

I nodded hesitantly, leaning into him as I clung to his arm. "I'll be fine. Just psyching myself up to face the firing squad."

"They can't be that bad." He smiled, tucking a loose curl behind my ear, fingering the large diamond stud in the lobe. The earrings were a present from my grandfather before he died, and I treated them like armor when I was forced to interact with my family. "These are pretty. You look nice, all cleaned up."

"I'd rather be dirty," I laughed, winking at the roguish grin that pulled at his mouth.

"I'll be happy to help you out with that later."

"Me too," I breathed as I stared at his handsome face. He'd carefully styled his hair, his face clean-shaven, and his suit perfectly pressed. My mother would be distracted by his pretty face and impeccable manners; hopefully, that would be enough to keep her from appraising his pedigree.

If anyone ought to be worried about being found lacking, it should be me. Their elite breeding just made them snobs, not better people, and certainly not any nicer. I was terrified I was headed for the same path, despite keeping my distance, but the last few weeks had given me hope of finding something more than their empty existence.

As the elevator stopped, Sam squeezed my hand, winking before he leaned in. "We got this."

The doors opened into a spacious penthouse suite, floor-to-ceiling windows across the entire space with a view of Manhattan most would kill for. It'd been remodeled after I left for Harvard, all of the historic touches I once loved erased to accommodate my mother's need to spend ridiculous amounts of money to make herself look important.

"Kristine," a deep voice to my right startled me, "nice of you to join us this evening. We weren't sure if you could step away from your commitments."

My father, Mason Willard the Third, stood just outside the door to his home office, the requisite glass of whiskey in his hands. His imposing height—well over six feet—and his severe features were intimidating to most. But to me, they represented a lifetime of not measuring up to expectations.

"Of course, Mason. I was invited by the birthday girl personally. It'd be rude to decline when I already planned to be in the city."

One heavily grayed eyebrow arched on his immobile forehead before he looked over my shoulder to Sam. "You must be the colleague we've heard so much about. Not from Kristine, of course. Her family is quite the point of embarrassment for her."

"Well, can you blame her?" another voice laughed. A slim, perfectly man-icured hand slipped around my waist. "Every time she comes home, you corner her and try to foist another brainless heir in her direction."

"Nana," I smiled, turning to give her a tight hug. "Thank you," I whispered in her ear. Being cornered right inside the door had not been a pleasant surprise.

"Mason, did you find that bottle of champagne I requested? The poor caterers had no idea what I was asking for. What a shame your wife can't manage to oversee a simple birthday party for an old lady. They couldn't find her anywhere."

"I'll see what I can do, Mother," he assured as he stepped around us, his face blank as he looked back toward me. But that was understandable since I knew he'd been getting more Botox injections than my mother since turning fifty. Not that he'd been all that expressive to begin with. If people called me heartless, I'd inherited it from him.

"Thank God you're here," Nana smiled, pulling me toward the main seating area and glaring at a few overly perfumed women seated on the couch.

Once they realized who she was, they hastily gathered their things and fled. "I don't know half the people here. Your mother invited all her succubus friends, and they've been gushing over how great I look *for my age* since I got here. They somehow think their poor performances as trophy wives for a few years before they were put out to pasture entitles them to my respect."

"Well." I smiled as I sat down, tugging Sam down next to me. "You do look pretty spectacular."

"Oh, stop it," she laughed, leaning back into her chair. "Your place in the will is secure. You don't need to flatter an old biddy like me."

She shook her head, glancing across the room, her features softening. She raised one hand, gesturing to someone, and then tipped back the rest of her wine glass.

"If it weren't for Pietro, I'd be hiding right now. He was talking to your father's boring business partners about profit forecasting. I was about to stab myself in the temple with one of your mother's prized heels. Lord knows why that woman needs an entire room full of shoes she can barely walk in. She's never been the most graceful creature."

I glanced at Sam, who'd been silent since we sat down, quietly rubbing his thumb over my hand as he scanned the room around us. I was sure it all looked intimidating, but none of these people held any real substance. It was all smoke and mirrors and millions of dollars of cosmetic enhancement. "If you couldn't tell, there are more artificial body parts in this room than in a Barbie factory."

He chuckled, squeezing my hand, but his expression was still distant.

"Were you planning to introduce me?" Nana interrupted, wiggling her eyebrows as she gave Sam a pointed glance.

"Sorry, of course. Daphne Willard, this is Sam Langley."

"I can see why you'd be so taken with this one," Nana winked as Sam leaned forward with his hand outstretched.

"It's nice to meet you, Ms. Willard. Kris speaks very highly of you."

"Oh, aren't you adorable? Call me Daffy, Sam. Chicklet told me you were a charmer, but you're just darling."

My cheeks heated as Sam looked down at me, obviously memorizing my grandmother's nickname to bring up later.

Nana's smile widened as she looked past us, Pietro stopping at the arm of her chair.

"Come meet Chicklet's young man, Piet. He edits those mystery books you love so much."

"Ah, another logophile," Pietro smiled. "What authors do you work with? Or is that a secret too?"

I scooted down, pulling Sam with me so Pietro could sit on the end of the couch closest to Nana. They held hands while the two men talked, and I could practically see the heart eyes Nana was throwing in Pietro's direction.

"What?" she mouthed as I smiled at their public display of affection. I was sure it drove Mason up the wall that she'd brought her new boyfriend home for her birthday party.

Nodding my head at the two men, deep in discussion over the latest crime drama Sam had edited, I realized that the only person in my family who mattered was giving Sam the stamp of approval.

BY THE TIME CAKE was served and Nana was called away to blow out her candles, Sam had spent half the night chatting with Nana and Pietro, easily keeping the conversation flowing.

"She's not so bad," Sam whispered as I leaned against his chest. We'd successfully avoided the rest of my immediate family, my mother steering clear because she and Nana only tolerated the other's presence in small doses.

"She's the only normal one in the family," I whispered back, still in awe of how she'd been casually dismissing the lingerers of my parents' social circle with grace and her sharp wit. They'd tried to work their way into our little group a few times, but she'd quickly driven them off with a few well-placed, thinly-veiled remarks on their character—or lack thereof.

I envied the subtle way she could put people in their place. My methods were a stark contrast, and I envied that my grandmother had never been called an ice queen. She'd made the most of her life, handling her situation gracefully, and I could only hope for half her character.

"This hasn't been as horrible as you'd worked it up to be." Sam's palm was running down my arm as we avoided the crowd, but my hackles rose as I looked toward the kitchen.

"Well, strap on your cup, Langley, because we've got an incoming."

It appeared that my mother had sobered up enough to confront me now that Nana was distracted, and my leech of a brother was hot on her teetering designer heels.

SAM

NEW YORK

"Oh darling, I'm glad you could take time out of your busy schedule to see your family. It's been quite some time. I was starting to think you'd forgotten where we lived."

Kristine's grip on my hand tightened as a slight woman, a full head shorter than her, despite the towering heels, stopped in front of where we were standing. She must have been the notorious Missy Willard, the woman Kristine rarely mentioned and usually only with disdain.

"Sam," Gregory greeted, holding his hand out in my direction, his gaze dropping to where his sister's hand was tucked inside my own. "I was wondering if you were the guest Kristine told Nana she was bringing along tonight. She seemed to think it was a boyfriend, but I knew she'd never bother to bring someone she was interested in romantically to a family gathering. That would entail her realizing she had a heart."

My hand clenched. Kristine's quick intake of breath at her brother's words caused my temper to flare.

"She did bring a boyfriend," I smiled, dropping my hand and pulling her into my side. It wasn't technically the truth, but my desire to get that self-satisfied smirk off his smug face was stronger than my need to define my relationship with his sister.

"Oh," he laughed, tipping his glass to his lips. "Did he step out for a moment?"

"Greg. Quit being a dick," Kristine sighed, reaching up to finger the button on my suit coat. "Sam is my date for the evening."

"You don't need to pretend," Gregory laughed. "It's insulting to your beard here to use him as a prop to distract our parents. Even Mother knows not to try to set you up after last time."

"Well," Missy smiled, "Trevor asked about you earlier. He's still single, and I'm sure he'd forgive your behavior from the last time you were in town."

"There's nothing to forgive," Kristine growled, her hand clenching into a fist. "I am not dating another of your friends' horrible offspring, no matter their bank account balance. I have no interest in being a desperate trophy wife grasping at straws to keep their husband's interest to remain flush with cash like someone I know."

"Honey," she smiled, her face eerily devoid of emotion. "I know you think this office romance is exciting, but trust me, they never last."

"Oh," Kristine scoffed, shooting daggers at the woman across from her. "You mean like the one you had with Mason?"

"My relationship with your father is different," she started, lowering her voice and leaning toward Kristine. "We came to a mutually beneficial arrangement a long time ago, and maybe it'd be in your best interests to look for something similar. Us Willard women just aren't built for all that romance nonsense."

"I'm nothing like you, and you married into the Willard name," Kristine hissed. "Don't pretend you know anything about giving a shit about people. Well, not beyond what they can give you. You couldn't even be bothered to raise your own children. They were just another way for you to secure your future."

"Krissy, I think you've had enough," Gregory frowned at the glass in her hand. It was full of water. Kristine had warned me earlier about keeping a clear head around her family, but it was apparent that didn't matter.

"Or maybe I haven't had enough," she laughed, tipping back the last of her water and leaning around me to deposit the glass on an empty table. "Sam and I came here tonight to celebrate Nana's birthday, not deal with you egotistical jerks. You want to know why I don't come home? Because I haven't felt welcome here my entire life. Nothing I do is good enough for you. And maybe staying in Boston, where people give a shit about me, is easier than coming here to be criticized or passed around like I'm some broodmare. I have a life, love my job, and don't come back here because I didn't choose to be related to you."

Her mother and Gregory shifted nervously, opening their mouths to talk, but Kristine held her hand up, indicating she wasn't done. "Sam came here despite my hesitations tonight because he cares about me." She paused, looking up at me and shaking her head. "And I care for him—a lot—even though I treated him like shit for months because no one in my life has shown me what a healthy relationship looks like."

"Keep your voice down," Missy sniffed, glancing around at the people who'd stopped talking around us.

"No." Kristine grabbed my hand, stepping back toward the entryway. "You don't get to tell me what to do. I'm not shrinking myself to please you any longer. I came to spend time with Nana, and now that I have, we're leaving. You terrible people don't get the privilege of knowing Sam. I'd choose him over you any time because he's a billion times more interesting than most people in this room. I'd pick him every time."

Her mother stood there with wide eyes, her mouth slack. Gregory didn't look much better, but I could tell he was holding back as his hands clenched at his sides.

I felt like yelling *Mic Drop* over our shoulders as Kristine grabbed my hand and dragged me back toward the private elevator in the ornate foyer.

"Do we need to say goodbye to your Nana?" I asked as she jabbed her finger into the call button.

"No. She saw the whole thing. Piet was holding her back from coming over. I'm fairly sure she started clapping when I dragged you out of there."

The elevator doors opened, and the older man inside nodded passively as he selected the button for the lobby. This entire world was foreign to me. Doormen and elevator attendants. Penthouse suites in Manhattan that were nearly as large as my parents' comfortable middle-class home in Michigan. Trust funds and marriages of convenience. It was clear we'd both grown up in vastly different environments, and the protective part of me wanted to take Kristine away from this place and never return.

These people didn't love her; they joked about her not having a heart, but they were emotionless zombies. She'd admitted everything I'd wanted to hear from her in the last several months to her mother in one vicious sentence.

Despite the ways she distanced herself, she cared for me. She may have even loved me, but this morning, I'd cemented things for her in a way that showed that I cared about her just as strongly. I knew her priorities and ensured her career went exactly where she wanted without me in the way.

"I'm sorry," she sighed as she slumped against my shoulder, glancing up at me with a look of open sincerity. "I knew they'd probably try to corner me, but I..."

"It's okay. I think that was a long time coming. Watching you stand up for yourself was amazing. You're stronger than you give yourself credit for. You may be convinced you're heartless, but I see you. I see how fiercely you care for the people who matter."

"I didn't mean to drag you into that, but I wanted you to meet Nana, and having you there made everything not feel like such an obligation..."

She was getting herself worked up again, and I couldn't resist her anymore. Even if this was the last time she spoke to me, I needed her. I needed to show her that I cared about her far more than even I'd confessed. And the things that would happen over the next few days were done for her. Because she'd worked so hard and deserved good things to happen to her, even if I wasn't around to watch them.

"Relax," I smiled, leaning down and softly capturing her lips, cognizant of our company in the elevator car. "You were astoundingly fierce in there. They deserved everything you said. Don't apologize for standing up for yourself."

"Sam, I…" Her voice cracked as her eyes watered, her hands grasping the front of my suit jacket and pulling me forward until my forehead rested against hers. Knowing how things would play out was the worst kind of agony, but I couldn't deny her the future she deserved. The future she'd earned.

"It's alright. I understand now. You don't need to explain anything to me," I whispered, my hands cupping her cheeks. I brushed away a stray tear with my thumb, leaning forward and kissing her softly. She'd probably hate me in a few days, but I wasn't taking this time with her for granted.

I wanted to lean forward and whisper my true feelings in her ear, but I knew that wasn't fair to her. This whole situation wasn't fair, but I was making the best of the options I was presented with.

The Uber I'd ordered was waiting at the curb as we walked through the heavy glass doors of the building, ready to take us back to our hotel. I wasn't sure what to say to her tucked in the backseat of the car. Nothing seemed like it'd make what she was feeling magically disappear, but I selfishly enjoyed how she clung to me in the back seat, her nose buried against my chest. The whole ride back, I ran scenarios through my head, trying to figure out how to fix what I'd done this morning, but whatever decision I made, she would pull away again, regardless. Every decision left her hating me, so I needed to stick with the plan and see it through.

When she swiped her card across the digital lock, I knew I shouldn't follow her inside, but when she looked at me over her shoulder, her hand extending to grasp mine, I knew I was too selfish to walk away.

"Can you hold me? Please…" she whispered as she steered me toward the bed and pushed me to sit on the edge. "I need—"

"Come here." Pulling off my jacket, I tossed it toward the chair and opened my arms. She didn't hesitate as she kicked off her heels and wrapped her arms around my shoulders, clinging to me tightly as she settled on my lap. "I've got you."

As her body trembled, I tucked her into my chest tightly, reaching up to pull the pins from her hair. I could feel the wetness from her tears against my neck, her breaths uneven as she finally let me see her walls break down. My fingers combed through her hair once it was free, a soft, dark cascade over her shoulders and down her back.

She seemed so fragile in my arms, this dichotomy of a woman who was so fierce yet so heartbreakingly alone in the world. I'd never felt this kind of desperation in my life. Sure, my family could be obnoxious, but I never doubted they loved me. I knew what it felt like to have the unconditional love of a parent who would make sacrifices for you. I knew what it felt like to have the friendship of a sibling, freely given without strings.

All this time, I'd thought she was incapable of feeling any real emotion, her heart locked up tight and inaccessible no matter how I tried to get her to open it to me, but now…

Now, I realized she didn't know how to express her emotions because they'd been conditioned out of her by the people who were supposed to care for her most. The love of her grandmother had kept her from turning into an emotionless robot like the rest of them, but she could only do so much.

"Please," Kristine whispered, her lips dragging along my throat as her hands gripped the back of my shirt. "Please pretend you love me, just for tonight."

My throat tightened, wanting to tell her that I didn't need to pretend, that I did love her, but I couldn't do that. I couldn't confess those things and then walk away. It was hard enough as it was.

"Kris, I..."

She leaned back, cupping my jaw and crushing her lips to mine before I could tell her to stop. Tell her that we shouldn't. That I needed to confess to her something that might make her despise me, but a selfish part of me couldn't resist how she felt in my arms. Just this once, I wanted to forget everything driving us apart and hold her as tightly as I could, for as long as I could.

"Touch me," she breathed as she unbuttoned my shirt, her lips sucking my neck.

Her hair slipped through my fingers, and I grasped it, pulling her head back and kissing her with all the desperation I felt. There was no solution to this that left us whole, where we could move forward without resentment or settling for things we didn't want. Tonight was all we had left, and I would embrace it while I still had the chance.

"You're so beautiful," I whispered against her lips as I pulled away. She was. She was glorious in her vulnerability, in the raw emotion she was letting me see, finally. "I don't deserve you."

She shook her head, tugging at my shirt and pushing it back from my shoulders. Her desperate fingers sought purchase on my chest as she leaned back in and nipped at my shoulder. "Don't talk. We have plenty of time to talk about this later. I just want to feel you. I want you inside me, Sam. Please, let me have this."

The sadness she'd been feeling faded into intense desperation that I returned as she stood and pulled her black dress down her shoulders, revealing the dark lacy underwear she'd covered up before I came out of the shower earlier. I'd been trying to distance myself, to step back and keep myself restrained for her sake because she didn't have all the facts. But I couldn't resist her.

"Take off your pants," she breathed, reaching behind herself and releasing her bra, the straps sliding down her shoulders and revealing a luscious expanse of soft skin. My fingers flexed on my zipper as I watched her cup her breasts, her heated gaze fixated on my barely concealed erection. "Don't stop."

She stepped forward as I slid them down my hips, eager fingers yanking on the material and hooking into the waistband of my boxer briefs. She climbed back into my lap as the material pooled at my ankles, grinding her hips into me as I tried to slow her movements. The scratch of the lace covering her against my sensitive skin was a welcome pain, the wetness seeping through the material making me throb against her.

Kristine's hands grasped the side of my neck as she undulated in my lap, my hands framing her hips. As I began to work the material down her hips, she shook her head, leaning in to nip at my earlobe. "Now," she panted, tugging on my earlobe with her teeth as she dug her fingernails into my neck. "Please. I want you. Just like this."

A moan tore out of my throat as she desperately pushed her hips down, grinding into my lap.

"Fuck," I grunted as she tugged on the hair at the back of my head, craving the pain mixed with the pleasure of having her in my arms. My fingers pushed the scrap of lace covering her to the side, sinking into her wetness as she gasped against my neck. She was almost dripping, her moans loud in my ear as I pressed against her clit, enjoying the way she moved with my hand, chasing her own pleasure.

"Oh God, it feels so good," she panted as I fucked her with my hand, working her up in my lap until she rode my fingers with desperation. "I need you, just you." Kristine's voice was a needy whisper as she clung to me. "I don't want anything between us."

"Are you sure?" I groaned as I tried to keep up with her frantic movements. I knew she was on birth control, but we'd always used additional protection.

"Yes."

Unable to hold back any longer, I tugged the lace further to the side, lining up my throbbing cock and pulling her down, groaning into her hair as I seated myself fully inside her warm body. Her fingers grasped my neck tightly, shifting her hips forward frantically as I thrust up from the bed, both of us desperately clinging to each other.

It was raw and needy, tinged with pain as we came together quickly and roughly, using each other to chase that intense pleasure we knew the other could provide.

"Fuck, Sam," she panted as she leaned back, her breasts swaying as she slammed her hips into mine, using my shoulders as leverage, her fingernails biting into my skin. I found myself egging her on, my fingers digging into her hips, helping her fuck me roughly, hoping she left marks I would feel for days. So, I'd remember how it felt to be with her like this. So, I'd know I did this all for her.

Leaning forward, I sucked on her nipple, biting down as she moaned louder, her hips faltering. I could feel the clench of her muscles against my shaft as I pressed my hand between us, strumming her clit as she fucked me. Her muscles spasmed around me, her back bowed, and her head fell backward as she ground against my lap, moaning hoarsely through her orgasm. It was the most uninhibited she'd ever been in my arms, and I gritted my teeth, forcing myself to hold off and watch this moment unfolding.

She was panting as she settled in my lap, her legs trembling as she sagged forward, burying her face into my sweaty neck. I clung to her, trying to record how she felt, her warm skin, her sweet smell, and how she felt when she came around me.

"You're so hard," she breathed as I throbbed inside her, right on the edge but not wanting to let go, wanting to hold onto her for a few more seconds. Kristine's soft lips dragged against my shoulder, sucking lightly as she began to rock in my lap, the wet slide of her satisfied body making me groan loudly. "I want to feel you come inside me," she whispered as her movements sped, my fingers clasping the lace against her hips so tightly I was sure it was digging into her skin.

"Oh, fuck, Sam," she moaned as I pulled her against me roughly, unable to resist the feeling of her any longer.

"With me," I panted as I pressed the lace into her clit, my thrusts uneven as I started to pulse inside her. She gasped against my neck, moaning out her second release, her hips grinding into my lap frantically.

"Holy shit," she laughed as she leaned back, kissing me softly, her fingers sweeping the sweaty hair from my forehead. Her eyes glowed with something I wasn't ready to acknowledge as she panted in my lap, a soft smile on her kiss-swollen lips. "You continue to surprise me, Sam. That was..."

I nodded, afraid to speak, as I stood from the bed, stepping out of my pants before turning and laying her against the sheets.

We kissed softly, her fingers slipping underneath the fabric on the back of my open shirt and grasping my shoulder blades. I settled between her hips, smoothing her tangled hair away from her face as I lost myself in the feel of her lips, knowing it might be the last time she let me in like this.

Knowing when I'd finally captured her heart that I'd only get to hold it for a few stolen hours...

THIRTY-FOUR

KRISTINE

BOSTON

"Welcome back, you two," Sloane smiled as she gestured to the two seats directly in front of her desk. The view behind her was just as impressive as the last time I'd been in her office. Downtown Boston displayed in the backdrop of her floor-to-ceiling windows.

"I know you're probably both anxious to hear the final decision of the hiring panel, but first, I wanted to congratulate you two on all the work you put in to make sure this book tour went off without a hitch. Diana filled me in on all the behind-the-scenes work you carried out, and I have to say, I'm a little disappointed this promotion will likely keep you two from working together regularly. You're quite the team."

Sam and I exchanged a look, his fingers idly tapping on the arm of his chair. Neither of us had slept well after the flight back from New York, the weight of returning to our real lives weighing heavily on this new fledgling romantic accord.

We hadn't made any grand declarations, but I could feel the love he had for me—at least I was still hoping it was love—in every little gesture, touch, look...it was overwhelming and scary, but I felt like we were finally on the same page.

I'd thought being with him constantly for the last several weeks would spell disaster and mean the end of our arrangement, but something had shifted that night in Seattle. I was done hiding from him, and I was done fighting to stay emotionally detached. And after his quiet support at Nana's party, I was pretty much head over heels. I just needed to build up the nerve to tell him.

"Anyway," Sloane continued with a bright smile. "As you know, we've offered the Non-Fiction position to Amanda from the New York office. And with some last-minute adjustments, Meg has also decided to stay in her current position within that office."

Looking over at Sam, his fingers still restlessly tapped out a steady beat on the armrest of his chair as he stared at something in the corner of Sloane's office. Something was going on, and he avoided eye contact, making me even more anxious for her to put us out of our misery.

"Meg isn't leaving? But..." I stuttered, but Sloane held up her hand to stop me from interrupting. I'd been ready to take on that position, but if she wasn't leaving the New York office, that meant...

"That leaves the position for the fantasy division as the last position open. You two were the final candidates, and each impressed the hiring panel with your work on the manuscript developmental edits and your performance on the tour the last few months."

This was it. The moment that determined both of our futures. My usually competitive nature was surprisingly quiet, hoping Sam and I could work things out, no matter the outcome. If he earned the promotion, I'd be happy for him. There would be other opportunities to advance my career. I'd never have the same chance to finally be with him in a real relationship.

"It was nearly neck and neck until our final virtual interview..."

Just spit it the fuck out already, Sloane.

"But we agreed as a panel that Kristine was the best fit for the position given the circumstances."

"Wait, what?" I frowned. Sam was still refusing to look over at me. I'd have thought he'd at least say something. We'd both been waiting for this moment, and he was acting out of character. He had been anxious all morning, and I didn't understand why.

"What circumstances?"

"Sam's availability to move into the open position at the Chicago office made this decision much easier because you two were equally qualified."

Chicago. What the fuck was she talking about? Sam was taking a position in Chicago? Since when was that even an option? Why hadn't he said anything? How long had he known about this? The interviews were three days ago. He hadn't said a word.

"I'm sure you'll both excel in your new positions, and I'm looking forward to working with you more directly, Kristine."

She continued to talk, but it sounded like the teacher from the Peanuts cartoon. Nothing she was saying made any sense. Sam was leaving? He was leaving, and he hadn't told me. Chicago was a thousand miles away.

I hadn't wanted to go to New York, but I'd been willing to try to make the four-hour distance work. Two hundred miles was a long distance, but a thousand...that was insurmountable.

Sloane kept talking as I stared at a red pen she had next to the closed laptop on her desk. Was this one of those moments when one decision changed my entire future? A decision I didn't make?

"HR will be in touch with both of you in the coming weeks about your transitions, and the relocation agency will contact you within the next day or so, Sam. I have to say. I was relieved when an alternate position opened because it was so difficult to choose one of you over the other for the position here. We'll miss you, Sam, but I have no doubt you'll do wonderful things in your new role within the house."

Miss him? Miss him... She didn't even know half of it. And apparently, neither did I. I didn't know a damned thing. And now I was left with the job I wanted, and the man that I...*fuck me*...the man that I loved—and now possibly despised—was going to be a thousand miles away as if the last several months meant nothing.

As soon as she was done talking, I stood, shouldering my bag and taking off for the door without a backward glance. If he could make this kind of decision without even talking to me first, I didn't want to hear it. No amount of cold feet or fearing commitment deserved this kind of treatment. I'd confessed things to him. He'd seen me cry...

"Kris, wait."

Sam's voice carried down the hallway, but I didn't stop, heading toward the door to the stairwell. I was seconds from crying or ripping someone's head off, neither of which I wanted to do in an elevator.

"Come on, seriously? Stop!" Sam shouted as I pulled open the door and started down the stairs as quickly as I could manage. Thank God for small favors since I wasn't wearing heels today.

"Kristine!" he shouted angrily over the sound of his footsteps on the concrete above me as I reached the first landing. Almost there. Then I could barricade myself in Isobel's office and fall apart over what a colossal idiot I'd been.

Grasping the strap of my bag tightly in my hand, I ran down the last set of stairs, ripping open the door to our floor and jogging across the tile in front of the bank of elevators.

Andrea looked up from her desk at the sound of the door banging into the wall as Sam tried futilely to catch up. "Are you okay?" she shouted as I took off past her desk and into the hallway that led to Isobel's office. I could hear her talking to Sam behind me, hoping she kept him distracted long enough that I could get away.

"What twisted your panties in a wad?" Carson fell into step beside me, his long legs easily able to keep up with my determined stride.

"Fuck off, Carson. Leave me alone."

"Geez, who pissed in your Cheerios this morning?" he laughed, but I was not in the mood to deal with his crap. It was bad enough he'd weaseled his way back into the office before his university semester resumed. "I hear you got a promotion. You too important to talk to the little people in the office anymore, Krissy?"

"Don't fucking call me Krissy, you colossal waste of good oxygen! Go back to your desk and pretend you never met me."

"What has you so... Oh, I get it. Lover's spat."

I made the mistake of glancing over my shoulder as I reached Isobel's door, and Sam was right there, a few steps behind us, with a determined look on his face.

"Don't even fucking think about it," Sam growled, reaching his hand out and pushing the door open, dragging me inside before I could protest. "Fuck off, Carson." Before Carson could reply from the hallway, Sam had closed the door and pressed me against it, his hands caging me in with his palms flat on the door on either side of my head.

"Why did you run?"

Oh, I don't flipping know, Sam. Maybe because my long-dead heart is lying on the floor of Sloane's office along with my dignity.

Instead of biting his head off—like I wanted to—I started crying. Loud, gut-wrenching, ugly sobs escaped my mouth as I clenched my eyes shut and pressed my entire body back into the door.

"Shit," Sam hissed as he cupped my face with his hands, pulling me forward and moving to wrap his arms around me. "I'm so sorry. I didn't see any other way. I couldn't let you give up your dreams for me. I couldn't make you go to New York either. Then when she told me that was no longer an option anyway... I'm so sorry."

His voice sounded as defeated as I felt, but he'd underestimated me again. I would have. I would have gone to New York or waited for a different position. I would have pushed my career goals aside for a little while, changed my course, or made any number of different compromises if it meant I'd get to see where this relationship with Sam went.

"Shhh," he whispered into my ear as my arms hung limply at my sides. There was no way I would clutch at him desperately and beg him to stay.

My sadness was quickly morphing into anger. Complete and utter frustration at his unilateral decision that blew up both our lives. How dare he?

"Let me go." My voice was low and rough, but he stepped back, grasping my shoulders. As my eyes opened, I saw his frazzled appearance, and my anger ramped up a notch. "Don't fucking touch me."

"Kris, I..."

"No." I shoved my hand into the center of his chest, causing Sam to stagger back a little, his hands releasing my shoulders. "You don't get to touch me, not anymore."

He nodded, shoving his hands into his pockets and looking like a dejected puppy. If I weren't so fucking angry with him, I'd laugh, but right now, I wanted to knee him in the junk. How dare he make this kind of decision without even mentioning something to me? I knew it was his career too, but was he fucking kidding me? He decided to move halfway across the country instead of risking the chance he might not get this promotion. He was just as bad as my father. Okay, not that terrible, but still. He should have said something. I thought that we... I'd convinced myself I was in love with him sometime in the last few days, and now...now that was all for shit.

"I'm sorry." His head was angled down, shoulders slumped forward.

"So you've said. But I don't think that makes any fucking difference right now. You didn't even tell me. What does that say about me? You can't trust me enough to talk about this before making this kind of rash decision. You let me think you were falling for me, Sam." My voice cracked a little, but I was still going to hold onto being pissed about this corner he'd backed me into. "And the scary thing is, I thought I was falling for you too, but obviously, that's a fucking joke."

"It's not a joke. I *am* falling for you. I've pretty much fallen," he confessed quietly, shyly looking in my direction. Goddammit. Those damned blue eyes of his were making it hard to remember why I was so fucking livid with him.

"No." My voice cracked again as I stepped back, flattening myself against the door. What I wanted to do was wrench it open, make a break for the elevators, and never come back into this damn building, although it's not like he'd be here anymore to remind me why I was such a fucking idiot.

"You don't get to tell me how I feel about you." Gone was the shy apologetic Sam, a fierce look of determination taking the place of the puppy dog eyes. "You have no fucking idea how horrible this decision was to make."

"Oh, please," I scoffed, crossing my arms over my chest. Normally, I'd adopt a stance like this to intimidate people, but I was fairly sure I was using it to hold myself together right now. "If it were that hard, you would have said something. Or were you too busy fucking me to consider how this might fucking destroy everything?"

"That's not what happened..."

"Are you kidding me? Of course it's what happened!" I shouted, no longer caring that Carson probably had his ear pressed up against the frosted glass in the hallway. "You made this decision for you, Sam. Not for me. You would have talked to me if you were making it for me. I was ready to go to New York for you, but no...you had to be secretive and blindside me."

"You were doing the same damn thing!" Sam started pacing in the small area in front of Isobel's desk, his jaw clenched, and his hands balled into fists at his sides. "I knew you didn't want to go to New York. I saw firsthand how horrible your life there would have been. You tried to convince me you stayed in the running because Isobel wanted you to, but I knew you were doing it for me."

"You didn't tell me about Chicago, you fucking asshole! It's a thousand miles from here. How exactly did you think that conversation would pan out for you? My decision only potentially took me a few hours away, not halfway across the country!"

"I didn't have any choice!"

"Bullshit. There's always a choice. My opinion just didn't matter enough to you."

Angrily swiping at the tears that were continuing to leak out of my eyes even though I was furious, I felt my throat closing at the thought that this may be the last time I saw him. I'd only worked briefly on one project in the last few years with someone from the Chicago office, and it was entirely through email correspondence. When Sam finally went, he'd be gone for good, and if this conversation indicated anything, I wasn't likely to see him again. The thought was enough to bring me to my knees.

If I questioned my feelings before, I didn't now. I loved him. But I didn't mean the same to him.

"Of course it mattered. *You* matter to me. Sloane told me that Meg's husband's transfer fell through, and she was considering staying on in her current position." He paused, running his hand angrily through the dark hair on the top of his head, shaking it roughly before he exhaled. "She told me that the panel wanted me here, but they had an editor leaving the Chicago office. You weren't going to get the promotion if I didn't leave. And then you told me you'd never want to make the mistake of getting married, and I panicked. Instead of risking you walking away from me, I selfishly chose to protect myself. Because you were going to break my fucking heart."

"So instead, you broke mine." The air in my lungs escaped in one heavy exhale, my body deflating even further as I leaned heavily against the door behind me. I didn't get the job. He did. And he gave it to me. "Fuck you, Sam."

"Chicago is only a few hours from my family, and I knew how much you were looking for a chance to prove yourself. I didn't want to be the reason you didn't move up since they gave the other job here to Amanda." He paused as he stepped forward, tilting his head to look into my eyes. "I didn't want you to hate me because I got the job, so I took the other one."

"But..."

"But you hate me anyway, so I guess it doesn't matter because we both know you would never let me into that locked-up heart of yours. I shouldn't have to beg you to love me."

"That wasn't your choice to make. For someone who said he could never despise me, *you* clearly couldn't love me either."

"I couldn't bear the thought of seeing you look at me like you're looking at me right now...every day. So, it's better if I leave." He lifted his messenger bag from the floor, pulling it over his shoulder as he took a few steps toward me. Stopping just shy of touching me, he closed his eyes. His pained exhale was loud in the otherwise quiet room. "Just so we're clear. I do care for you, Kristine. And that's why I had to make this decision because I knew no matter what you feel for me, you would have resented me for taking the job here, and you would have resented me if you found out I turned it down for you. There wasn't any way I would get to keep you, so this will make it easier to let you go. I'm sorry."

My mouth opened a few times, but I couldn't even formulate words right now, my throat tight and my eyes stinging. I'd thought telling my family off was hard, but this...

Sam grasped me gently by the shoulders, moving me away from the door before he pulled it open. My heart beat wildly in my chest as I watched him slip through the opening, giving me one last sad smile. I blinked back more tears as the door shut with a quiet click.

When Isobel had asked me if I'd ever change my career goals for a man, my answer had been a gut reaction. But now, I could see a gray area where relationships were concerned. You made compromises. You talked about your options and made decisions together. But Sam had stolen that from me and any chances of a relationship between us, even if his intentions were pure.

We were done.

I was done.

And I didn't see any way to come back from this. To find a way back to *us*.

THIRTY-FIVE

SAM

MINNEAPOLIS

FOR THE FIRST TWO hours of the six-hour drive north, my mind was working overtime, trying to figure out how I would stand being in the same room with Kristine for more than five minutes. In the six weeks since I'd seen her last, she had completely wiped me from her existence.

My emails bounced back, and the desperate calls were rejected, my text messages didn't send, her profile from Tinder had been erased—not that I'd opened it an obsessive number of times to look at her profile photos—and Isobel was refusing to act as a messenger. She'd cut me completely out of her life in the length of time it took me to settle in Chicago, and I couldn't stop thinking about her. I'd fucked up, I knew I had, but there was nothing I could do to change the decisions I'd made.

My stomach had churned when I sat on the video call the morning after Evan's proposal, but I'd been terrified that there was no future with Kristine. So, I'd cemented that reality.

My new team in the Chicago office was solid, and I loved being able to take on a new role working directly with the authors instead of just being a side note in a Word document. It felt like my input in the creative process mattered, and I'd finally found my stride out of Adrian's shadow. The head of publishing was invested in my success with Vivid, and I was finally within a few hours' drive of my family.

It should have been perfect. I was close enough for them to visit but not close enough for my mother to meddle or show up at my new apartment unannounced. Not having roommates was quiet, but I'd heard from Taylor and Caleb often. Blake had settled into my space in the apartment back in Boston as if I'd never been there. Making new friends was going to be a challenge, but a few other young professionals at the office weren't married yet and had no kids. With a little time, I could see myself being happy in Chicago.

But I wasn't. I loved my job and the challenges it presented, but I didn't feel the same excitement I'd felt going into the office over the last several months. I tried to tell myself I could move on, that if she could turn her back on me without letting me truly explain myself, then I was better off.

If only it were that easy to erase love from your heart. She'd imprinted herself there, and no matter how much I wished for the marks to fade, they didn't. I loved her, and I'd missed the chance to tell her that for real, not just while she was crying and staring at me like I'd broken her heart. The way I left Boston would probably haunt me for years, possibly the rest of my life, but I didn't see any other alternative.

She could hate me all she wanted, but I made the decision for her. I could have easily stayed in Boston, settled into the position there, and let her stay on with Isobel, but I knew she would never have been happy maintaining the status quo. She wanted more, and I wouldn't take that opportunity away from her.

Daphne had texted me a few days after I'd left the city, telling me that Kristine was heartbroken and my dumb ass needed to do something about it, but it was a lost cause. She'd kept me at arm's length for months while I was already a goner for her, and she saw my actions as a betrayal. It felt like a betrayal, but I'd been throwing myself at a brick wall for months. We'd both made mistakes that I wasn't sure we could fix.

Seeing her CC'd on emails from Sloane was the worst torment. She'd even asked if we would be interested in working on Chase and Evan's new novel, but I couldn't keep torturing either one of us like that. Stepping away was the mature thing for me to do, but it felt like swallowing a bag of nails.

"Thanks for riding up here with me." I smiled over at the brunette sitting in the passenger seat, feeling a little guilty that I'd been silent most of the ride through Madison. When she'd suggested carpooling to the engagement dinner in Minneapolis, I was a little skeptical, but Kelly had been a great resource while I was getting used to Chicago.

"It's not a problem. We were both going to the same place, so we might as well save on gas."

Kelly's head bobbed in my peripheral vision, biting her lip before turning to face me. "Have you spoken to her?"

"Hmm?" I hummed. I'd wondered how long it'd take her to bring up Kristine. I knew she'd picked up on our behavior toward each other in the bar that night we'd gone out with her during the tour. Part of me lamented that the sun was setting, meaning Kelly couldn't continue typing away at her laptop like she'd been doing since we left the city.

"Kristine. She's coming, right?"

"I don't know." Adrian and Isobel had flown in last night, along with a few others from Boston, but I had no idea if Kristine was coming. She'd been invited; Evan had asked me what was going on between us when he called to invite me to their engagement party, but I'd tried to keep things vague.

Chase and Evan weren't stupid. I think they knew something was happening during the tour, but Evan wasn't the type to pry into other people's personal lives. On the other hand, Chase seemed exactly that type. She'd just been too busy finishing up her romantic comedy series to make a big fuss over it, and she was closer to Kristine anyway.

"Weren't you two…" she trailed off as she made a crude hand gesture, poking her finger into her closed fist. "Ya know, playing hide the sword."

If she only knew what Kristine and I had done the last time that swords had been mentioned with a sexual connotation.

"It was complicated."

"Didn't look all that complicated to me. You two had some major chemistry. You weren't all over each other like my brother and Chase, but it was still there. I was low-key jealous that you two seemed to be pulling off working together and *working it together*."

"I thought there was something, but she hasn't talked to me in weeks." I knew it was my fault, but it still stung that she'd been able to push me out and move on.

"Long-distance can be challenging. Maybe if you give her some time, she'll come around."

"It's not that easy, and I'm fairly certain she hates me."

"Why? It didn't look like she hated you when we hung out." I started to open my mouth, but she held up her hand, stopping me. "And don't give me that—*it's complicated*—bullshit. Turning your back on that kind of connection must have taken something pretty major."

"We were both up for the same position, and I was told they planned to give it to me. Another position opened up in Chicago at the same time, and if I took it, they'd give her the promotion in Boston."

"Ah, I get it now. You sacrificed what you wanted to ensure she got what she wanted."

"It also moved me closer to my family in Michigan, so it wasn't completely altruistic, but yes. I didn't want to be responsible for her losing the job." I didn't want to be responsible for coming between her and her freedom. That may sound dramatic, but I knew if things hadn't fallen apart with the position in New York, even thinking of sending her back to her family was like clipping her wings. After seeing the light go out of her eyes at her grandmother's birthday party, I couldn't do that to her.

"Did you ask her if that was what she wanted?"

"If you hadn't noticed, she isn't the easiest person to get close to. I know I should have talked to her before I took the job, but I didn't see any other way. Two other candidates were waiting in the wings, and Kristine worked her ass off for that position. She deserved it as much as I did." She also never gave me any indication until our last night together that she felt for me what I felt for her, but by then, it was too late. Things had already been set in motion that I couldn't stop.

"Maybe she wanted *you* more than a promotion."

"It's too late now." I shrugged, glancing down at where my phone was mounted on the dashboard. We had another few hours until we got to the hotel, and while talking to Kelly was keeping my mind off what would be happening tonight, dredging up my past mistakes wouldn't change anything. "Can we change the subject?"

"Neither of you is dead yet, and last I checked, modern technology made it pretty damn easy for people to stay in touch. You should try to talk to her." Of course, she'd ignore me. Parts of her personality reminded me of Kristine, tactlessly bulldozing her way into getting what she wanted.

"She's blocked me on everything. I don't think she wants to communicate with me."

Kelly tapped her fingers on her knees, squinting as she looked over at me. It made me want to squirm, but I was still trapped in the car with her until we got to the hotel. "You don't seem like the type to give up easily, Sam. You love her, right?"

A few months ago, it would have been hard for me to answer that question easily, but the phrases 'hindsight is 20/20' and 'absence makes the heart grow fonder'—while terribly cliché—were startlingly accurate.

"Alright, don't answer, but I could see it then and still see it now. Beneath that armored exterior is just a woman who wants to be loved. So, if you love her, you need to tell her, no matter how many ninja stars she throws in your direction. She is your feisty little samurai right?"

"I'll think about it."

"You do that," she ordered as I turned off the highway, letting the conversation drop for now. If I had to stop for gas every time she tried to corner me, neither one of us would be getting to sleep at the hotel tonight.

WALKING INTO THE RESTAURANT with Kelly the following evening, after she'd forcibly dragged me out of my hotel room, I scanned the bar area and saw a few familiar faces. At the other end of the long counter, Isobel sat on a barstool next to Adrian, who had one arm loosely draped around her back. She looked different. I couldn't quite place why, but as Adrian's other hand slipped into her lap, his palm settling against her abdomen, I knew I'd missed something major since I'd been gone. It seemed all those long working lunches and dinners had produced something significant.

"She's here," Kelly whispered, tugging on my shirt sleeve, drawing my attention back to the open doors of the event room where Chase and Evan were hosting their engagement dinner.

Kristine wore a short black dress reminiscent of the one she'd worn to Nana's birthday party in New York. Her hair was down and loosely curled around her shoulders, several inches shorter than when I saw her last.

"Close your mouth. You're drooling," Kelly snickered as she squeezed my hand. "Go get her, stud."

Then she veered off to a table in the corner that held an older couple. The man looked to be an older version of Evan, and they were vaguely familiar, so I assumed they were her parents. They'd come up a few days earlier, so Kelly couldn't catch a ride with them.

I knew she had a car in the city, but Evan had asked if I minded giving her a ride since we both lived nearby one another. My modest one-bedroom apartment wasn't quite in the same price bracket as her trendy condo, but we did live within a few blocks of each other.

Kristine turned away from where she'd been chatting with Chase, her eyes narrowing as she watched Kelly walk away.

"Hey, you made it." Evan stood from a nearby table, reaching forward to shake my hand. I smiled as I made eye contact with him, glancing back toward Kristine, noting the glare she had aimed in my direction. So, she magically hadn't decided to forgive me in the last few weeks.

"We weren't sure if you could come up, but thanks for letting Kelly tag along. She may look like a responsible adult, but my parents were worried how many speeding tickets she'd rack up if left to her own devices."

"Of course, man. Wouldn't miss it. Although I'd have thought you and Chase would be sick of me by now. I know we were all ready for that tour to be over."

"Eh, it had its moments. Have to admit, Chase and I had a bet going about you and Kristine, but we were clearly wrong about what was going on between you."

We were all off the mark on what had happened, but I knew they'd been whispering about us when they didn't think we were paying attention. I'd told Kristine she was paranoid, but maybe we were more obvious than we'd thought. Not that any of it mattered now. We'd both gotten what we wanted professionally, and I knew that truly mattered to her.

The rest of the night was a choreographed dance of avoidance on her part. I tried to sit near her at dinner, but she conveniently appeared at a different table after going to the bathroom the second I sat down. I attempted to corner her at the bar, and she pointed Adrian toward me. I tried to get Kelly to play wing-woman and get her to acknowledge me, and she gave her the cold shoulder.

It was like the beginning of our working relationship all over again. She was doing anything she could to avoid talking to me. But this time, at the end of the weekend, I wouldn't be able to corner her in any elevators. This was my last chance to convince her what happened between us wasn't over, but she was shutting me out at every opportunity.

By the time dessert rolled around, I'd all but given up and decided maybe it was best to return to the hotel. Kelly's parents were still holding court at one of the tables with some of Evan's relatives who'd made the trip up, so she asked to catch a ride back to the hotel with me.

"She's still holding quite the grudge, isn't she?"

"You think, Captain Obvious?" I knew I was being a dick to Kelly for no reason, but I'd mistakenly thought that I might be able to talk to her since Kristine had a few months to cool down.

"Don't be an asshat, Spamela." she laughed as she flicked me in the side of the neck.

"Please don't call me that." Kelly's face sobered as she looked at me, probably sensing that I was emotionally wiped after being outright rejected all night. At least if she'd talked to me, even if it were to yell at me or tell me to fuck off, I'd be able to gauge how she was doing. Icing me out as she had just prolonged the torture for both of us. But she wasn't exactly known for facing her problems head-on. I should have known better.

"You're not giving up, right?"

"What the hell am I supposed to do? She made her opinion of me glaringly obvious."

"So, you're not even going to try? I thought you said you loved her. Maybe you need to man up and figure this shit out. Make her listen."

"No one makes Kristine do anything." I didn't want to admit defeat yet, but it was clear that I was losing the battle. And I'd probably already lost the war.

Kelly let me wallow in my misery, heading up to her room after we returned to the hotel. I was tempted to drown my sorrows in the hotel bar, but even I drew the line at drinking alone. Normally I'd text Adrian, he was always up for a fun time, but he'd left the dinner a little early when Isobel started getting tired. They hadn't said anything, but the small bump she was sporting was hard to hide in the form-fitting dress she'd been wearing. I'd been around enough pregnant women to know when someone was expecting.

It was still strange not to see them at the office every day, and now I didn't even get to sit on the sidelines with popcorn as Adrian tried to figure out how not to screw up fatherhood. Kristine was probably losing her shit over it, but she wasn't working with the same team anymore, either. I wondered if Isobel would stay in her current position once the baby came, and I also wondered what would happen if the romance position was up for grabs. Would Kristine want to step into her place?

LOUD KNOCKING AND A few muffled curses from the hallway startled me. I'd just been lying in the dark, trying to get my brain to turn off. My reservations were for another night, but I might drive back to Chicago early tomorrow after tonight. There wasn't anything keeping me here. Evan and Chase were here looking at wedding venues, and despite them asking me to be an usher, it'd be a little weird for me to hang around while they were busy.

As I padded across the carpet toward the door, there were two more sharp knocks; whoever was out there was impatient.

"Hold on a sec. Let me unlock the door."

"Hurry the frick up!"

My eyes widened as my hand paused on the lock. Only one person used that word, and she'd spent the entire night pretending I didn't exist. Why would she be showing up at my hotel room?

"Kristine?"

As soon as I pulled the door open, she shouldered her way into the room, pushing it closed behind her and dropping her purse on the floor by the door.

"What are you doing?"

She narrowed her eyes, placing her hands on her hips as she glared at me.

"What do you think I'm doing here, Sam? I came to find you, you asshole."

"Could have fooled me. I tried to talk to you several times tonight, and you avoided me like the plague."

"Well," she huffed. "I'm here now, so shut up and listen to me, Spamela."

As soon as I opened my mouth to respond, she reached forward and pressed her palm across my mouth.

"Shhh. I didn't say you could talk."

Nodding, I took a few steps back and sat on the edge of my bed.

I expected her to take a seat on the desk chair a few feet away, but she shocked the hell out of me when she kicked off her high heels and climbed right into my lap.

Instinctively, I grasped her hips, noting the scent of wine on her breath once she was settled.

"Are you drunk?"

"No," she snapped, resting her hands on my shoulders. "I've never been more clear headed."

My brain was confused, but other parts of me had perked up as she settled on my thighs. She was staring at my mouth and claimed she came here to talk, but she was being quiet for someone who had so much to say.

"I'm so fricking angry at you," she hissed as one of her hands grasped the side of my neck. After a few moments of tense silence, it slipped toward the back of my neck and gripped the hair at the nape.

"I hadn't noticed." Poking the bear on my lap probably wasn't smart, but things had never been easy between us. One of us was always being a smartass. It was just how we worked.

"Shut up, Sam."

She licked her lips, and my fingers tensed on her sides as she scooted closer, bringing her in direct contact with the growing problem in my sleep pants. Clearly my dick had missed its playmate. A soft gasp rang out as she ground herself against me.

Afraid to move, I tried to sit still as she shifted, but it only worsened my problem. She was sending mixed messages for someone who hated me.

"Why are you here?"

"I don't know," she whispered as she leaned her forehead against mine. "I honestly don't know. I should stay away from you, but..."

"But?"

A single tear tracked down the side of her face, and I hated that I'd been another person who'd let her down. She'd been blindsided when we returned to Boston, and I knew I was the cause. She was right. I should have talked to her after my video interview with Sloane, but I was afraid she'd resent me eventually if she found out she'd been passed up for the job. Going to Chicago meant she got what she wanted. I never factored in her wanting me instead.

"It hurts too much to stay away."

I'd never had faith that she'd choose me without hesitating, so I'd run to protect myself. I'd accused her of running for the same reasons, hating it when she pulled away when things became serious. But in the end, I'd been the one to flee instead of figuring out the future with her. The decision had already been made when I realized she might love me too.

"Kiss me, please?"

Those words were all I'd wanted from her a few months ago. Her acknowledgment that she needed me too. That our relationship hadn't been one-sided.

"Please?" she murmured, cupping my cheeks and tilting my face toward her, dragging her soft lips against mine.

"I'm sorry," I whispered, momentarily leaning forward and losing myself in her taste. "I'm so sorry. I didn't want to leave you."

"Everyone does," she whispered brokenly, making my heart hurt. She rocked over me frantically, desperate whimpers escaping her throat as she kissed me again, over and over. We poured everything that had gone unsaid into each other's lips, only pulling apart momentarily as she lifted my shirt off, her fingers digging into my shoulders as she dove back in for more.

"We should talk," I gasped as she ground her hips against mine, her fingers pulling down the straps of her dress, letting it pool at her waist.

She grasped my hands, pulling them to cover her breasts. "I don't want to talk. Talking makes things more difficult. Touch me. Pretend you felt the way I thought you did that last night."

"But..."

She leaned in, letting her lips close around my earlobe. "I want you to fuck me, Sam. I'll beg if you need me to. Isn't that what you want from me?"

"Fuck," I groaned as she pushed me to the bed, digging her fingernails into my chest. "I want so much more than that, baby."

She grasped the material of the dress around her waist, pulling it over her head and roughly pitching it off the side of the bed. Her breasts heaved as she ground her hips against me, the lace barely containing the swells of her chest.

Flashes of the last time we were together like this wound their way through my thoughts, the desperation of that last time we were together fueling my need to do this differently, to make this better for her. I'd been selfish the last time, but I could make this time better.

Grasping her hips, I leaned forward, kissing her shoulder. She dug her fingernails into my shoulders roughly, growling in my ear as she ground into my lap.

"I don't want tender, Sam. I want you to make it hurt. I want to remind myself why I should stay away from you."

My fingers slowed her movements, urging her sideways as I laid her down against my sheets, her dark hair spreading out behind her on my pillow. "I don't want you to hurt anymore. Not because of me."

"Just fuck me."

"You know it's not fucking anymore. It hasn't been for a long time." I pushed down my pants, climbing back toward her naked. She dragged her hand down my chest as I pulled at her panties, drawing them over her hips and down her legs, leaning forward to softly kiss her stomach as I reached behind her to release her bra straps. My fingers traced the exposed skin, my lips following and cupping one swell as I sucked at the other. She tugged at my hair as my other hand traced across her hip, my fingers teasing her before they settled against her throbbing clit.

"Fuck me anyway," she moaned, pressing her hips into the movements of my fingers and grasping at the hair on the back of my head. "Don't play with me. I'm tired of the games. Please. I need you inside me."

Kissing my way up her chest, I softly captured her lips, settling between the cradle of her thighs, the head of me pressing against her.

"Sam," she groaned as she pulled my hair, breaking the soft kiss. "I want it hard."

"No," I whispered, lining myself up and teasing her with the head of my cock. "Do we need anything?"

"No," she gasped, and I pressed my thumb into her clit as I slipped inside her.

"God, you feel…" I moaned as I shifted my hips forward, slowly sliding into her body. It was just as intense as I'd remembered, the raw feel of her surrounding me.

My hands framed her face, watching her eyes drift closed as I set a slow rhythm inside her, rolling my hips into hers languidly. She wanted me to take her roughly, but I couldn't. I needed her to feel every inch of me, to know that I hadn't meant to hurt her.

She gasped against my lips, her eyes fluttering open as I tilted my hips, using my knees as leverage to drive into her. Her soft hazel eyes bored into mine, her lashes wet as I joined my body with hers unhurriedly, reveling in the intense feelings of being with her swelling in my chest.

"I…" I panted; my throat tight as I tried to find the words to tell her how I felt.

"No," she shook her head, her fingers covering my lips as she thrust her hips into mine from the bed. "Just feel. Please don't say anything," she moaned, her back arching as she pushed against my shoulder.

I leaned back, grasping her hips tightly in my fingers as I settled on my knees, thrusting forward into her, watching her breasts shake as my thrusts increased in intensity.

"Oh, fuck, just like that," she moaned as her head rolled to the side, her back arching as she pushed her hips into my movements. A soft pink flush spread across her fair skin, covering her neck as her moans increased.

I gripped her hips tightly, thrusting into her as her fingers grasped the sheets tightly, her knuckles turning white as her moans rang out around us. My body tensed as I felt her clench against me, a loud cry slipping between her parted lips as she arched up, gasping through her climax.

Falling forward, I grasped her hip, pulling her legs tightly around me as I drove into her, claiming her mouth as I chased my release. She kissed me desperately as I stilled, moaning into her mouth as I came inside her.

My chest heaved as I pulled her against me, rolling onto my side and tightly holding her to my chest. She intertwined her legs with mine, her fingers digging into my shoulder blades as she burrowed into me.

There were so many things I wanted to say to her, words burning in the back of my throat. I held her instead, running my fingers through her soft hair and closing my eyes, content to fall asleep with her in my arms.

My fingers grasped cold, empty sheets when I awoke, and I saw no traces of Kristine from the bed other than the indentation in the pillow next to me. Her purse was no longer by the door, and her dress wasn't on the floor with her heels anymore.

Squinting, I grabbed my glasses from the nightstand, focusing on the piece of hotel stationery that was tucked into the doorframe.

Getting up from the bed, I knew I would not like whatever she'd left on that note before she snuck out while I was asleep. I had a feeling I'd just been *Dear John*'d.

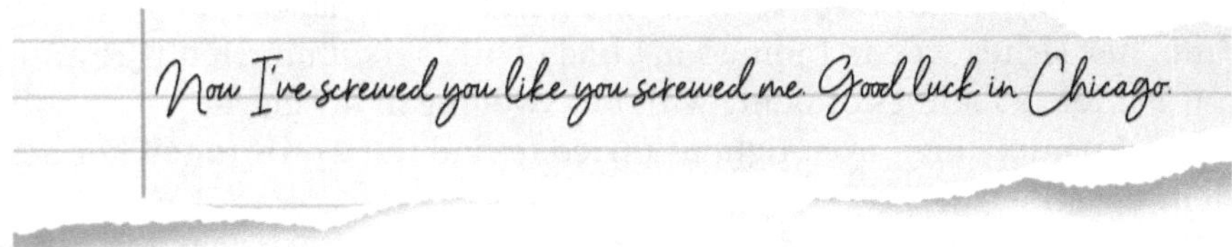

My pulse pounded as I read the hastily scrawled words. I wasn't even sure how to respond to that. She was still mad at me, but she'd been the one who showed up here last night and initiated everything. I knew having sex with her again wouldn't magically solve our problems, but I thought she'd at least stick around so we could talk. Clearly, it was just about revenge for her or taking back the power. Whatever it was, the message was loud and clear. She didn't want anything to do with me.

I almost balled up the paper and threw it to the floor, but then I saw *TURN OVER* printed neatly in the bottom corner.

I wish things were different but I don't see any way past this. I would have given up this job for you. I hope you know that. I would have let it go if it meant you staying with me. I don't know how we come back from this, so I snuck out and did the fucking walk of shame back to my room because I couldn't let you go again without falling apart and begging you to come back.

I ~~loved~~ love. I'm fairly sure I love you, Sam. But I screwed things up between us from the start and for that I'm sorry. I hope you have a good life in Chicago, closer to your family and everyone who means something to you. I wish I could take back every time I pushed you away, but sometimes things aren't meant to be, no matter how much you want them to be.

That sounded like one of those cliche lines I tease Chase about so I'm just going to stop writing now. I want you to be happy, so please just let this go. I only wanted to see you one last time. Now we can both move on.

All my love, Kristine

Shit.

I wasn't sure what I was supposed to do with this letter, but I wasn't letting her walk away again, not knowing how she felt. Moving on was the last thing I wanted to do right now.

Throwing on my clothes and flinging open the door to my room, I nearly collided with Kelly in the hallway.

"Hey there, lover boy," she laughed, rubbing her hand over the mess of my hair. "I take it she found you."

"What?"

"Kristine." She frowned, taking a step back. "She showed up at my door last night looking for you. Told me Evan gave her my room number."

"What?"

"She seemed to think something was going on between us. Thought you'd be with me, but I gave her your room number." She leaned around me, peeking around my partially opened door. "Huh, I thought she'd still be in there with you. Did she go back to her room to get something?"

"What?"

"Man, she really must have screwed the brains out of you," she cackled, and I grasped her shoulders, pulling her away from my door.

"She left. Do you know which room she was in?"

"What?"

"God, Kelly. Do you know which room Kristine was staying in? I need to talk to her. She was gone when I woke up this morning, but..." I raised the letter that was still clutched in my fist.

"Oh shit, did she fuck and duck?"

"Kelly," I huffed, shaking her shoulders and glaring down at her. "Focus."

"Oh, yeah. She's on the third floor. Let's go."

"No, just tell me the room number." I shook my head, stepping around her and heading toward the elevator.

"Yeah, right. I'm totally coming for this. I love a grand gesture. Let's do this," she clapped her hands, following me onto the elevator with a slightly crazed look of excitement.

By the time we got near room 347, I was a mess, but I stopped a few doors down, grasping Kelly by the shoulders again and stopping her in her tracks. "Stay."

"I'm not a dog, Sam," she laughed as she tried to take a step forward. "I don't just stay because some guy commanded me to."

"Nope." I shook my head. "You stay here."

"Oh, come on," she pouted. "You're no fun."

"Yup, just call me *joy killer.*"

"Fine."

"Stay." I pointed at her feet before I turned around and stepped up to Kristine's door, knocking three times and holding my breath as I listened for signs of life. She'd had a few drinks last night, but I think the nonstop sex half the night would have burned away any chance of a hangover.

Silence stretched down the long hallway. The only sounds were my breathing and a rustle of clothing with the barely restrained bouncing that Kelly was doing in my peripheral vision.

Knocking again, I waited, still not hearing anything.

"Are you sure it was 347?"

Kelly nodded, stepping forward, shouldering me out of the way, and rapping her knuckles on the door. "Kristine, it's Kelly. Open up."

"Why would she open for you but not for me?"

"Shh," she chided as she leaned against the door, her ear pressing to the surface. "I don't think she's here. And the Do Not Disturb sign isn't out. Did she...?"

Fuck. She'd left. Of course, she wasn't answering the door if she'd checked out.

"Would the front desk tell me if she checked out? Where would she go?"

"Let's go." Kelly grabbed my hand, towing me toward the elevator, riding silently to the ground floor.

Kristine wasn't in the small seating area where the complementary breakfast was being served. Somehow, I knew that we wouldn't find her.

"Let's ask. Maybe she's still here."

Kelly trotted over to the desk, and I followed, my footsteps heavy as she talked to the clerk.

"I'm sorry, Ms. Willard checked out and had the shuttle take her to the airport about an hour ago..."

Fuck...she was gone. She panicked again, and I couldn't blame her. After all, hadn't I been the first one to leave?

KRISTINE

BOSTON

So, MAYBE THE NOTE was a little much, but I'd panicked when I'd woken up at four-thirty in the morning with Sam wrapped around me. That night hadn't changed anything. He was still in Chicago, and I was still in Boston. Things between us would never be resolved unless something major changed.

No matter how much I missed him, a long-distance relationship without any plans to change wasn't an option. He'd eventually find someone who wasn't constantly pushing him away, and then I'd have the painful privilege of hearing about his perfect new girlfriend through social media. Maybe he'd even show up with her at Chase and Evan's wedding in a few months.

Nana had read me the riot act when she found out what had happened with the job, telling me I was being an idiot if I just let him go without a fight, but there wasn't anything left to fight for. Sam had left. He'd gotten a better offer than anything I could give him and jumped at the chance. I couldn't blame him, not with how I'd treated him. He was right to accuse me of breaking his heart. It may not have been intentional, but I probably would have ruined him with my tendency to close out everyone and everything close to me.

Work was busy, and it'd been a steep learning curve, having to go from answering to only Isobel to working with several different departments and supervising my own team of three copy-editing interns. I enjoyed it, but it wasn't as easy a transition as expected. And I wanted to talk with Sam about it, but I'd cut him out so brutally. I knew he'd balk at me coming to him for advice or even to have a friendly ear. The office felt more isolated than ever, and I realized how dependent on his company I'd become in the months leading up to the book tour.

It also bruised my ego more than I wanted to admit that I wasn't the first pick for the position. Sam may not be the manipulative asshole that my father was, but he'd diminished my achievement by passing off the job to me. Sloane seemed happy to have me in the position, but I still felt I hadn't earned it. It may not have bothered anyone else, but being the second choice ate at what was left of my ego. Not that my ego and sense of self-preservation had gotten me anything but a broken heart and wounded pride.

It also sucked that now I had no one to talk to about whatever weird relationship was still going on with Isobel and Adrian. She was pregnant—I knew that much from the ginger ale and saltines she kept on top of her filing cabinet—but my new job duties left me extraordinarily little time to spend with her lately. She was training my replacement, and knowing I was almost her equal was weird. I'd been with her so long; it was bizarre to walk to my own—albeit much smaller—office in the morning instead of hers. It was on the other side of the floor, so I didn't even see her in passing. Loneliness had also settled in over the last several weeks. My interns had all been assigned cubicles, so I was often in my office by myself. Isobel wasn't on the other side of the room, and I didn't even have space for a table and chairs in my office like she did if I decided to invite my interns to work there.

The private conference rooms were still mostly vacant, but I got a weird pang in my chest every time I looked at those closed doors, so I'd started avoiding that corner of the floor.

Several months ago, I was perfectly content to work in peace and quiet, and now my brain was filled with nonsense I didn't want to focus on. I missed Sam fiercely some days, almost to the point of tears, which would have shocked me before I'd fallen for him, but now, he was gone. If only my heart got the memo.

His absence didn't make my heart grow fonder. It just ached like I was missing a limb instead. He'd slowly worked his way into my heart, and now I didn't know how to get him out.

I was surprised when Chase had called to invite me to the engagement party, but I guessed with all the time we'd spent with them on the tour, we'd all grown closer together. She'd fished around a little about Sam when we'd talked, but all I had to tell her was that he was in Chicago, and no, I hadn't talked to him since he left Boston, and she dropped it.

He'd tried to call me several times a day until I decided to finally change to a local mobile phone number, turning off my old one from New York. It had the bonus of making it harder for my family to contact me, not that they were speaking to me since I'd embarrassed them at Nana's party.

I knew it was shitty of me to ghost him, but he'd broken something inside of me. For the first time in my life, I felt like I'd finally connected with someone and let my guard down enough for them to see the real me, and he'd pulled the rug out from under me. It hurt worse knowing I deserved it because I'd been so horrible to him for so long that he didn't expect anything else from me. I'd realized my feelings for him too late and hidden behind my insecurities.

I was supposed to be the one with the commitment issues, but he'd left when things got messy. It was a bitter pill to swallow that he'd left without saying goodbye, but I hadn't given him much of a chance to anyway. Isobel had castigated me for asking if I could work from home the last two days he was in Boston, but I couldn't face him. Now, I was kicking myself for not getting some closure. But closure wouldn't have helped anyway because that meant letting go of him and moving on.

I'd thought he'd been close to telling me he still loved me, but I'd stopped him, knowing it'd make my heart crumble even further. Sam had broken me, and all it would have taken to glue me back together were those three magic words but knowing there was no way for us to be together would have shattered my heart into more pieces than before.

This was why I didn't date, why I didn't put myself out there emotionally, because it gave someone the power to tear your entire world apart.

I knew if I'd stayed that morning, I would have said things I couldn't take back, and he would have told me things that probably would have made it harder to walk away again, but I'd lied in the letter. We weren't better off apart. We fit together. He softened my sharp edges, and I—I became the person I wanted to be when he was around.

I'd been trying to absorb everything about him into my skin that night, knowing it would be our last time together. I hadn't known before that the final night in New York would be the last time I was with him, but now that I had been with him one more time, the ache was worse than I'd anticipated.

"You planning to sit there in silence, brooding the entire day?"

"What? What are you doing here? Aren't you supposed to be at a signing or something?"

"Oh," Chase smiled as she settled into the small solitary chair across from my desk. "Evan's fine. Diana is there. He doesn't need me anymore."

"I doubt that. I didn't realize you two had the self-control to do things separately." I smiled, only a fraction of my typical sarcasm present. I couldn't help noticing how she seemed softer around the edges lately. Chase was never an outright bitch like I tended to be, but she hated how some genre editors, Adrian included, treated her just because she wrote romance novels.

She invariably came into the office armed with quick wit and always had Isobel to back her up if needed. Still, I'd noticed she seemed much more content since she'd started spending most of her time in the middle of nowhere Connecticut with her husband-to-be.

"Ha-ha, you think you're so clever. He's fine. He's gotten so much better at being around crowds in the last few months, even all by himself, like a big boy." She paused, a sly smile pulling at her lips. "So, how's Sam?"

My fingers stopped tapping at the corner of my desk as I narrowed my eyes in her direction. She either knew something, or she was fishing. Which one of those was debatable.

"Why would I know how Sam is? If you hadn't noticed, he doesn't work here anymore."

"Someone sounds defensive." Her posture was relaxed as she leaned back in her chair, unaffected by my tone. "I just figured you might know since you spent the night with him after my engagement dinner."

"Where did you...?" The smirk on her face answered for her. "Kelly," I sighed, knowing that she'd seemed closer to Sam while we were in Minneapolis, and I'd made a total idiot of myself thinking they were dating. "...but?"

"How did my future sister-in-law find this out? Well, she had to comfort poor heartbroken Sam the six-hour ride back to Chicago after you *wham, bam, thank you ma'am*'d him."

"I doubt he was all that heartbroken," I muttered. I may have cried the entire shuttle ride to the airport—and most of the plane ride home—but I was sure he was finally glad to be done with me. Some days I was done with myself, or at least the person I'd been before him. She was a lonely, defensive, and sometimes horrible person, but I didn't want to be her anymore. I couldn't return to that, but I didn't know how to move on either.

"What the hell is going on with you?"

I blinked hard, realizing I'd probably been quiet for more than a moment. "Nothing's wrong. I'm fine."

"No, you're not. I can tell from here that you're not. But I don't understand why you're being so freaking stubborn still. I thought seeing him would finally put things in perspective for you. Evan and I..."

"What? What does that even mean?" I interrupted.

"You think we didn't notice how you acted the last time we were in the office? Do you think Isobel didn't notice how...not hostile...you've been toward Adrian since the book tour? She said you'd completely lost your fire. She was worried it was the job, but Evan and I saw the two of you together for weeks, so I knew it wasn't that. The night Evan proposed, you and Sam seemed so in sync. Then when I heard he was leaving and we saw you acting like a zombie afterward, I knew something must have happened. I tried to ask Is, but she's got her own shit going on right now—anyway, back to you. What's going on?"

"Why do you even care? I don't work for Is anymore. I'm not working on your new series. You don't even like me." I hated being a Debbie downer, but I knew what people thought of me. Unfortunately, I'd been left with the gossip mill speculating about Sam's abrupt departure and my refusal to acknowledge his existence before he went.

"Seriously?" She sat back in her chair, one perfectly groomed eyebrow arched as she shook her head. "We're back here? I thought we'd finally become friends over the last few months, and you're pushing me away now too? Doesn't it get old keeping everyone at arm's length?"

"You think I don't know what people think about me?" I hissed, getting defensive, even though I knew she wasn't trying to back me into a corner. "You think I don't know what everyone thinks about the fucking office ice queen with her frozen solid heart? I heard the whispers for weeks. They thought Sam and I had gotten together on the tour but then dismissed it because he'd never possibly be interested in me. He was too nice for a bitch like me."

"Oh, come on. That's bullshit," she laughed. "Calm the fuck down and talk to me."

"About what? About how I screwed up my life and pushed away the only man I've ever loved over my fixation with a stupid job? How I don't really like this job I wanted so badly if he isn't here? Is that what you want to talk about?"

"Well, yeah. That is what I want to talk about. You think I haven't seen this all play out on the page a million times?"

"I'm not one of your characters, Chase." I snapped back, hating that I really *did* sound like one of her characters.

"Yeah, you're right. If you were one of my characters, you'd get off your ass and onto a plane to get your man."

"Isn't it the male characters who always swoop in at the last moment and throw down some grand gesture to win back the girl?"

"Fuck that. Women can screw up too. Let's face it, you don't exactly make it easy for anyone to get close to you. Maybe finally telling him how you feel will fix things," she shrugged. "Maybe it won't, but you'll never find out if you don't try. You wrote him a goodbye note. He thinks you're done. If you're not and you do love him, it's on you to tell him. He's not a mind reader."

"He's the one who left."

"And did you give him any other option? You didn't ask him to stay. Is told me how savagely you cut him out before he left. You ran away from him in Minneapolis. I'm guessing Sam had no idea when he took that job he meant anything more to you than just a disposable fling."

"I don't even know where he lives. Am I supposed to show up at the Chicago office and make some obnoxious public declaration in front of all his new coworkers? Isn't that how it works for all your male leads?"

"Fuck you. My readers love a happy ending," she giggled, taking a business card out of her pocket and placing it in front of me on the desk. "That's his address. But he won't be there this weekend."

"And you know this because?"

"Because Kelly hates seeing him being so pathetic, and you need a kick in the ass. So here I am," she spread her arms out as she sat back. "Kicking your ass. Flip the card over. That's where he'll be if you take this." I frowned as she leaned down and pulled a long white envelope out of her bag, thrusting it in my direction. "And finally get your shit together."

It was a one-way ticket to Kalamazoo, Michigan, connecting through Chicago for the next morning. "Um, why am I going to Michigan? Shouldn't I be going straight to Chicago?"

"It's grand gesture time, Kristine. Are you ready for this? Because if you're not, that's fine, but that also means you need to let him go, and I don't think you're ready to do that either."

I looked down at the card in my hands, not recognizing the name or address printed in Evan's neat handwriting but unwilling to risk losing this chance.

"What do I need to know?"

"Oh, no." Chase shook her head, standing up and shouldering her bag. "I've done my part. The rest is on you. If you want him as much as I think you do, make it right."

I tried to return to work for twenty minutes after Chase left, but she was right. I did need to make this right. She'd given me the pep talk and the plane ticket, and I had to figure out how to clean up my mess.

"Fuck," I sighed as I pulled up my contacts list. In my fit of despair, I'd symbolically deleted his contact information. Not that he'd talk to me if I called.

Sam's Facebook page provided the information I needed. Isobel had often teased Chase about her Internet stalking skills, but I'd learned a few things from her, easily finding a few of Sam's sisters tagged in a photo from a family birthday a few weeks ago. Sam looked tired, his smile the fake one he reserved for interacting with people he wasn't that comfortable with.

I knew he loved his family, so it couldn't be them. Was he as miserable as I was? With his new job, the new city, and new friends, I'd expected that he'd be too busy to think about how epically things had imploded between us.

The first two of his sisters had their profiles locked down tight, only having a profile picture and information on where they lived and their spouse. The third one was more promising. She had an online boutique with a phone number listed.

My pulse pounded as I input the number, waiting for it to connect. I hated calling people instead of texting or emailing, but I was desperate.

"Hello. Thanks for calling Ever After Boutique, Claire speaking. How can I help you?"

Fuck. I was supposed to talk now.

"Hi, uh. I'm looking for help with something. You're the Claire Baxter related to Sam Langley, right?"

Rustling noises came through the phone, and when she returned, her voice was lower, and the background noise faded away.

"Who is this?"

"You don't know me..."

"Clearly, but I'm interested, nonetheless. How do you know Sam?" she laughed. "Are you the reason he's being such a grump lately?"

Pausing, I decided transparency was the way to go.

"My name is Kristine. I worked with Sam in Boston..." I took a deep breath and told her why I was really calling. "I'm in love with him. I need your help."

THE NEXT CALL I needed to make wasn't so easy.

"What do you want, Kristine?" Kelly's tone was abrupt. It was clear she wouldn't take my side in this break-up. I knew she'd befriended Sam after he'd moved to Chicago, but I didn't realize how close they were.

"I need help."

"Yeah, you do. But psychiatric services aren't part of my friendship package."

"I'm sorry."

She scoffed, a dry chuckle carrying through the line. "I'm not the one who deserves your apology."

"I know. I screwed up. Leaving like I did..."

"Was fucked up," she filled in when I paused.

"It was. I was mean to you too. I didn't mean to accuse you of fucking him."

Her laughter that time was a little more relaxed. "Well, he is cute, but I don't make it a habit of sleeping with other people's boyfriends."

"He's not exactly my boyfriend," I sighed.

"But that's what you want, right? Because if it isn't, you need to leave him the fuck alone."

I knew I had one chance to get her to help me. I paused to gather my thoughts and then simply declared, "I love him."

"Love doesn't magically fix everything."

"According to your sister-in-law, it does," I laughed.

"Well, she also thinks orgasms make the world go-'round, and she's sleeping with my dorky brother, so let's not use her as a credible source of realistic information." Part of me was jealous that Sam was closer to her now. Not because I thought they'd get together but because when we'd met, Kelly had been easy to talk to; I could see her being a valuable friend. But I had to fix things with Sam first.

"Chase said you talked to him after everything went down in Minneapolis. Do you think he'd forgive me?"

"I think that guy would walk through fire for you. But you can't play with him anymore. He doesn't deserve the way you treated him, and I don't know if I can help you unless I know you're serious about things this time. What's your plan?"

"I'm trying to figure that out," I confessed. Having spent the last hour on the phone with Claire and her older sister Becca figuring out travel arrangements.

"He's not in town this weekend. You can stay with me if you fly in, but he's got something going on. And I won't be around much because I got a project dumped on me, and I need to be in the office all weekend."

"I don't need to stay with you. I talked to his sisters, and Chase gave me a ticket to Michigan."

"You're going to the wedding?"

"Is that a stupid idea? How pissed would he be if I just showed up there? Claire and Becca thought it'd be fine, but now I'm wondering..."

"My God, you're as much of a drama queen as he is," Kelly laughed, cutting me off. "As long as you don't plan on making a scene, I think the wedding is a great idea. Actually... Give me a second."

My phone chimed, and I pulled it away from my ear. A text message with Kelly's confirmation number and hotel address had arrived.

"What's this?"

"My help. This was my room for the wedding when I was supposed to go as his replacement date. It's yours now. I'll call and get it transferred to your name. Just don't watch pay-per-view hotel porn while you're there since it's my credit card on file."

"Well, now that you've planted the seed..." I laughed, and she growled in my ear.

"I know where to find you."

Putting my phone on speaker, I pulled up the hotel information and saved it.

"Thank you, Kelly. I mean it."

"Well, don't think you're off the hook with me. You need to prove you're serious about him. But now you owe me a favor."

"Is this *The Godfather*?" I chuckled.

"*'One day I may call on you to do me a service...'*" she mimicked in a deep voice.

"Yeah, okay, what do you want from me?"

"Not sure yet, but I'll let you know."

I glanced at the time, knowing that I needed to get home so I could get things packed. The next 24 hours were going to be tight.

MY PULSE WAS ERRATIC as I glanced at my watch for the tenth time in the last twenty minutes. We were still sitting on the tarmac, the darkened skies of Chicago obscured by the rain streaking down the small oval window to my right. This plane was supposed to take off four hours ago, but an unexpected thunderstorm had kept the flight before mine from landing, delaying my connection to Michigan. With each minute that passed, I began to feel like my chance was slipping away, that maybe I'd waited too long, and this was the universe's way of telling me I was too late.

> *Kelly: Have you boarded yet?*

Glancing up toward the front of the plane, I watched the flight attendant talking on the handset next to her jump seat, and a frown pulled across her lips. She sighed loudly and briefly reached up to put the handset back into its cradle before pressing a button next to it and pulling it back to her mouth.

"Unfortunately, it looks like we'll be waiting a little longer. The good news is they've started letting planes take off now, but we're twentieth in line, and one runway is still shut down."

> *Kristine: On the plane, 20th in line for takeoff.*

She sent back a cringing emoji, and I sighed as I leaned back into my seat, glaring at the blurry lights outside the window. This whole grand gesture thing was turning out to be a nightmare. The heroes in Chase's books made it look much easier than reality.

> *Becca: Rental car will be ready when you get here. Keith went to get it for you before they closed. Keys are behind the visor. We'll meet you at the hotel.*

Sam's oldest sister sent a picture of a nondescript red sedan and the license plate number.

> *Kristine: Won't someone steal it?*

> *Becca: Welcome to the Midwest. It'll be fine for a few hours. Can't wait to meet you. Although I'm sure it might have to wait once my brother steals you away.*

I wasn't so sure it would still be there once I finally arrived, but I had to believe that something would eventually go my way today. With all the delays, I felt like maybe karma was finally catching up with me.

Sam's sisters had come together with Chase and Kelly to help me pull this plan off, but I was still nervous. Chase had given me a pep talk about believing in love and jumping in with both feet on the way to the airport this morning. She told me I'd know what to say to him when I got there...if I ever got there.

Thankfully, the weather had cleared up when my flight eventually landed. I'd quickly—awkwardly in the confines of a tiny airport bathroom stall—changed into the figure-hugging black dress and heels I'd picked out last night and found my midsize rental car in the parking lot. The keys had been tucked into the visor along with a key card to the hotel room Kelly had booked for me.

The address was already plugged into the navigation app on my phone; my luggage was in the back seat and, thankfully, hadn't been lost despite the delays. I was ready to go.

Firing off texts to Becca, Chase, and Kelly that I'd finally arrived, I threw my phone into the passenger seat and started the four-mile journey toward taking back control of my future.

SAM

CLIMAX, MI

"You two need to go back upstairs. Uncle Sam is sleeping," my sister's voice hissed as I blindly reached for my glasses on the end table next to the pull-out couch.

"He's not asleep now," a little voice giggled as a solid weight settled across my legs.

"Yeah, Uncle Sam's awake. He wants us down here!" yelled another.

"Uncle Sam was asleep," I yawned, sitting up and wrapping my arms around the two little giggling boys perched on the end of the mattress. "But now the tickle monster is awake!"

They both squealed, trying to get out of the cage of my arms, seemingly stronger than they'd been since the last time I did this. Or maybe I hadn't been working out in the last few months and had gotten weaker. Whichever it was, the tickle monster was soon vanquished, and I was being attacked by two determined little six-year-olds who were surprisingly agile.

"Okay! Okay! Truce!" I laughed as I tried to pull a pillow over my head. "Quit! No more kidney shots!"

"Never!" They squealed as they both jumped onto my back, and one of the twins tried to put me in a headlock.

"Alexander! Let go of Sam, right now!" my sister, Claire, shouted, her *mom voice* eerily reminiscent of the way our mother sounded in our childhood.

"Moooom," my nephew whined as his little arms dropped before he scrambled across the mattress and hopped to his feet beside Felix. Alex always took things a little too far, and I knew my sister had difficulty reining in his energy. For all that Felix was like my mini-me, often referred to in our family as Little Sam, Alex was all his father. This was probably why he was my sister's favorite despite all the gray hairs he would inevitably cause as he got older. Felix was the dutiful rule follower with a sweet disposition, and Alex was a wild child with absolutely no impulse control.

"No," she said, pointing up the stairs. "You two, get back upstairs and finish your breakfast. You know there's no roughhousing until after you've cleaned up after yourselves, and grandma would kill you if you broke anything down here."

"Fine," they pouted, their dark little heads of messy hair hung low as they trudged up the stairs into the kitchen.

"Sorry," Claire cringed as she wiped her hands off on a dishtowel and sat on the corner of the mattress of the pull-out couch that was my bed for the weekend. "They snuck off when I let Paisley back in from the backyard. Dad's watching a war movie with Brad in the family room; you know those two are worthless as babysitters. They're more likely to encourage the mayhem than they are to stop it."

"It's fine. I should probably get up anyway. I just wasn't expecting quite the exuberant wake-up call."

"I still don't understand why you canceled your room," she laughed. "Staying on Mom and Dad's pull-out couch isn't exactly comfortable. Aren't they paying you well with your new fancy job?"

"I didn't see the point in driving an extra twenty-five minutes there and back when I'd be here anyway. It's not like I haven't slept on this couch every time I've visited since college. Mom turned my room into the boys' bunkhouse. At least I fit on this mattress. The bottom bunk isn't exactly designed for people over five feet tall."

When I'd gone off to college, my mom used her empty nesting energy to remodel the house. My sister's bedrooms had been converted to an office, a home gym, a sewing room, and a guest bedroom. Mine had been initially converted to a nursery for her grandkids, but now it was wall-to-wall bunk beds for when my nephews spent the night.

It was easier to stay down here where I wasn't right on top of people. I could have stayed in the guest bedroom near my parent's room, but the basement had always been where I hid from my sisters anyway, so I didn't mind. I also knew that the thumping coming from my parent's room wasn't a ghost like my sisters led me to believe when I was younger.

"Sucks that your date wasn't able to come." She frowned, picking up the pillows the boys had knocked to the floor and fluffing them before stacking them back on the arm of the couch. I knew she wasn't digging, but I'd been closed-lipped around my family since the move. Claire knew when something was bothering me, but I was afraid to confess how much of a disaster I'd turned my life into.

"Kelly's got this big project due, and I didn't want to drag her away from the office to do me a favor."

"So, you two have been spending a lot of time together lately?"

"Don't," I warned as I shook my head, not wanting to get into this conversation with her. Mom was bad enough with the questions and far less subtle. "Kelly is just a friend. She felt sorry for me not knowing very many people yet and offered to come with me to the wedding, only so I didn't have to fly solo. We booked separate rooms at the hotel. It is most definitely not like that between us."

"Didn't you two go to that engagement dinner in Minneapolis together too?"

Where I ended up getting my heart ripped out by the woman who I still somehow have feelings for because I'm clearly a glutton for punishment.

"Don't you start too. I'm single. It's fine. Mom already has enough grandkids. She doesn't need me to give her any."

"We all just want you to be happy, Sam. I know she pressured you to come back home more often, but if this job makes you miserable, we'd understand if you didn't stay in Chicago. If going back to Boston would make you happy..."

"It's not the job," I sighed. I was becoming a grumpy asshole because I was depressed and felt stupid for falling in love with a woman who pushed people away when things got hard. "The job is actually pretty amazing. I'm just having a tough time letting go of things I shouldn't have gotten attached to."

"That sounds like there's a story." The sheer amount of barely restrained interest on her face made me cringe. Claire had always been able to get information out of me.

"There was a woman in Boston..."

"I knew it!"

"Seriously?"

She cringed, miming zipping her lips, and motioned for me to go on.

"We were both up for the same promotion, and she got upset when I took the position in Chicago." It wasn't the whole story, but I was embarrassed to confess my self-destructing role in our relationship.

"Oh, come on! That can't be the whole thing. What's her name? Is it that Kristine you went on the book tour with? Are you in love with her? Why didn't you invite her to the wedding if you're dating?"

"Nope." I shook my head. "We're not...we weren't dating. She..." I didn't even know how to explain what had happened between us without making her look bad. We were both guilty of screwing this whole situation up. I wasn't honest with her about my feelings or the job in Chicago. And she never let me past her defenses enough to trust me.

"You love her."

"What?"

She smiled, reaching forward to grab my hand. "A big sister knows these things. Maybe you need to talk to her."

"God, would all you women quit fucking meddling? She doesn't love me. Well, she does, but it's all fucked up, and she won't really talk to me. It's over. I just need some time to move on. She's made it clear she wants to move on."

"Don't close that door yet, Sam," she urged, reaching over to squeeze my hand. "Sometimes, you just need to step back to get a little perspective on life. Things will work out how they're supposed to, you'll see."

LOOKING AT MYSELF IN the bathroom mirror, I sighed as I recalled the past twenty-four hours. My mother had been in rare form, taking every opportunity to poke at me when I'd shown up without a date this weekend. Kelly had originally agreed to be my plus one, and I knew it was a pity date, but I'd hated that I couldn't use her as a shield this weekend, as shitty as that sounded.

If she were here, I wouldn't have to answer the questions from my mother about why I was still single. Like I was supposed to fall for the first woman who showed interest since I'd moved to Chicago, and fast forward to a quickie wedding and two kids. I'd told her that Kelly was only a friend, but after the trip to Minneapolis and all the time we had spent together lately, my mother was convinced I'd been lying to her.

I'd told Claire more than anyone else in my family, but I didn't really tell her anything. She'd told me to keep my heart open, but I was struggling.

The truth was, I was still hung up on the woman I'd left behind in Boston who crapped all over my heart and used me. The note crinkled in my pocket everywhere I went for the last several weeks, and I knew it was pathetic that I'd been carrying it around like some lovesick douchebag. I'd become that guy. The one who let a woman break him, but I couldn't close the door. Kristine would always be the one who got away. Whether that was my fault or hers was up for debate. I'd missed the opportunity, and she'd made it clear that our night together in Minneapolis was goodbye.

Standing at the door to the ballroom on my way back from the bathroom, I watched my parents on the dance floor for a moment before I resumed my pathetic seat by myself at our table. My oldest sister, Becca, and her husband, Keith, had been keeping me company now that dinner was over, but I still felt like a third wheel. They should be enjoying their time away from their three boys, and she was still stuck babysitting her little brother even twenty years later.

My sister smiled brightly as I turned toward the table, waving me over as I planned my speech for cutting out early. Brett and his new bride had already made the rounds to the guests on our side of the room, so it's not like anyone would care if I left.

"Hey! I was wondering if you'd run away," she laughed as she lifted her wine glass in a mock toast. My sister had been enjoying the freedom of being out without kids and an open bar. "Sit down, sit down. Tell us about your new apartment again."

"It's not that interesting, Bec," I sighed as I pulled my jacket from the back of my seat and shrugged into it. I hesitated at sitting back down because she'd try to suck me back into the conversation. "Actually, I think I'm going to take off. Go back to Mom and Dad's house." Where I was staying in the basement on the pull-out couch like a loser for the weekend. When Kelly was supposed to come as my date, we'd booked—separate—rooms at the hotel where the reception was being held, but I'd canceled mine when I found out I'd be flying solo.

"No, no, no," she slurred slightly, her eyes flashing toward the phone resting on the table in front of her and then leaning around me to look toward the door. "You can't leave yet. Come on. We never get to see you."

"I was here a few weeks ago." I'd been an asshole the entire trip, but I'd shown up for our other sister's birthday dinner like the dutiful son, brother, and uncle that I was. Now that I was only a few hours' car ride from home, I was trying to be more present.

"Yeah, but we didn't get to talk to you about how you're settling in. Are you all unpacked now? Have you had a chance to explore the city? Are you..." she paused, her eyes flashing to her phone as a text message scrolled across the screen.

"Am I?" I prompted as she frowned at the screen.

"Are you..." she trailed off. "Oh, sorry. It's just the babysitter. Are you dating anyone?"

"Am I dating anyone since I saw you two weeks ago? And you asked the same question then." I looked over at my brother-in-law, who seemed more sober than his wife but still acted strangely. "I'm not ready, Bec. Maybe in a few months."

"Things can change in a few weeks or even a few hours." She shrugged as she passed her phone to Keith, nudging him in the elbow. "You never know. It wouldn't hurt you to be open-minded about things."

"No, I'm not interested in dating anyone," I sighed, looking back toward my parents again. "And Kelly is just my friend. I told you all that. It's..."

"Complicated, I know," she laughed. "You made it clear this morning when you laid into Mom about calling her your girlfriend. I'm just worried about you, Sam. You've seemed sad since you moved back, and I'm worried you moved to Chicago to appease Mom. I'm sure she'd understand if you want to go back to Boston. If you want to go back to work things out with..." Her eyes widened as her words cut off, but she pulled her drink glass in front of her face, glancing away.

Shaking my head, I reluctantly dropped into my seat, looking toward where my brother-in-law had disappeared. I was glad they'd been invited to the wedding—my sister was the bride's babysitter when we were little—so I wasn't stuck with Mom and Dad all night, but they'd seemed distracted by their phones all evening.

"There's no reason for me to return to Boston. My job is in Chicago now. I like my new position and my team. It's just..." Claire was the only one in my family I'd talked to about Kristine, but even she didn't know she was supposed to be here tonight. When things had fallen apart, I'd assumed that her promise to be my date to this wedding wasn't on the table anymore. Since she wasn't talking to me either, I'd kept quiet about our relationship and how it'd all blown up in my face.

"It's complicated, or at least it was." I wasn't going to pour my heart out to another sister. It'd been decades since she dated anyone, and she'd been with Keith since they were teenagers. My life in Boston wasn't like that. I didn't have a college sweetheart and a life in the suburbs. My love life had been spotty, uncommitted, and, more recently, messy. "I was seeing someone, and it didn't work out."

"So, talk to her and figure it out."

"Have you been talking to Kelly?" I laughed, squinting my eyes at my sister when she choked on the sip of wine she'd been swallowing.

"No," she sputtered, sitting upright in her seat, her cheeks bright red. "Why would I talk to Kelly? How would I even get her phone number?"

She glanced back at her phone again, tilting the screen away from me as another text scrolled across the center of the screen. "Trouble with the babysitter?"

Keith still hadn't come back yet, and I felt like there was something I was missing. Becca wasn't the type to keep secrets, but they'd been acting weird all evening.

"What?" she asked absently as she looked down at the phone she'd pulled into her lap. "Oh, no. Keith was taking care of something for me. He's on his way back now."

"The boys okay?" I knew they were with their regular babysitter tonight, but my sister still had trouble letting go sometimes.

"Oh, they're fine. Hailey was making slime with them. I warned them about putting it in each other's hair this time, so I'm sure they'll be good for her. They seem to behave for everyone but me. They love having a babysitter. Probably because it means they get pizza and ice cream for dinner."

Keith rejoined us ten minutes later, his hair a little wet, but he seemed satisfied with whatever errand he'd been on for the last twenty minutes for my sister. I knew they planned on staying at the hotel tonight, so maybe he was taking care of their room. Not that I wanted to think about my sister and her husband having a hotel room together. There were just certain things you pretended weren't happening. Like your sister's husband planning to get laid after they'd fulfilled their duty to keep her little brother entertained after his date to a wedding ditched him.

"I can get out of your hair if you two want some time alone," I offered as a slow song drifted over the speakers, the group of wedding guests starting to thin out as people headed home for the night.

Their heads started shaking in unison as Keith's eyes darted up to the doorway, his lips pursing as he glanced down at his lap.

"Well, at least go dance." I nodded to the dance floor, "Don't let me keep you from enjoying yourselves. I'll be fine here by myself for a few minutes."

"Are you sure?" she asked, tucking her phone into her purse before she took her husband's outstretched hand. "You can't sneak off while we're gone."

"I won't. It's fine. I'll be here when you get back."

"Promise?" She held out her pinky, and I shook my head as I reached over and linked mine with hers.

"I promise."

"Don't make me hunt you down," she teased.

"Go," I growled as I pulled my phone out of my pocket. "I'll check my email while you're gone."

Unlocking my phone, I scrolled through my inbox with one hand, trying to block out the music as I toyed with my empty glass in my other. Maybe I needed a refill. Becca and Keith were wrapped around each other, not paying any attention to the rest of the room. I wouldn't sneak out, but if they insisted on me staying longer, I needed more alcohol.

The bar was relatively empty, only a few of Brett's groomsmen lingering with the promise of free beer. We'd gone to high school with a few, but I'd been gone for a long time. I sat down heavily at one of the stools, not wanting to sit by myself at the big empty table. It wasn't like anyone would miss me, and I was biding my time until I could get out of here.

Chapter
THIRTY-EIGHT

KRISTINE

KALAMAZOO, MI

When I arrived at the address programmed into my phone, the parking lot was full. Music poured out of an open side door as I grabbed my bag and headed toward the lobby. The wedding was still in full swing, but I could only hope Sam was still here with how late I was arriving.

"Do you need help checking in?" The clerk asked as I wheeled my suitcase toward the desk.

"I'm already checked in, but would it be possible for someone to take this to my room?" I asked, gesturing at my small suitcase.

"Of course, let me verify your room number," she said with a smile, holding her hand out for my keycard.

Handing it over, I glanced down the hallway, seeing flower arrangements on a large table just past the sign for the ballroom.

"Oh." She smiled. "You're part of the wedding block. Let me take this so you can get back to the reception."

"I'm running a little late," I apologized, my flight delays having thrown off the original plan.

"Dinner finished a little while ago, but the seating chart is by the door. Do you know which table you were assigned? I can have catering send out an extra plate since you missed dinner."

"You don't need to bother." I waved her away, my nerves rising. Maybe it'd be better if I headed upstairs instead and left Sam alone. "I ate at the airport."

My phone buzzed in my pocket, and I pulled it out. An alert was on the screen for my group text with Kelly and Chase.

> *Chase: Are you there yet?*

> *Kelly: Did you find him?*

> *Chase: We're dying for details!*

> *Kelly: But we'll leave you alone since you're probably getting laid.*

> *Chase: Fingers crossed, but hopefully not your legs!*

An animated gif scrolled across the screen of Kevin Hart with the words: *It's about to go down.*

> *Kelly: Or at least someone is! Get it, girl!*

Shaking my head at their ridiculous banter, I fired off a text to let them know I was at least at the hotel, even if I was too chicken to find Sam.

> *Kristine: Here, suitcase dropped off, big girl panties on.*

I saw the dots scrolling across the screen as I walked toward the closed double doors.

> *Kelly: Should have left the panties off. Becca texted me a few minutes ago they were stalling him in there. Hurry up!*

It was disturbing how much of a group effort this whole thing had turned into, but I appreciated all the help they'd given me, along with Sam's sisters. They all could have easily told me to stay away from him.

> *Chase: I will fly up there and beat you if you screw this up!*

> *Kristine: Okay, okay. Going. I'll find him.*

Now that I was here, all the ways I'd screwed this up over the last several months wouldn't stop running on a loop in my head, and I hesitated. I understood firsthand why the heroes in Chase's books freaked out while trying to pull off their grand romantic gestures. This was hard. I could walk through that door, and he could refuse to talk to me like I'd done to him at the engagement dinner. He'd have every right to blow me off, I'd been horrible, and I had no idea where we'd go from here, but I'd experienced losing him. And that hurt.

I was miserable in Boston. And as long as he was in Chicago, I'd continue to be miserable. It was time for me to be brave and take the chances with my heart. If it meant quitting my job when I flew back to Boston and leaving behind the promotion that'd seemed so important a few months ago, I would. I'd do it for him. He was worth taking the risk.

Steeling myself with a deep breath, I pulled open the door and slipped inside, scanning the table numbers to find the number twelve his sister had told me they were seated at. Half the tables were empty, a crowd of people on the dance floor, but I hoped he was still there somewhere.

A loud whistle from the dance floor drew my attention, and a petite brunette waved wildly in my direction. I glanced behind myself, then back toward her. She pointed to the back of the room where a large bar was located and a small group of men in tuxes gathered off to the side. Frowning, I looked back toward her, shrugging as she continued to point. Obviously, she was trying to get my attention, and I felt like an idiot as I realized this must be Sam's sister and her husband.

Hoping that their eagerness to help meant that Sam wouldn't tell me to leave, I scanned the tables again, seeing the empty chairs around the one numbered twelve. Becca was still pointing at the back of the room.

I didn't see him at first glance, but when I looked back, a dark-haired man was facing the bar staring at his phone next to the men in tuxes.

I hadn't recognized Sam because he wore his glasses, but my heart ached when I saw how alone he looked. I'd caused that. I was supposed to be here with him, but we'd screwed everything up. I'd screwed most of it up, but I would ensure he wasn't here alone now. Late was better than never, right?

Glancing back toward the dance floor, I saw the woman giving me a thumbs up and nodding her head, holding onto the arms of the man behind her, both watching me stand by the door like an idiot.

Sam's attention was wholly focused on his phone as I approached him, terrified he'd look up and glance in my direction. I wasn't sure what I would say, but I couldn't let a little stage fright stop me now.

"Geez," I cleared my throat as I stepped behind him, wiping my sweaty hands on my dress. "It's a real cockfest over here, isn't it?"

Probably not the most romantic line to lead with, but the corner of Sam's mouth pulled up in a fraction of a grin as he placed his phone down on the bar, and I knew I'd gotten his attention.

"Yeah," he smirked as he turned to face me, his eyes scanning down the form-fitting dress Chase had pushed on me before returning to my face. "But the real question is, who's got the big dick energy?"

"Well, certainly not them," I cringed as I hooked my thumb over my shoulder at the group of young guys doing shots at the other end of the bar.

His eyebrows rose, and I saw his hand clench in his lap like he was trying to keep himself from reaching for me. "And what about me?"

"Are you fishing for compliments, Langley? Isn't your ego big enough?" It felt good to fall back into our usual banter, but he still hadn't indicated that he'd wanted to see me.

He shook his head, standing up from his stool and taking a hesitant step toward me, forcing me to look up to maintain eye contact. He smelled good, exactly like I remembered. It sent a pang of intense longing through me as he continued to stare at me with a half-amused, half-annoyed look on his face, not unlike how he had looked at me a few months ago before all this started.

"What are you doing here, Kris?"

"Well—" I cleared my throat, slowly reaching forward with my hand and grazing my fingers against the back of his hand. When he didn't pull away, I hoped it was a good sign despite the serious look in his eyes. "I was invited. I'm a little late, but I hoped the invitation was still good. I heard you needed a date."

"Hmm," he hummed as he turned his hand and clasped my fingers, tugging me another step until our chests were just a hair's breadth apart. "Took you long enough to get here. Were you washing your hair again?"

The fingers on his other hand reached up to toy with a curl that'd settled on my shoulder, my pulse going wild at his proximity.

"Yeah, you caught me. Hopefully, it's not too late for me to join you. I'm sorry for keeping you waiting. I'm just...sorry." I was sorry for all of it, but I was afraid if I started confessing my sins, it'd all come out like word vomit and scare him away.

"I'm sorry too, but it still doesn't explain why you're here. You're a little late if you're here to fulfill some obligation to me. You made it clear where you stand. More than once."

Shaking my head, I put my hand on his chest, resting it over his heart. It was pounding like mine was, so maybe he wasn't as unaffected as he was trying to appear. "But I didn't, Sam. I wasn't honest with you. And I know I screwed it all up, and you probably don't trust me. But I had to try. I had to come here to tell you in person that I..."

His expression wasn't giving anything away, but his hand was still clenching mine as his eyes slowly scanned my face.

"That you?" he prompted, the fingers on his other hand tracing the sliver of my shoulder that was exposed above the neckline of my dress.

"That I..." my voice squeaked as I squeezed his fingers, tears pooling in the corner of my eyes. Clearing my throat, I tried again, taking in a stuttering breath. "I love you."

My heart was hammering in my chest as he gazed down at me, not saying anything. He was completely silent, his face guarded but his eyes fierce, not breaking my gaze as his hand paused on my shoulder.

"I mean, I know I was a total bitch, and you didn't deserve how I treated you for the last few months, but I'm sorry. And I'm an idiot, but I had to try. Because I hate not seeing you every day, and I hate that I pushed you away at every opportunity. I should have realized how I felt about you sooner and stopped trying to be afraid, but..."

"Shut up," Sam growled, cutting off my nervous stream of verbal diarrhea as his hand slipped along my neck.

"But I..." I sputtered, my chin trembling as I tried to fight off the urge to burst into tears.

"Kristine, shut up," he whispered as his hand slipped into the hair behind my head and tugged, forcing my head back. I was panting as he loomed over me, barely restrained energy pulsing through him as his jaw clenched.

"Okay," I gasped as his fingers tightened at the back of my neck, my scalp prickling as he held me still.

Expecting him to push me away at any moment, I clung to the fabric of his lapels, holding on to his suit jacket to anchor myself. If this was the last minute I spent in his arms, I wanted to remember it, even if it hurt when he rejected me.

"Tell me again," he whispered, his eyes focused on my mouth.

"I'm sorry," I whispered back, licking my lips.

"Not that part, the other part," his voice was soft, much softer than I was expecting, with the tension that seemed to be rolling through his body as he held me. I wasn't sure what he was asking me for, my mind not holding onto anything more than fleeting thoughts under his intense stare.

"You've got big dick energy," I whispered, my voice shaking.

"You're such a pain in the ass," he huffed as a smile finally crossed his features, relaxing his face as his hand gentled in my hair. Leaning down, his lips grazed my ear as he held me to him. "Not that part either, but I'm glad you noticed."

I sagged in his arms, my nerves settling as he nuzzled the side of my face, his thumb rubbing lightly over our joined hands trapped between our bodies. "Tell me what you want me to say, and I'll say it, Sam."

"Why are you here?"

My thoughts raced as I tried to recall what I'd said to him, what he was asking me to tell him. And then it clicked.

"To tell you that I love you."

He dropped my hand, and I felt a momentary pang of desperation before his hands grasped the sides of my neck, and his mouth was on mine. The first contact was gentle, just a graze of his lips before he pulled me forward, nipping at my mouth as his slanted over it, possessing my lips as he stole the breath from my lungs. My fingers clawed at his jacket as I tried to hold on, my grasp on him the only thing anchoring me as I tried to keep up with the frantic pace of the kiss.

He broke away a moment later, pulling me forward, tucking his face into my hair, and panting as I tried to keep myself from climbing up his chest.

"I love you too." His whispered confession caused the tears that'd been building to finally fall, a sob catching in my throat as I clung to him. I wasn't sure what I would have done if he didn't still feel the same way. If he'd decided I wasn't worth it and told me to leave.

"I'm sorry," I sniffled as I buried my face in his chest, shaking as he held me.

"Stop." His voice was firm as he pulled back to look down at me, his thumbs smoothing away the stray tears that'd tracked down my cheeks. "You're here now. We both fucked this up, but I'd like to try again. I mean, if you want to. We can figure this long-distance thing out. How long are you here? Do you have to go back to Boston tomorrow?"

"I want to figure it out, too," I agreed, reaching up to tuck his hair back from his forehead. It was a little longer than the last time I saw him, curling against his skin. "I don't know how long you want me to stay, but I have nothing worth returning to if you aren't there."

"But the promotion," he frowned.

"Doesn't mean anything if it means I lose you."

"They filled my position with Adrian, but I could ask Sloane if..."

"No. Don't take that opportunity away from Andrea." I shook my head, leaning forward to rest my head on his shoulder. "From you either. You wanted the job in Chicago, Sam. I see that now. I was so focused on what I wanted that I didn't realize you weren't happy in Boston."

"I'm not exactly happy in Chicago either, not without you," he confessed, his fingers combing through the hair on the back of my head.

The music changed to something faster, the volume rising as I pulled back to look at Sam. "What are your thoughts on a roommate?"

He squinted, looking down at me with amused annoyance at my weird tangents. "My apartment has one bedroom, Kristine."

"That's more than enough room," I told him, stroking the hair on the side of his head. "I don't take up much space."

"What are you going on about?"

"Unless you'd rather I get my own place or stay in a hotel or something. It might take a little while to sell my apartment in Boston, but I'm sure I can find somewhere to stay near you while I look for a job."

He was shaking his head as I babbled on. I'd gotten ahead of myself, asking to live with him while figuring out what to do with myself in Chicago. I had savings. I could afford several months of hotel rooms if I didn't find something immediately. Sloane would probably kill me for quitting already, but I'd chosen the promotion over Sam once and regretted it. I couldn't do it again. Even if it meant starting at the bottom in the Chicago office or elsewhere, I'd gladly return to being an intern.

"Do I need to pull your hair again to get you to shut up?" Sam teased as he jokingly tugged at my nape.

"But..."

My mouth snapped shut again at his raised eyebrow, but I wanted him to pull my hair again. Sam bossing me around had always made my pulse race.

"You really want to come to Chicago?"

"Yes," I confessed, opening my mouth to talk again, but his narrowed eyes made me bite my lip to stop myself from continuing.

"To be with me?"

"No, to be with Kelly," I delivered with a straight face, but he still rolled his eyes at me. "Of course, to be with you. I came here to tell you I loved you. Did you think I would do all this and return home?"

He opened his mouth to respond, but I touched his lips. "Point taken. Moving is going to be the only way we can be together. You've always made concessions in this relationship, and it's time for me to make some. It makes sense for me to come to Chicago because there isn't a reason like my family to stay in Boston."

"But what about Nana?"

"That's what vacation time is for. I can fly back to visit Nana whenever. I can even bring you to the Cape. I'm sure she'd love that. But I'm tired of making excuses about why we can't make this work."

"If you move out here, you won't have anywhere to run." His smile was nervous as he said that, and I reached up to smooth out the wrinkle between his eyebrows. I'd done a number on him.

"I don't need anywhere to run. I'm sorry for making you doubt me, Sam. But I love you, and I want to make this work. Please let me have another chance?"

"On one condition," he conceded, kissing me softly. "If you get scared again, you've got to let me in."

"I will." And I would, too. There was too much at stake here. Running away from my problems got us to this point, and continuing to do so would only break us for good. I knew what my life looked like without Sam. I wasn't willing to go back to that.

"Where are you staying tonight?" he asked, brushing the hair away from my temple.

"Upstairs." His eyes widened as I showed him my keycard. "Do you want to see my room?"

"Are you coming on to me?"

I laughed, loving the way he smiled at me in return. "Duh. I thought I clarified that part earlier when I told you that you had big dick energy. You think I go around randomly complimenting men's junk for fun?"

"What am I going to do with you?"

Grasping his hand, I pulled him forward and leaned my head against his chest. "Hold me?"

Sam wrapped his arms around me and held me to his chest. The steady thump of his heart was comforting, and I knew this was where I was meant to be, with him.

"Do you want to get out of here now?"

I leaned back, resting my chin on his chest and looking up at him. "Did you need to talk to your family or go back home with them tonight, or…?"

"Or…" he laughed, interrupting me. "Are you going to throw a tantrum about having to share a hotel room again, or can I take you upstairs and peel this dress off you now?"

"I didn't throw a tantrum," I pouted. "Shouldn't we talk more about this, or...?"

"Do I need to go over this again? I'm choosing or. We have plenty of time to work out the rest later. Much, much later. Once you've regained your voice." He nipped at my ear, pulling me toward his chest and holding me tightly.

"Regained my...?" *Oh...*

"I'm sure. Let's go upstairs," he urged. "What happened to the brave girl who dragged me into my apartment a few months ago? She had no problem bossing me around and telling me to remove my pants."

"Then get your ass upstairs, Langley," I laughed, reaching down to grab his ass. "Let's do this."

"Finally, we're on the same page. Yes, let's," he grinned, and I knew all the details we needed to figure out would be there later.

Mission accomplished. I'd come here to make a grand gesture and get my man. Now it was time to trust that we'd get it right this time. Finding the courage to make yourself vulnerable was utterly terrifying, but when you found the right person, it was easy to make the leap and trust that they'd catch you.

Epilogue
PART ONE

SAM

CHICAGO

REACHING FOR THE ZIPPER on my suitcase, I tamped down the urge to laugh at my girlfriend. Kristine was roughly digging through her small closet, the wire hangers squeaking on the bar as she abused her poor wardrobe.

"You need to calm down," I chuckled, leaving my already packed luggage next to the bed as I crossed the room and halted her frantic movements. "My mother is not going to care what you wear. I told you it was casual. You can wear jeans and a sweater. It's really not a big deal."

She leaned back into my chest, heaving a deep sigh as her fingers found mine, weaving through them and holding on tight. "Easy for you to say, you've met my nightmare of a family. I don't know what to expect here. Our first meeting didn't exactly make the greatest impression."

Kristine had briefly been introduced to my family the night of Brett's wedding shortly before I stole her and escaped to the sanctuary of her hotel room. We'd attempted to talk for about two minutes before we couldn't resist the draw of ripping each other's clothes off. And they stayed off for two blissful days before reality pulled us apart, and we had to return to our respective cities to do damage control.

Sloane had initially been resistant to Kris leaving her new position, insisting she stay on until they could secure one of the other candidates for the role. It didn't take them long, but then we faced the problem that the Chicago office had no copy-editor positions open. Ironically, the position of my copy-editing intern was still not filled, and the management agreed to let her temporarily step into the role until they could find a spot to best utilize her talents.

While it would have been easy to fall into old habits and sneak around the office skirting rules on fraternization, we kept our hands—and other parts—to ourselves in the office. Out of the office was another matter.

As soon as she moved into my modest apartment, it'd been like we were never separated. Each day when we returned home, clothes were roughly shed within minutes, and we fucked on every damn surface we could think of. Without the pesky hindrance of roommates, we christened all the furniture, the kitchen, and the bathroom, including a very slippery but satisfying interlude with her perched on the edge of the sink with my face between her legs.

Now she was freaking out because I'd invited her to spend a long weekend in Michigan for the Thanksgiving holiday with my family. It'd be different than my last visit, mainly because I wouldn't be sleeping on a pull-out couch in the basement. My mother had giddily offered the guest bedroom down the hall from theirs, but I'd immediately passed, knowing I'd never be able to keep my hands off Kristine for four days.

"My mother is dying to get to know you," I promised, toying with the button on her jeans as I tucked my face into her neck. "She's excited to meet my future fiancée."

Kristine growled, exactly like I knew she would, still a bit resistant to the idea of that kind of commitment. "Don't get ahead of yourself, Langley. Just because you've got long wood doesn't mean I want to tie myself to it for the rest of my life."

"You don't need to tie yourself to it. Just embrace it with open arms...and hands...and mouth...and don't forget this," I teased as I snaked my hand down the front of her pants, tracing the lips of her pussy through the silky material of her panties.

"You're such a tease sometimes," she sighed, leaning her head back into my shoulder, letting me continue to stroke her lightly. Nothing calmed the savage beast like an orgasm, and lucky for her, I'd mastered pushing her buttons with my fingers and the contents of her little black box.

"I'm only a tease if I don't make you scream my name," I whispered, ghosting my lips along the column of her throat. "Now, why don't we get out one of your toys and see if I can do just that? We've got thirty minutes until we need to get on the road. I only need ten."

"That sure of yourself, Spammy?" she taunted as she reached back, cupping me through the material of my pants where I was already hard for her.

"It's that big dick energy."

Kristine laughed as I released her, nodding toward the bottom of her closet where the little black box now lived. While she turned the dials on the lock, I got to work, deciding there was no clearing the disaster of clothes strewn on the bed, but the new full-length mirror on the wall beside the closet would work fine for what I had in mind.

"Want to try out the new one she sent?" she asked as she held up a small, handheld toy with a round opening on the end. Air pulse technology proved a wonderful addition to our bedroom activities, coaxing out her ability to squirt, which we'd rediscovered since our steamy night in Seattle.

"Sounds like fun." As she began to strip off her clothes, I mirrored her actions, my cock bobbing as I finally pulled down my pants.

"Where do you want me?" she asked, tracing her palm down my abdomen and grasping me in her fist.

"Hands on the wall on either side of the mirror. Let's see how dirty we can make it."

She didn't hesitate, pushing her ass toward me as she braced herself. Leaving the perfect target for a handprint.

"Fuck, Sam," she squealed as I made contact but shot me a challenging look over her shoulder that meant she wanted more. Not wanting to leave her waiting, I brought my palm down again, enjoying the matching red marks on each cheek.

I pulled the toy from her hand, turning it on and smiling as I saw a shudder ripple down her spine at the soft thumping noise.

Crowding her against the mirror, I bent my knees and slowly pushed my cock between her legs, teasing her with the length of it as my hand brought the toy to her clit.

"Oh, god," she panted as I centered the opening, knowing this little wonder would make her cum in less than a minute at the right setting. While some men would be intimidated by such a feat, I knew it'd only make my mission easier, priming her to explode once I pushed inside her in tandem with this little beauty.

"That's right," I whispered roughly, tilting my hips so my tip just barely caught in the opening of her pussy, slipping easily against her as I coaxed the first of many climaxes to come. "I'm right there. But I need you to come for me if you want it. Show me how much you want my cock."

She obeyed commands in the bedroom more readily than when I was her supervisor and fell apart in moments, gasping as her hips gyrated against mine. I continued to press the toy into her, lining myself up and thrusting inside, groaning at how tight she was after she came.

I watched over her shoulder as her tits swayed, her eyes clenched shut as I fucked her. Squatting lower and tilting her hips so I could hit the spot inside I knew would make her soak both me and the mirror. While it'd taken some experimenting, since I knew she could do it, I stuck with it once she'd moved in, making it my mission to get her there as much as possible.

"That's right, baby. I want you to cover me. Just breathe. I can feel you tightening again. Fuck, yes, just like that," I encouraged as I pressed my finger on the button on the side of the toy, reveling in the scream that tore out of her mouth at the increased intensity.

I groaned as I felt her start to come, her muscles tightening as she flooded my hand, my grip on the toy faltering and it falling to the floor. Determined to prolong it, I gripped her hips, driving into her as her fingers flexed against the wall in front of her.

"I can't," she panted as her legs began to shake, and I knew she was close again, the desperation as she moaned ricocheting off the wall in front of her.

"Yes, you can," I grunted as I felt myself riding close to the edge, desperate to do this for her. "Fucking come, right now."

Despite her stubborn independence, she listened, moaning loudly as she came, barely able to hold herself up as she squirted almost violently, soaking the mirror in front of us and my legs as I let go inside her.

"Now we need to shower again," she sighed as she made eye contact with me in the mirror, her mood much lighter than before.

"Worth it." It was all worth it with her. Even braving my crazy family to have them meet the woman I was equally crazy about.

Epilogue
PART TWO

KRISTINE

CLIMAX, MI

SAM'S CALMING TECHNIQUES HAD worked long enough for me to get my suitcase packed and loaded into the car. But over three hours later, as he slowed to turn into the driveway of his parent's surprisingly large house, my pulse went a little haywire.

"Home sweet home." His boyish grin made me smile, knowing how much he adored his family. He kept telling me I would too, but I wasn't sure. His sisters had gone to bat for me to pull off my grand gesture, but I hadn't really talked to any of them other than to assure them I wouldn't break their baby brother's heart.

"You ready for the chaos?" he asked, unbuckling his seatbelt, reaching over to grasp my hand, and tracing his thumb over my knuckles. I'd never been the type to seek physical comfort from another person, but Sam often knew what I needed before I did. "My sisters promised they'd try to keep a leash on Mom. But I'm sure she'll ask some invasive questions trying to keep you on your toes. I promise she's not that bad."

"Really great job calming me down there, Spammy."

"Six months ago, that would've driven me nuts, but I know that's just how you show you love me, baby." The grin didn't leave my face as he kissed my cheek, sneakily releasing the buckle on my seatbelt. "But you're here. So we might as well get this over with."

"Again, with the ringing endorsements," I laughed, blowing out a breath before I reached for the door handle.

"You know you're stuck with me now. I know where you live."

Rolling my eyes, I opened the door, waiting until Sam rounded the front of the car, offering me his hand as he helped me stand. While I always wanted to open my own doors—both in life and my career—Sam was there to support me, always.

"What do you think?" he asked as we walked up the front steps, the blue two-story colonial looming over our heads.

"It's bigger than I imagined." I knew real estate was more affordable in the Midwest, but this rivaled the space in my parent's obnoxiously large multi-million-dollar penthouse. Just not as pretentious. By a long shot.

"Yeah, it is," he snickered, winking at me as he squeezed my hand.

"I'm about to meet your mother. Can't you behave yourself for two minutes?"

He smiled, shaking his head as he reached for the front door handle. "You want me to answer honestly?"

Before I could chastise him for making jokes while I was freaking out on the inside, the door swung open, and while I'd been expecting his mother to jump out at me and begin pestering me with questions, it was a little boy covered with a powdery substance that looked like flour.

"Uncle Sam is here!" he yelled, leaving the door open as he pulled a super soaker from behind his back and shot it up the staircase behind him.

"Um." Looking over at Sam with wide eyes, he didn't seem fazed, just shrugging as he pulled me inside and helped me remove my coat, tossing it on a couch overflowing with them in a sitting room to our left.

"That's how the twins normally are. They're a little feral, but they're cool little dudes."

So far, this visit was not what I expected, but in the best way possible. This was already proving to be as far removed from my family holidays as you could get.

"Sam, get your ass back here," a feminine voice yelled from somewhere down a hallway to the right of the stairs. "Your dad is trying to ruin the turkey. Come get this electric carving knife before he cuts off his finger again."

Again? I mouthed as Sam chuckled, towing me toward the origin of the noise, thundering footsteps and squealing sounding from up the staircase as we passed.

As Sam pushed open the door at the end of the hallway, the aromas of a home-cooked meal invaded my senses, and my stomach growled as I followed behind him. It looked like something out of a Norman Rockwell painting, a mouth-watering spread of classic Thanksgiving foods covering the entire surface of the kitchen island.

"Sam," his mother cooed as she turned, spotting her son. She gave him a big hug, oven mitt cladden hands cupping his cheeks as she released him. "I'm so glad the weather cooperated so you could get here. I'd hate for you to miss another family holiday now that you're closer to home."

I knew she meant well, but I had to bite my tongue to tell her he'd missed family gatherings before because he was trying to create a successful future for himself. But he'd warned me about her sometimes passive-aggressive commentary. And that it was mostly harmless.

As she released him, her eyes caught mine. She quickly pulled Sam behind her, opening her arms as she stepped toward me.

"Kristine! It's so great to see you again. Maybe we can get to know you a little better this time." She wrapped her arms around me, surprisingly strong despite my being at least five inches taller than her. "Now that you two have come up for air." I thought that she was done, but she wasn't. "I know I couldn't stay away from that Langley wood when we first started dating either."

"Mom," Sam scolded, but she smiled wider, waving her hand at him to leave her alone.

"How do you think you got here?" she teased, winking at me. "Langley men are virile too. Hope you two are using birth control. Unless you're ready to give me a few more grandbabies, not that I'd be opposed to that."

"Not right now," I squeaked, glad I was religious about the birth control shot I'd started getting in lieu of the pill. I knew it wasn't foolproof, and I'd recently begun to think about long-term plans with Sam, but I wasn't ready quite yet. "Maybe after we're thirty."

"We'll see. Five years is a long time," she smiled, patting my arm as she released me, turning back toward Sam. "Get that knife away from your father. He's not ruining the meal with another trip to the ER. I told him Brad was on his way over here, but he's squirrelly and got the knife from the cabinet before I noticed."

Sam, ever the devoted son, relieved his dad of the sharp implement, laying it down on the counter while he reached down to unbutton his cuffs, methodically folding his sleeves up his toned forearms. Before I could ogle my boyfriend anymore, an older version of Sam stepped into my line of sight, holding out his hand. I didn't see any fingers missing, but I wouldn't argue with Sam's mother about knife safety.

"She's not as scary as she appears. Don't let her steamroll you. She means well, but she's not known for her tact."

"Thanks for the warning," I said with a smile, shaking his hand.

He pulled me in slightly, leaning down to whisper in my ear. "But she's right about the virility thing. You might want to wrap it before you tap it. Isn't that what the kids are saying nowadays?"

Before I could respond, the back door to the house swung open as a crowd of people filled the small kitchen. I could see that the Langley genes ran strong, Sam strongly resembling his sisters. I recognized Becca, who'd been at the wedding, and a few of their voices seemed familiar, but they paid me no mind, filling up the rest of the counter space in the kitchen with various covered dishes.

The chaos continued as the sound of the carving knife drowned out the voices, Sam expertly wielding it to carve up the large bird sitting on the stovetop in a roaster pan. It was oddly arousing to watch him, but I kept it under a lid, trying to figure out who was who as I eavesdropped on the conversations going on around me. Sam had prepped me with details of his sisters and all of their families, but now I felt like I might have needed an illustrated family tree to keep it straight.

Despite my attempts to blend into the background, I was unsuccessful, my eyes catching Sam's as his sisters seemed to turn as a pack and set their sights on me.

"We're stealing your girlfriend," one called over her shoulder as she hooked her arm in mine and started walking toward the door to the hallway. Sam smiled at me from across the room, winking before he returned his attention to his task.

"Don't bother fighting," another sister teased as they led me to another door, revealing a staircase as it opened.

"Down the stairs, Kristine." I was a little freaked out as they surrounded me, dragging me into their lair.

Their lair turned out to be a large finished basement, one half filled with a large sectional couch and the other piled high with toys and various baby equipment.

"How was the drive over?" Another asked as she sat down to my left, pulling a leg underneath her to face me. "I know when we lived in the city, fighting traffic on a holiday was a nightmare."

"It was good. Not as bad as traffic in Manhattan on Thanksgiving."

"Don't scare her with a ton of questions," another chimed in, settling on the other side of the large couch. "They just got here, and you haven't even introduced yourself."

"The whole reason we dragged her down here was to ask her questions. It's not like Sam has given us many details to go on. But his mood seems greatly improved over when he first moved back."

Seeming to remember their manners, they went around, introducing themselves. I'd met Becca briefly at the wedding, Claire had been the one to run point on the grand gesture, but I'd only heard about the other two, Alison and Fiona.

"Tell us about yourself," Fiona encouraged, crossing her arms and settling back against the cushion behind herself. "Why exactly would you give up a promotion to follow Sammy out here?"

That question was easy. "Because I love him. The promotion was nice, but after a few weeks, I knew I couldn't live without him and didn't want to."

My answer seemed to open the floodgates to their easy acceptance, and their postures relaxed, the conversation flowing easily as they fed me embarrassing stories about Sam's childhood, making sure I knew all his dirty secrets. While I'd feared gaining their approval, it had been easy. As long as I loved their baby brother, they'd treat me like part of the family.

"Mom!" The little boy from the front door came thundering down the stairs, the flour mostly missing from his damp hair. On the other hand, the water gun was still gripped tightly in his small fist. "Nana said it's time to eat. She made me help Felix set the table, but he had it handled. That little brown noser didn't want to share the ice cream she promised us after dinner."

"Alex," Claire scolded, shaking her head. "We have company. You could behave yourself and let her believe I haven't raised a pair of savages."

"I could," he agreed, shrugging. "But that sounds boring. It was more fun to shoot water at Uncle Leo's crotch and call him pee pants."

Fiona burst into laughter, clearly entertained by her husband's run-in with his nephew.

"Alex, enough. Go wash your hands and put that gun away, or you won't see it until the end of the school year."

"Party pooper," he muttered, his pout eerily resembling his uncle's.

"Yes, I am. No more shenanigans. I already know Uncle Sam will encourage the chaos, but he's not the one you have to answer to tomorrow."

The little boy stomped up the stairs, clearly not thrilled with his mother's threats.

"Maybe you can keep your boyfriend from giving him any ideas later," Claire laughed, winking.

"That's cute. You think I can control Sam," I laughed, and his sisters joined in before we all stood and ascended the stairs.

The first floor had been transformed in the short period we'd been downstairs, folding tables in every room and every spot at the large dining room table set with what looked like holiday-themed china.

It also seemed like the number of people in the house had exploded, children of all ages running around and laughing, some with plates full of food, others headed toward the kitchen.

"Grab a plate from the big table. Sam got upgraded from the kiddie table since you're here." Claire instructed, grabbing one of her own and heading to the buffet cabinet along the wall to check out the offerings. "Stay away from any of the casserole dishes with the blue glass. Fi means well, but Leo cooks at their house for a reason. Anything in the china serving pieces is usually safe but avoid the stuffing with the Cheerios. It's the gross gluten-free stuff Alison's husband likes. It tastes like cardboard."

Navigating was a little overwhelming, but Sam appeared at my side as my plate filled, kissing me on the cheek and beaming. Being around his family suited him, and I was glad we'd decided to come here instead of considering returning to Manhattan. Fuck my parents, and my ass kisser brother. I wouldn't let them make me feel obligated to behave how they wanted any longer. We'd agreed to spend the week after Christmas with Nana and Piet, and I could give a shit less if I saw my parents.

Sam squeezed in at the crowded table by my side as we sat down. I grabbed his hand, squeezing, a little overwhelmed at how natural it felt to be here.

I love you. I mouthed as tears gathered in the corners of my eyes.

"I'm so happy you're here," he whispered back, wiping my tears before leaning over to kiss my temple and propping his arm across the back of my chair.

As his father started the blessing prayer, I said my own, eternally grateful that whatever higher power was up there somehow deemed me worthy enough to be a part of this family and deserving of Sam's love.

THE END

THE DIRTY WORDS SERIES

Foreplay on Words (Amazon)

Book One of The Dirty Words Series
Evan and Chase
Preview of Foreplay on Words: https://BookHip.com/WCJHJGA

Mark my Words (Amazon)

Book Two of The Dirty Words Series
Sam and Kristine
Preview of Mark my Words: https://BookHip.com/QHWGXTZ

Bound by Words (Amazon)

Book Three of The Dirty Words Series
Nathan and Kelly
Preview of Bound by Words: https://BookHip.com/NRRHRBN

More Than Words (Amazon)

Book Four of The Dirty Words Series
Adrian and Isobel
Preview of More Than Words: https://BookHip.com/TARMSTL

MASKED MEN OF SAGE SPRINGS

Accidental Abduction (Amazon)

Book One in the Masked Men of Sage Springs Series
Hudson and Charley
Preview of Accidental Abduction: https://bookhip.com/CDPWXAB
Coming to audio soon!

Illicit Illustration (Amazon)

Book Two in the Masked Men of Sage Springs Series
Reid and Hazel
Preview of Illicit Illustration: https://bookhip.com/CDPWXAB

Smokin' Situation (Amazon)

Book Three in the Masked Men of Sage Springs Series
Annie and Tristan
Preview of Smokin' Situation: https://bookhip.com/FCDAKTZ

STANDALONES

The Midnight Voyeur (Amazon)

Now available in Duet audio featuring Branden Davis-Butler, Cole Eubanks
and Troy Duran: https://books2read.com/themidnightvoyeur
(Wide at all audio retailers)
Spicy, taboo, reverse age-gap, stand-alone – Ginny
Preview The Midnight Voyeur: https://BookHip.com/SZXGKKQ

The Mystery Correspondent (Amazon)

Steamy Christmas novella, stand-alone – Ryder and Stella
Preview of The Mystery Correspondent: https://BookHip.com/XPBVAMB

Meet Him at the Altar

New Adult coming of age, written like a romcom/mystery
Kendall & The Groom
Preview of Meet Him at the Altar available on ELKoslo.com

Social Media

Website: ELKoslo.com

Instagram: @elkoslo_writes
Threads: @elkoslo_writes
TikTok: @elkoslowrites & @elkosloauthor

Facebook: E.L. Koslo
Page: EL Koslo Romance Writer
Private Reader Group: E.L. Koslo's Dirty Words Brigade

Pinterest: @elkoslo

X: @ELKoslo
BlueSky: https://bsky.app/profile/elkoslowrites.bsky.social

Amazon: amazon.com/author/e.l.koslo

Linktree: linktr.ee.Elkoslo

Newsletter: https://elkoslo.beehiiv.com/

www.ingramcontent.com/pod-product-compliance
Lightning Source LLC
Chambersburg PA
CBHW021219310726
48971CB00006B/1619